METANOIA

Total Conversion

Also by Joseph P. Cody

THE TIGER'S FURY

DRAGON FANG

HUBOT - Human Robot

PHANTOM TEAM

WILD VIOLETS - Growing Up
In The 1940s And 50s

METANOIA

Total Conversion

JOSEPH P. CODY

A Mystery

Autotech Industries

St. Paul, Minnesota

This is a work of fiction. Any resemblance to persons living or dead is purely coincidental. Names, characters, place and events, except where noted, are products of the author's imagination and are fictional. The views expressed herein are solely those of the author and do not necessarily represent the position of Autotech Industries.

This book is written, printed, and bound in the United States of America

First Edition: 2010

ISBN-13: 978-0-9791167-5-9
ISBN-10: 0-9791167-5-9

A Publication of:

Autotech Industries
688 – 11th Avenue NW
St. Paul, Minnesota 55112

Note: Autotech Industries is a publisher; it does not sell books. This and other books by Joseph P. Cody may be purchased from Amazon.com or any book store.

To anyone in need of conversion

Metanoia (met-*uh*-**noi**-*uh*) noun, composed of two Greek words *meta* = after or beyond, and *noeo* = to think. In Classical pre-Christian times metanoia meant to change one's mind or heart about someone or something. In the Greek Old Testament, it is used twenty-eight times with essentially this meaning. When the context specifically mentions sinful practices about which a person was changing his or her mind the meaning is construed to be repentance. (Repentance is man's action taken to right a relationship with God, broken by sinfulness, for which he does penance.) Through the centuries after Christ, the meaning becomes that of a profound spiritual transformation or conversion; a turning away from the old (sinful) self. It is more than a firm resolve to "change the mind" but also encompasses the need to produce demonstrable results.

One of the Church Fathers, Lactantius (240-320), wrote his **Divine Institutes** in the early fourth century. In **Book VI, Chapter 24** he has this to say: ". . . For he who repents of that which he has done, understands his former error and on this account the Greeks better and more significantly speak of metanoia, which we may speak of in Latin as a return to a right understanding. For he returns to a right understanding, and recovers his mind as it were from madness, who is grieved for his error and he reproves himself of madness and confirms his mind to a better course of life."

— 1 —

February, 1953, Sauk Centre, Minnesota

"I'm Margaret," the young woman said to the man as he turned away from the freight office window. The man in his early-twenties looked at the woman before him trying to place her. Her greeting sounded as though she thought he was expecting her, but he was at a loss.

Finally, he said, "Should I know you?"

"I'm Margaret Kerry. I was told to meet Stephan Johnson at the train depot here in Sauk Centre today. I got off the train a half-hour ago. The few people who arrived with me all had someone to meet them and immediately left. I assumed you must be Mr. Johnson, arriving a little late."

"Sorry. I'm Carl Wessen, and I'd like to help you, but I have my own problems."

"Yes, I couldn't help overhearing. You have some parcel here and the freight charges are more than you have with you. Is that it?"

Sadly nodding his head the man said, "Yes. I bought a new cast iron stove out of the Sears and Roebuck. Based on the listed weight I know I sent enough money to cover the destination charges. Now I find the weight was more than expected and I'm a dollar twenty short. I really need that stove. My wife is quite ill, and I'm afraid the house will burn if I fire that old thing we have enough to keep the place comfortable."

"Do you know Stephan Johnson? I asked at the ticket counter and he didn't know him. I called central on the telephone, and they had no record of him."

"Are you sure you got off at the right town?" he asked really noticing the woman standing before him for the first time. She bore a resemblance to his wife, about twenty, brown hair, even features except for a bit of a turned up nose. She was even close to the same height and build. She wore her hair differently, and quite attractively, he thought, with a loose wave held back by gold clips. Her dark brown coat was well cared for but worn enough to show threads on the collar below her chin. The slightly tattered suitcase she held fit the profile as did the lace shoes that had seen better days.

Carl was six feet one inch tall with a slim build, but hard. He had spent much of his life with a pitchfork in his hands. His black hair had a natural wave which together with large very blue eyes and a strong chin made him a handsome man in anybody's book.

"Why yes, I am sure. Here is the letter I received from Mr. Johnson's wife offering me a position as a hired girl to help with her eight children, and doing housework."

Carl took the letter out of the envelope and quickly read it. It seemed to be as she said. The letter was signed by Mrs. Johnson with clearly a woman's hand.

"This may be very forward of me," Margaret said presenting her best smile and blinking her soft brown eyes a few more times than necessary. "There seems to be no Stephan Johnson, the snow is falling pretty fast, and you need a dollar twenty. Could I suggest that I loan you the money, you get your stove, and I go with you for a day or two and help look after your wife until she's well. I have no place to stay until I find out what went wrong. I have some nurse's training."

After some hesitation, Carl agreed to the woman's offer. After he loaded the crate into the back of his black nineteen thirty-eight Ford pickup, they set out for home. Carl operated a farm five miles northwest of Sauk Centre. He, his wife Ruth and their son Timmy had moved on to it the previous spring. The summer had not been terribly successful. They had stayed even with their mortgage payments but little else. Besides the payment to the bank, there were almost an infinite number of things that required updating from fences to the roof on the barn. The stove had become a necessity that left little for gas and groceries until the next cream check. They sold whole milk to the creamery, but the payment had always been called the cream check.

They rode in silence for some time. The snow was beginning to drift in at places causing them to nearly become stuck once. When they turned off the road onto the hundred yard long driveway, Carl was struck with the desolation of the place. The house was blurred by the falling snow. The thin windbreak trees had not grown enough to provide protection. His heart sank as he thought of Ruth and Timmy, who'd be three in the spring. They'd be wondering what happened for him. He hoped against hope that Margaret would be more help that burden. One never knew when bringing a stranger into the house without references.

Carl's reservations were not entirely unwarranted. Margaret had not been completely honest. She had written the letter from Stephan Johnson's wife herself. Carl in his concern for his other problems did not think to look at the postmark. It had been mailed two blocks from her last place of residence, a charity center associated with an orphanage that was used to house the older parentless children. His oversight was according to plan.

Margaret was an orphan who was staying alive the best way she could. Times were good for any woman who could find a man and get married. Her present plans did not extend to getting married or anything of the sort. She needed a job, or at the very least a situation that included room and board. Up until the day before she had been mopping floors in a hospital. The pay was hardly enough to cover the rent for a real apartment. Besides, the air in the hospital filled as it was with the smell of sick people, disinfectants, medicines, and other chemicals, made her nauseous and lightheaded, if not a little depressed, at times. It was her hope that if she got away from it, got out of the city, she would feel better, and become a part of life by living with real people.

The year before, she had gone off on a similar excursion to southwestern Minnesota. From a chance meeting in the hospital, she had learned that she might have relatives in that part of the state. On that occasion, she had written ahead and actually had the offer of a trial position with a family on a large farm. It turned out they were distant relatives, and sadly, were gossipy. When it became known in the community that she was a poor relative living on what amounted to charity, people regarded her coldly. This was not what she wanted. The nuns at the orphanage had done a good job of teaching her the basics of reading writing and arithmetic. They had also insisted that the children read classics to broaden their education. She was disciplined and capable and refused to settle for being a castoff.

Her present vagary was really a leap of faith. It was the middle of winter, and the snowstorm, while not part of the plan, could work in her favor by adding a sense of urgency. She had to ingratiate herself with some family very quickly, prove her worth and become established. At the very least she needed to stay in a position long enough to get a good reference.

Her nerves were raw to the point of causing panic. She had enough sense to know any sign of fear or hopelessness would be counter productive. Yet, her stomach churned from lack of food that day, and worst of all the faintness and fatigue she had often experienced in the hospital was back.

As they dove, neither occupant of the pickup said anything since each had worries of their own. Carl stopped the truck and backed toward the steps that led to the porch off the kitchen. Fifty feet from his destination his progress was halted by snow. His attempt to drive forward and try again was unsuccessful. That was as far as he was going.

"Sorry, your arrival wasn't more pleasant," he said to Margaret.

"I've tromped through snow before," she said resolutely with no malice in her voice.

Carl forced open his door pushing back snow, and they both got out his side. He stomped down the snow the best he could leaving the start of a path for Margaret. She followed with her suitcase getting her shoes full of snow. As they entered, Timmy was there to greet them.

"Mom's been asking where you been. It's getting cold in here." The little guy was clearly worried and didn't know what to do. He had been ordered never to attempt to put wood in the stove. They had set up a bed for Ruth in the living room so she could be near the wood fired heater.

"Yeah, Timmy. It's okay now. You've been a good boy looking after Mom."

"I got her a glass of water. Who's that?"

"You're a good helper. Her name is Margaret. She's here to help out for a few days."

By this time Carl had his coat and boots off and went into the living room. He knelt by the bed and saw how pale his wife was. He put his hand on her forehead and knew she had a fever. "How ya doing?"

"Not so good," her voice weak. Almost at once, her eyes focus on Margaret. "Who's that woman?"

"I brought her from town. We need some help for a few days. I can't leave you alone. The cows have to be milked, and the rest of the chores have to be taken care of. I have the new heater for the living room so we can keep you warm. She'll cook and look after Timmy and you while I'm outside. Is there anything I can get you?"

"Carl, we can't afford hired help."

Carl knew that when Ruth began a sentence with his name it was a solemn occasion where she deeply disagreed with him.

"Don't worry. She was stranded at the train depot with no place to go, and there's a blizzard blowing up. She'll only be here for a day or two, and agreed that she won't be paid."

Carl knew Ruth's concern, of course. With her flat on her back, nine months pregnant, and running a fever, it was not good to have an unattached young female running around the house.

He rose and went to the kitchen. The light was already fading and the wind howled. Turning to Margaret he said, "I hope you're good at making do. See what you can get on for supper. There's some stew in the enameled kettle on the porch. Ask Timmy if you can't find what you need. I'm going to bring in the stove."

Carl put on his boots, coat, and mittens and headed out. The cast iron stove with crate was two hundred pounds. He dumped the crate off the back of the truck and tipping it end over end wrestled it to the steps. Working a farm made a man hard, and having been raised on a farm he had been hard before he started his own place. Yet, he was not an overly large man so his back was aching by the time he got it that far. Pausing, he stood up straight and twisted the kinks out of his back. Now, the hard part began. With the crate on end by the kitchen door, he had no choice but to open the door for as long as it took to get it in.

First he went in and closed the door to the living room so Ruth wouldn't get a chill draft. Then he was at it. Luckily, the kitchen floor was one of the things the needed work so if he gouged the worn-through linoleum it wouldn't matter. A half-hour later he had it placed beside the existing stove. He had the foresight to buy new stovepipes so he could get the new stove set up and ready to go without moving the old one. When he was ready, he had only to douse the fire in the old stove, let the steam and smoke work its way out and then dismantle the old pipes and connect the new.

By five-thirty night had fallen, and the new stove had a fire roaring in it. The room filled with smoke as the preservative oil was burned off the outside of the new iron. They opened the door and a window and eventually it was livable. Ruth moaned from time to time but said nothing.

For supper Ruth sat up, ate some soup, and drank a little tea. The others ate at the kitchen table with hardly a word. Margaret had shown initiative in getting together what there was. Of this, Carl was pleased. She also seemed content to eat the somewhat common fare.

"I'm behind on the chores. The livestock have to be fed, and the cows milked," Carl began. "If you need me for any reason come to the barn and yell for me."

Margaret nodded, and said in a low voice. "Ruth is pretty sick. I'll do what I can, but she should be in a hospital."

"There's no way we'd make it. The roads are snowed in by now. Even if we had left as soon as we arrived home, we wouldn't have made it.

"Could you call a doctor?"

"You think she's that bad?"

Margaret's medical training was next to nothing, but from working in the hospital, she knew a sick woman when she saw one. After all, the only people in hospital beds were sick people. It was another reason why she was happy to be quit of the place. She was young and healthy. Why should she spend her time around sick people? She nodded rather emphatically.

Carl went to the telephone on the wall and took the receiver off the hook. He turned the crank to ring central on the party line. Nothing. It wasn't uncommon in storms for the lines to go down.

"Lines are down," Carl said. With that the lights blinked. "Power will likely go out before long, too," he added. "I'll show you where the candles are."

Suited up again, Carl stepped out. A few moments later, he was back. "On second thought, under no circumstances are you to try to come to the barn. The path is drifted over and you could easily become disoriented and lose your way. This looks like a big storm. Okay?"

She nodded.

Carl had most of the necessary work done in the barn when the call had come that his stove had arrived. In a half-hour he had silage spread out in the feed troughs and opened the door to the barnyard. The animals were stoically waiting to be let in. He had to beat on some noses with a stick to keep them back long enough to brace the door open against the wind. Then, they flooded into the cavern they knew would offer food and shelter. The several inches of snow heaped on their backs cracked and slid off as they moved. The milk cows went to the left and the young stock to the right. The stock was trained and offered no problems.

More than an hour later, he was done milking and proceeded to heft hay in the mangers. The power had remained on, for which he was thankful. Minutes before he left the barn he was left in the dark. He had a kerosene lantern, but thought better of trying to light it in the barn. One match dropped in the wrong place would ignite the whole tinder-dry place. He took it with him as he left, knowing he'd need it in the house.

He set out. There was no sign of the path once he was ten feet from the barn, but he had always had a good sense of direction—except tonight. It was darker than he could ever remember. Normally he left the barn and followed the path to the house lights. It was never a problem, even with an overcast sky. Tonight was different. There was no path, and no house lights. Nothing but blinding snow and relentless wind. After enough steps, he knew he should have been at the house. No house. The snow was hip deep which meant he was off course. His foot landed on something under the snow. He pawed it clear with his mitten. It felt like the front bar of the cultivator. If that was so, he had veered to the left. On the other hand, it might be part of the plough which meant he had gone to the right. It was too confusing in the total darkness with the wind and snow to determine which. If he went the wrong way, he'd be hopelessly lost. He went to the right, into the wind, under the assumption the wind had shoved him off course to the downwind.

He wandered about for a long time, and was about to panic when the wind started to buffet. He was entering the lea of something. It was a building. Thank goodness. As he approached it, he stumbled on a foundation. That wasn't right. The house wasn't like that. He was back at the barn. Never had he encountered anything like this. Not once while growing up could he remember a storm this bad. Why did it have to be tonight?

He went back into the barn, felt his way to the milk room and lit the kerosene lantern. With the globe down, he'd chance it. He had no choice but to try for the house again. Once out of the turbulence of the barn he carefully determined the wind direction. The lantern helped with this by making the blowing snow visible around him. He'd take five steps and look back at his tracks. In this way, he could see when he was getting off course. Finally, he practically bumped his head on the corner of the house away for the porch. A couple of steps to his right and he would have missed it entirely, been lost again, and died in the snow. He followed the wall with his hand until he was in the porch. Exhausted, he leaned against the door as the turned the latch.

The door swung open and he tumbled in, pulling his nearly frozen legs to the side as he slammed the door. From the living room he heard, "Is that finally you? Where have you been? You've been gone almost three hours."

Carl looked up and his eyes focused on the woman standing in the doorway. "Oh, no! You look like a corpse, too."

Margaret went to him and helped him sit up. "Come on into the living room. The new stove works good. I've got it nice and warm."

He brushed the melting snow off his eyebrows, and pulled off his cap and mittens. Struggling to his feet, he staggered into the living room.

"No!" he yelled. The stove was glowing red and the chimney was bright orange. That girl had never fired a wood stove. He grabbed his mitten and using it he closed the draft adjustment near the floor, and set the damper in the chimney to nearly closed. He examined the stovepipe and all seemed to be holding up.

He turned to Margaret and said, "You're a city girl aren't you? I didn't think. You could have burned the house down. I'm serious, you could have." She was ready to defend herself but he held up his hand. "I'll explain how this works in a minute. How's Ruth?"

"The bed's wet. I think her water broke. The baby wants to come, but she's too weak."

Timmy edged over by his dad. Carl put his arm around him as he spoke to Ruth. "Can you hear me?"

"Baby's coming. Need a drink." Margaret handed him a glass of water. The girl seemed to be doing what she could.

Carl helped Ruth raise her head and she drank. Carl let her lay back again. "We'll make it sweetheart. We'll make it."

He pulled Timmy to him. The little guy was nearly in trauma as he watched. His life was falling apart. Taking Timmy aside he sat down heavily on an easy chair that had seen better days and held him.

As the two of them relaxed for a minute Margaret said, "Try this," as she handed him a cup of hot coffee.

"Thanks." He could feel the warmth of the liquid inside him like a river. He hadn't realized how close he had come to freezing to death. He didn't think he was frostbitten any place, maybe a little on his right cheek, it was just that his overall body temperature had gotten dangerously low.

It was starting to get cool in the room again. He looked at Margaret. "Okay. Now, open the draft by sliding that silver handle near the floor toward you. That controls how much air is allowed to enter the stove. That keeps the wood burning at an even rate. The damper on the stovepipe is normally opened to light the fire so there's a good draft. But, it must be closed most of the way when the fire is going. If it's too far open all the heat goes up the chimney. We'll get just as much heat in the room with those two controls set right as you had with everything red hot. I'm not faulting you. There was no way you could have known."

She did as instructed and the room started to warm again. He motioned her to come to the chair near his. He looked at her and in as kindly a voice as he could manage said, "You're doing fine. I got lost in the storm coming to the house and nearly froze to death. I realize this isn't what you signed up for, but it has all the marks of being a long night."

Staring straight ahead she said, "I wish I had stayed at the train depot."

"If wishes were horses, beggars would ride." He said gently.

"What?"

"That's a line from a nursery rhyme."

"What's it mean?"

"Nobody ever read nursery rhymes to you when you were young?"

"No. I'm an orphan."

"Oh. I'm sorry to hear that. I guess this isn't the first piece of tough sledding you've seen in your life."

She shook her head. "No."

"Well, the line means that if everyone's wishes came true we'd all be rich, smart, and a king. You're not at the train depot, you're here. And, thank goodness. We'll need all the nurse's training you have."

Margaret looked uncomfortably at her clasped together hands in her lap. "I was a little dishonest. I don't have any nurse's training. I worked in a hospital mopping floors and watched nurses doing their work sometimes."

"Have you ever seen a baby being born?"

"No. How about you? How about when Timmy was born?"

"Are you kidding. They won't let a husband within a country mile of a delivery room."

In the weakest voice he had ever heard, she replied, "Looks like we're on our own."

They sat both with their own thoughts. Timmy had fallen asleep. Ruth moaned, followed by a cry. Carl took Timmy to the small bedroom off the living room, and opened the guest bed. He was awake. "Timmy, I'm going to have you sleep in this bed tonight because I have to stay with Mom. Okay?"

The little head nodded up and down. "Now, I have to tell you something. When babies are born sometimes the mother gets scared. So she cries out, sometimes real loud. Don't worry, though. Okay?" Another nod. "I'll come in and check on you now and then. Lay down and try to go to sleep."

It was a long night. The baby finally entered this world at three a.m. They managed to get the umbilical chord tied off and cut, and the placenta removed. For the two neophytes, it was ghastly. Margaret cared for the baby while Carl tried to help Ruth. She was alive but weak and ran a fever. For the moment, she was sleeping.

Carl went to where Margaret was sitting in an easy chair holding Vincent Carl. Ruth had decided on the name with no objections.

Margaret held out the baby to him. "I don't feel so good," she said. In the pale light, he could see a waxy perspiration on her face.

"Do you feel like you'll throw up?"

"Yes, I do. I first noticed sweat and nausea this morning but it passed and I didn't give it another thought." That was the truth, but she was afraid it was a reoccurrence of what she had experienced working in the hospital. With the stress of the unknown she had faced all day it was starting to tell.

"Get the wash basin from the kitchen."

She was no sooner in the kitchen when he heard her wrenching. This got better all the time.

Carl laid the baby in the easy chair and found an old bucket for Margaret. Against some halfhearted protests, he took her upstairs and put her in their bed. He left her a candle, some matches, and a tin cup of water on the nightstand.

"Here, I'll open the register in the floor. Heat will come up from downstairs. It should keep the water in your cup from freezing. Get some sleep if you can."

When he returned, Ruth was awake. He went to her. The first thing she said was, "Where's Margaret?"

"She's sick too, looks pretty bad. She brought it with her ignoring early symptoms from this morning. I put her upstairs in our bed. I'll stay down here with you for the night."

This appeared to relax Ruth. "How's the baby?"

"He looks fit and strong. Sleeping like a champ."

Her voice was a little woozy as she asked, "What day is today?"

"Let's see. It's early on Wednesday."

"Oh! Ash Wednesday. Vincent was born on Ash Wednesday."

"Yeah. I guess so. Can you sleep? You're still sick and you've been through a lot."

"Stay with me for a few minutes. I know you're tired, but tell me about Margaret. How did she latch on to you?"

"I first purchased a few groceries and the new stove pipes. That took the last of the money. Then I went to the train depot. The freight for the stove was more than I had included with the payment. She was waiting for a Stephan Johnson. I guess she got off at the wrong town. Anyway, she loaned me the money so I could pay the additional freight and bring the stove home. I could hardly tell her to get lost after she had done me that favor. Now that I think of it, she didn't look too good at the time."

"How sick is she?"

"Very sick, I'm afraid. She vomited in the washbasin in the kitchen. With only a candle on the kitchen table, she could not have seen what came up. Later when I went to throw it our, it looked awfully dark. With the flashlight, I saw there was a lot of blood in it. I don't know about these things, but she may not last out the night."

"You don't suppose she brought tuberculosis into the house, do you?"

"No. This is different. She never coughed once, and in my family, as I've mentioned, there was TB. I'd have noticed that immediately. Maybe it's stomach ulcers or something like that."

"If she was at death's door, why would she be out in the country side in the middle of winter going to a new job."

"She said she was an orphan, and from the way she said it, the look on her face, I tend to believe her. If that's true she has nobody to turn to. She had no choice but to follow through on plans already made."

Carl was silent for a time resting his eyes. He was thinking of how while he was growing up everyone received the Mantoux Test quite regularly as they were searching for TB. Anybody that was positive from the Mantoux Test went in for a chest x-ray. Those who showed spots on their lungs were sent off to sanatoriums where they were quarantined until they either got well or died. Only survivors of TB with the acquired immunity were allowed to work in those places.

"There was the case," Carl began, "of a cousin in the family, maybe thirteen. I remember it well because there was a lot of anguish over it. She brought in the mail one day and saw the notice that her x-ray showed that she had TB. Having heard so much about it, she knew what it meant and refused to face it so she threw the letter away. By the time the second notice arrived, the disease had spread. She lingered in a sanatorium for some months. They can do certain things that help if it's caught early enough. For her, it was too late."

Ruth's eyes were moist. "That's so sad. It goes to show that even though we have little, there are still others who have less. I wonder if Margaret knows she doesn't have long to live and decided to die away from the cold impersonal city. God sent us this chance to be a good neighbor. She's here so we can make her feel like family before she dies."

Carl was pleased. "You're feeling better. Even though you have a long way to go, you're thinking about others already. With the baby born there's a tremendous load off your system. You'll do fine now. Enough of this. You need rest, and I'm about dead. I'll see your bright face in the morning."

She smiled at him, closed her eyes, and was soon sleeping peacefully.

— 2 —

The Oval Office smelled of cigarette smoke as it always did. The President didn't notice because he was the one smoking. Representative Norma Holleran noticed the odor immediately as she entered at six-thirty this Wednesday morning in May. It was the one public room in the country where the strict enforcement of no smoking was not observed. The cigarette Nazis should have been going berserk about this, except that the President was so far left that he made most liberals look conservative. Hence, he was their man so if they decided to look the other way it was all right. Only the moronic masses were to be kicked into compliance by their whims. The President was a two pack a day addict—on an abstemious day. Normally, he was a chain smoker. This, as well as a covey of other fetishes and deficiencies, were scrupulously kept from the public by the compliant media. The multitude of oily courtiers expecting to curry his favor by kissing various of his body parts weren't about to complain either.

The President looked as he normally did in the morning—terrible. With a cup of coffee in his hand and a cigarette hanging from his lips, his slim frame slouched in the chair behind the huge desk. He wore a dark blue suit, as he always did, which could have been the same one he wore for his high school graduation, assuming he did graduate—there were no records of that or anything else about his life. The suit wasn't in any way worn that was readily visible; it just looked lived in. The man didn't clean up well.

Norma wore a yellow suit that had seen a few days, not as many as the dark blue suit. The summery color of her attire was set off by a dark red coordinated scarf tied off with a loop just in front of her left shoulder. The shoes were off-white low heeled pumps that she'd trade for lace shoes as soon as she got to her office. Her hair, died black, its original natural color, was waved, but not a fancy hairdo that took a lot of care.

As speaker of the House of Representatives Ms. Norma Holleran was arguably the second most powerful person in the country. The President had even mentioned once that the fix was in so that if anything happened to him, the Vice-President would be dead within two days, and she'd be president. It was also rigged so she'd stay president, and not simply be a place holder until a new president and vice-president could be put in place. She wasn't sure that was true, but her ideas were far more in tune with the President's than those of the Vice-President—except something had changed.

Therein came the rub. She'd been out of town the evening before giving a routine speech at a small college. She wasn't sure why she had made the remark, it surely had not been on the Teleprompter, and it was not something that had ever entered her mind at any time in the past. She had slipped in the sentence, "It does seem like we've pushed a little too far on abortion, and some rethinking is needed there." Immediately, a firestorm of media hype erupted. A speech that would have had no national coverage would be on the front page of every newspaper this morning, and it would lead every TV and radio newsbreak all day. She had received the call at five-fifteen this morning telling her to be at the meeting with the President at this hour. It, of course, meant he had been awakened earlier than normal, too. There were no doubts in her mind that this meeting would come as she left the auditorium after the speech the night before. As such, she had had time to prepare a defense as she returned to Andrews Air Force Base in the Air Force biz jet she had at her disposal. She had spent much of the night lying awake thinking about it, too.

It was still a mystery as to what had happened. There was no doubt she had said the words. It was as if someone else was talking for those few seconds. Further analysis would have to be set aside until later, maybe this weekend. For now, there was the President glowering at her with every line in his face in bold relief. She was never sure what, if any, makeup he used for TV appearances. It was clear, though, that she now beheld the pure, unadorned, man. For her, a woman, at least she knew how to apply makeup herself, and was never—that is never—seen outside her bedroom without it.

"What on earth could you have been thinking!" It was not even a rhetorical question. It was an accusation. "As sensitive as that issue is, that was inconceivable. What's worse, that subject's not even on the radar screen at the moment. There was no reason to poke a stick in that hornet's nest. Is the job too much for you? Should you be stepping down? I don't know if I'll ever be able to trust you after that. Okay, let's have it. What do you have to say for yourself?"

It was like going back to the third grade and being scolded by Mrs. Tollenwich. Suddenly, the man whom she had admired since he had come on the political scene seemed not so admirable. At least, the frontal barrage had not been as long as she had expected. She was somewhat surprised at actually being given a chance to defend herself. And, being something of a political street fighter, she had no intention of taking a beating without pushing back.

"I've been in national politics for thirty-three years. This fall I'll be running for my seventeenth term in the House of Representatives. I know politics a fair piece better than you do. I grant you, that it was not a statement that we would want to have said. But," here she paused for a couple of heartbeats, a timing thing she had mastered, "there are political realities that must be faced."

"I have set the political realities since I started running for president and I will continue to do so! If you are so political astute, why am I here, and not you?"

Because jerk, you are putty in the hands of your handlers. *You* have not set the political agenda, *they* have. Why was she thinking this way? Over the past two years, she had at regular intervals sat back and consciously thought through the direction these people were taking the country. Every time her conclusion had been the same. She didn't care which way they took it as long as she kept her power with all its perks. Of course, after so many years of pursuing the liberal agenda, at times, she actually believed that the women, minorities, and the poor were exploited by the wealthy. The fact that all of these categories faired better in the United States than anywhere else on earth never seemed to enter her mind.

"Mr. President, why you are there, and I am here is not the topic of discussion this morning. There are some political realities that must be addressed, and best initiated by us rather than us having a response forced upon us. The first is that partial birth abortion is opposed by at least seventy percent of the American people. Some polls have it as high as eighty percent. Don't forget, forty-seven percent of the electorate voted against you. That seventy plus percent is getting organized to make an assault on the democratic control of the Senate and seriously erode our lead in the House this fall. I especially have a formidable challenger. They're pulling out all the stops. In my speech I didn't say anything would change, only the way things seem to be.

"This will give all of those knee-jerk Catholics who would vote for a groundhog if it were labeled a Democrat a continuing reason to cast their ballots for me as well as for other pro-abortion Democrats. When Catholic Democrats vote, myself included, they trample on most of what they would believe if they were really Catholic. You with your strident pro-abortion record would not be President had it not been for those Catholics. But, there comes a limit. The liberal bishops of the past two generations are gradually being replaced by more conservative ones. This is another political reality that cannot be dismissed."

The President drew himself up and tapped the ashes from his smoke in the little ashtray. Not an ashtray, really, rather a porcelain candy dish with the cover lying near it. It was easy to pop the cover on when certain people were admitted to the room. A remarkably efficient air filtration system had been installed that could circulate and clean the air in the entire room in minutes, though it produced a minor hurricane. The upholstered furniture, drapes, and carpets were steam cleaned weekly. To a nonsmoker there was still a hint of smoke lingering, but most of them were easily convinced that was from the one or two cigarettes the President allowed himself during a week. Mindless morons!

He poured more coffee into his mug. Nothing had been offered to his guest, but he was not that type of man. "I have the crew working on damage control. Make sure you don't say anything like that again. In fact, keep a low profile for a week or so. You only address issues when I say to address them."

This brought up another issue so she began. "I know no other way to broach this subject than to simply say it. You are not supreme dictator for life in this country, at least not yet. Until you are, there is another political reality that will not go away. I cannot be seen as being nothing more than your mouthpiece, your lap dog. Two of you is one more than the voters will swallow. We have to be seen as being at odds now and then. Those klutzes in the voting booths must have the feeling there is a reason to vote. As it was, we had to lever them off their fat behinds last election. This fall is an off-year election. You, as one of the first minority candidates to have a shot at the presidency, will not be on the ballot. Face it, a large number of people turned out to vote last time for no other reason than they thought it would be a hoot to have something different. They didn't know why it would be so cool, nor did they care what you planned to do. There is even a name for that attitude. It's called *recreational voting*. Everything in life is supposed to be fun, so why not voting. Don't expect them to bother voting this fall."

The President leaned forward and coughed. "Fine! Think of it that way if you must. I know you didn't care about the issues when you started into politics. You latched on to those that you thought would bring you to power. Where your allegiances lie now I, frankly, don't know. But, here is a political reality for you. Don't bite the hand that fed you and brought you to where you are. That could be dangerous to your health."

He laced his fingers together and placed his hands behind his head. He leaned back and yawned. "Any more speeches planned in the next couple of weeks?

"Certainly. I have one at a pharmaceutical convention in my district. There's no avoiding that. People have to see me and know that I'm still there for them. My opponent has nothing to do but give speeches and make other appearances. I'll have a tough race."

Leaning forward and placing his forearms on the desk again, he said, "Stick to the prepared text. Nothing off the cuff. We were planning to dominate the media with the nuclear treaty starting today. Now you've thrown that off target."

She could see he was angry. In his place she would be, too. But, life had its little hiccups.

With that the President rose and headed to the washroom off the Oval Office. She found her own way out. Walking the hall to the elevator Norma was pleased at how well it had gone. The man, an ideologue, was not very smart, though his handlers were. It was almost as if her escape had been planned. What was he, or rather, what were they planning? Maybe the meeting was nothing more than a perfunctory first skirmish until the real attack could be formulated. This was a brutal game and her future performance would play a critical part in what was to come. It was a good bet that if she didn't run for reelection the Republican would win in her district. The one most likely to be the next Speaker of the House did not command the following that was hers. It was in their interests to keep her in the position she now held. That is, she'd remain if she continued to be in lock step with them. The gnawing question was, would she?

Alone in the back of her limousine, Norma stared out the bullet-proof glass as they wove their way through the barricades leaving the White House compound. The dawn spreading across the city was masked behind a gray sky. Raindrops streaked the window producing a bleak empty feeling inside her. Fatigue was part of it, but more than that was a deep sense of the transience of it all. How much longer would she be a part of it? Part of what? The power she wielded—was it really power? It struck her that is was a whole bunch of people doing a whole bunch of things that didn't really have to be done. The only anchor she had was the fact of the limo, and her alone in it. What she did must be important, or this vehicle wouldn't exist, and she wouldn't be the one in it. She wouldn't have the large office to which she was being taken. There wouldn't be the staff waiting for her instructions. The whole microcosm of the country's capital and its surrounding buildings must be needed for something. The social structure like a colony of insects, the minutely controlled status of who had what seat in the house chamber, how close it was to the front or to the aisle would not matter if it weren't important. It must be terribly important, but for the moment, Norma could not remember why it was.

There had been down times in her life when it seemed all was lost. She was of sturdy stock and had always come back. The darker it appeared, the more she doggedly forged ahead. This was different. The thing that had bothered her most from the previous night wasn't what she had said. Rather, that she had made a spontaneous remark at all. It seemed as if she could have stated reciting a nursery rhyme in the middle of the speech. No, that wasn't right, either. It was like something took control of her and forced her to say something negative about abortion, anything at all, in her own words, but necessarily on that subject. Worst of all, there had been at the time a pleasant something, she didn't know what to call it. It was different from what she'd normally refer to as a feeling, an aura? It wasn't pleasant now. In fact, she was horrified at the thought of it.

Norma Holleran had been raised a Catholic by devout parents, too devout in her opinion. When in college, she had fallen in love and been married. Yeah, real love. She had admitted how unrealistic that was a thousand times. It was sex and nothing more. Inevitably, the promiscuity that was rampant at Berkeley flooded into her marriage. It affected both her and her husband. The result was a divorce after a year. It didn't matter to her, because the marriage had the desired effect of giving her a new last name thus separating her from her parents. Her liberal acquaintances saw, in her keeping her married name, a conservative side of her and that she wasn't the liberated female she claimed to be. In that they were wrong, but for reasons they would never have guessed.

The issue of artificial contraception came up. The papal encyclical, *Humanae Vitae*, came out in nineteen sixty-eight forbidding it. It didn't take long, though, for the word to get around that if you found the right confessor, shopped around as it was called, that you'd get a free pass—not a sin at all.

Through the ensuing years, she had argued the point at times with those holding the opposite view, usually at parties when most of the people, herself included, were half in the tank from alcohol or drugs. From these shallow discussions, she was alerted to an interesting scientific finding. With some research on her own, she found that the evidence was in. Most artificial contraceptives did their jobs by means of early abortions. Yet, it was still easy to find confessors who would acquiesce on contraceptives. The conclusion was obvious to her. If the Catholic Church was divided on artificial contraception, it was divided on abortion as well. She, like millions of others, followed the logic until she arrived at the position of her liking and from the point on stopped thinking. The beliefs or opinions of some priests, and even a few bishops, did nothing to change the constant teaching of the Catholic Church through the ages that all forms of artificial contraception were seriously sinful.

As she got into the political game, it became equally obvious that a liberal was going to get ahead a lot faster than a conservative, so she became a Democrat. That was a no brainer. It was easier to sell hedonism to a hedonistic culture that to preach virtue. This was especially so because the conservative politicians were caught off the virtue reservation as often as the liberals. Of course, they all recognized the double standard the media took toward such matters. They meticulously searched for the slightest infraction on the part of conservatives, while largely looking the other way for liberals. This was another reason to be a liberal, the press was in your back pocket.

In this respect, she was very different from the President. Ideology was the stuff he was made from. For her, she was in the business of selling what people wanted to buy. A thought suddenly occurred to her. Was that what happened? Did she subconsciously detect that the market was changing? Was her inner sense directing her to a more moderate position because that was the way of survival? That was ridiculous. In the upper circles of power, there was no such animal as a Democrat who was not totally pro-abortion.

With a sharp noise, her driver opened the door, thankfully. The distraction should have been welcome. It wasn't. There was an unruly crowd of reporters yelling questions at her.

"Ma'am. Your briefcase. You left it on the seat. Did you mean to do that?" the driver said standing between her and the microphones thrust at her.

"Things on my mind," she responded so only he could hear. She mechanically turned and bending into the vehicle snatched the small handle of the familiar object. Thank God for familiar things.

She pushed her way through the vicious onslaught saying, "No comment." As harsh as the enveloping horde of vultures was, her greatest misery was her shoes pinching her feet. She'd be glad to get into some comfortable footwear.

Vincent Wessen came into the kitchen carrying his sport coat at a quarter to six. He slipped the coat over the back of a dinette chair. His wife Camilla stood by the counter slicing an apple for her breakfast. They both got their own food in the morning.

"Hi, sweetheart. Top of the morning to you."

It was an Irish greeting, which was a little odd seeing as they were both of German extraction. The response was supposed to be, "And the rest of the day to you."

She gave him the raspberry. It was her way of saying she was glad to see him, too. Or, he had no alternative but to assume she was, though he thought it would be nice if once in a while she'd answer in a more civil way.

He retrieved his usual from the refrigerator, roasted almonds, and a piece of cheese. If there was a banana available, he ate that, too. Making coffee was too time consuming, so he drank water. According to his schedule, he'd be leaving the back door of his three bedroom ranch style home in Arden Hills, Minnesota a few minutes before six. With flextime at AB Equipment Company, where he worked, he'd arrive by six-thirty which was the earliest he could officially start his day. This permitted him to leave work at three o'clock to miss the rush hour traffic. All in all, it worked well for the twenty-mile commute to the opposite side of town. Besides the sport coat, he wore an oxford shirt, necktie, and dress slacks at work. The dress standards were becoming more slovenly each year while the work attitude slipped with the attire. It was easier for him to act and work professionally if he were properly dressed.

"I thought this was one of your days off." She spent two to three days a week working for a charity.

"I switched with Jane so I'm off tomorrow."

"Paul gone yet?"

"Yes. Since I was going in, he had to take the bus."

Paul Sanders was Camilla's nephew who had graduated from high school that spring, actually only a little more than a week before. In the fall, he would be starting at the University of Minnesota and living with them. Since Vincent and Camilla lived on a bus line, it would be possible for him to avoid the expense and disruption of living in a dorm on campus. From everything they had heard, the dorms were little more than an earthly Pandemonium. There was loud music and goings-on until after midnight that started anew by five in the morning. How anybody managed to study was a mystery. Not so much of a mystery, they didn't.

"I hope this summer's involvement gets him out of his shell a little. He's so quiet." Paul was spending the summer working for a pro-life candidate for the U.S. House of Representatives.

The summer job was another reason they had agreed to the living arrangement. Although he was the middle of five children, he was very quiet. It seemed that with so much going on as he grew up, he'd be more sociable. It was the difference in people. They'd see him walking around the back yard seemingly aimlessly. When asked what he was doing he'd say he was thinking, or sometimes praying. It was hard to argue with a young man who never got into trouble, and whose main fault was minding his own business.

One evening while they were sitting on a patio bench a few days before he had asked Vincent about prayer. The question struck him as odd, though it shouldn't have. Vincent had said that if a person had faith God would answer his prayer. Unfortunately, most of us think that the things we pray for are nearly impossible, that God isn't listening, or any number of reasons that our prayers won't be answered, so our faith lags. Paul had said he had faith and would pray to change some things in the pro-life movement. Vincent had said, with prayer and a lot of hard work, his candidate could win the election. That made sense. Vincent had no way of knowing that was not what the young man had in mind.

A sandy hared young man of eighteen alighted from the metro transit bus at the corner of Snelling and University in St. Paul. Though it was sunny the crisp late May wind was a scant fifty-five degrees and appeared as if it might whisk the slender figure down the sidewalk like a dry leaf. Contrary to the intent of the bluster, the figure faced it and tripped along the sidewalk all but oblivious to its presence. His jacket flapped as his scuffed sneakers lightly padded along with the determination of their wearer. The clear blue eyes set in a long serious face set atop the five foot-eleven frame were alert, though somewhat distant. The mind behind the face was lifted in a morning offering to God with the sure hope that his work of the day would be to His glory.

As Paul Sanders entered the store front door at the campaign office on this Wednesday morning, there seemed to be more than the normal amount of chatter. He was among the last of the regulars to arrive when he used the city bus system. It was a long ride with a transfer in down-town Minneapolis. Sometimes he could use Camilla's car if he had to stay late and she was not in need of it.

Chad Gigsby noticed him immediately and as was his wont started talking before the door was closed. Chad was as much an extrovert as Paul was introverted. His black hair and round face gave him a comedic expression that went with his jovial demeanor.

"Hey, Paul. Have you heard the news about Holleran?" Before Paul could say anything, Chad continued, "Last night she was giving a rah-rah speech on a college campus out East, and she slipped in a pro-life state-ment, 'It does seem like we've pushed a little too far on abortion, and some rethinking is needed there.' I know that's exactly what she said because the sound bite has been replayed on the radio a dozen times. What a gaff. Wonder what got into her shriveled brain?"

"Maybe she's subtly signaling she's changing her stand on abortion."

"That was about as subtle as a bulldozer sneaking in the back door."

Paul enjoyed Chad's outgoing personality, his use of similes, meta-phors, and hyperbole. Chad seemed to take to Paul, too. Maybe it was their being such total opposites that produce the camaraderie.

Chad continued, "The media talking heads are in a tizzy wondering what's going to happen next. They're scrambling to get an interview with her for 'clarification.'"

"Either way," Paul managed to slip in, "it puts some media attention on the issue."

While they talked, Paul was making his way to the table where he worked. His job was to cross check computer lists weeding out duplicates to prevent multiple mailings to the same person. This was important because contributors might think that if the campaign had enough money to send two or more identical solicitations, they were flush with cash. He knew it was menial work, but he was in a small way part of an energetic enterprise for a good cause which he enjoyed.

———————

That afternoon as Paul was riding home on the bus he thought about the excitement over Norma Holleran's statement. His attention, as always, was distracted by the blacks in the back. Of course, in the back. He had seen public television programs about the race riots in the fifties and sixties associated with the civil rights laws. The issue of the blacks being second class citizens had been accentuated by their having to ride in the back of buses. Now that that was a thing of the past, they wouldn't be caught dead sitting any place else. They always seemed so garrulous, too, with their vocabulary limited to little more than the "N" word and the "F" word. They seemed to be forever the underclass with that caste now codified by the legislature. The media didn't help by conferring victim status on them. It was pathetic, but there was nothing he could do about it.

As his thoughts returned to Holleran, it occurred to him that prayers were answered. He remembered Tuesday evening praying to end abortion. He was in his bedroom, after that program on TV about modern physics, string theory, and stuff like that. Sitting in his chair, he prayed that she in particular would change. Being the Speaker of the House, she was in a powerful position. He had prayed for her soul, and for the pro-life cause. It would be such a blessing if someone in a position like that would be staunchly pro-life.

Of a sudden, he had a strange feeling. He remembered praying for her to make just one statement that was pro-life. It would be so helpful. He prayed with deep faith, knowing that if he truly believed his prayer would be answered, it would be. He believed it would be. Things were falling into place. The TV program had ended at eight. She had made the statement shortly after nine. But, that was in the Eastern time zone. He was in Central, an hour earlier. She had been scheduled to speak at eight-thirty Eastern but things were delayed so she started ten minutes late. The statement had come toward the end of the half-hour speech. In a moment, the world closed in around him. He flushed and the ruckus behind him dimmed to nothing. It was shocking, unnerving. She had made the statement, as close as he could determine, at exactly the same second he made his prayer. Wow! He felt weak and his hand shook.

He was pulled about inside by conflicting feelings. Was it right to control another person's actions in this way? After all, people had free will. Free will was a terrible thing in that it could lead to eternity in hell. Yet, if he could influence her so she would turn to God, was that bad? Through each person's life, God made ample provisions for them to be saved. Maybe, he was one of the ways this woman would be helped. Moreover, how'd he know she'd be making a speech at that exact time? Another thing suddenly occurred to him. Sometime during the morning, he had made a similar prayer. He was bent over his printouts with nobody paying any attention to him. It was only a few moments, but he remembered feeling he, once again, prayed with a pure faith. Unconsciously, he shrugged. What was done, was done.

— 3 —

The President sat listlessly behind his desk in the Oval Office. Alone for a few minutes, he tapped the ash from his smoke into the candy dish. It occurred to him for the hundredth time that this wasn't such a great job. Why did so many people have to fight him at every turn? Of course, the fact that he was intent on destroying their way of life, decadent as it was, could play into the matter. He looked at the time, six o'clock. That lifted his spirits a little. Three times a week at this hour he chaired a meeting with the strategy committee composed of his unofficial inner group of advisors.

Minutes after leaving his desk, the elevator door opened two levels lower than the Oval Office. He proceeded to a little room which, a half-hour before, had been swept for listening devices by his special security detail. As he entered, the four were in their places. This was a totally off the record meeting. Therefore, there were no file folders or papers on the table, no pens in hand. The only information entering into the meeting came in the minds of the five men, and the only conclusions produced by the meeting left the same way.

Of the four men seated, two were known to the public. They were David Adams, his chief of staff, and Seth Goldman, his national science advisor, both of whom came from his former days in Chicago. The other two were not on any official roster, though they had ties to his former place of residence, also. They were Joab Feinstein, and Sal Khruz. All, except the President, were at least third generation Americans. The five made up a clique that had formed over a decade before. When they started their plans, they had the vision to see that they would arrive at this point. The surprising thing was that it had happened so soon.

As the President entered and took his place at the round table, he was greeted with hi, and hello. No names or titles were used in this meeting. Someone listening to the proceedings would have to learn the participants' identities by voiceprint, or the process on elimination. Presumably, they would not speak about themselves in the third person.

By common agreement, the President began. "What do we do about Holleran? It sounds like something is happening to her mind. She has been useful up until last evening. Looks like it's time she took her leave." He finished his remark by pointing to Sal.

"I think it would be best to be rid of her. After all, she's old enough to have a stroke or something like that. She works long hours and has a lot of stress. No one would question it."

Seth shook his head in disapproval.

Feinstein raised his index finger. He was a lean man in his fifties with a pointed chin and close cropped hair streaked with gray. His steely eyes gave no hint of warmth. The others turned their attention to him. "The next in line for her position would be a problem, and we can't have them start falling like flies to get to the one after that. It think we're stuck with her for the time being."

The President pointed to his chief of staff.

Adams' eyes glinted a little as he spoke portraying the fact that he knew he'd pass the deciding vote. "She has to go."

The President nodded as he said, "Any discussion?" There was none. That ended the matter. Three of the five had voted in favor of getting rid of Holleran. Holleran's remaining time on the job, that is, her life, depended only upon the amount of time it would take to organize the activities to end it.

For a brief moment the President, for the hundredth time, thought how great it was that he was the one leading the discussion since he was the last to join the happy group of conspirators. In reality, he did not lead it. What he failed to realize, was none of the other four had any interest in getting his opinion on the matter of Holleran. He was shown a certain courtesy because he was, after all, the President. That meant he was the conduit through which the others had to operate. And, he could not be alienated so he would come to oppose them. He completely failed to grasp the reality that a vote similar to the one just taken regarding himself would result in his being eliminated, too.

Oblivious to how tenuous his position could be, he began the next item on the agenda, *The Plan*

The Plan was the over all structure that guided their day to day activities in achieving the goal of changing the United States of America and with it the world. In addition to their other duties, each member of this group was assigned tasks related to the plan. Seth and Joab did most of the work because they had no other official duties. The other three had to be careful lest committee work they did alone or in concert with others be seen as other than routine activities.

The President turned his attention to Seth Goldman the architect of the plan, and accepted by the other three as the official leader of the group. He began on cue, "Let's hear from political affairs first. Then I have some ideas I'd like the rest of you to think about."

Sal Khruz headed another committee called political affairs, or more commonly known as dirty tricks. Its purpose was to derail promising Republican candidates long before any particular election cycle began. Once in the run-up to an election, they put their efforts into bringing public embarrassment directly onto the opposition candidates or by infiltrating their campaign staffs to generate the appearance of illegal or uncouth activities. It was a no holds barred activity, with the only rule that of not being caught. With the major media so compliant toward the liberal agenda, the revelation of such activities was seldom a problem.

Sal nodded as now the attention was on him. "Leaving aside any effects of the plan, we stand to lose many seats in both the House and the Senate this fall. Though that is typical of an off year election, it will likely be worse than normal. Our goal is to target those races where a long term Democrat appears at this point likely to be defeated by a Republican. The philosophy is to demonstrate that entrenched Democrats don't go down. There are five such races, and for all but one, we have a plan in place to handle it. The one hold out is the fourth district in St. Paul, Minnesota. In addition, there are many other contests that flop from one party to the other on a regular basis, and we are actively working on these."

"What's so hard about the guy in Minnesota?" Seth Goldman asked. "That Ellefson's been around their state capital, and Washington for years. There must to be something you can get on him."

"We've scrubbed him hard, and come up with nothing. He's good looking, articulate, and for some reason his message is resonating with the people. We're looking through his campaign staff, now. If anybody hears anything, let us know. He's proving to be a hard nut to crack."

This was nothing more than normal political back-stabbing. An opportunity would turn up, all they had to do was be patient and keep their eyes open

The President looked at Seth. "Where are we on the plan?"

"Cyber attack is still the best all around threat to push the plan to completion. It worked so well in the fall of 2008 that it's hard not to look that way. Of course, we can't expect something so unprecedented as the Republican candidate suspending his campaign to go to Washington to attend to it. Are you sure the Republicans aren't part of this committee?"

Chuckles emanated around the table.

"Even though it worked well in the last campaign, no person or organization took credit for it, as they well shouldn't have, because they were us. It was a good practice mission, though. This time, I'm working on a group to blame for it. To achieve the ultimate goal, we'll need a defining event. In that regard, may I suggest that we get things moving with our action against Holleran? Rather than make it look like a medical condition, we could make it an assassination. This won't be the defining event, but it will start things headed in that direction. I haven't finalized who should take the fall for it, but that's not important just yet. Comments?"

Joab was head of the *messy* dirty tricks department. That was the department that left "remains." If Holleran's demise were to look like an assassination, he'd be in charge of doing it. He had a long history of being a terrorist, while looking like someone who was fighting terrorism. Though born in the U.S., he went to Israel in his early teens, was trained by the Mossad, and later migrated to Chicago where he joined this gang.

The President was staring stony faced between two of the others. His ascent to power had been accomplished by smearing his opponents, destroying people's good names, and generally lying and cheating. Killing had not been necessary. The total amorality of these four with regard to murder sent a chill through him. Although, the successful completion of *The Plan* would result in the untimely deaths of millions, he had decided to deal with that in the future.

"Can the assassination be handled in a timely manner?" David Adams wanted to know. "It would be best if it could be associated with her remark last night before that becomes old news."

"I'll work the problem," Joab replied. "If it can't be handled by the end of this weekend, we may have to rethink it."

David nodded his assent.

The President looked around the table. "If there are no other pressing issues, we'll have to break this up. I have commitments for the evening."

The meeting ended and all filed out as they had entered, empty handed.

At seven o'clock the same evening, Norma Holleran was in her D.C. apartment working at her laptop computer. She had already eaten. Her housekeeper, Hilda, had left by the time she arrived home. That was normal. However, her supper had been prepared, and the table set. Things were ready for the morning, too. The coffee maker was filled with the timer adjusted to have fresh coffee waiting when she arose. There was even fruit and yogurt prepared for breakfast.

For the moment, her attention was fixed on a speech, more of an off the cuff "discussion," that she would have with some of the wavering democratic representatives the following morning. She would do most of the talking so it was important to have a good outline, with the most significant points written out in detail. As she sat at her rostrum in the house chamber during the day, she did a lot of work on her laptop. Most of what the house members had to say on any subject was predictable. Acknowledge someone and it was like playing a recording. They all wanted their chance to get their views into the Congressional Record, though, it was no longer necessary to actually say something on the House Floor to get it inserted in the Record.

She froze as if stunned by an electrical shock. Where did that comment come from? "It is important that we make it possible for doctors to opt out of performing abortions if, in conscience, they are opposed to it." It was one of the main goals of the new health care philosophy the President was pushing to remove conscience from medicine. She had signed on to it, not seeing it as a big deal. Doctors served their own interests, which was to make money. Who ever heard of a poor doctor. After all of those years of college, internship, and residency, they were entitled to a good income. What did conscience have to do with anything? It was a foreign concept that a doctor would care about the Hippocratic oath. However, there was an astounding number who did. No matter. Politics were politics. Conscience had to go.

All of the rationalizing begged the question of how that sentence had managed to appear on her computer. She had not used it to access any network nor the Internet that day. It could not have been put there by a virus. She was certain there was no time the computer had been left unattended while booted up. Yet, as she thought about it, she was working on this file while a conservative house member, an M.D. in real life, had been speaking. She sat back and realized that she could remember typing that line. She connected her printer and made a hard copy of the speech. With a yellow highlighter, she noted each pro-abortion statement. Eventually, the whole page was yellow except for one sentence.

She rose from her chair with her coffer mug and went to the kitchen. After sprinkling a few crystals of instant coffee in the mug, she filled it with hot water from the little hot-pot she kept plugged in during the evening. There was a sense of relief as she realized she had caught this one before actually saying it. Twice in a week would have finished her. This was serious.

She needed to get away and sort this out. Her mind spun through what was left of the week. It could work. A desperate mind can solve otherwise huge problems with ease. The following Monday, she was due to go to Albany, New York to do some chain jerking of that loose-as-a-goose governor. While there, she'd give a short talk to some of the party faithful at a reception, something that was part of the game. People worked and contributed as much for the ability to get up close to the politicians and hear inside gossip, as for ideology. If she could arrange it for Thursday, it would leave most of Friday open as well as the weekend. The legislative agenda pushed things that way, too. Several key house members had asked for Friday out of town for campaigning. This would make them happy and give her some favors to be called in.

In the little living room, she sat in her reading chair and put her feet up on the footstool. Sipping the coffee, she could only think of one person, Wally Stern. He was a shoestring relative, but more of a friend. Not a close friend, but an understanding man. She reached over to her handbag and retrieved her cell phone. Irritated that his number wasn't in her speed dial list she had to get up and go to the Rolodex on her desk. It rang three times and then was answered.

"Hi, Wally. It's Norma."

"How ya doing? It's been a while. Life on the top floor of the political poop pile must be keeping you busy."

"Yeah. As always. Listen, I have to talk to you. It's urgent and personal in a professional sort of way."

"Let's see. In women-speak that means 'my personal life is starting to interfere with my job.'"

Wally was a professor of a lot of things. He studied and gave courses on philosophy, linguists, and the paranormal, to name a few. An all around bright guy, she had always turned to him with perplexing problems.

"That's about it. Unexplained personal things are happening to me that are affecting my professional life. And, I do mean *odd* unexplained things. Does that grab your interest?"

There was a pause. "You mean like hearing voices?"

"No. I say things I never thought in a hundred years I'd say."

"You mean the statement earlier in the week?"

"Yes. Now, it's happened again."

"You need a break."

"No argument there. I'd like some time to talk and think about this away from everything. I just don't have any place to go. You mentioned a hide away in the Adirondacks once. Do you still have that?"

"It's not mine, but yes, it's still there. You telling me you want to spend a few days in a bucolic setting? To say it's rustic is to put a positive spin on it."

"Yeah. I'm that desperate."

"You're a such-much important personage, though. Can you drop out of sight for a few days without anybody caring?"

"It might surprise you how little anyone cares. I'll have to tell someone where I'm gong, and I always carry a little beeper with me. If it goes off it says there's an emergency. Then I flip a switch on the thing and that will locate me so I can be brought to Washington. No emergency, nobody cares."

"How do we do this? I'll see about the cabin being available. You work your schedule. I have your personal email address. You have mine. We'll set it up that way. That sound okay?"

"Good. I have to go to Albany, New York sometime soon. If I can arrange it for tomorrow, you could meet me in Albany, early Friday afternoon. Could you do that?"

There was an extended pause accompanied by rustling paper sounds. "I'd drive up, it's about eight hours, and we'll meet there. Let me know as soon as you can. You'll need warm clothes. It'll be cold at night, and during the day if it rains."

"That's okay. I'll manage. And, Wally, thanks."

Immediately, she called her office. There was always someone there this early in the evening. "Yeah. Hi Donna, it's me." Donna was not her top appointments broker, but coming up fast.

"What do you think about getting that trip to Albany moved up to tomorrow afternoon? I could meet with the worker bees in the evening and have a sit-down with the governor Friday morning. There are some friends in the area who have invited me over for the weekend and I could really use the break. I'd like to sort of disappear shortly after noon on Friday. Think it could work?"

"Don't see why not. Let me see," she clacked away on a computer. "We can free up your schedule here easily enough. We'll jolly the governor around and he'll do it. He's always been accommodating, even if a little off the reservation at times."

Another pause, and then, "Okay. It looks like a go. We'll firm it up in the morning. Let 'em know you'll be there."

"Oh, thanks, Donna. You're a jewel. Bye."

Ten minuets later Norma sent the email to Wally and leaned back. Done. Now, all she had to do was make it through a day and a half without destroying her political career.

If Norma Holleran had been shocked by the sentence on her laptop, it was certainly not a greater blow than that experienced by Alvin Freidmuth as he listened to the recorded conversation between his father, Eugene, and his father's lawyer.

"The bastard!" Alvin seethed as he saw his fortune slipping away.

"After all I've done for the creep, he gives me this as thanks."

Actually, Alvin hadn't done all that much for his dear ol' dad. He had tried at times, but what could you do for a man who had everything? Besides that, there was never any love lost between the two. The old man had more millions than he could count, and continued to be a miser. He certainly didn't need Alvin. True, at times his father had helped him out of messes when things had gone sour on some of his attempts to duplicate his father's financial acumen. Why did one man have so much talent and wealth while the rest of mortal men ended up with zip?

The recording was from a week that ended about noon that day. Hours ago the private investigator Alvin had on retainer had delivered the recording to him. It was a thirty-two gigabyte flash drive, commonly called a thumb drive. Marv Wilson, his PI, had bugged the office of his ninety-six year old father. This was not the normal "bug" people think about. Those devices transmitted continuously or perhaps only while there were sounds in the room. The shortcoming of those was the ability of the target to "sweep" the room with a receiver that could detect the transmissions and find the bug. The way to defeat the sweep was to have a recording bug that did not transmit unless commanded to do so. All Marv had to do was stop his car within a half block of the house when he knew no one would be sweeping the room for bugs. Upon receiving the correct code, the recording device would download the information to him in a burst transmission.

Alvin's concern was his father's increasing desire to change his will. After his father had alluded to the fact that he might leave Alvin essentially nothing, Alvin had instigated the eavesdropping program. As with any bug, it required a lot of time to review the recorded conversations in order to extract useful information. However, modern technology took much of the drudgery out of that. Marv had, for a fee, given him a piece of software that did some useful things for this sort of shady activity. First, it was fairly good at converting speech to a text file that could be searched for key words using any conventional word processor. Then, there was a mode where it searched the recorded sound data for words. He'd type in a word like "will." The program would put together what that word would sound like and search the data for a match. A third method was to speak the search word into the microphone attached to his computer and have it search for the word. Using the three methods, he had what he needed, and what it revealed did not leave him a happy man.

Some time ago Eugene had expressed a desire to locate the family of his first wife. Recently, he had become almost obsessed with locating someone from her relation. Eugene was operating on the assumption that his daughter from his first marriage was dead. Alvin had never learned why he felt that way.

Alvin had always thought his sister, Norma, and he would share the inheritance. Alvin's wife was especially looking forward to wallowing in millions. He had his orders to insure that nothing interfered with the plan. The recording revealed that his father had hired a PI firm to see if his first wife's family could be found. As the old man's days were drawing to a close, he seemed to be feeling increasing guilt about forsaking his first daughter. He had a driving need to make it right. In one of the conversations with his lawyer, he even suggested leaving his entire estate to whomever he could find of his first wife's family. In Alvin's opinion the man was clearly no longer competent, though, now was not the time to try to prove it.

The old man openly discussed his two children from his second marriage, Norma and Alvin. He said he hated to leave anything to Norma due to her far left feminist views. In the position she held as Speaker of the House of Representatives, she could do enormous damage with a large sum of money. Alvin was well meaning, most of the time, but a bumbling man in his opinion. The money would soon be gone with nothing to show for it so he was reluctant to leave him much.

The conversations with the lawyer, Fen Lions, were almost daily. Charitable causes came up in one way or another most days. Four days previously they discussed leaving all of his money to charity. They wrangled on about it with his father's opinion being that a little here and there would be fine. But, he knew from experience that no charity could adequately stay on mission after a big windfall. A substantial infusion of money required new staff to administer it, which always led to corruption and public scandal after which the charity was dead. He certainly had no intention of putting it into the public treasury at any level of government. He didn't get rich without his battles with various bureaucracies. As a result, he always reverted to his children, as undeserving as they might be.

As Alvin skimmed through the text file of the eavesdropped conversations, he found that earlier today, his father was excited about a new strategy. Alvin's software keyed the text to its location in the recording. At this point, Alvin reverted to actually listening to the two men's conversation.

"Have you heard what's on all the newscasts today? Norma made a clearly pro-life statement in a speech Tuesday evening. The media are going nuts about it and she's not commenting. You wouldn't suppose she's coming around and seeing how destructive to society that whole liberal agenda is, would you? What if I leave all the money to Norma, on the condition she repent of her radical leftist attitudes?"

There was a long pause in the conversation. The lawyer then spoke. "My suggestion would be to wait a while. That might have been a slip. It would be unlikely she could be reelected in the fall after jettisoning her liberal views."

Eugene countered, "But, with enough money she might have a change of heart, and drop out of the rat race. Money can do strange things to people. I want you to see how this could be set up. We'd have to be careful that she didn't grab the money and then go back to her old ways."

The old man seemed to be grabbing on to the idea like a bulldog. "Years ago she opined that she had no causes other than herself. The route to success was the way society was headed. It was going that way with or without her, so why not ride along."

The lawyer added, "There's always hope, I guess."

"Here's a way my money could do some good, and at the same time stay in the family."

Alvin was startled. He had not heard so much animation in his father's voice in years.

His father's parting words were, "And, I'll keep the PIs on the trail of Joyce's people."

There followed the rustling of papers, and parting pleasantries.

One of his father's statements was particularly apt with regards Alvin. "Money can do strange things to people." How true. He tapped in the number for Marv Wilson and made an appointment to see him at seven in a sports bar.

Shortly after seven, they were into their first beers as Alvin presented the case. Marv listened attentively his head leaning over the table only inches from Marv's. As expected the sound level was high with a dozen large screen monitors presenting sporting events of various kinds. There was no important game at the time so each screen presented something different. One even had a lacrosse match underway.

Alvin was concluding the facts, "Norma's quite an important person. How does one even get close to her? If I were to go to Washington, it wouldn't help. We hardly know each other any more. She'd only allow me a perfunctory visit. And, besides what could I say that would help the situation?"

Alvin had already arrived at the conclusion that talking was not the course of action to produce the desired results. He hoped that Marv would suggest what he had in mind. That would make it easier to get him on his side since Marv would be the one to execute the plan.

Marv was at home in this particular type of establishment. He had played tackle on his college football team, ten years before, and had stayed in shape. Being six-three and two-forty, he was a formidable man. He actually had a hint of a neck because his head was a little larger than normal. Barring the oversized head, he would have been the typical fireplug lineman. In spite of his size, his movements were smooth and sure. Unless standing beside a more normally proportioned person, his size was not evident.

Standing beside, even setting across the table from, Alvin, Marv's size was evident. Alvin was five-ten and one-sixty, even with a little paunch. He was out of shape and not particularly handsome. Their physical disparity had no effect on their relationship. In the old west, the six-gun was the equalizer. In today's world, it was money.

Marv leaned a little closer to Alvin. "It sounds to me like you think the solution is to take out Norma."

That was close to what Alvin had been thinking. The way it was phrased was a little off. Who cared? One way or the other the subject had to be broached.

"Now that you mention it, that is a particularly direct way to solve the problem. Would it even be possible, though? She must have all sorts of protection. In addition, it would have to be very cleverly done. The investigation would be intense. Me, my father, and a lot of money, all point in one direction. And, I don't like the direction."

"But, you see the dearth of alternatives, don't you?"

Alvin sipped his beer as the waitress appeared. They both ordered another beer and a burger with fries.

"Unless," Marv continued when the attendant gave her attention to the next table, "you think she'll pass up the money."

"Well," Alvin drew out the word. "No. I wouldn't think she would. We aren't close anymore, but she hasn't changed. She'd take it in a minute. What dear old dad doesn't understand is that while his lawyer is a canny man, she has access to the world's finest. Everyone around her would want both the money and her continued support of the causes. Once Dad was dead, she'd be back on message and they'd figure out how to keep the money."

"That brings up another point," Marv said. "What time frame are we talking?"

"Pretty short. He doesn't have much time left. It could be a matter of weeks before he no longer has a full deck and can't change his will, that's why he's pushing the lawyer and PIs so hard. I'm afraid he'll make the rash decision to leave it all to Norma, or the relatives of Joyce his first wife. Or, any other hair-brained idea that strikes him. His plan would be to change it back to the way it is now if the other options fell through. But, by that time, he could be declared incompetent thus leaving whatever he had in place as his final will."

"Okay. We have to move on this. Step one of any project is what's in it for me?"

"It depends on what you do. If we take the 'direct approach' as we've mentioned, and you are the one doing it, you get ten percent."

"And, that would be how much in any ball park you want to use."

"Twenty to twenty-five million as of the statement I saw a month ago."

"This would be transmitted to my deserving, poverty stricken, hands in what manner?"

Alvin had known for some time that he could draw money out of one of his father's assets at any time to raise liquid money. That investment was a high stakes international mutual fund that paid better than ten percent a year. The minimum deposit or withdrawal was one million dollars.

"Cash to an off shore account, if that's what you want. Tax consequences would be your concern. However, with the right moves my broker should be able to help along those lines."

If Marv had known how inept Alvin had been in the past with each of the operations required to accomplish the outlined means of remuneration, he might have extracted himself from further involvement in the project at that moment. Lacking that knowledge, however, he pressed ahead.

"It's important we learn as much about the habits of your sister as possible. It would be especially important to know what she does in her off times. There's no possibility of reaching her where she works. Those people are totally paranoid about security. And well they should be. There's hardly a day goes by that they don't pass some law that destroys the livelihood of at least a few thousand people."

"Fine for you to say. But, how are we going to find out anything about how she lives?"

"What's this we, *Kemo Sabe*? You're the one who'll find out, or there's no deal."

"Why me? That's what I pay you for, *Tonto*."

"Because, Running Bull, we are discussing more than snatching a little information. If we did pull it off, you or I would have to immediately remove the latest bug that I left in your dad's office. After that we act dumb and wait for the old man to die. First, though, you have to get information on the woman. With some facts in hand, I may be persuaded to take a trip out east as my only further obligation to consummate our above mentioned deal."

"Then the deal's dead because I wouldn't know where to start."

"Not dead. I'll show you what to do, and then you'll do it. You will enter the world of ones and zeros. The cyberspace of communications. We all live in it. When you called me on your cell phone to set up this meeting, the information was out there to be collected. If it was not, the only reason was that nobody took an interest in it. Look how easily I bugged your father's office, and all the neat software tools I gave you to sift through it. Expand that a trillion times and you have what the FBI can do. Which, by the way, means if we proceed with this, we cannot call one another again in any way. We will have to set up meets at prearranged times and places. Or we can plan to leave written messages at prescribed places like bulletin boards in Laundromats."

Alvin's face twitched as he considered the situation. Might as well take the next step. Nothing needed to be decided until they had information. "Okay. When do we do this?"

"Now. Tonight. You leave and drive away. Return and stop along the street in five minutes. I stay and finish my beer, leave and take a little walk to stretch my legs. We go to your place and I show you what to do. After that, you return me here. We'll figure out how to get together." After a pause, "What about your wife?"

"She's already got half the money spent, in her mind, that is. I've insisted that there are to be no transactions until we have the money. This is her night out for dinner with the girls so she won't be home for a couple of hours."

"That'll be enough time."

Alvin was half standing and then slumped back into this chair. "Something just occurred to me. What if my place is bugged?"

"Then we're both toast."

They finished their meal and set out on the first step into their world of crime.

— 4 —

Alvin's study was reasonably nice, though nothing special, no fireplace, no French doors opening onto the veranda, simply an extra bedroom that was his private space. There was the computer table immediately on the left upon entering with a wooden desk to the side of it that was too cluttered to be functional. The two easy chairs and footstool took up most of the room to the right. The single maple bookcase graced the space on the wall opposite the door. The two black speakers standing as sentinels on either side did nothing for the decor. The DVD player and a pile of discs occupied the top shelf. The few books were not dusty because the maid came in once a week and dusted them. They were never opened.

As they had driven from the bar Marv inquired if Alvin had any email contact with Norma. To his satisfaction, they communicated a couple of times a year with the last time at Christmas.

While the computer was booting up Marv asked, "Where'd you get the machine? It looks a little old."

"A place I worked upgraded all the computers in the building and sold the old ones off for fifty bucks apiece. It's done everything I've ever needed."

"Did they write down the serial number of the one they sold you, or did they just take one off the shelf and give it to you?"

Alvin gave a slight chuckle. "All sales were final with no guarantees, so the computer geek asked which one I wanted. I pointed to one, wrote a check and walked out with it."

"That's not bad. Depending on how things work out, you may be dropping this one on a rock and buying a new computer. I'll explain in a minute."

With the computer on line Marv said, "I hope you didn't delete that last email from your sister."

"No. I save family correspondence in the file called 'Family.' Pretty clever, don't you think?"

"Would've fooled me. Call up Family."

Alvin didn't have a clue where this was going, but followed instructions.

"The thing you have to remember is that email is about the most non-private means of communication ever invented. The only thing less secure is to have a shouting match with someone in the middle of a crowded room. We all like to imagine it's secure. Rubbish. You must also realize that although it's not secure, it's complicated. When you send an email it's like sending a letter in that it first goes to the local post office, and then through a series of sorting stations before getting delivered. An average email makes fifteen to twenty stops. At each stop, it leaves a 'note' that it was there, and has a code attached identifying the station. Most people don't care about that so the average ISP, Internet Service Provider, strips it off before displaying the message. Let me show you. Highlight that email from your wife, but don't open it. Now right click on it. There you see a lot more information about the email. We'll start there, though you won't know what's happening."

"So when do we find some useful information?"

"We'll get there. With billions of emails sent each day, it's necessary to handle them as efficiently as possible. One way to enhance the through-put of the system is to make sure every chunk of data that it processes is the same size. Therefore, each email is broken up into several packets. Each packet has the sending and receiving address in it as well as the place of the packet in the email so the receiving station knows how to put it back together. It also tags it with station information as it goes along. In addition, your BIOS number is included in the email."

"Huh?"

"BIOS stands for Basis Input Output System which is some software that's hardwired into your computer. Its number is the unique serial number of your processor. That's why it's nice your computer is not exactly traceable to you. Any email you sent to your sister would contain your computer's BIOS number. However, if nobody could prove you bought that computer, and if you in fact didn't have it when someone came looking, it would make connections to you more difficult. I tell you this so you understand a little of what we are to do next."

Marv opened the little soft sided case he had brought in with him and removed a CD. "There's a program on this disc called a packet sniffer. It chases after those packets that result from the Internet system doing its job. These programs actually have useful purposes such as network troubleshooting. But, face it, most of them are used by hackers. Nearly all emails are sent in clear text and can be scooped up by packet sniffers, that includes user names and passwords."

"Wait a minute. Wouldn't someone as important as Norma encrypt her messages?"

"Her business correspondence, yes. However, not her casual personal messages. There's a good reason for that, too. If she wanted to send you an encrypted email it wouldn't do either of you any good if you couldn't decrypt it. That means the two of you would have had to agreed on an encrypt/decrypt system in advance. And, that's too much bother for the vast number of the incredibly boring emails that are sent. They're secure because no sane person would care about them—except us. That's where we win."

As the sniffer program loaded, and installed itself, Marv continued. "Our strategy will be as follows. We'll start with Norma's message to you. From that, we should get her password. Then we'll make one sortie into her inbox hoping to get some idea of what she will be doing this weekend, or next. If we can connect to a friend's email, we'll never have to touch her end again. We'll watch the friend's email instead. It's possible, being who she is, she might have a 'ping detector' which is another type of program that tries to detect our sniffer. Then, of course, we could have a program that could detect if our sniff has been pinged. As you might guess, there's a lot of people in the world with way too much time on their hands."

"What if she doesn't have her computer on? Do we have to wait until she gets up in the morning and logs on to the net?"

"Of course not. You're not getting it. The emails in her inbox aren't on her computer, but in a storage space allocated to her on her Internet Service Provider's hard drive. That's up twenty-four-seven." After making the final entries in the installation process, the packet sniffer was ready to go.

"Okay. You're armed and dangerous. Here we go. Type in her email address."

It took less than five minutes to have Norma's password. With that they entered her email account and two minutes later had downloaded all the messages in her inbox, and her sent messages.

"Here's one that's only an hour old. Who's Wally? Any idea?"

"Yeah. Wally, no, *Doctor* Wally Stern."

"Doctor of what?"

"Don't know. Not medical, though.

"What's he do?"

"Professor of something or other at a college in the D.C. area. He's a shoestring relative, second cousin, twice removed, or something like that. His parents and my parents knew one another as friends rather than relatives."

They both read the email.

Wally,

It looks like I can be free in Albany in the early afternoon on Friday. If you can get dibs on the cabin, we should be good. I just have to discuss this with you. Hope you can come through.

Regards, Norma

"This looks promising," Marv said, all business.

"The cabin would likely be in the mountains around Albany. That'd be perfect. The question is, would he fly up there to meet her at the airport and rent a car, or drive up?"

Alvin knew this was PI stuff so let Marv think. After a bit Marv continued, "Suppose it depends on the type of cabin. If it were really plush, he'd fly because it would be fully stocked. It could even come complete with a butler. If it were back woodsy, he'd want to bring along groceries, sleeping bags, and a ton of paraphernalia. In that case, he'd drive. Any ideas?"

"This is just a hunch, so don't blame me if it's wrong. If Norma were getting the loan of the cabin, it'd be plush. She knows a lot of high rollers. Wally's another story. His friends are not likely to, on the average mind you, be rich. He might know somebody here and there that's well to do."

"Okay. While we're at it let's hit Wally's email."

"Wow! Look at that, pay dirt again."

They had an email from Wally to Norma that had been sent a few minutes after they had hit Norma's account.

Norma,

Got the cabin. We're on. As soon as you can, let me know where to pick you up. I'll buy some food and bring along what else I think we'll need. Brace yourself for rustic.

Wally

"Get off the Internet and start again. Then call up MapQuest, or Google Maps. We have to see how far it is from D.C. to Albany. Then, you have to get me Wally's home address, car model, and plate number. I'll have to leave in the morning. I'll need some money for time and expenses for the trip just in case they're heading to Albany, Minnesota, rather than Albany, New York, or any of a million other things go wrong. I never work on my own money. If it pays off, we'll settle up, so don't worry. Can you write me a check for, let's see, twenty-five grand?"

"That much?" There was shock in Alvin's voice.

"Gotta fly out which means I have to buy what I need locally. This isn't a case of following a teen who has a shoplifting habit. Can you do it?"

Alvin winced. "Yes . . . I think so. You sure you'll need it all?"

"No. There's some contingency in that. You'll get back the unused money when I return."

"I can't write a check for that much. I'll be able to give you a bank draft as soon as the banks open in the morning. That okay?"

Marv agreed and they began working the net again. It looked like a seven or eight hour drive to Albany, so Marv assumed Wally'd drive up in the morning. However, he had to be prepared for the eventuality he left the evening before. Alvin continued to be amazed at how easily Marv managed to find Wally's home address, and car registration off the Internet. He was struck by how little privacy anyone had any more.

After they had finished, Alvin drove Marv to the sports bar where he had left his car and returned home. He sat in one of the easy chairs in his den sipping Scotch. What could he be thinking? This was madness. It didn't occur to him at the time that he was in as much shock over the twenty-five thousand dollars as he was with the fact that he had ordered his own sister assassinated.

Thursday, June 3

Eugene Freidmuth, at ninety-six, believed in staying active. Every national news broadcast had at least one item about a health issue. For the out of shape and aging population anything to do with health was news. Even for people in good shape, it was an issue of importance because upward to twenty percent of the gross domestic product went to medical care. The research into various aspects of Alzheimer's disease was of particular interest to Eugene. All the data indicated that the more active, both physically and mentally, a person was the less likely he was to get the dreaded affliction. With exercise equipment, rain or shine, he did his daily workout. Over the years, his weights had shrunk in size, and the speed of his treadmill had tended downward as well. But, he kept at it.

For mental stimulation, he continued to manage his own affairs, as well as being active on the board of directors for a couple of charitable organizations. In the evening, he read books of all kinds. His eclectic selections covered everything from spiritual works, to novels, biographies, and histories. Someone had told him that reading required much more mental activity than watching television. He enjoyed a movie on DVD now and then, but that was passive entertainment requiring little imagination. Reading novels in particular was beneficial because it was a participatory activity. First, it required the calculating ability of the brain to decode the characters on the page into words and sentences. Then, the reasoning function was required to follow the plot. Further, the reader was forced to access memories stimulating mental processes different from the first two. The reader became a partner with the author by fleshing out the scenes from his own experiences. In short, reading a novel exercised more mental functions than almost any other activity.

Eugene lived in the Highland Park neighborhood of St. Paul. The house was non-assuming from the street. The highly pitched roof and white stucco exterior with the characteristic dark wood planks embedded in it gave it an Alpine look. Fifteen-foot high long-needle pine bushes around the front added to the impression. He maintained a large airy room in the front of the comfortable sprawling home as an office. Each morning, after a balanced low fat breakfast, he was to be seen behind the ornate oak desk checking stock prices, and other financial news that affected his investments. It was here that he met with business associates. He did little traveling to the business districts of either Minneapolis or St.

Paul letting others come to him rather than the opposite. He had the money, they could do the driving.

This morning at precisely eight-thirty Eugene's house keeper showed a thirty-something man into the room. His name was Dillard Sulk who was employed by The Alpha Agency. Names fascinated Eugene. Who, but a man with the name of Dillard, would work for a detective agency? He mentally corrected himself. They were now called professional investigators. The name of his employer was sleuthy in itself. With an opening like, "Hello. I'm Dillard with Alpha," nobody would have any more information than before he had spoken, yet the introduction would have been made.

That aside, The Alpha Agency had done good work for him in the past so it was only normal that Eugene would ask their assistance in the matter of locating relatives of his first wife.

"Have a seat Dillard. Care for a cup of coffee?" He held up a thermocarafe as he spoke. The man shook his head. "I always allow myself two cups in the morning," Eugene continued, "it clears away the settled dust from over night."

With the coffee declined and pleasantries out of the way, Dillard could see Eugene was intent on the purpose of the visit that had been set up on the previous evening so Dillard began. "As I reported before, after the first week of searching we had not located any likely relatives of Joyce Sutton." Sutton was the maiden name of Eugene's first wife, Joyce. "However, using the lead you gave me a few days ago, we've located a woman who might be related to her, perhaps a younger sister. This woman's husband is dead, and she has one surviving son that we can locate. There are hints there may be another son, but we haven't found him yet. We have not approached the son. If we could find this woman's county of birth, we should be able to trace her to your first wife if there is a relationship. However, that might not even do it because she was born during the Great Depression, and people moved around a lot back then looking for work. After so many years, there is frequently almost no way to establish a person's lineage for certain. We surreptitiously made an inquiry of her personally but she gave no hint of the fact she might be related to Joyce. She was most noncommittal. It was as if she were hiding something."

"You said 'almost no way' which implies there is a way."

"Yes. There is a way brought to us by modern technology, and that's DNA testing. I mentioned this at our first meeting on this case. Have you thought about that? You remember I mentioned that to do that test, we need a sample of DNA from Joyce or your daughter, Margaret. If we had it, we could determine if there was a relationship. Our agent, a middle aged woman, approached the woman we located, under the guise of selling cemetery plots. While in her apartment she asked to use the bathroom and lifted a hair sample from her brush. Now we need reference DNA to do the test."

Eugene opened a side drawer of his desk and pulled out a thin hard cover book. "Have you ever heard of a baby book?"

Dillard shook his head.

"Joyce started one for Margaret. It was common in those days. Mothers used it to record the growing up years of their children. It contained information about the birth and christening as well as when the child had the measles, and other childhood diseases. Where possible it contained pictures of birthday parties, and later school plays, that sort of thing. A common practice was to put a lock of hair either from the first birthday or the first haircut in a little envelope in the book. There is such a lock of hair in the book. It's very old and may have deteriorated, but it is of a certainty Margaret's."

"That should do it." Dillard opened his attaché case and produced a plastic sample bag and a tweezers. "May I?" he said reaching for the book.

He carefully extracted a few stands of hair and deposited them in the bag after which he zipped it closed.

"Give us a few days and we'll see."

Eugene could see the pleasure in the man's expression. The fees he paid to the agency were on a time and expenses basis with a bonus for success.

The man, looking every bit of his ninety-six years, swiveled his chair around and watched through the window as Dillard closed his car door and drove away. A melancholy mood fell on him as thoughts of the past welled up. How could he have forsaken little Margaret the way he had? Having been young and dumb didn't help once one was old and regretful.

Since shortly after Eugene's first wife, Joyce, had died, Eugene had given little thought to Margaret. Joyce's death was sad, but sad things did enter people's lives. He and the daughter's mother had been married during their teens. They had, against the odds, fallen madly in love. Their happiness flowered despite it being the Depression and times were hard. It was something they rarely talked about, but both felt deeply and truly. His wife liked to read and often they'd discuss stories and the specific characters in them. One such was *The Scarlet Letter* by Nathaniel Hawthorne. There was a line that caught her fancy and she read it to him. It was so poignant that he never forgot it. "Let men tremble to win the hand of woman, unless they win along with it the utmost passion of her heart." She had come to him and hugged him close as she whispered in his ear, "You have the utmost passion of my heart." He had made a feeble attempt to say it was reciprocated, finally saying that though he had nothing, he had everything. She said that was the sweetest thing she had ever heard. It was a moment he never forgot.

The arrival of Margaret brought them closer still, more than they had ever imagined it could. Some time after the baby's first birthday tragedy struck. His wife unexpectedly took ill and shortly thereafter died. He knew such a love was only to come to a man once in his lifetime. The gift of angels had been taken away. Though, in sorrow to the depths of his soul, he was not bitter. They had not squandered their gift with petty grievances. They had been young and in love, as only the young can love. In a day, he was old.

Grief stricken, he didn't know what to do. He had no marketable skills, something Joyce never seemed to mind. Neither of them having relatives who could manage another mouth to feed, he was advised to put the child up for adoption, which meant she went to an orphanage. The little girl, having been brought through the first year of her life in an idyllic family with doting parents, became irascible with the loss of both parents and therefore was not a first choice for couples seeking to adopt.

The first few years he tried to visit her when he could, but then his first break at acquiring a worthwhile profession took him to Chicago. After that the visits stopped. He always hoped to get enough time and money to bring the girl to Chicago and hire someone to look after her. One thing led to another and it never happened.

His daughter wasn't even three when he remarried. He inquired into her status at the time, feeling not a little remorse for not having kept in contact with her. The response he received from the orphanage was that a couple was proceeding with the legal work to adopter Margaret, and that they would be given first consideration. His second wife, being none too keen on the idea of a stepchild, caused the matter to be dropped. Some years later when Eugene had a pressing need to locate Margaret, he learned that the adoption proceedings at the time of his second marriage had fallen through. As such, Margaret grew up in the institution.

His second marriage, to all outward appearances, met the norm of a good marriage. Both were faithful, and lived in harmony. It was a simple fact of the calculus of the heart that nothing would ever fill the void left by the loss of his first love.

———————————

Marv Wilson arrived at Dulles Airport south of Baltimore Thursday afternoon. His schedule was tight, though doable as long as things went right. After picking up his rental car, a gray Ford Explorer, his first stop was at a place that in another world would have been called something like Detective Technologies and Equipment, but was in fact called The Hill Company. It was a one stop shopping center for the things he needed. Most of the things were easy like a GPS cell phone transponder and receiver with display for mounting inside his vehicle. In addition, he needed a simple hand held GPS locator of the type used by hikers. Completing his list of electronics were a couple of non-contract cell phones that were traceable to no one. He didn't expect to need them, but unforeseen things happened at times. He also bought hiking boots and a camouflage suit that was made of a modern fabric that was waterproof and vapor breathing to let perspiration escape. The nasty item was a nine-millimeter pistol with silencer. Included in his purchases was the return policy which meant he could return the items and have them disposed of. That location was different from the point of purchase for obvious reasons. This meant the burnable items like the boots and suit were incinerated, and the other items would be ground into powder or melted. It was the surest way. No matter where a person dumped something, it could be found, and worst of all he might be seen dumping it. The electronics were obvious. There was no telling what incriminating evidence those little microcircuits would retain in their shriveled brains. The boots and clothing were also a problem. They could retain fingerprints and samples of DNA in perspiration, scuffed off skin and a dozen other ways. The boots could leave telltale prints in the mud, as well as carry away samples of the soil from the scene in the tread. A clean-up of his vehicle was also included.

After his shopping spree, he was off to find Carl Campus, a.k.a. Dr. Wally Stern. A half-hour later he slowed to a stop on Stern's street. The number on the mailbox gave the location, except that there were four mailboxes on the same stand. Two he could eliminate as not the right houses since they could be seen to the west side of the street with house numbers matching mail boxes. The other two were obviously on the east side and were not visible. There were shrubs along the street and the land leading to the houses went over a slight rise before descending to a shallow ravine making for abnormally secluded properties. He could see the lots weren't terribly large in this area of Silver Spring, Maryland. That being the case he wouldn't know what awaited him if he drove into either of the houses that seemed to be associated with the other two mailboxes. He could drive up as Stern was doing yard work in the front. He'd be seen and remembered as a stranger arriving at an odd time.

Marv had been stopped for a full minute and was forced to move on. He hoped his pause had not attracted attention. As he drove, he was dismayed that there was no place near the houses, such as a park, where he could inconspicuously wait. A mile down the curving street he turned around and headed back trying to see something that would aid in his mission. A car in front of him set the pace so his speed would be normal for the neighborhood. In cases like this, it was of extreme importance not to draw attention. He passed the location of the four mailboxes seeing nothing more than he had on his first inspection. A hundred yards past them, as he rounded a bend, he caught sight in his mirror of a car emerging from one of the suspect driveways. It appeared to be coming his way as it was lost from view by the turn. And, it was blue.

Dr. Stern owned a blue GMC Yukon. Marv slowed a few miles per hour until the blue vehicle came into view behind him. It was an SUV. Could it be? If it was, this was prefect. Who ever suspected they were being followed by the car in front of them? They approached a stoplight that was red. Seeing the following car put on his left turn signal well before the intersection, Marv waited two seconds and put on his, too. He was still fifty yards from the intersection so it would not seem obvious he was mimicking the blue car. They got a green before they had to stop and turned onto the four lane cross street. Immediately, Marv guided to the right lane and accelerated slowly. The blue SUV turned into the left lane and sped past. It was easy to verify the plate. He had his man.

He let two more cars pass him on the left before pulling into the left lane. A couple of miles later the blue Yukon turned left into the parking lot of a large supermarket. Marv went past the market, and proceeded down the street. He turned around and entered the parking lot from the opposite direction. The Yukon was parked into the double row of spaces with the back facing the traffic lane. That was the obvious way to park if the owner expected to have a large order of groceries and wanted the rear hatch unobstructed for loading.

Marv pulled in nose to nose with the Yukon. He got out and looked at his tires as if he expected one might be going flat. He used a ballpoint pen as one would use a tire pressure gauge and pretended to check one of his front tires. Stooping at the front in the two-foot space between the bumpers, he looked under his vehicle. The whole exercise was to give the impression to anyone who might be watching that he thought there was something wrong with his Explorer. While on his knees, he tore the paper off an adhesive strip on an object the size of a pack of gum. As unobtrusively as possible he slipped it between the slats in the grill of the Yukon pressing it firmly against the back of a slat. This was a good place because all automobile grills were plastic which wouldn't interfere with transmission and reception. He had to marvel yet again at how miniaturized these things had become. It was a GPS receiver that would transmit the location of the vehicle by means of the cell phone system. All he had to do was dial it up on the receiver in his vehicle and it would display the location of the Yukon on a moving map. He could be a thousand miles away. If the Yukon were within a cell phone system, he'd know where it was within three feet.

The operation completed to his satisfaction, Marv stood up and shrugged as if finding nothing wrong. He walked to the entrance of the supermarket, went to the service counter, bought a newspaper, and left by the same entrance. It would not do to be seen coming into the parking lot, fooling around with his car and leaving without going into the store. Ours was a purpose driven society. Nobody did anything without a specific end in view. With this in mind, his precautions were not without merit. Occasionally, someone drove another to a store and then waited in the car. With nothing but boredom for company, any activity within sight was of interest.

Exiting the parking lot, Marv drove a mile in the direction of Wally's house and found a place to park. A half-hour later the Yukon was moving. He saw it drive past him exactly as his display showed it should be. All systems were go.

— 5 —

Major Pat Harbor had the Learjet C-21A holding on the south end of the taxiway at Andrews Air Force Base located to the southeast of the District. The C-21A was the Air Force designation of the civilian Learjet 35. In the passenger compartment that could accommodate twelve passengers were two women, the speaker of the House of Representatives, and her assistant. One of them would be questioning the delay any second. He'd rather be diving on a heavily defended target than chauffeuring VIPs from this stinking city.

Click. "Major! What's holding us up? We haven't moved in ten minutes. Kick it in the ass!"

"Sorry, Madam Speaker. There are a couple of F-15s holding at the end of the runway. Their refueler isn't on station yet. They don't want their fuel state falling below minimums before they can top-off."

"I don't care about fuel state. Contact the tower and tell those other things to get out of the way. Tell them who I am. Do it."

"Yes, Ma'am."

Major Harbor looked over to his copilot and rolled his eyes. The tower was aware of who his passengers were. It didn't matter. You don't risk two F-15s and their crews for some hot shot female ego from inside the beltway. He was about to call the tower and get an estimate of the remaining delay, when the F-15s start to roll. Halfway down the runway they rotated and hit the afterburners for a few seconds a maneuver designed to gain altitude quickly and lessen the noise over the power jungle.

Norma Holleran was about as irritated as she'd ever been. That airhead governor had better have a limo waiting for me, she thought. Taking a deep breath, she was counting the hours. Tonight and Friday morning were the only hurdles left. It had happened again earlier in the day. This time, luckily, it had been a comment to a staffer, who was told in no uncertain terms he'd better keep his mouth shut or she'd personally slit his throat. What was it about that cursed abortion issue? Dammit! Who cared about some chunks of nothing, not even born yet? There was growing talk in liberal circles that even normal babies weren't human until they began to be conscious of others around them, that is, until they were two or three years old. The idea was by no means new, but it had been getting traction in recent months. The strident pro-life opposition was trying to get a constitutional amendment that said even embryos were human from the moment of conception. Not in her lifetime!

Her frustration level lessened when the plane started to move. Was the job starting to get to her? She kept asking herself that question. Why should it? She recalled her first term as a freshman representative. It had been the most stressful time since becoming involved in politics. Every-thing since then she compared to that, and nothing had even come close. Nothing, except that brief time earlier in her life, but she didn't think about that much any more. Yes, life at the top had its demands, but she had learned how to handle the career she had chosen. Of that, she had always maintained an iron certainty. She had chosen the life, the life had not chosen her. There was a seminar she had attended years before where the moderator had repeatedly drilled into them that an important means of handling stress was to be sure you were there to happen to life, and not the other way around. People suffer stress when they lose control of their lives. That is precisely what she felt now. She had to find out what was going on so she could take counter measures and regain control. It was unacceptable to be blurting out anathema statements at unpredictable times.

There was reading she should be doing, but decided she was too tired. Her assistant, Minna Simmons, didn't speak. From long association, she knew when not to disturb her boss. The plane rushing down the runway and rising into the sky always gave her spirits a lift. Not today. As the plane gently swayed, she relaxed only to be abused by a nagging doubt. She had started down the liberal path as an expedient means of advance-ment. What if the concepts had gradually become ingrained and now she was a fanatic? Was that the problem? As long as the ideas hadn't meant anything one way or the other, it was logical that she could change course with the direction of the prevailing wind. The opposition was nothing more than background noise. If her thinking had become doctri-naire, then opposing views became threats. Even worse than that, maybe the idea that a two year old child was nothing more than an animal was too much and her subconscious was rebelling.

Though she had no children of her own, she had been around tots that age, and the idea of them being anything but human was disturbing. During the Christmas recess, she remembered vividly the little girl of about two. The person whose house she was visiting had a toy poodle. The little girl, also a guest, squatted as small children do and grabbed its hair. Her mother said, "No. Pet the doggie gently like this." The little hand rubbed the fir the wrong way pressing too hard, but the animal was accustomed to children and didn't fret. The little half formed questions about the doggie's name, why does he have a fuzzy nose, and a dozen others were so charming. Anyone who said that little girl wasn't human had to be an animal themselves. Had this gone too far?

Her head ached with a tightness behind her eyes. Oh, she longed for the releasing oblivion of sleep.

Norma was jolted awake as the wheels made contact with the runway. She casually glanced out the window. The setting sun cast an extorted shadow of the plane that skipped along the ground as they taxied to the waiting limo—that had better be there! It was her fondest hope that the face time with the political hacks did not include a meal. She hated the mass produced plates of so-called food provided at public functions. Her plan was to give a twenty minute talk, take some questions, and then mix with the crowd trying to say hello to everyone. If you don't like it, stay out of politics. As she considered it, she didn't entirely hate it. The adulation was good for the ego.

She had her talking points prepared for the governor in the morning. She would at all cost avoid the issue of abortion. It was not an issue in this state, nor even remotely the reason for this appearance. She felt safe on that score.

———————

Wally left his driveway at six the next morning, Friday, planning to be in Albany around two p.m. Marv was on the road at eight. His tracker put the Yukon a few miles past Wilmington, Delaware. It didn't matter because he had all day, literally. It was possible he could make his move this evening, though there were significant drawbacks to that. The most important was he'd be fatigued after a long drive. The other was the need to locate their destination and reconnoiter the area. He was always open to see what developed, though.

A little after two, the Yukon was maneuvering around in downtown Albany. Marv was passing Newburgh, New York. His plan was to continue for another hour and see which direction they went. As the minutes passed, he saw them on the toll road heading in his direction. That was easy. At Kingston he paid his toll and pulled off, filled his gas tank, and waited. There were mountains all through this area to the west of the throughway. Maybe they were headed for the Catskills. That wouldn't be terrible. Twenty-five minutes later they turned off at Athens, New York and headed west.

"Are we headed to the Catskills?" Norma asked.

"Close. The place we're after is a little to the north. It's secluded as you'll see."

After twenty-five miles of weaving around in the valleys, Wally turned onto a gravel road and switched to four-wheel drive. They bounced around until finally crossing a stream. The ford had fist sized rocks laid over the stream's bed to maintain a solid road surface with a uniform water depth flowing over it. This caused the stream to be three times its normal width at that point. The water was only a couple of inches deep at the moment.

"If it rains hard, we'll have to wait until the water level falls before we can get out," Wally commented. "Don't worry, though. I don't think there's any rain forecast. But, I brought plenty of food, just in case."

The road rapidly deteriorated until it branched with either option looking equally bad. Wally went to the right. A quarter mile later they emerged from the trees into a clearing a couple of hundred yards wide. To the left of center sat the cabin with the mountains thrusting steeply upward fifty yards behind it.

"Home sweet hide away," Wally said as he pulled to a stop twenty feet from the front steps that looked like they could use a few nails. The siding was unpainted shakes, weathered gray. The shingles were split cedar. A stone chimney thrust above the gable roof on the right indicating a fireplace. It was after four and the cabin was on a southeast slope of the mountain so it was already in shade.

"Let's carry in the stuff and get things squared away first," Wally suggested. "There should be time for a walk before we eat. I've done a lot of driving today, and I could use it."

Norma nodded lethargically and got out. She was more than a decade older than her companion. Halfheartedly she carried her suitcase into the cabin. Wally followed with a box of food that he set on the small kitchen table to the left of the door. The inside of the building wasn't something that showed the hand of an interior decorator. There was nothing covering the studs in the walls making the one inch pine boards that formed the outside sheeting visible. There was no insulation because with little means of heating the interior there was nothing gained by trying to keep the nonexistent warmth inside. The nails that held on the shakes came through the pine boards, and were bent over in areas where one might put a hand on them. It was obvious that in this shack, like similar shanties in the woods, the walls were no more than needed to hold up the roof.

The layout consisted of two rooms. To the left was the only bedroom with a full sized bed and a cot in it. The main room had a stone fireplace in the right wall. A counter protruded half way out from the far wall separating the kitchen area from the living room with the kitchen on the left. Behind the counter were a propane stove, and a sink. In the living room were a couple of wicker chairs, a small sofa that had seen better days, and an easy chair.

Norma was headed for one of the wicker chairs when Wally clapped his hands. "Not yet. Ya have to help carry the stuff in. The whole idea is to move around and get the blood flowing, snuff out the bad air, snuff in the good. Come on, now, get moving." His voice was only slightly chiding, more encouraging. He was beginning to hope he wouldn't have to wait on her like an invalid the whole weekend.

"Give me time to change." She was still wearing a black business pants suit, the standard female power uniform. Ten minutes later, she reappeared wearing new denim jeans, a red plaid shirt, and running shoes. Though she helped, Wally made two trips for her one.

"When do we start working on my problem," she wanted to know when the last of the provisions were in the cabin.

"Not tonight. Not a word. I've been behind the wheel ten hours today, and I'm shot."

She made a beeline for the sofa and flopped on it. It squeaked as she shifted from one lump to another trying to get comfortable. "I'm not so sure this was a good idea. This woodsy stuff isn't my line. I wanted to get away, but I miss my servants already."

"We for sure aren't going back tonight, and you haven't seen anything yet. Let me show you the bathroom facilities. Come," he said beckoning with his hand.

She heaved herself to her feet and he led her out the door and to the bedroom end of the cabin. There solemnly standing fifty feet from the cabin was the outhouse complete with a crescent moon carved in the door? "Oh! I had no idea," she said softly.

"The good news is there is running water of sorts in the cabin," he said. "A small stream up in the rocks behind the cabin has been dammed and a pipe run to the kitchen sink. The only problem is the drain from the sink goes into a bucket that must be emptied periodically, best if it's done before it runs over. How about a short walk? You must move! You're in lousy physical shape, aren't you? Maybe your problem is nothing other than your mind and body atrophying from lack of exercise. You might have been able to push yourself day and night when you were younger. Now, your mind is rebelling. You'd better watch out or you'll have a stroke."

"Who appointed you to nag me?"

"You did." He then mimicked her voice, "Wally, I need to get away."

Ten minutes later they began walking. The clearing was rocky with stumps, tall grass, and weeds. There were trails probably cleared of debris by people, but clearly first laid down as game trails. Beyond the clearing to the right as they had driven up to the cabin, they were in thick hardwood forest. The trail stayed at about the same elevation as it ducked around rock outcroppings and jogged to prevent collisions with trees. Wally smiled as he thought about it. Thank God for animals. If people had laid out the trail, either the trees would have been cut down, or everyone would bump their noses into trees. He wasn't sure which. The forest had been logged more than once since the white man arrived so there were stumps of various sizes and degree of rot.

After fifteen minutes Wally said, "Okay. Let's turn around and get some supper. I'll fry hamburgers, and we'll have a glass of wine. How's that sound?"

She answered with the first word she had spoken since starting the walk, "Finally."

After eating, Norma perked up a little. She washed the dishes after heating water on the propane stove. Wally had brought a tank of propane with him. He carried in several armloads of wood from a pile on the bedroom end of the cabin. He pulled the cot out of the bedroom and put it behind the wicker chairs by the wall opposite the door.

The chores done they sat in front of the fire and didn't say much as they sipped the last of the wine. "Are there bears in this forest," she asked at one point.

"Haven't seen one around here for a long time. It wouldn't be a problem if there were, though. The only kind in these parts would be black bears. They're more like large raccoons than anything else."

"I don't care. Lock the door."

There was a hasp like one would use for a padlock on the inside. Hanging on a string near it was a wooden peg. Wally fastened the door.

After dark, Norma heated water to wash her face, especially to remove the makeup. It was annoying to do everything by the light of a candle. The last chore was the worst. With a flashlight she made her way to the outdoor facility, not sure she believed Wally about the bears. It was still early by the schedules they normally kept, but both were tired and the stillness made sleep come easily.

Marv followed their progress until they stopped. He had to assume they were at their destination because it was not near any town or even on a recorded road. They had exited the turnpike at Athens and turned west into the mountains. He signaled the tracking device to shut down because it used less power in its quiescent state. It wouldn't do to have the battery in the tracker go dead. Checking the map, he saw that Athens had a population of only a couple thousand. Where he was in Kingston was better. It was a larger city and hence easier to remain anonymous. He'd drive the twenty-five miles up to Athens in the morning staying off the toll road.

That same evening, Vincent was having a beer with his brother, Tim, on the patio. Vin's brother lived and worked in Southern California as a writer in the TV business. His brother was born Timothy Wessen, but now was Don Fuller. As he always said, it was an obvious switch. In reality, when Tim started writing he used the pseudonym of Don Fuller. As time went on, everybody in his work community came to know him as Don. Finally, his tax accountant suggested it would make things easier if he officially changed his name, so he did.

After getting caught up on their lives and work the conversation lagged so Vin said, "I learned something odd a few weeks ago, and don't quite know what to make of it."

"What's that?"

"I flipped to the back of my desk calendar looking for the page with the whole calendar for next year. I noticed a special page called perpetual calendar that gave a formula for calculating the day of the week for any date of any year. On the back side of that page was a means for determining the date for Easter in any year. You remember how Ma mentioned many times that I was born on Ash Wednesday?"

"Yeah. She said that every year when your birthday came around."

"So, on a whim, during my lunch hour, I decided to test the formula. With the date for Easter, it was easy to find Ash Wednesday by counting back forty days not counting Sundays. It turns out I was born eight days after Ash Wednesday in nineteen fifty-three. I find that strange since she was always so sure of that connection. She never mentioned anything special about your birthday."

"Are you sure you calculated Easter for the right year?"

"That came to mind right away so I ran the numbers again. No mistake. Then I thought there might have been a printing error in the method given on the calendar. On the Internet, I found several sites with formulas different from the one I used. It didn't matter. They all came up with the same answer. I have a copy of my birth certificate in the house and I checked. My birthday is as I had always known. So, why was Ma so wrong?"

"All I can say is you'll have to ask her about it some time."

"Yeah. I'll be sure to do that."

They sat in silence for a few minutes. Tim mentioned the flowers around the patio. "It's interesting to see the different species of flowers here. I wonder of any of these would grow in Southern California."

When Vin didn't comment, Tim said, "The thing about your birthday is kind of bothering you, isn't it?"

"Yeah, I guess it is. Maybe I'm adopted or something. How much do you remember about what happened back then?"

"Come on. I wasn't even three years old and I wasn't taking notes. There are a few things I remember, though. They are probably a combination of my impressions at the time and what I recall from hearing Mom and Dad talk about them when they thought I was still too young to remember anything.

"When you were born there was this woman, really just a girl in her teens, I guess, named Margaret who came to help. She was supposed to look after me while Mom was in the hospital. In those days women were in the hospital for a week and more when they had a baby. Times have changed, haven't they? Now, they have them out in a day, or even less.

"Do you remember how even long after that, whenever Mom got upset with Dad, it didn't matter what about, it always ended with Ma haranguing about the winter on the first farm. And, Dad would say something to the effect that he couldn't go back and change things, that she should let it go. If she thought nobody was listening, she'd persist and the name of Margaret would come up. I never knew what that was all about, but Dad would say 'We don't talk about that' and that would end the matter. It was as if Ma had to be reminded every so often that that topic was off limits. Whatever the spat was about, that ended it."

Vincent could remember something like that but only in the foggy recesses of his mind. On the other hand, Tim, he couldn't help thinking of him as Tim, was a three-year-old and even one so young remembers a lot especially if it's associated with strong emotion.

Vin replied, "Yeah, I remember the name Margaret coming up from time to time, and maybe once or twice in the context you remember. I did ask Ma about it when I was maybe four or five, and she said Margaret was a hired girl they had come in to help when I was born. Apparently, they didn't get along or something. Mom said the girl didn't help at all. She was so fussy and meticulous that, in fact, she ended up causing Mom more work than if she hadn't been there. Seems to me, Ma said she got sick while she was there, and for some reason the girl had no place to go. That always seemed curious. You'd think she would have been from the area, so why didn't they send her home if she couldn't do anything?"

"Funny you should mention that," Tim replied. "That's stuck in my mind, too, that she didn't leave. There must have been more to it than that."

At that, both fell silent, as they took a pull on their beers. Finally, Vin said, "So, why would Mom bring up Margaret? Sure, she was nine months pregnant and out of sorts, but having her around couldn't have been that bad."

"Like I said, it wasn't simply that she brought it up. Something was eating her about that girl."

"If the girl was very sick, it stands to reason there would have been a lot of commotion at the time. But, even if she had no place to go, wouldn't they have been able to call a neighbor or someone else to help out a little?"

After more silence, Tim said, "Both Ma and Dad talked about a terribly snowy winter one of those years. I think it was the one when they were on the farm by Sauk Centre. They may have had a blizzard about that time because you were born at home. I'll never forget that. After you were born Ma got really sick, and yeah, the hired girl got sick, too. Sure. It's funny. Not until now did I put it together that the reason things were in such chaos was that they were both sick. On top of it all, we were snowed in for several days. And, Dad had to do the farm work, look after both of them, keep food on the table for himself and me, and care for you. He must have been exhausted. It's too bad he's gone. I'd like to ask him about that. They sure didn't talk about it other than the way we've discussed. That in itself is odd. Such a traumatic time and not a word. Ma sure could go on about other things that happened."

"That's starting to make sense. They were only at Sauk Centre for one year. Then we moved to Uncle Fletcher's place. Dad ran the farm and Uncle Fletch retired, but helped out some. He never mentioned a blizzard, but I remember he said that dad had taken on more debt than the other farm could handle."

"That was when a small family farm could provide a nice living if the debt wasn't too big. Dad said we came to the city when Uncle Fletch died because the corporate farms were taking over, had to get big or get out. He decided to call it quits."

"Do you remember anything else about Margaret?"

"Only that she was there, and you were due to be born and weren't coming. And, the girl got on Ma's nerves." Don paused. "Ma changed after she got real sick once. You remember that. They both mentioned it."

"Yeah. But, that was a different time."

"They made a point of saying that. You'd have no way of knowing, being a tad young. But, it seems to me that it happened then. If both women were sick at the time you were born, and that was compounded by the storm, think of the stress she would have been under. That could change anybody. Of course, I can't say for sure."

They left it at that but it made Vincent think. He had no clear notion of what difference it would make if he found out more about Margaret. Still, he decided to pursue it. Maybe if he could find Margaret's last name something would click.

— 6 —

Wally was up at first light. He had not slept well tossing and turning through the night. It might have been from all the driving the day before or the slight musty smell of the mattress. He dressed and pulled back the curtains from the front window. Fog covered the forest causing condensate to drip from the eves. He sat in the easy chair using the light from the window to read some of the material he had collected before leaving town. What Norma was experiencing was a subject of interest to him. When they started to discuss it, he wanted to be prepared so she wouldn't fluff off what he had to say.

At seven-thirty, hunger was starting to gnaw at the underside of his belly button so he knocked lightly on her door. There was some rustling and moaning. He knocked again, "Daylight in the swamp." He didn't know why he said that other than it was something his father always said when rousting him out.

"Okay! No need to pound the door down."

At least she's alive, he thought. We're off to a good start.

"I'm going to start breakfast, that okay?"

"Wait fifteen minutes. I need time to put myself together."

Minutes later, while Wally had his back turned, he heard her shuffle out to use the facility. He had found the bacon and eggs, and was digging for the bag of bagels and the pack of cream cheese. While she was gone, he placed a basin of warm water on the dresser in the bedroom. He was about to see if she had gotten lost when the outside door opened. As she walked past, she glared at him. Apparently, he had been unable to suppress his shock. Without makeup, she looked twenty years older. Clearly, the media and cameras were very accommodating in showing only her best angle, and not revealing those candid shots when the makeup was smeared, or the light was wrong.

After fifteen minutes, he said, "Come and get it. Breakfast is ready." He had the places set with a glass of juice by each and the bagels cut. The bacon was on a couple of layers of paper towel to absorb the fat.

She appeared wearing the same thing as the afternoon before, including makeup. As she sat down, he brought the fried eggs.

"I can't eat that crap! My cholesterol is too high as it is."

"One egg and a couple of pieces of bacon won't hurt you. We're going to walk up the mountain this morning and you'll need it. Your cholesterol is high because you never move. A big part of what we're doing this weekend is to get you some fresh air and exercise. There's no guarantee anything I can offer you as advice will be of benefit. You have to be prepared to pick up the pace in the self help department."

Wally was, as always, surprised to see the extreme two-facedness of politicians. Here, where there were no reporters or cameras, she was what he assumed to be her normal self, sharp and rude, as opposed to the public self when on stage. How they could keep track of when to use which or even who was who, he found hard to imagine.

After cleaning up, they left the cabin. Wally wore a light jacket that he would stuff in the small backpack he carried when the sun hit them. Besides that, he had on a baseball cap, old dress shirt, worn Dockers, and his hiking boots. She wore a jacket, but preferred not to wear a cap lest it affect her hair. One never knew where a TV camera might be lurking.

After twenty minutes, they had climbed to a small clearing where a tree had conveniently fallen ten years before to leave them a place to rest a bit. They could see out across the valley where there was still fog lying in the lowest areas. The sun was bright in a cloudless sky. Birds were chirping with the harsh calls of crows in the distance. Wally offered her a bottle of water and opened one for himself.

"Okay. Where do we start?"

"This is a hell-of-a couch. What kind of shrink are you, anyway?"

He wasn't sure if there was any humor in the statement or not. "It's not going to be like that. You tell me, in detail, what's bothering you, and I'll offer some suggestions. You first."

"It's not difficult. In fact, out here, away from all of that, it hardly seems important."

"That's the idea. You have to step back and ask if it really *is* important. Is it?"

She kicked over a chunk of bark and watched the disturbed ants rush about. "There," she said pointing. "Those ants were quietly going about their business harming no one, doing their part to keep the ecology balanced when I upset their whole world with one flip of my toe. That's how it is."

"Are you sure you're not saying that because you happened to kick at the piece of bark? Maybe it's a spiritual obsession or something from within you. Have you been working extra hard because of a certain law you're trying to pass? Have you experienced stabbing pains in you chest, headaches, anything like that?"

"Sure. It could be anything. However, it seems like someone is doing it to me. You don't suppose it's the spirit of some dead person that has come to haunt me, do you?"

"I would doubt that. That's not normally their style. You're sure it's someone?"

"Yes."

"If I understand right, then, you're saying it's like someone is stalking you, leaving nasty notes where you're sure to find them."

"Yes."

"What else?"

"It's always been about abortion. That's part of what's so confusing. It's not about any of the legislation that the country is stirred up about, nothing important."

"Abortion is *not* important?"

"That's been decided. Nothing's going to change about that."

"Setting aside the possibility of any changes, it is an important issue. Every single year on January twenty-second, there's a huge collection of demonstrators on the National Mall. That is the coldest month of the year. The media virtually ignores what would be the lead story if that many unwed mothers or any other fringe group showed up in like numbers. People care deeply about it and just because your persuasion is on the top, legally and politically, at the moment, doesn't mean everybody is happy about it. The pro-life issue will not go away."

"There, you made the classic mistake. It's pro-abortion and anti-abortion."

"That distinction is significant?"

"Yes. Very. Being 'pro' is to be for something, and 'anti' against it. It's always advantageous to be 'for' and a disadvantage to be 'against.' To be against implies a person is a negative thinker rather than a positive one. Plus, the term pro-life brings life into the issue where there is no need for it. It muddies the waters. Beyond that, pro-life expands the debate to include other issues like euthanasia. That's not fair."

"Before you can get to the bottom of what's disturbing you, you must accept the fact that abortion is an important issue. If it's not important, why don't you change your stand on it? Then, whenever you make a pro-life, excuse me, anti-abortion, statement you will simply be reiterating your stand. In that scenario, your problem goes away."

"Wally, don't be stupid!"

She stood up and marched toward the trail that wound its way up the mountain. He followed. This was going to be more difficult than he had imagined. He doubted he'd be able to be of much assistance to her.

They climbed a total of nearly a thousand feet above the cabin and were at the top. The trail led along the crest for some distance and they followed it until there was a clear area. The view was spectacular, even inspiring. They sat again, this time on a rock covered with lichens. The cabin was long lost from view tucked away down there somewhere. It was possible to see the place the gravel road broke off from the paved one that snaked along in the valley floor. Wally pointed it out to her. As they watched, a gray speck moved along the paved road, slowed, and turned on to the gravel road. After a hundred yards it turned off and slid beneath the trees not to reappear.

"What's that car doing?" Norma asked.

"Hard to say. Might be a day hiker, bird watcher, or someone like that. It's Saturday and there are people who come into mountains like us to get away and sit on a rock where they can enjoy the solitude."

"So," he said trying to get back to the issue, "you think that, in a matter of speaking, there is someone stalking you."

"Yes."

"Do you sense it's one person or a group? Was there any thing different from one time to the next that comes to mind?"

"I get the feeling it's one person because they were the same. First, I did it, said the sentence, as in the first and third cases, and wrote it as in the second. Then, there was a brief pleasant feeling. That immediately gave way to the horror of it all, though."

"Let's assume for the moment, it's one person, a live person. It is logical to assume that person is antiabortion because no pro-abortion person would be interested in having you make statements against the cause. Does that make sense?"

"I suppose so."

"I think it's important that you start to think about this person as pro-life because he would certainly think of himself that way. For the sake of argument, I'll use "he" to move things along by using the conventional usage."

"You *are* a male chauvinist, aren't you?"

"And, you're so bound up in politically correct issues, it's a wonder you can function. Let's not get off the track, though."

"What track are we on?"

"It's still an indistinct track like some of those game trails that crossed our path as we were walking. But, it's not nothing."

"Almost nothing. There are millions of people in this country who are antiabortion. Any one of them could be doing it. In addition, just what is it *she's* doing? It's not as if I'm getting strange calls on my cell phone. *She's* connected right to my mind."

Wally chuckled. "It is entirely possible we may be able to say that the person who is doing this is more likely to be male than female. We'll get to that in a minute. This person can be affecting you in one of two main ways. The first gets into the paranormal, which is mental telepathy. The second is prayer. We're not sure the two are all that different. But, deciding which it is will help narrow the search."

"Why limit it to those two. What about some sort of demonic possession channeled through a human?"

"You're not going to like this, but that would be counter-productive for Satan. You've been playing from his sheet of music all your life." He held up his hand to stave off the retort he knew was coming.

"Yes. I know you think that making it legal for some poor unfortunate girl to have an abortion is only being compassionate. You have convinced yourself that you are being altruistic. The facts show it differently. To take only one thread of the argument, the enormously documented post traumatic syndrome that women experience after abortions is undeniable. These women curse people like you for the hell you have caused them. There are other things I could mention, but no need to push a point. We can categorically rule out it being something from the devil. It is either a neutral person who is using mental telepathy to ring your chimes to see what happens, or someone who deeply believes that abortion is an abomination, and is praying to change it through you. Where would you put your money?"

Wally could tell Norma was not at all happy with the way this was going. For him, the first time she had mentioned what was happening, it seemed obvious what it was though he knew it would be hard for her to accept. She dug a groove in the clay soil with the heel of her shoe as she considered the alternatives. In her defense, he knew it was easy for him to talk. It wasn't his life that was being turned upside down. He hoped his value system was sound enough so this would never happen to him. She certainly thought her values were on a sound footing. The strange events themselves were one thing. Having to analyze the situation and hear the things that he was saying was another.

Since she made no response, Wally started again, not sure how far he'd get. "I would guess, you are like millions of people who have come to accept that abortion is something they decide not to think about. They think of it only as a word. I recall a man I knew years ago who was pro-abortion. He had seen a picture of a torn apart baby that was the result of an abortion. He said, 'Don't ever show me one of those pictures or you'll change my mind.'"

She looked at him. "You're babbling. Get back to my case. You think there's little doubt that it would be the religious fanatic."

"Fanatic might be the wrong word. Let's say he feels as strongly as you do."

"There you are again. What makes you so sure it's a man?"

"Not sure. Call it a hunch that has some experimental data behind it. In the class of people who take their religion seriously, it is generally conceded that women pray more. That may be true owing to the fact that we usually think of the little old ladies in church alone. That's mainly due to women living longer than men and therefore leaving widows who have lost their companions. They gravitate to church to pray, and to find like minded people for friends. However, in tests where people pray for something, such as the recovery of a sick person, if it's just men or just women, men get better results. And, if it's one man compared to one woman, the results are more dramatically in favor of men. There's no explanation for that as far as I know other than the spiritual and psychological makeup of men and women are far different than is commonly believed. Here again, it's considered politically incorrect to acknowledge any fundamental differences between the sexes. That's another PC trap that keeps modern society off balance. Furthermore, I'd hazard the guess that the person doing this is relatively young, perhaps in his teens."

"You're really out on a limb now, and you look ridiculous there."

"Not as much as you'd think. What is happening is rather amateurish. Mature prayers wouldn't do something like that. They would have learned the problem of unintended consequences. Someone once gave me a prayer card with a prayer to St. Joseph. It said to make a novena. That means to say the prayer every day for nine days in a row, for any intention. But, it warned to be careful of what you prayed for because you'd get it. Mature prayers, like cloistered monks or nuns, would pray for more general things. If they prayed for you, it would be that you be converted from your evil ways so as to get to heaven."

She looked at him. "You're not a pro-lifer for God's sake, are you?

"I never thought of myself that way. In what I do, I try not to settle for platitudes. Many professors are comfortable with that. I'm not. I wouldn't go so far as saying I'm a seeker of truth. That's putting the bar too high. I try to separate fact from fiction in some of the nonscientific areas. Let's say I feel compelled to look at what abortion really is, or never settle for a statement like 'all religions are equally good.'"

"Yeah. Fine. My legs are starting to feel stiff and we still have to go down. We climbed too high."

"Maybe." He unzipped his backpack and took out a granola bar. "Eat this and we'll head down. That's a lot easier, and we'll take it slow."

— 7 —

Around a slight bend and there it was. Marv tried not to be too attached to gadgets but this was great. The gravel road was where the display said it would be. He took a left and started up the gentle grade. After a minute, he saw what looked like an over grown road off to the left. Without hesitation, he turned into it. A hundred feet in he was out of sight of the gravel road. He turned around so if he had to make a hasty retreat the vehicle would be pointed in the right direction. It was to the side of what was really a wide trail and was masked by bushes. Someone coming in the way he had come would have to look back to see it. It was good. Well off the paved road, and out of sight of the gravel.

With the engine off but power on, he took one last look at the distance and direction to where the tracking device placed the Yukon. He didn't dare drive any closer, and his parking place was what he wanted. He took the little GPS receiver he'd bought with the rest of the equipment and pressed the button to mark the location of his Explorer as home. Then he punched in the coordinates from the tracking device as destination. That done, he powered off the vehicle, put the string on the GPS around his neck and the device in his shirt pocket. He donned his camouflage suit, and took the pack with the equipment, food and water he needed. He dared not walk any part of the distance on the road so he set off through the forest hoping to find a game trail going his way.

As Wally and Norma were about to start their hike down the mountain, Marvin arrived at the cabin. In the brush off to the rear corner of the bedroom, he waited a full fifteen minutes. Nothing stirred so cautiously he made his way up to the cabin. He noted an old log nearly three feet in diameter lying ten yards behind the bedroom. It had shed its bark, and the upper parts of the ancient tree had been chopped off for firewood. The log, itself, showed signs of having been whacked away at with an axe by someone wanting to let off energy or frustration. There was evidence of lesser efforts, too. Weather faded initials had been chopped and cut in the black deteriorating surface over many summers.

As he approached, he saw split firewood piled to within a foot of the bottom of the bedroom window. Looking in while shielding the glare of the window with his hand, he saw an unmade bed and no activity. The window was either locked or jammed. At the corner, he looked toward the door. Nothing. In a few long steps, he was at the door. It was unlocked with the padlock hanging in the hasp. Gun in hand he entered sweeping it around as he did. Nobody. Good. Immediately he observed the layout. The cot in the living room against the far wall was understandable. He made a hasty search of the building and the belongings the two had brought with them. There appeared to be no gun, though there might be one in the car, or less likely, Wally carried one. He observed the inside hasp and the wooden peg. The woman would insist on the door being secured from the inside at night.

He had his plan. He'd wait until they were asleep, first the man, then the woman. He observed in detail the location of the cot and the pillow on it. With his hand spread wide he measured down from the corner of the back window and over to the location where the head would be. He'd mark that location on the outside of the wall. The walls were three-quarter inch pine with wood shakes on them. The nine-millimeter slugs would go through them like a sheet of paper. He'd do a pattern of three shots at the head and two more at the location of the heart. If one or the other hit a stud, it wouldn't matter.

Regardless of what the woman did, he'd immediately use a piece of wood to break the bedroom window. With a bright flashlight he'd find the woman and finish the job. She'd be disoriented, and it was unlikely she'd immediately dash out the front door into the darkness. Any amount of hesitation she displayed would be enough.

Finished inside, he made his way to the rear of the building and after measuring, noted the location of the pillow by a chip out of the shake. He closed his eyes and felt from the windowsill down and over to his marker. It would be easy to find. There was one last thing to do. At the Yukon he reached into the grill and removed the tracking device. Quickly he retraced his steps to the cover of the forest behind the cabin. He found a comfortable place opposite the bedroom corner and settled down for a long wait. Where he sat his view of the cabin was partially obstructed by leaves as he wanted it to be. By slowly moving a branch he

could open the view and see the whole building and its immediate sur-
roundings.

From his pack, he pulled out a bottle of water, beef jerky, and granola
bars. This provided a satisfying meal, though not something one would
want to eat on a regular basis. Rain was predicted for the evening. Planning ahead, he had worn a wool shirt because even with waterproof
clothing, rain drew off body heat rapidly. The foliage provided heavy
shade so it wasn't overly warm, in fact, comfortable, too comfortable. He
should have moved about, perhaps rehearsing a couple of paths for
egress.

Waiting was boring, and he had not slept well the night before. Why
did he always get the room with noisy neighbors? His eyelids drooped,
and immediately snapped open. This went on for several minutes until
finally sleep won out.

As Marv dozed, another figure cautiously made his way to the cabin.
Strangely, this man went through a pantomime matching that of Marv in
all its important details. His clothing was even the same. After completing his mission, this man retreated to the forest off the living room corner
seventy-five yards from Marv. If they had been thinking the same as far
as a place to wait, they might have met, though the meeting would not
have been social.

————————————

It was long after noon when Wally and Norma reached the cabin. Her
knees were hurting and there with blisters on her toes. Both were to be
expected since going down took less exertion, but put more force on the
knees while pushing the toes against the front of the shoes. Wally had
found a walking stick for her so she could use her arm to take some of
the load off the knees with each step, though by the end Wally was supporting most of her weight. He failed to realize how fragile people become if they don't exercise regularly. At least, she was at her normal
weight. An extra fifty pounds would have spelled disaster. How she
managed to survive the stress of her job without regular workouts and
sweating mystified him.

Due to her saintly demeanor, she only informed Wally of his abject
stupidity with every other step rather than every one. He began to wonder if her problem was due to being unmarried. There was no husband to
tell her to stuff a sock in it now and then when she got into a bitching
session. Whether or not that was the case, he bore the abuse fearing that

if he stopped her she'd pout and refuse to talk. Alternatively, the tirade would expand to include his being responsible for all the ills of the world. In neither case would they get to the root of her problem. If it were not resolved she could go off the deep end. And, for someone in her position that did not add up to a good thing in his opinion.

They didn't even stop at the cabin heading instead straight for the crescent moon establishment. She pulled the door toward herself and said, "I can manage! Go inside."

Ten minutes later she came through the door and took the few steps to the easy chair. "What could you have been thinking! I'm not some amazon."

"You must walk during the day. That capital is a big complex with long halls and lots of steps. How do you manage?"

"My office is close to the house chamber and I take the elevator. RHIP! Rank has its privileges."

"That not withstanding, may I suggest that you start an exercise program or you'll be having knees and hips replaced in no time. Can I get you anything?"

"Yes. Bring me that little blue case from the bed and some water."

She twisted the cover off a prescription pill bottle and popped two capsules into her mouth. "Those are for the pains I get in my head at times. They're generic pain pills so they should help with my sore muscles and joints. The thing with my head, it's nothing serious. I'm not terminal—until today!"

Wally pulled over a box and put a blanket on it so she'd be able to put her feet up. She accepted it without comment. Then he put together lunch. She agreed to a sliced salami sandwich, a small one, and sliced apples. Wally brought the food into the living room so she wouldn't have to move. They finished with Fig Newtons.

As they were finishing, he asked, "Did anything we discussed earlier help?"

"It only helps if we can find the little creep and make him stop."

"What if he doesn't want to stop? We might want to proceed cautiously. If we alert him that his praying is having an effect, it will only encourage him to pray harder."

"Then we stop him."

"How?"

"We do whatever it takes."

"Like kill him?"

She drank some more water. "I must have become dehydrated. That was a punishing ordeal." After a pause, "Aren't you getting a little carried away with this praying."

Wally noticed the change of subject when it came to following her logic to the end.

"A lot of people pray," she continued. "I even do now and then. But, nobody expects prayers to be answered in such a literal, specific way. You pray for nice weather for the picnic and it rains. You pray for someone to get well and often as not they die. That's the way it is. Not this direct linkage. What if one person prays for a sunny day and another for rain? They can't both have their prayers answered."

"First of all, that's not really true. If the person praying for rain is a farmer, and the day were sunny for the picnic, and it rained that night, both prayers would be answered. However, that's not what we're talking about. The question is the level of faith of the two prayers. If you believe in prayer, you are accepting on faith that God has the power to answer prayers, and the inclination to do so. Most of us don't doubt His power. It's the inclination part where the uncertainty lies. How can we be assured that He will answer our prayers? It's in our faith. For Christians, we have his solemn assurance that if we have faith he will answer our prayers. For example, if memory serves me its in *Mark 11* where He says: 'Amen I say to you, whoever says to this mountain, 'Arise, and hurl thyself into the sea,' and does not waver in his heart, but believes that whatever he says will be done, it shall be done to him.' And in another place, He said, if you have faith as large as a mustard seed, you shall say to this mountain, remove from here and it will be removed.' He meant it literally. There's no other interpretation for those verses. The obvious conclusion is that for most of us we don't have faith the size of a mustard seed.

"I mentioned earlier that mature prayers aren't normally so specific. That's because it's sort of like tempting God. It's akin to saying we don't trust divine providence. If the mountain is there, we must trust God that it's better to have it there than someplace else. That's not to say that if the mountain were found to be composed of high grade iron ore that it would be intrinsically evil to 'move' the mountain to the steel mill so the iron could be extracted for the good of mankind. That not withstanding, if someone has a deep faith that a very specific prayer will be answered, God will answer it."

"You mean he writes a script of what I'm supposed to say, and then prays me to say it?"

"I'd bet against the script. He'd pray that you say or do things that help the pro-life movement. And, he prays for that specifically, maybe at random times, or on a schedule. It doesn't matter. And, from tests, it doesn't matter how far away the prayer is from the object of his prayer."

"This is totally bizarre. I can't believe it."

"I'm afraid that's the most logical answer."

"And, what did we conclude about *illogical* explanations?"

"That you are having a complete and probably permanent mental breakdown."

"So, it's some crazy person who's good at praying."

She removed her shoes and shuffled around in the cabin. Clearly, she was working on what to do about the unprecedented situation she faced. Wally asked her if she wanted to come out and enjoy the many varieties of wild flowers in the clearing. She was not interested in walking any place outside. She sat on the sofa and promptly fell asleep.

He left her to her slumber and wandered among the flora in the clearing. There was a profusion of blooming plants. Wally assumed one reason the owner of the cabin kept the clearing open was for the flowers. In the heavy shade of the trees, there were fewer varieties. It was peaceful as he roamed the area. The clouds began to thicken in the late afternoon. He surmised it might rain after all, though the weather report from the night before last indicated it was unlikely.

They ate their supper while Wally had her tell him about maneuvering bills through the House of Representatives, the politics, the back biting, and the unlikely alliances that formed on certain issues. The whole place seemed to operate on an animal level where it was eat or be eaten. Even among one's own kind, it was a constant battle similar to mating rights or nesting territory. It was a total snake pit of egos that had nothing to do with representing the constituents. His head reeled. This was more than he cared to know.

Shortly before seven, on his way back from the outhouse, he stopped at the Yukon and picked up a sleeping bag, and a foam pad. He'd sleep on the floor tonight. Norma popped down two more capsules and took a last trip outside before the rain started. She was ready for bed by seven o'clock. The rain started shortly thereafter.

Marv had watched the pair emerge from the forest at the end of their hike to the ridge. She was hardly capable of walking on her own. This was going to be so easy. He had been listening to a pocket radio with ear plug to pass the time. The forecast was for rain this evening, heavy at times. That was his time to act. It would insure darkness and covering sound. Tracks would be washed away. He was not a professional assassin, but he had enough experience from high risk surveillance jobs to know patience was a virtue that paid off.

It was now seven and the heavy clouds made it nearly dark. He had seen the two of them, at separate times, make a trip to the toilet. The guy had stopped at the Yukon to get something, though he couldn't see what it was. The rumbles were drawing closer. The candles in the cabin went out shortly after seven. He gave them another half-hour to settle down. It wasn't long before the rain came in earnest punctuated by flashes of lightning and cracks of thunder. He could not have planned it better. Then he moved.

The flashes of lightning helped him maneuver around the rocks and stumps. It was like walking in a darkened room with a strobe light flashing at random times. In the midst of a step he stopped. Gently he set the foot that had been in motion on the ground. The last flash had revealed a tall stump between himself and the cabin. The height was wrong. There were no trees in the clearing and all the stumps were cut two feet high and largely not visible in the tall grass and weeds. Out of natural caution, he slowly lowered himself. A flicker of lighting in the distance provided enough light to see the stump had moved. Man or animal, something was making its way toward the cabin. A bright flash followed immediately by crashing thunder showed a man standing under the eves at the location of the cot inside.

Above the steady throb of the rain, Marv heard the unmistakable sound of a silenced pistol being fired. Under other circumstances, a person might have put it off as associated with the thunder. This was different. It was the time of darkness, the time of silenced guns dispensing death. Most of all, the time when death could catch an assassin unawares.

Marv understood the purpose of the other all too well. As such, he sought cover and concealment. The log was the obvious place. Inching along on hands and knees, he felt the ground for branches that could, with a snap, announce his presence.

Weeds taller than the log grew along the end where Marv now knelt. The rain and lightning had not slacked with flashes every few seconds.

The other man was moving along the rear of the cabin and was about to round the corner to the end of the cabin with the woodpile. He froze in place as light played on his wet camouflage suit.

A pair of headlights came bobbing out of the trees accompanied by the whining sound of an off road four-wheeler. It was followed by another. The figure stooped slowly as the vehicles approached the cabin. Both men saw the lights of the second illuminate the rider of the first. He wore an unmistakable "Smoky the Bear" hat that was the standard uniform of many law enforcement departments. On the rain suit, there was a shoulder patch.

Marv's first impulse was to take off running for the trees to the right, then he thought better of it. His suit, while camouflage, would be shinny with the rain. If a light should point his way, it would cause one of the officers to investigate. If his presence were detected, the obvious connection would be made to the dead man in the cabin. The rocks immediately behind the cabin were too steep to climb especially when wet, so escape to his right was the only way.

Both officers had disappeared out of sight in front of the cabin. What would the other man do? He might kill both officers and then the woman. In any case, it was imperative for Marv to get away from the clearing as fast as possible so he would be ahead of the other man. It would not be a good thing to come upon the assassin as he was making his way down the rough country in the dark.

Marv still held his gun. He was beginning to think of himself more as the prey than the hunter, though not so much as to be debilitated, more to increase his caution. The lightening was not as frequent as it had been so the situation could get out of hand in a second. There was a glow from the vehicle headlights in front of the cabin that did nothing to help him. The next flash of lightning revealed the other man had disappeared. Marv's heightened sense of wariness caused him to sweep his gun slowly around hoping not to encounter the other man unawares.

Resolved to make his way to the trees beside the road where it came into the clearing, he took one last sweep of his gun in the opposite direction. A sudden flicker of lightning chilled his blood. The other man had been making his way to the cover of the log and was less than twenty feet from him pointing his gun at Marv. It was a standoff, each man pointing a silenced nine-millimeter at the other in the pulsating light and dark. The other man had night vision goggles, but they were tipped up against his forehead. It was clear he wasn't using them because the view would blossom into a solid green with every flash of lighting. The storm provided intermittent illumination for some seconds. The other man held up the palm of his left hand toward Marv and started backing away. Marv did the same. The electrical part of the squall was passing, and the rain was settling into a steady downpour. After twenty steps backward, Marv crouched down and stepped to the side. The situation had gotten worse. The fact of the man pointing a gun at him was only part of it. He had been close enough to see a small microphone extending around his cheek to beside his mouth. There were more of them!

Norma was dozing off when the cabin seemed to shake. It wasn't thunder; it was too rhythmic for that. Then she knew. Someone was pounding on the door. She opened the bedroom door.

"Wally, somebody's at the door," she whispered.

By this time, He was sitting up on his sleeping pad trying to clear his head. The soothing sound of the rain had caused him to fall asleep immediately. The lights from the two vehicles produced a dim glow in the room.

From outside came the voice. "Ms. Holleran. Sheriff Conures here. Will you please open the door?"

Wally was kneeling by the window in his boxer shorts and cautiously pulled back the corner of the curtain and looked out. Then he said to Norma in a voice just above the roar of the rain, "He's wearing a uniform. You'll have to open it. He's probably here to check on you."

"Darn. How'd anyone find out where we were?"

"Ms. Holleran, are you okay?"

"Not as hard as you might think," Wally replied. "Yell that you're coming."

"I'm coming!" she shouted.

She went to the bedroom and reappeared with a bathrobe wrapped around herself. At the door, she opened it holding her hand palm forward in front of her eyes.

"Yes, sheriff. Why are you here?"

"Sorry to disturb you, Ma'am. I'm Sheriff Ted Conures. The man there is my deputy, Jim Wentmore. We were notified late this afternoon that you were taking a weekend out here and were asked to drop by to check on you. We didn't know the exact location so it took us a while to find you. Nothing special, just routine. Sorry we didn't get here sooner."

"Yes. Well, I did a lot of hiking today and was tired, so with the rain and all, turned in early. Is there something I should be concerned about?"

"No Ma'am. Nothing much untoward happens out this way. Apparently, someone in your office was concerned. Are you alone?"

"No. My cousin Dr. Wallace Stern is with me. We're fine. You've done your job. Now, I'd like to try to get back to sleep."

"Yes, Ma'am. Sorry to have bothered you. Good night."

She closed the door, put the peg in the hasp, and flopped into the easy chair. The rain still pounded on the roof.

"What else?" she said lethargically, "I was just dropping off."

Wally had his pants on and watched beside the curtain. The two men stood near the front of the cabin so they were under the overhang. He could hear them talking loud enough to be heard above the rain, though he couldn't understand what was said. After that they walked to their machines where the engines still idled, mounted, and drove off.

"Comes with the territory," Wally replied.

After the door was closed the sheriff said, "Jim, we'll drive off and after a couple of hundred yards I want you to stop and walk back to the clearing. Stay in the trees and watch the place. She's second in line. No way I'm taking a chance of something happening to her. You have your night vision. I'll send someone to relieve you at midnight. In the morning we'll see. Once it's light, there should be no worry. They'll probably leave on Sunday, anyway."

They mounted up and were off.

Marv watched the vehicles drive away. Why hadn't there been a scream from inside the cabin when the woman discovered the body? It didn't matter as he thought about his situation. It made no sense to try to finish his job with other assassins lurking about. With the lightning passing, the others would start using their night vision capability. His only hope was to return to his vehicle and disappear before all hell broke lose. The woman in the cabin had a cell phone and it would work in the mountains since his tracking device had. Once the alert went out, the place would be locked down.

The fear of being pursued fell on him. He started running for the trees a hundred feet from where the road entered the clearing. He was moving too fast for the conditions. His foot caught a rock sending him sprawling. He skinned his shin and a stump connected with his left shoulder. He hissed through clenched teeth knowing he dare not give vocal vent to his pain and frustration. Checking that he still had his gun and his backpack in place, he was off, more cautiously this time. Under cover of the trees, he worked his way down slope frequently checking his GPS still on the string around his neck. The display brightness was turned down so as not to destroy the dark adaptation of his eyes. He heard the stream some distance ahead. When he approached it, he saw a savage torrent. On his way up, he had discovered the footbridge upstream from the ford and entered it into his GPS as a way-point. Using it, he crossed over. Twenty minutes later he arrived at the Explorer. Moving as fast as he could, he ran to the gravel road. In the dark, it was hard to tell if the sheriff's vehicle was still there or not, though he saw no sign of it. He decided he had no choice but to leave.

The rain had slacked off for the moment. Back at his vehicle, he opened the passenger side door and grabbed a heavy plastic garbage bag. He had thought to switch off the interior lights before leaving for the cabin so there was no light to give away his position. Pulling off the top of his rain suit, he stuffed it into the bag. Then the bottoms. After that he sat on the passenger side seat and took off his muddy boots, and into the bag with them, too. He pulled the door closed. In stocking feet, he slid behind the wheel. Key in the ignition, it started. Without lights, but with windshield wipers slapping he drove to the gravel road, and turned down hill. His severest dread was that the body had been reported, his Explorer had been found, and they would be waiting for him to drive onto the paved road to be arrested.

He stopped some distance back from the pavement. He didn't want a passing car to see him driving out of the side road at this hour. He intended to turn to the right, but saw the muddy tracks of the sheriff's truck and trailer go to the left. He went to the left so his muddy tracks would join with the others.

It started raining harder again. If it rained long enough, all tracks would be washed out. He had his escape route planned to go the other way, but the idea of turning around and driving past the gravel road again was more than the wanted to endure. He'd tangle around in the night until he found the toll road. The spray of the water from the road would wash most of the mud off the Explorer. In any case, his equipment return agreement included a complete cleaning of the vehicle.

It was fully light and Norma was first up muttering to herself in the bedroom as she put new bandages on her blistered toes. Her activity roused Wally. He sat up on the sleeping pad and pulled on his pants. Standing up he pulled back the curtain. The sun was up and everything looked clean and bright. It would be a beautiful day. It was bright in the room with the sun coming through the window. He was sitting in the easy chair tying his shoes when he noticed the wood splinters on the floor. Then it occurred to him there was a tear in the upholstery in the arm of his chair. He knew it hadn't been there before. What was this?

Walking across the room to the cot, the holes in the wall were obvious, a total of six. Many splinters covered the blanket over the mattress. He was on his knees examining the exit holes on the front wall when Norma came up behind him.

"What are you doing? Lose your contact?"

Shaking his head slowly he rose and fell heavily in the easy chair. "I'm supposed to be dead."

"Now what? You're not having a heart attack on me, are you?"

"Very funny."

"I'm not trying to be funny. What are you talking about?"

He took her by the hand and showed her the holes in the wall, and the splinters, and what looked like sawdust on the cot. Then he showed her the holes in the opposite wall, as well as the cut fabric on the chair.

"While we were out on our hike yesterday, somebody came in here and noted exactly where I had slept the night before. Last night he came up behind the cabin during the rain and put six bullets through the wall all of which would have hit me if I had been sleeping in that bed."

She sat down in a wicker chair stony faced. "What if he's still out there?"

"Not a chance. If he wanted to kill you too, he would have done it in the dark while it was raining. What possible reason would he have for risking full daylight? During the rain any tracks would have been washed away. Now there's mud everywhere that would leave permanent tracks."

"Okay, okay. He's gone."

"Why not *she*?"

"Not now Wally! The question is, should we call the sheriff?"

"Why, wouldn't we?"

"Because it's complicated."

"Well, let's uncomplicate it. Somebody tried to kill me. That seems pretty uncomplicated to me. He didn't try to kill you."

"Come on Wally, you are so naïve. Are you a high level drug distributor who has decided to thumb his nose at the Colombian drug cartel?"

"No."

"Have you been messing around with a coed who happens to be the Vice-President's daughter?"

"The Vice-President doesn't have a daughter in college."

"You know what I mean."

"Are you saying he tried to drill six holes in me because he was trying to kill you and we look so much alike and he couldn't tell us apart?"

"Don't be stupid. He wanted to kill you first because of the totally insane stereotype that all guys are macho and carry guns. With you out of the way I would offer no problem."

"I see what you mean. You are known to pander to another politically correct following which are the anti-gun wacos. He'd know categorically you wouldn't be armed."

"Guilty as charged."

"Even if it would have gotten you killed? Oh, excuse me, gotten *me* killed? Okay. For the sake of argument, let's assume that he was after you. Why didn't he kill you? He had to assume he had killed me?"

"I can think of two reasons why he didn't kill me. The first is that his plan was interrupted by the arrival of the sheriff. The second is killing you would send a message to me."

"Hmm . . . . That's pretty logical for a girl."

"Stop it!"

"Okay, okay. Just trying to add a little levity to a serious matter. Let's analyze the two. The first reason doesn't make sense. Why didn't he wait a half-hour so the sheriff would be long gone and then continue his attack."

To his surprise, she didn't have a retort. Finally, she said, "I hadn't thought of that."

"I can tell you why. Because the sheriff left his deputy to stand watch."

"But it was dark and raining. How'd the assassin know the guy was there? We have to assume the deputy was smart enough not to sit on the front step."

"If he was after you, this is the big time with lots of money. The guy had those night vision glasses that see the infrared heat of things. As he waited he would have been able to see where the deputy was and make his escape."

"Why not kill the deputy first and then me?"

"Doesn't work. We're back to there we were yesterday. You are seen as the evil one. The deputy is probably a nice guy with a wife and kids. He'd have orders not to kill someone like that." He paused. "No. That doesn't work because he did try to kill me and I'm a nice guy, too."

She glared at him.

"Maybe killing the deputy would complicate matters. The guy might be able to send an emergency signal with his last breath. They'd block all roads and the assassin would be trapped."

He paused, thinking. Then slowly said, "As for the second option, that he would kill me to send a message to you, that's over the edge. Who kills someone simply to get another's attention? I know this happens in the movies, but real people don't do that."

"Don't be so sure. This is really the big time. That order would have to come indirectly from the President. Of course, he'd maintain plausible deniability. It'd start out with five million dollars and go through several intermediaries until the guy got ten thousand for the job. The President is a slimy enough rat to do that. I don't doubt that for a minute."

"Let's have something to eat and go for a walk."

"I don't want to walk. I want to get out of here, now."

"Sorry. Can't. The stream's too high. It'll go down by this afternoon."

"That's dumb. Why have a road if you can't use it. Why isn't there a bridge?"

In his reply, Wally tried not to be condescending. "The reason that road is maintained at all is because it's a fire road. There are only fires when things are dry. When it's dry, the stream is only a trickle. If they were to build a bridge for a cabin or two it would be like the famous bridge to no-where in Alaska."

After breakfast, they set out. Wally could see the tracks of the second deputy who had left at sunrise. With a little searching in the wet bushes, they found the place where their guard had maintained his vigil.

"That seems to answer option number one," Wally said. "Let's walk down to the stream and see how high it is."

Fifteen minutes later, they were at the stream. The two four-wheelers the sheriff and deputy had ridden in on were parked nearby. "See. By the time they returned, the stream had risen so much they couldn't chance crossing it."

"So, how'd they get across?"

Wally pointed to a footbridge two hundred feet upstream. It was only two logs that had been thrown across at a point where rocks forced the water into a deep narrow gorge.

She nodded.

"The sheriff would have known about the logs. They know every back road in the county. And, the idea of a foot bridge like that is common."

Their walk back up the muddy road was in silence. The birds were enjoying the sunny morning producing a cacophony of calls. Neither human saw the new day in such an uplifting way.

In the cabin, Norma put her feet up again and looked at Wally who was looking at her. "What are you looking at?"

"You. This is serious. There is no doubt someone tried to kill me, and that it was done because I was with you. I never realized what a vicious world you live in. Suffice it to say, after I deliver you to your fancy jet I want to be done with this. Don't call me, don't email me, don't write a letter. I will never acknowledge that I even know you. If you want to take that personally, that's your business. My purpose is to stay alive. That means if you want anything more from me, you have the rest of the day. That's it."

She was not accustomed to having anyone speak to her that way. In a begrudging way, she could see his point, yet thought despairingly of him for being such a coward. Bottom line, she needed him, his insight.

Wally began again. "I think you should consider a few obvious facts. The first is that if you make more pro-life statements, there will be no more warnings, assuming this was a warning. The second is, you are not likely to find who is doing this. It follows that you will make more statements and therefore be killed. You call yourself a Catholic, a pro-abortion Catholic. That's an oxymoron if there ever was one. However, I suggest you find a priest and make an extremely sincere confession. And, do the penance he gives you—no penance, no absolution. We both know that."

"Are you a Catholic, Wally?"

"No. I was brought up a Catholic, the same as you. But, I haven't been to Mass or anything else for decades. I'm not such a hypocrite as to say I am one. The events of this weekend might change that, though. And, I'm going to buy a gun and enhance that totally insane stereotype that all guys are macho and carry guns. So, there."

"Wally. I'm shocked . . . no I'm not. You can't help it. Enough of this. How do I find this guy?"

"To do what? Kill him?"

"To talk to him. To try to convince him that the world isn't as black and white as he seems to think."

"Whether or not you want to call abortion murder, it certainly kills a human being. Death—life. That's pretty black and white."

"You just said it, though. If he keeps doing this, I will be killed. He would be, in effect, murdering me. If he's such a virtuous person, it seems he wouldn't want to do that."

"Now that you're the one who could be murdered, it's different, is that it?"

She was stumped again as she stared straight ahead. He could see her grappling with the contradiction. Her belief that she or some other anointed one could decide who lived and died had come full circle with someone else deciding that she was the one to die.

"Do you suppose he'd write me a letter? I get a lot of hate mail as do all the other high profile members of congress. It doesn't matter if you're conservative or liberal, there's always someone who hates what you're doing."

"Possible. But, it wouldn't exactly be hate mail. It would be more of the type that the final judgement awaits you, you are in danger of spending eternity in hell, time is running out, and to repent before it's too late. Something like that."

"What else? Would these be the ones that say go to hell, bitch, or even to accept Jesus as my Savior?"

"Not likely. That second type of letter would come from born again Christians. That's not what we're talking about. The ones that say to go to hell aren't either. In that context, hell is used as a four letter word. It's basically coarse language. The different uses of the word hell are significant, especially in this case. This is what we study in linguistics. You'd be looking for someone who was more specific. He would connect hell with eternity, which is part of the meaning of hell. Also, expect some reference to time because any time, even the age of the universe, is nothing compared to the infinity of eternity."

"When would I get such a letter?"

"You may have already received it, or will get it soon. For some reason, you did or said something that made him notice you. If he wrote a letter it would all be part of the same set of circumstances. He's trying every way he can to influence you."

She was thinking about what they normally did with the toxic mail. That's what they called hate mail. How much was still around? It wasn't trashed as soon as it came in. What would it sound like to ask a staffer to start digging through it looking for a letter that was trying to save her from hell? What story could she use that wouldn't sound totally crazy?

The conversation switched from one topic to another. At one point they reexamined the bullet holes and concluded there was no other explanation. Someone clearly intended to kill Wally, and maybe Norma. They could not settle on which of the two possibilities was the truth. Did the sheriff's deputy scare off the assassin before he could complete his job, or was he long gone by the time the sheriff arrived, having done all he intended to do?

Wally mentioned calling the sheriff or other law enforcement again. She remained adamantly against the idea. First of all, because of her position, it would be a federal crime and the FBI would become involved. One of the other reasons she mentioned was that since nobody was hurt, they could say she and Wally had staged the shooting to get publicity, or for some other nefarious reason. He hadn't accepted any of it. There seemed to be some deeper reason she didn't want the FBI looking into her background any more than they normally did for someone who became Speaker of the House.

The watershed for the stream wasn't large so by three o'clock the water had subsided and they were able to ford the stream. Wally drove Norma back to Albany and delivered her to her waiting Learjet. He drove straight home arriving after midnight.

— 8 —

It was Sunday afternoon when Vincent knocked on his mother's door. She had moved to the assisted living building six months before at his insistence. She felt she didn't need it but there were times when it was helpful to have someone who would check on her. He tried to see her once a week with this time of week being most convenient.

"Vinny, come in. You're looking good. How are Camilla and the boys?"

Vincent had three grown sons who stopped by now and then to visit him. They hadn't been by since the last time he had seen his mother, so assuming no news was good news he answered, "Everybody's fine."

They chatted about nothing, which was the norm. Finally, he said, "Ma, something odd happened to me the other day. I ran across a chart that made it possible to calculate Easter for any year. Since you mentioned that I was born on Ash Wednesday so often, I decided to check it out. It turns out I was born eight days after Ash Wednesday. How can that be?"

He noticed how she looked away immediately, as if looking out the window.

"What do you think? How could that be?"

"Oh. Must be some mistake. The chart must be wrong."

"No," he said softly. "I went on the Internet and found other ways of calculating it. They all agree. My birth date is eight days after Ash Wednesday."

"Why is that important? You have other things to do. Why waste time on this?" After the briefest pause, "Are you and Camilla going anywhere on vacation this summer?"

By eleven-thirty on Sunday evening, Marv was in the vicinity of Camden, New Jersey, where he exited the toll road and found a motel room. During most of the drive, he was wondering about what had happened back at the cabin. Two things wore on him. Why hadn't the dead man in the cot caused total bedlam? The only conclusion was that the cot had been moved, and the man wasn't dead. Things like that did happen. In the dim light, they would not have seen the holes in the wall or the inevitable wood chips lying about. At this point, that didn't matter.

The other shooter did matter. The fact that he was not acting alone meant a conspiracy at the highest levels. That meant power and resources beyond what he could imagine. If the source of his equipment could be trusted, he was clear on that score. Even if the other people knew about the Hill Company, it wouldn't matter. All he had to do was get there first and witness all of his stuff being destroyed. There would be no evidence, only their word against his. Not good, but beatable in most courts. His main concern was the court of revenge, where evidence didn't matter. Going after a VIP of that magnitude had been a big risk. He knew that Alvin saw it as all in the family, but Holleran's position put it a smidgen beyond that. He should never have agreed to it. Poor ol' Alvin would be mad, though. A large part of the advance was spent. But, that's the way it went with risky investments. Some worked, some didn't.

The next morning he stopped at an out of the way business in Maryland north of the District. He showed his return slip and was told to drive in. As part of the purchase, he had been give plastic covers to put over the license plates so none of the employees would be able to sell that information to others. He handed over the materials to be destroyed and was asked if he wanted to witness it. He said yes. He had also purchased the car clean up option for three hundred dollars. It consisted of the car being cleaned on the inside with a vacuum cleaner that had suction stronger than the ones the police use which were stronger than household cleaners. The fibers and particulates form of forensics was becoming more automated so this was necessary. If anyone connected the vehicle to the scene on the mountain, it would be clean. After the vacuuming, it was steam cleaned inside and out especially underneath. After the complete cleaning, and at no extra cost, the clean up crew tracked some dirt and grass clippings from the Maryland area into the front as well as the back.

As the first step in the equipment destruction process, the clothing was placed in a gas fired incinerator with a quartz glass window so the client could witness them being burned. A high speed hammer mill was used for the electronics. Each piece was slipped down the chute and a fine powder was the result. The gun was placed in an arc furnace. It too had a quartz glass window, though it was highly tinted. The gun was reduced to a pool of molten metal as Marv watched. That done, he drove to the airport and caught his flight back to Minneapolis.

Norma Holleran's knees and toes were still bothering her as she reached her office this Monday morning. Donna was the first to greet her. "Was the weekend relaxing?"

"If he hadn't insisted we climb Mount Everest it would have been. We struggled all the way to the top of that mountain behind the cabin. He said we had climbed almost a thousand feet. To him the view was spectacular. As far as I'm concerned, one tree looks the same as all the others. Coming down was the worst. It put a lot of pressure on my knees and they still hurt. And, I managed to get some golf ball sized blisters on my toes."

"I'm sorry to hear that. But, was it in any way therapeutic? I'm hoping it was because I was alerted an hour ago that you would be having a call from the President at any time."

Norma sat behind her desk and loosened the laces on her shoes. "Yes. I suppose he will call. If it weren't for those talk show guys, last Tuesday's slip would have gone away by now. Darn it, I wish there was some way we could stop them."

The phone rang. It was the President.

He didn't beat around the bush. "It's time you put an end to this. It's distracting attention from the things I want to do. What good are you if you cause me more trouble than help? Do it today, is that clear?"

"Yes, sir. I have planned a news conference in a couple of hours to address only that issue. I'll put it to rest."

"It had better go away. And no more slips, clear on that?"

"No more slips." The phone went dead.

She sat back and closed her eyes. And, what if one of those things happens again? she thought. There was no dodging this metaphorical bullet. She had to take her chances.

"Donna."

"Yes, boss."

"Contact the newsies and tell them I'll talk to them at ten in the meeting room down the hall. All that can get in, that is. It will be strictly to address the abortion comment."

"Consider it done."

"Thanks."

At ten o'clock the place was packed. Norma had a prepared statement, after which she would take at most three questions. She walked in and began.

"There had been a lot of to-do about nothing over the last week. I thought it was trivial enough as not to bother making a statement, but it is still going on. Therefore, I have this to say to you. First, I have not changed my position on abortion. That should end most of it. As to how that statement slipped into my speech, I have the following somewhat lame excuse. That was a prepared speech and for the most part I was following the Teleprompter. Yes, I use one at times, too. There was a minor disturbance in the audience, something of a catcall. I was momentarily distracted and read the next sentence as it appeared. That was the one that has caused all the furor. Someone had hacked into my final draft and there it was. The moment came and went. In hindsight, I should have stopped right there and corrected it. I didn't. That's it.

"There are an enormous number of details associated with an appearance like that. I do not have an unlimited budget to have dozens of technicians double and triple checking everything. Mistakes will happen. In addition, yes we are trying to find how the sentence came to be there, but it isn't easy. Now I'll take a couple of questions."

The questions were pithy as they always were. After the perfunctory equally pithy answers, she was off to the House chamber.

Norma had lunch brought in to her office for Donna and herself. She had an office manager, Doug Bradley, who took care of scheduling her day, assignments of staffers, saw to payroll, and all the other things that it took to keep one of the most important people in the country going. There were also her advisers who watched over the political scene, and in an election year, the campaign. Donna was a staffer, and as close a confidant as she had around the office. Though much younger, she was becoming hardened to the brutal bureaucratic games that this city was famous for.

Donna poured coffee for both of them as they sat at a small table off to the side of the room. The lunch was a sandwich and a custard cup. Donna was a petite lady, quite pretty actually in her mid-twenties. She wore a flowered long sleeved dress and conservative flat shoes. The possibility existed for her to make some man a fine wife if she managed to escape this mad house before it was too late. Maybe it was too late already. The two of them had lunch together now and then, so Donna wasn't surprised by the invitation.

"I invited you to lunch because I need a little favor. You're resourceful and discreet, not that there's anything sinister about what I need. You understand?'

Donna nodded as she ate. It was a free lunch after all, and the pay for someone at her level was not the best.

"I want a review of the fan mail we've received recently, good and bad. How long do we keep it?"

"At least a month's worth, usually it's six weeks. It depends on how much we get and how far behind we are on answering it. The FBI wants us to keep it six weeks as a minimum. You know, in case there would be an attempt on your life they'd scour the letters for clues."

"When I met with the President last week to get my ass chewed out, I was struck with how dictatorial he was. I've seen it before, but it was particularly obvious that day. I suppose it had something to do with the issue we were discussing. As I've considered it, I'm concerned that, as strange as it may seem, my statement was closer to the mark that I realized. He is too shrill on abortion. We've been making steady headway on all the progressive issues over the years. He's too doctrinaire. What I'm saying is he might be galvanizing a new base of opposition that could be disastrous. That's the purpose of reviewing the mail. I want to see if a new constituency is emerging so we can take steps against it now."

Donna had been listening intently while not losing track of the other activity which was eating. Norma had hardly taken a bite of food as she was intent on choosing her words carefully.

"I should think that by now we'd know about all the antiabortion worms that could crawl out of the woodwork."

"They may have made an appearance in the past and have lain dormant until this guy we call a president pushed too hard. Anyway, over the weekend Wally and I discussed this so here's what I want. The letters that are favorable go in one pile, as always, to get a nice answer. The horrid ones damning me to hell go in another. Don't throw them away because we may have to sift them again. Then we know about the born again types and their message of accepting the Lord, as well as the ones about the fetus is a baby. These all go on their own piles. Then, we see what's left. Wally said they would be aimed at me personally, not the babies, they would be polite and sincere, and oddly, they would contain a reference to eternity."

"Excuse me, but that sounds positively weird. You really trust Wally on this?"

Trying to appear as thoughtful as possible Norma answered, "Yes I do. He made quite a good case for it. I couldn't do as good a job of convincing you as he did me. He studies linguistics, and not only the meanings of words, but the motivations people have when using them."

"We'll do it if you're sure it's worth the expenditure of the resources. It'll take people away from other activities."

"Let's give it a try. Start with the mail of a day or two ago and go back a couple of weeks. I'll talk to Bradley and see that you get a couple of people."

As Donna rose to go she noticed Norma had hardly touched her food. "Are you feeling all right? You hardly ate anything."

"Got a little headache again. I'll take something for it and then finish eating. And, while there is no secrecy to the sorting, the fewer people who know about it the better. Hopefully, it will amount to nothing." She immediately reproached herself for having used the word secrecy. There was nothing like a little mystery to get everybody interested.

Donna left and Norma wondered how crazy her request had sounded. She knew Bradley would pose an objection. It didn't matter. He'd do it because she was the boss. Besides, there was no other way to find the little creep. She popped a pill in her mouth and washed it down with coffee. She wished her appetite were better.

The sandwich didn't look good, though it couldn't be the fault of the sandwich. Donna ate every bit of hers. She forced herself to eat part of it while leaning back in her high backed chair. With her eyes closed, she chewed thinking about when she'd make the next false statement, or when the next attempt would be made on her life. She had almost convinced herself that it didn't matter if she never made another slip. They'd want to get rid of her anyway, feeling they couldn't trust her. They were more paranoid than anyone could imagine. Having done it once they'd think she would be lying in wait for the absolute worst time and then let out a barrage of antiabortion rhetoric.

How would they do it? Poison? She opened her eyes and looked at the half eaten sandwich in her hand. Was that why it didn't look appetizing? A sixth sense was telling her not to eat it. That was stupid. Who took which plate was completely random. Not necessarily. She had read about how it was possible to influence people's decisions. The dill pickle on one plate could be turned so it looked appealing, while on the other so it looked fingered and messy.

A chime sounded. The House was ready to go back into session. The afternoon would be more contentious than the morning so she had to be there for it all, right to the bitter end, even if it went into the night.

Eugene had the TV on as he started his lunch. The noon report led with Norma's news conference. He was angered for having even thought the girl might be coming around. After all those years, he should have known better. He'd call his lawyer after he'd eaten and have him stop work on the idea of leaving his money to Norma. He hated to be taken in that way. From long experience, though, he knew to cut his losses and move ahead. There was nothing to be gained by hanging on to what couldn't be changed. The PI had called and would be in at one. That might be interesting. It was a brighter spot in his day.

After lunch, Eugene made his way in his office. He had to rely on his cane more than normally lately. He spent as little time as possible thinking about his health, but when hardly anything was working the way it should, it was hard not to. He knew he had little time left, and that was why he felt so compelled to settle his affairs. The money he had fought so hard to accumulate all his life had become a burden. How may other old people found themselves in a similar situation, he wondered. He lowered himself wearily into his well-padded chair. His cardigan sweater was open. Funny, even at this time of year he felt compelled to wear a sweater. Not so funny at all, he thought. He pressed the speed dial for his lawyer and left a message to stop work on the will in which he left his money to Norma.

It was one o'clock as he swiveled his chair to look out the window. His attention was drawn to the car pulling to a stop in front of the house. It was his PI, Dillard Sulk, a good man, one who understood the importance of promptness.

Two minutes later, the man was shown into Eugene's office. There was a puzzled look on his face, he thought. He wore a glen plaid sport coat, with a starched oxford shirt and coordinated tie. His dark slacks had creases in them. Here was a man who cared about the impression he made on people, a professional, Eugene's kind of man.

Eugene smiled, "How goes the chase?"

"It goes well, Mr. Freidmuth, but not great. The DNA test comparing the hair sample you gave me the last time with the one from the woman we had tentatively identified as a relative of Joyce was positive."

"A close relative?"

The PI held up his hand. "Before we go any further there's something I must tell you about DNA matching tests. The first thing is we are all led to believe it is a simple thing like using a piece of litmus paper to test for acids or bases, it turns red for acids or blue for bases. DNA tests are much more complicated. There are at least two reasons why the test results can be confusing or inconclusive. The first is there is clearly contamination of the lock of hair. Here, we mean not just any contamination, but other DNA. The test procedure is very sensitive to small amounts of DNA from another source. Maybe someone handled the sample over the years. For all we know, it could have been Ruth Wessen, herself. She may have been a friend of your first wife who was shown the book. If that's the case, then the match could be coming from the contamination rather than the hair itself. There is other evidence, which I'll mention in a minute, that indicates that may not be the case.

"The other reason these particular test results could be inconclusive is that most DNA testing is used in forensics. There are people who have been on death row for years and who are one day set free because the DNA tests of the evidence shows they did not commit the crime. Another important use is in cases like child support where men have DNA tests made between themselves and the child. Sometimes, it turns out the woman was promiscuous and the man is not the father. That means, in simple fact, that most of this testing is done to determine direct relatives as in child support. Or in crimes, is it me or not me. You see what I mean?"

"Yes, I guess so. Continue."

"It should come as no surprise that there is less precision when it comes to more distant relatives, and less practice on the part of the technicians who do the tests. In this case, there is clearly no direct match as in forensics. This we expected. But, we know two things. There is a relationship, and there is contamination."

Eugene nodded. "Is there any indication about what the relationship is?"

"I spoke with a microbiologist at the lab about it. He said it could be as close as a sister, or as distant as a cousin."

"Would it help to run another test?"

"I asked about that, too. With the testing as complicated as it is, he said we could come up with a variety of possible relationships. As I mentioned, with a direct match or not a match, the tests are reliable. But, with contamination indicated, determining the type of relationship would be unreliable."

Gene nodded. "I see what you mean." After a moment he asked, "What about an aunt?"

"Sure. It fits in the range of relatives we're talking about. There is a Certificate of Marriage for Carl and Ruth Wessen in Luverne, Minnesota. It shows Ruth's maiden name was Sutton. Your first wife was a Sutton, too. It's a common name, but not like Johnson. What are you thinking?"

"Maybe Ruth is Margaret's aunt. Joyce was the oldest of several, I don't remember how many. She was from South Dakota, Sioux Falls area. It was the height of the Depression and there were crop failures to boot. She was sent off to Minneapolis to make her own way. We met and ten months later were married. By the time Margaret was in her teens, she could easily have run across some relatives. She was getting to the age where the orphanage would turn her out for good. Who knows?"

They were both silent for a few moments. Then Eugene asked, "You're sure Margaret was related to this other woman?"

"The microbiologist was certain of that. So, however she fits, there is a relationship, the contamination not withstanding, as I mentioned."

Gene leaned back in his chair looking at the ceiling. "Well, some relation is better than no relation. What else do you know? How did you find this Ruth Wessen in the first place?"

"That's what you hire us to do. We investigate. And, this shows that it's more likely the relationship from the test is real rather than being from contamination. From the records of the now defunct orphanage, we found that in nineteen fifty-two Margaret disappeared one day leaving a note that she was going to southwestern Minnesota. She had found a job as a hired girl. Since the nuns at the orphanage were legally responsible for her, they went to the train station and upon giving her description learned she had purchased a ticket to Luverne, Minnesota."

"She had her own money?"

"By the time the children were in their teens they were expected to work as well as attend school. They helped in the laundry, shoveled snow, that sort of thing. If they did a good job they were paid a small amount as a means of teaching that reliable work paid off, and the importance of thrift for when they were out on their own. She could have saved enough for a train ticket."

"I see. Go on."

"We've been in a position like this before, so we sent one of our people out there to ask around. We found an old women who remembered Margaret. It's odd. Some of these people can't remember what they did yesterday, but are clear as a bell on what happened sixty years ago. She was employed by one of the larger farmers named Wessen for several months. This woman remembered her coming to church with the family, and seeing her in town now and then. Then she was gone. The orphanage records her coming back after six months. The following February she disappeared again, only this time she left no note. That was the last anybody heard of her.

"Luverne is a county seat so our investigator checked in the vital statistics at the court house for that period of time. That's when he came across the Certificate of Marriage of Carl Wessen and Ruth Sutton. Checking in the metro area we made some informed guesses and the DNA test shows we guessed right."

"All right. We strongly suspect Ruth Wessen is a relative to Margaret, and hence a relative of Joyce. We can't find Ruth's other son." Eugene paused. "Wait a minute. Why don't you talk to Ruth Wessen? She could clear this up for us."

"We tried. When our agent visited her to get the hair sample, she wouldn't even reveal Vincent's name that's listed in the St. Paul phone book. Our woman mentioned she had never run into anyone who was so tight lipped."

"Okay, scratch that idea. Did you check on Vincent Wessen?"

"We subscribe to several for-fee data bases so a quick check was easy. He lives in Arden Hills and has no arrests or warrants, no traffic tickets. He owns his house and cars, and has no credit card debt. He has some certificates of deposit, and a savings account all totaling about a hundred sixty thousand. His wife doesn't have a job, but we found she is active with a small pro-life organization. We called the organization. She volunteers there three or four days a week. Nice upstanding, law abiding couple."

"Hmm. Wonder what Vincent Wessen would do with it," Eugene said to no one in particular. Then, to Sulk, "I want you to spend a little more effort on Vincent Wessen. Also, see what you can do with the genealogy of Ruth Wessen. Maybe we can find out how the families are connected. Let me know as soon as you learn anything."

— 9 —

Monday afternoon 5:00

"Marv? Alvin."

"I told you not to call me."

"Who cares. I can see you did one fine job. Turn on your TV. She's got her face on it big as life."

"Yeah, but that's the problem, and I mean problem. Since you did call me, remember the first meeting place we decided on? Be there at seven. Don't tell anyone where you're going, and try to see if you're being followed. Got that?

"What's this . . . ?

"Do it."

Alvin's phone went dead.

Monday evening, 6:00

The five were assembled at the round table deep in the White House. Joab Feinstein began without letting the others take a breath.

"As you all know by now, Norma Holleran is alive and well. That means we have something of a situation. I had it set up to kill her as she was taking a long weekend at a cabin in upstate New York near the Catskills. You were briefed on this last Friday. Totally beyond anything we anticipated, our assassin was prevented from completing his mission by another armed man. It was dark and raining with almost constant lightning. They saw one another at the same instant, each pointing a silenced gun at the other. Rather than both dying, both backed away. At the present, we have no idea who the interloper was, though we will not rest until we find the answer to that. It means that we must find another way to deal with her."

The President's expression went from shocked to grave. "A leak!"

"A leak, or someone trying to do the same thing we were doing at the same time in the same place."

David Adams, the chief of staff, was shaking his head. "No. If it was another assassin, that guy would have killed her, or stayed out of sight as our guy did it. This seems to say she's hired her own security. How about that doctor guy who was with her?"

"Not likely. He's a college professor. It was a driving rainstorm at the time, so he would have had to have rain gear and equipment, to say nothing of special training. The professor has none of that. Our guy was highly trained. He wasn't out smarted by a dummy."

"Why'd you send only one guy?" the President asked.

Joab was feeling whipped by this, though he knew he dare not show it. "It was a one man operation with backup. This wasn't something like taking out a terrorist cell where we could retask satellites, use several levels of law enforcement, send in SWAT teams, helicopters, and all the rest. We sent one man. He knew that there would be a man and a woman at the cabin, though he didn't know who they were. He was told to kill them both. A second man dropped him off a couple of miles from the cabin. The driver didn't know what the object of the mission was, only that upon a call from the assassin he was to pick him up at a prearranged location different from the drop off point. They communicated by radio using codes. Not knowing who else might be around in the dark and rain, our man sent the code and was picked up as arranged. The two in the cabin, in all likelihood, knew nothing about it."

There was silence. Things like this were not supposed to happen. They were to control events, yet this gave the feeling someone else was exerting control. It was the first messy dirty trick they had undertaken since the inauguration. What had been easy back in Chicago, now, at the national level, appeared to have a level of complexity they had not expected.

Seth Goldman, the National Science Adviser, spoke. "Have you learned anything about what security Holleran laid on, if she did? Was it just for that weekend, or does she have her own private Secret Service now? Get a handle on it. We can't be caught blind sided like this." There was agitation, not quite accusation, in the last of Goldman's remarks.

"A cursory look shows nothing. She called this professor and they made arrangements for the weekend. That's all. We've checked his emails and phone calls and he didn't set it up."

More silence. The subject they were all assiduously avoiding was the possibility of a leak. A leak could point to one of them.

Sal Khurz spoke for the first time. "If she didn't set it up, who did? Who else knew she was going to be at that cabin? We must consider the possibility that our plan leaked."

To that Joab replied, "I know it points to me because it's my department. I told only one man where the operation would take place. The driver didn't know what was up on that mountain nor what was to happen. Of course, he knew it would be an assassination. That's what they do. When the shooter made the rendezvous later that night, that essentially ended it. They know enough not to discuss operations like this.

"There was a leak, but I discount the possibility that it come from our side. We learned of the trip to the mountains by listening to Holleran's calls and snooping through her emails. Someone else could have done that, too. Beyond that, according to existing policies she had to tell at least one of her staff members what she planned to do. The leak came from her side."

There was a sense of relaxation around the table. When arbitrarily wielding the sword of death, it was all too easy to suffer self-inflected wounds.

"That still leaves us with Holleran," the President said. "Maybe she can be disposed of as collateral damage from *The Plan*. We'll wait for your ideas about that when we meet on Wednesday," he said looking at Khruz. "And, let's find that other guy."

That ended the meeting.

Minneapolis, 7:00

With the summer solstice only a couple of weeks away, the days were long. The sun was shining and the air warm and humid. Marv nonchalantly sat on the opposite end of the park bench from Alvin.

Without looking at the other man, Marv started, "Things really went to hell. I have to tell you about it so you'll understand the seriousness of the situation. Let's walk."

There were other people strolling in the park which was good in that they would not be conspicuous. "The object of my trip and the other guy were in the very rustic cabin. It was night and raining hard with a lot of lightning, as prefect as it gets. I had entered the cabin when they were out hiking and saw where the man had slept the night before so planned to shoot through the wall and do him first, then her. A flash of lightning showed another man in front of me. He did just as I had intended, shooting where he expected the man to be on the other side of the wall. Then some law enforcement guys rolled up on four-wheelers, the sheriff, I suppose. I had hidden behind a big log behind the building. During a dark period between lightning, the other guy decided to hide there too. We saw one another at the same instant, each pointing a silenced pistol at the other. We could have both shot and both been dead. If he was half as scared as I was, he was terrified of dying in the next second. Instead, he held up his palm and started backing up. I did the same. It was the best offer I had all day.

"I didn't see him clearly, but he did not look familiar. But, he had one of those little microphones beside his mouth indicating he was part of a team. My only hope was to get out as fast as I could. I thought it possible that some of that team would finish the job. I didn't care because if they found me they'd finish me. She's still alive so they must have called it quits, too."

Marv stopped talking as another couple met them on the trail. They said hi, and passed. Then he continued, "All of this means that there is someone else who wants your sister dead, and they have more resources than we do. They will not be happy about their plan been disrupted. Expect them to dig, and dig hard. That means we can't be seen together again for a long time. As I mentioned when we were using the net that night, drop your computer on a rock."

"That's a cute saying, but just exactly what do I do with it?"

"Drop it off at a county recycling center. They'll take it for five or ten dollars. That way it will be thrown in with hundreds of others." Marv slipped a cell phone out of his pocket. "Here's a non-contract cell phone. If you really need help, call the number on the slip of paper taped to it. Memorize the number and then destroy the note."

"Is it that serious?"

"Listen, buddy. Killing a high profile politician would have been bad enough, but messing with a professional assassin, especially one who has friends, is the worst. My concern is they will scrub Holleran's emails and find you. It they look hard enough, they'll do it, and these guys will be motivated. After that, even though I left nothing that could implicate me, they could still find me. I had to go to a certain not quite so respectable place to buy my equipment. They are very discrete, but with enough muscle applied to the right places, people talk."

They fell silent as they approached other strollers. "Destroying your computer may not do any good, but it's worth a try. Buy a new one so the room looks right, though. My point is this, they won't be trying to make a court case against you, none of the Miranda Rights thing. They will want to settle a score, which means punishing you, maybe even killing you, and by extension, me. Remember, they have to assume I ID'd the other guy. For sure, I know what he was up to. Maybe you hired me to protect your sister. That would imply you knew what they intended. It goes on and on."

Alvin could see Marv was upset. After all, he was a PI, not a killer. Marv continued, "I spent some time scouring the net for word of anything out of the ordinary happening in the woods south of Albany. The Albany paper, radio, and TV stations had a total of nothing. The guy must have moved his bed. That's the only explanation. In the morning, they surely found the bullet holes and chips of wood on the floor. However, with nobody hurt, what could they do? It would be obvious the shots were intended for the man. So, he has a few enemies. That would be the logical explanation."

Alvin sighed, "I hate to change this fascinating subject, but where does that leave us in our mission of getting filthy rich? I saw Norma's statement on TV. Wonder what the old man will do about the will? That statement doesn't look like she's had much of a change of heart. Maybe we're back to square one."

"I'll drive by and download another readout from the bug in Eugene's office and drop it where we had planned. That okay?"

"Yeah. We've gone this far. No point in dropping the ball now."

That same time, Washington, D.C.

It was something of a pleasant surprise for Norma Holleran that the House session had ended as early as it had. It wasn't even eight as her driver stopped at her apartment building. The doorman opened the limo door and she was about to step out under the awning that extended across the sidewalk. She gave a start when she glanced up at him.

"Where's Alfred?"

Alfred was the doorman who had been there longer than she had. He was so kind, almost fatherly, that she had grown accustomed to the few friendly words from him each time they met.

"He's taking a few days off. I'm Slade, his replacement. Watch your step there, Ms. Holleran."

He was big as a house, and not fat. One eyelid drooped, and when he smiled—a fake smile it seemed to Norma—there was a tooth missing. The uniform hardly fit as though there were no sizes large enough. She thought he'd be more at home as the bouncer at the most violent skid row bar in the worst neighborhood.

She suppressed a shudder as she hurried past him. But, he was quick.

"Here, let me get the door for you."

She nodded and slipped past him into the lobby, hurrying to the elevators, trying not to run. What was this? Why the gorilla in place of Alfred? After all that had happened, it was hard to believe it was coincidental.

The elevator door opened with a ding and she got in. Safe. Come on. Get a hold of yourself. Letting out a breath, she relaxed. Arriving at her floor she walked to her apartment. As she opened the door the light was on in the kitchen. She froze. "Hilda? Are you still here?"

No answer. She was never here this late. Pausing in the doorway, she wondered if she should call security. What if that *thing* in the bulging uniform from downstairs answered her call? She flipped the switch by the door for the lamp beside the sofa. The living room appeared normal. Clenching her teeth, she entered. "Anybody here?" No response, no movement in the kitchen. Slowly she made a check of the other rooms.

Hilda must have forgotten to switch off the kitchen light. There had to be a first time for everything. The neat note on the kitchenette table gave tonight's menu. Norma almost collapsed into one of the chairs and with her elbow on the table supported her head with her hand. "Have to get hold of myself," she whispered for the second time in ten minutes.

Tuesday morning, 7:00, June 8

Alvin and Marv followed one another to the McDonald's drive-up. Marv ordered coffee and a sausage biscuit. Alvin ordered only coffee and followed his compadre to an industrial area. Alvin parked beside Marv at the end of the parking lot in front of a building that housed a half-dozen businesses. He went to Marv's car and sat in the passenger seat.

Business was first, and they had their argument about the expenses, as Marv had expected. Marv insisted that he continue to get his one hundred fifty per hour. However, it was reimbursable against his percentage, if

Alvin scored in Eugene's will. It was a joke, of course. What was sixteen thousand dollars to Marv against his thirty million, and even more ridiculous against Alvin's three hundred million.

Eventually, they got down to work. The pertinent information from the latest download from the bug in Eugene's office came around one o'clock the previous day. The call to the lawyer eliminating Norma from the will once again was good news. The part with the PI was not. They listened to the entire conversation twice.

"That man just might leave the bulk of the money to that engineer in Arden Hills. He's crazy."

Marv looked at Alvin. "Al, one thing you must get into your head, he is not crazy. He might be old, and if his kidneys don't get him his heart will. But, those are mechanical things. It's not like he was having visions or couldn't remember his name. Listen to the meeting with the PI again after I leave. He's sharp as a tack. He followed what Sulk said, offered suggestions, and accepted the rationale why they wouldn't work. He's all there."

Alvin leaned back, stared out the windshield, and scratched his head. "Yeah. I know. It was more of a figure of speech, but what you said does bring things into focus. With Norma out for good, or so it seems at the moment, it leaves me. And, we both know what he thinks about me. He's been searching for something to do with his money. Out of the blue these Wessens show up."

"Thank goodness it's not the U.S. Treasury, or some other gigantic organization. A couple of mundane people we could handle, if the need arose."

"Funny. I was thinking the same thing. Spend a couple of hours and see what you can find on those people. Addresses, kind of cars they drive, where he works, that sort of stuff. If Gene gets serious about going off on that tangent we have to be ready."

Wednesday noon, June 9

It was the noon recess when Donna asked to see Norma Holleran. "Well, boss, we did two weeks' worth of hate mail and came up with these," she said handing a half dozen letters to Norma. "Do you want us to keep at it? Branley wants his people back."

"Give me a chance to look at these and I'll let you know after lunch."

After Donna left, she quickly scanned each of the letters. Each had the word "eternity" highlighted in yellow. None of them looked like what she had expected. Suddenly, something registered. She shuffled them again. There was one, hand written, by what looked like a younger person. She read it again, more carefully this time. It contained most of what Wally had said to look for. It was from Minnesota so the writer was not a constituent. Wally had mentioned that would likely be the case. Okay. This could be it. Now what?

It would be hard to take action on one letter. It would be better if there were a pattern. What kind of pattern? Then, something came to her. Why hadn't she thought of this before? There was no reason to think she would be the only one getting such a letter. Who else? She had to think of what this guy would know, not what she knew. She was obvious, a very visible pro-abortion Catholic. In addition, the next most visible pro-abort Catholic would have to be Senator Harry Rutlen. He was from an old blue blood family who had been a thorn in the side of pro-life Catholics for as long as she had. She hesitated to contact him because he might think she was losing it. Would it matter? She had to get this settled. She pushed back the papers on her desk so she could see the phone list of the senators and representatives under the glass. Picking up the phone, she called the senator's extension.

"Senator Rutlen. Hi. This is Norma Holleran. Glad I caught you before you left for lunch. Could we meet for a few minutes? Best if it could be today."

"Pretty busy. What is it?"

"Something I don't want to discuss over the phone."

"Sounds pretty mysterious."

She could hear a heavy breath being taken in and released.

He continued, "You're in session this afternoon, right?"

"Yes."

"I'll call you between three and four. We'll take a break together. That okay with you?"

"Fine. Thanks."

It was four-fifteen when the call came. Norma excused herself from the chamber and went to meet with the senator in his office.

"I'll try to be brief. It has to do with the stupid statement I made a week ago yesterday." She proceeded to tell him about Wally's analysis of the situation. He was surprised to hear it had happened two more times after the one in the speech. Then she showed him the letter.

"That's interesting," he said.

She didn't know what to make of the comment. Before she could respond, he continued.

"I received one just like that."

"How'd you pick it out. You haven't had the same thing happening to you?"

"No. It's the whole format. Hand written, and the way he says it. One of the people who opens the mail set it aside, as one of those that couldn't be categorized. That pile is sorted by a more senior staffer. He also set it aside. It rose to the top of the pile of its own accord. What do you propose to do about it?"

"I don't know. Do you see anything sinister in it?"

"Not until now. This professor friend of yours really thinks this is the cause of what happened to you?"

"I haven't shown it to him, but it fits exactly the profile he laid out."

Rutlen shrugged. "Have the FBI do a casual check. I can tell you, I don't want to start saying things that come out of nowhere. You can say I agree with you on having them look into it."

Norma smiled. "Thanks, Senator."

"Not a problem."

It was a problem, of course. Norma knew that. He'd be back for a return favor sooner rather than later.

— 10 —

Wednesday evening, June 9

At six o'clock the meeting of five was about to begin. This was the time when they were to get the report from Sal Khruz as to the next major goal of *The Plan* which was the total take over of the government. The first milestone had been to work themselves into a position where they had access to the levers of power. That had been accomplished. The second was to use that position to gain control of the government. It had never been part of their thinking that they would actually have the presidency directly under their control. Having that plum fall into their hands took some time to digest which is why only now were they preparing for the final assault. They knew that leading up to the total takeover lesser power grabs had to be carefully spaced so the general public didn't see a pattern—a law here, a few presidential orders there. It all had to be carefully concealed.

The four met regularly without the knowledge of the President even as he thought he was an equal member of the group. They sneered at how easy it was to lead him along under that misconception. He was the perfect stooge. Having no ability to speak in public without a Teleprompter, it was only a matter of dictating that appeared on the screen in front of him to control what he said. As a result, this was a ho-hum meeting for the other three, but necessary for the sake of the President.

Sal Khurz started his presentation. "None of the steps needed to accomplish our goal are very complicated. They were all laid out in Saul Alinsky's book *Rules for Radicals*. They are common sense when you strip away ingrained attitudes of fair play and morality. I'll summarize the thought process I've used in applying the rules and we can then discuss it."

It was understood that an event was necessary to achieve their ends. The event would cause a national emergency that would make it possible for the President to assume vast new powers. The case of the fire in the Rightstag in Germany shortly before Hitler took dictatorial powers was studied as an example of what they wanted. In addition, the case of President Bush grounding all the airlines in the wake of the 9/11 attacks was a good model. Only, they needed something that would not go away as fast as the 9/11 grounding did. It needed to last several weeks, better a month. Then it would be seen as the President's actions that relieved the situation. After the disruption was resolved, it would only be his continued control that would prevent it from happening again. And, it was necessary that anarchy not result. It must be an emergency, but one which only firm and total control by the government could resolve.

The national emergency would be aimed at one of the things the American people valued most. These included the following: government, money, cars, guns, food, TV, cell phones, security, the Internet, and sex. Significantly, no part of the Constitution nor any of the Bill of Rights were included.

The American people valued government, but that was in effect the goal, vastly increased governmental control. Naturally, that was out. Money, yes, but that was all over the place. If there were a lot of inflation, those with retirement annuities or savings would lose, but those with debt, most of the people, would win. Besides, the economy needed money to operate, and there was no point in destroying that, at least not yet. Getting rid of cars was like getting rid of money. The economy needed them to operate. High gasoline prices were bad for the economy. It would be good to get rid of the guns in private hands, but that might be difficult, especially in an emergency. Making food scarce would make everybody hoard food and fat people mad. And, it could not be made to happen fast. Food was out.

Television was certainly something Americans valued; it was part of the bread and circuses. If all the stations went dead, it would not be accepted that it would take as long as a month to get some of them back on line. More importantly, TV was the means of communicating to the people the need for tighter governmental control. TV was out. The addiction to cell phones was so deep that people would feel naked. It would be like taking away all illegal drugs. Anarchy would result. Security could be threatened in any number of ways, especially by the specter of a foreign attack. But that could be laid at the feet of the government itself. That would produce a ground swell to remove the incumbents.

The remaining two were cyber space, and sex. It was a combination of the two that they would use. The Internet was needed for commerce, so if that went away completely so did the economy. It was like money, only more so. Even the utilities couldn't operate without it. But, an attack on one sector controlled by cyber space would be perfect. The cyber attack on the banks a month before the election in two thousand eight was a practice run that they used to develop the techniques needed. Significantly, no one was blamed, or took credit for that attack. This time it would be different.

This left a two pronged attack on sex and cyber space in that order. Sex was good because while the crisis was going on, everybody still had access to his or her own particular addiction or perversion. By frothing up public animosity against those who sought to end the free sex society, that is, pro-lifers, the imposition of presidential emergency powers would be accepted. However, it would not work to blame only the pro-lifers. They were too benign a group. It was necessary to work the white supremacists into it. Although, that group was not against abortion as such, at times they applauded the murder of an abortionist for reasons far different than people suspected.

Khruz continued, "I propose doing something like Oklahoma." He was referring to the Oklahoma bombing by Timothy McVeigh on April 19, 1995 when McVeigh exploded a truck bomb beside the Alfred P. Murrah Building in Oklahoma City killing one hundred sixty-eight and wounding another four hundred fifty.

"The reason I feel that is a good model is primarily because the public has grown tired of fighting Islamic terrorists. It's been nearly a decade since the World Trade Center was hit, and there hasn't been anything since. We have to dust off a home grown enemy—white supremacists with pro-lifers thrown in for good measure."

The President interrupted, "Won't it seem odd if you duplicate what McVeigh did?"

"Why should it? It will be a copycat crime. Beyond that, I like it because it will be simple and easy. I've discussed this with our resident terrorist," they all looked at Joab Feinstein, "and he agrees it has little risk to us and a big payoff.

"I wasn't directly involved in the Oklahoma City bombing, but those who were said all they had to do was point McVeigh in the right direction, and he did all the rest. The World Trade Towers was too complicated and never would have worked if the Arabs were left to their own devices. We gave them a lot of help because those dogs can't hunt. If you want something done, find some white guys. It'll be different this time, though. The feds have all the white supremacist groups so infiltrated that we'll have to take a more active role. We'll be sure those fringe groups get the credit, of course.

"Let me be clear, the main event will be a cyber attack, and I'm still working on exactly what that will be and how we'll do it. However, leading up to it must be a series of disturbing preliminary attacks. The first will be a bomb attack on an abortion clinic in St. Paul, Minnesota. The Ellefson campaign is buddy-buddy with some of the pro-life groups in that area, and the evidence will show all those people were in on it."

The President nodded his approval. "Have you learned anything more about what happened over the weekend with Holleran?"

"We're getting close. By Friday, Monday at the latest, we should have it sorted out."

That ended the meeting.

Thursday morning, June 10

Paul Sanders was taking a coffee break from his job of sorting names. Chad Gigsby approached, sat beside him, and spoke in hushed tones. "There's a lot of talk about Holleran. You setting here with your nose in these printouts all day probably don't hear much. Some say she's cracking up, that she'll step down soon, even before the election this fall."

Paul replied, "As Mark Twain once remarked, 'The reports of my death are greatly exaggerated.' I'll have to see that to believe it. Why is that happing at this critical point in the election cycle?"

"That's kind of the point. Something funny is happening. It started with that out of place statement she made about abortion a week ago. And, apparently that wasn't the only case. Listen. Our candidate has had several staff positions in Washington over the years. He's connected. That's why there's such a good chance he'll win. It's all rumor, of course, but the word is that somebody is controlling her mind, like a trance, or something out of a seance."

"Wait. What do you mean it happened again? I don't listen to the news all the time but there was no mention of it that I heard. Wouldn't everybody be talking about it?"

"This wasn't public. She told it to someone in her office. She swore him to secrecy, but someone else heard the whole thing. It happened the morning after the slip in the speech."

"Come on. You don't mean to say you believe that mind control stuff. That's for fringe people who believe in Atlantis and Big Foot."

"Doesn't matter if I believe it or not. The word is they're turning over all the rocks to find who's doing it. If they're looking, it must mean they think they can find. If they do, poor guy," here Craig made a slicing motion of his finger across his throat, "he's history."

Paul took a sip of coffee hoping his expression didn't show what he was thinking. He felt he had to continue his devil's advocate position so he said, "Whoa. What if the press got wind of the fact that members of Congress began to think something like evil spirits were pulling their strings. And, not in the normal graft, greed, and corruption ways, but mental telepathy that determines what laws get passed. They'd go nuts."

"Must be it's so serious they don't care. What if it starts happening to others?"

"It's a crazy world. I have to get back to work. They want to send out mailings to this batch as soon as I get the duplicates cleaned out."

Chad started to walk away, then stopped. He returned and plunked down in the folding chair again. "Just one more thing from somebody else. They heard Holleran has been targeted. That's all. Wonder what that means?"

"Targeted by the Republicans to unseat her in the fall. That's obvious. That would be something wouldn't it? Imagine, knocking her off. Wonder who's next in line in the House to be Speaker?"

"Nah. I don't think that's it. She wins by getting seventy percent of the vote in her district. Can't be done. Well, now you're up to date." Chad got up and with a playful jab said, "Stop fooling around and get to work."

Paul replied, "You're invading my space." As Chad walked away, he added, "Go bother somebody else."

Paul appeared to be working, but he wasn't getting much done. There was no way they could find him. He had said prayers, sincere ones, but it wasn't as though anyone had been hurt. Besides, it had to be something or someone else. But, Craig did mention it had happened again, and the second time was mid-morning of the next day. That was a pretty good coincidence, if that's what it was.

Friday morning, June 11

A thirty-something man still within the weight range of normal entered the campaign office. He was in superb physical condition, though
from looking at him one would not draw that conclusion. His name was
Fred Clements, and he worked for the FBI. In truth, to say he worked for
that organization was a little off the mark. He didn't just work for the
bureau, he saw himself as a crusader against crime which was not the
same as saying he necessarily believed in justice the way other people
did. For him, the human race was divided into two groups, law enforcement at all levels, and the rest of the people whom society at large saw as
a herd of sheep with wolves mixed in. But, he knew this to be untrue. In
reality, there were no sheep only wolves some of whom wore sheep's
clothing. All were ready to tear apart others if given a chance. To prove
this one had to go no further than acknowledge the fact that everybody
tired to cheat on their taxes to say nothing of driving thirty-five in thirty
zones—criminals, one and all. It was simply the case that some of the
wolves were more advanced in their development than others.

He asked the first person he saw if he could speak to the campaign
manager. Queried as to his business he said he'd rather keep that between the manager and himself. He was asked to wait. Every eye was on
him for the minute that it took for Hal Worthington to appear. Hal was a
dark complected man of mixed blood, being half white and half Jamai-
can. He wore a suit most days, as he did today. He was over six feet tall
and his energetic nature kept any sign of fat from forming.

"What can I do for you, ah, Mr. . . . ."

"Clements. If we could speak in private, I should only take a few
minutes of your time."

Worthington nodded. "Of course. This way."

Inside the office, Hal motioned to a chair. As Clements took a couple
of steps toward it, Hal moved behind the man to close the door. Before
the door was completely closed, Clements began. "I'm from the local
FBI office. Here's my card." With that, the door clicked shut.

Worthington took the card and nodded. "What can I do for you?"

"This is a routine check. It seems someone from your staff has sent
threatening letters to some high profile members of congress. This happens quite often and in the vast number of cases it's an individual letting
off a little steam and amounts to nothing. But, when we are asked to

investigate we have no choice. The man's name is Paul Sanders. Is he part of this campaign?"

Hal was surprised. "Just who are these high profile members of congress?"

"I'm not at liberty to say. Does this man work here?"

"What is it he said in the letters?"

"I'm not at liberty to say that either. Now, does he work here or not?"

"Well, yes. He's volunteering for the summer. He's only eighteen. He works at sorting through mailing lists to remove duplicates. And, I might add, he's very good at it. He's out there now. Do you want to talk to him?"

"Not necessarily. Does he seem like someone who would want to bring harm to a politician he finds particularly disagreeable?"

Hal chuckled. "He's the kind of kid who'd gently brush a mosquito off his arm rather that kill it."

Without acknowledging the remark Clements continued, "How carefully do you screen the people that work for you?"

"Two of us interview them. It's important to know their views on issues. We don't want a vocal 'save the whales' person in the office if the candidate thinks there are more important issues. You understand that. Otherwise, if they're willing to work, we don't say no. We need all the hands we can get. Is there anything else?"

"No. That should do it."

"It's too bad, you know."

"Why?"

"He's such a good worker. I'll hate to lose him."

"Why would you lose him?"

"Oh. If he's being investigated by the FBI, we couldn't take the chance. We have to be so careful about any hint of impropriety. The candidate would be destroyed if the media found out. In that regard, I do hope you will keep this confidential. You understand, we don't have the resources to do background checks on all the volunteers. Is that agreed?"

"I suppose. You have to let him go, eh? Well, you have to weed out the bad ones, don't you."

The crass remark took Hal by surprise. "Now, if you please, be on your way." Hal's tone had become noticeably harder as he realized what he had to do. He accompanied Clements to the door and did not shake the man's hand which was not offered in any case.

The door to Worthington's office was hardly closed with Clements inside when the buzzing started. Chad was the one closest to it and had heard Clements' first words. Others were looking at him and he pointed at the door and whispered, "FBI." Several side conversations immediately started. Chad got up and went to Paul who had the ability to tune out the noise of the office.

"Hey, Paul."

Paul looked up.

"A guy from the FBI came in and is talking to Hal in his office. Wonder what's going on."

Paul cracked the slightest smile. "I told you not to party so much. They finally caught up with you, I bet."

Craig was pleased. "Paul. You're finally getting the hang of a little chitchat."

"We'll probably never know what it's about. I want to get the rest of this list done by noon, and time's a-wasting."

A half-hour later, Hal casually approached the table where Paul was industrially working. "Paul, I need to talk to you for a few minutes. Let's go to my office."

Paul, thinking nothing of it, left the table and followed. Hal had him close the door.

"I'll be done with those lists I'm on by noon. They wanted to know because they plan to have some mailings out by next week."

"That's not what I wanted to talk to you about. The man who was in here a while ago was asking questions about you. He said you sent some threatening letters to members of congress. Is that true?"

Paul's face went white. "That was the guy from the FBI, right?"

"How'd you know that?"

"Craig told me. I saw him as he left. He looked like a creep. But, about the letters, that's not true. How could anybody get all that so twisted up? Did he mention who I sent them to?"

"He wouldn't say."

"That's just fine. All secret. So secret he wouldn't even say who I was supposed to have threatened." After a pause, "So what? Do you believe him?"

"Paul, I doesn't matter what I believe. The issue is that the FBI is to some degree investigating you, and not for a security clearance at a defense plant. They think you have committed a crime, or intend to commit one. You have been doing a super job, and everyone likes you. The problem is, we simply can't have the appearance that something illegal is going on in the campaign. I have to ask you not to be part of the campaign any more. Take a few minutes to say good bye to whomever you want, and leave by noon. I'm really sorry."

"Just like that. On the say of one man who offers no evidence of any kind, you do this to me. Maybe it's not so bad. If that's how easily you guys cave in, it's no wonder the Democrats always win. My uncle has a saying, 'If you don't lie down, people won't use you for a rug.' You think that might be the problem?"

Paul left the office, walked to his table, and sank heavily on to the metal folding chair. Craig saw it immediately and went over to him.

"What happened? You look terrible."

In a sickened voice he said, "I've been fired. I can't even keep a job I do for nothing." It was so quiet in the room a pin dropping would have shattered glass.

"Why? What did Worthington say."

With that, they all saw Hal Worthington striding out of his office and out the door to the street, making eye contact with no one.

When the door was shut, Paul continued. "He said that FBI guy that came in earlier accused me of sending threatening letters to members of congress, and he could not tolerate having someone who was being investigated by them on the campaign."

"Did you?"

"No."

"Big surprise. Wait." Craig looked around. "What are all of you looking at?" He went into the office and came out carrying a business card. He placed it on the copy machine and made three copies. He returned the card.

Back with Paul he said, "Here's the card of the dork who accused you." He gave Paul two of the sheets. Others came up and told him they were sorry to see him go. There was little else anyone could say.

Paul retrieved his lunch bag from the refrigerator and put it into the little backpack he carried. Craig left with him.

As they walked to the bus stop at the corner, they exchanged phone numbers. They said good-bye and Craig returned to the office.

"Mr. Sulk. It's only been a few days. You've been working hard," Eugene Freidmuth said as the PI was shown into his office.

Dillard was wearing a different sports coat today and no tie. "What we found and didn't find wasn't so hard, and unfortunately most of what I have to say is in the category of what we didn't find. There are quite a few Suttons around Minnesota and the Dakotas. We found no obvious way the two families were connected. My suggestion would be to rely on the DNA test. According to that, there is a connection. We can keep beating the bushes if you want. I would not hold out much hope of doing better than the DNA if we did, though."

Sulk paused as if between subjects. Eugene waited.

"We were equally nonproductive in locating Ruth Wessen's other son, if there really is one. Assuming he exists, he could have died out of state and no record ever made of it here. Or, from problems with the law, the underworld, or any other reason, he might have changed his name. As long as he never applied for government employment or something like that, his former name would not come up."

Eugene thought a minute, then said, "We're left with Ruth Wessen and her son Vincent who are out on some branch of the family tree. Strangely, I'm drawn to them. I've been thinking of Vincent to get the bulk of the money, though I'm not sure why."

"That reminds me," Sulk said as he opened his case. "We did more work on Vincent Wessen. He's quite an upstanding citizen. I'll leave the report with you."

"You've done a good job Dillard. I'll call if I need anything else. Show yourself out, will you? I don't get around as well as I used to."

— 11 —

Friday morning, 8:20

Unaware of the kind of day Paul Sanders would have, Vincent Wessen drove northwest on interstate I-94. His destination was Sauk Centre, Minnesota. It was in a way a sentimental journey. In another, it was a detective mission. The discrepancy of his birth date from the one his mother had so many times described had become almost an obsession with him. The irking thing about it was there seemed to be no possible way of resolving it. He had been stupefied at how his mother had refused to discuss it. Through his entire life, any time a conversation turned to things about his growing up, she was unstoppable in her retelling of childhood stories, some of them embarrassing to him. With only a word or a phrase, she would be reminded of an incident, and out rolled the story to be repeated to friends and strangers alike. In addition, it seemed like she accurately remembered the events because neither his father nor any relative ever contradicted her. What was it about his birth date?

That brought to mind something else that had always puzzled him. It was the aloofness she had around the relatives, especially her own. She was that way around his father's relatives too, but nothing like hers. He knew little about her side of the family. Rarely had they gone to weddings and funerals, and there were virtually no casual visits. He wouldn't be able to pick his cousins out of a crowd because he had never met some of them. This all seemed to stem from some sort of feud that arose at the time of his parents getting married. Apparently, both families for different reasons were against it. And, the rancorous dispute had never been resolved. All his life he had accepted it as the way things were. Now, for the first time, he began to question it. From his mother's attitude, he knew there was something behind the birth date irregularity. His having been born on Ash Wednesday was one of her favorite stories like it cemented something into place because in her mind there was no way it could be questioned. Then, suddenly, it was as if she had been caught being dishonest. Something in a solid foundation had crumbled.

At Monticello, he almost turned around and returned home. That was the other side of it. There were times when he thought it was positively absurd that he'd care about such a small thing. What difference could it possibly make to anyone, least of all, him? But, he didn't turn around or even slack his pace. He was going to Sauk Centre. He had what might be a premonition that a gathering storm was about to unleash its fury against him, and that in some bizarre way his finding of this oddity about his birth was the suffocating calm before the tempest.

At the very least, he intended to drive out to the homestead where he had been born. He was sure he could find it because shortly after he had passed his driver's license test his father and he had driven up that way. He hadn't been a good enough driver to be trusted on the main highways. But once in town, he was allowed to drive out to the place. It's a strange thing how a person remembers a route more exactly when he's driving than when only a passenger. That was forty years ago. He wondered if the place were still occupied or more likely eradicated from the land as his parent's farm was grabbed up by one of the corporate farms that were becoming the norm.

At shortly before ten, Vincent was on the off-ramp at Sauk Centre. It was a nice rural town, large enough to have the businesses and services needed in toady's world, yet a small town. It was the home of Sinclair Lewis, and the setting of his famous book *Main Street*. In the novel it was called Gopher Prairie. The novel was not complimentary to the fine people of the town. This led to him being disowned for a couple of generations. As Lewis's fame spread over the years, the younger generation saw profit to be made in a tourist trade based on the author. Now Main Street was called *The Original* Main Street. The town also had a Sinclair Lewis Avenue.

Vin had gone on line and discovered there were ten nursing homes in town. The response from those he called was the same, stop in and let us have a look at you. They weren't against inquiries of this kind, it gave the residents something to do. On the other hand, they didn't want someone with a scam bilking their charges out of their savings.

He had picked his first stop at random. As he parked, he saw government money written all over it. The architecture was, in his opinion, appalling. That's the way it went, though. The entry was really a community room of sorts where people could meet and chat with friends. As he entered all conversation stopped and all eyes were on him. This he understood. After a few years, everyone knew everyone else's relatives, and when they came. Life was anything but unpredictable. Salesmen and those providing services had a separate entry.

A woman in a uniform looked at him from behind a small counter. She appeared scant years, even months, away from being an inmate herself. She asked, "May I help you?"

"Yes, I think you can. I'm Vincent Wessen. A couple of days ago I called asking if I could inquire about a local resident who lived here in nineteen fifty-three."

She smiled. It seemed genuine as she approached him. With a gesture of her arm, she indicated a vacant chair. "I sent a notice around to the rooms saying you'd be here. Many of the people in the room now responded. Why don't you ask them what you have in mind?"

She stepped away taking her place once again behind the counter with a phone on it. Its position was such that he could see her and know that he was being watched by someone in authority. One false move, and here come the cops, was what the body language spoke.

Vin considered the dozen faces looking at him. They were mostly alert, having come not so much from the motive that they would have something to contribute, but to be in the lead in getting the gossip. Such was life.

"I'm Vincent Wessen," he began. "I was born on a farm northwest of town in February of nineteen fifty-three. I was a little too young at the time to remember, but I was told it was during a fierce blizzard. Were any of you living here then, and remember the blizzard."

Several heads nodded. Nobody said anything.

"My parents were Ruth and Carl Wessen. They were only here for a couple of years . . . ."

"Less than that," a woman said. She wore a dark dress with brown stockings. Her shoes were of the lace type and looked new. She appeared to be about eighty so she would have been in her twenties at the time.

"You remember them, then?"

"Oh yes. They bought the Hanson place, but he didn't have enough money to get it started. Ran out of credit and the bank took it back. That was it. They lost it and left. Never heard from them again. Didn't your mom and dad tell you about that?"

This was starting out positive. "Yes, they did. The reason I'm here is to inquire about a young woman, maybe mid to late teens at the time, who might have stayed with them for a while during that winter. We think she was kin in some way. There's a matter of an inheritance, not a great deal, but enough to bother with. I'd like to find her if I could. Her first name was Margaret."

The woman didn't reply. Vin looked at her and raised his eyebrows as if questioning. Still nothing. So he asked, "Do you remember such a person?"

She didn't respond at first as a cloud came over her face. "In a way I do. There was a young woman living with them for a while. I don't recall when it was, though. They didn't mingle much. But, ya have to remember that to come in and start up a farm is a tough job. It took all the work the two of them could do. Worst of all, they got a late start, early June, it was. Seems like the community sort of forgot about them. That might seem unusual, but there was so little known about them. From when the baby was born, that'd be you, she must have gotten pregnant about the time they arrived. I remember hearing she was off her feet most of the time, had a tough go of it. Might be the girl came to help in the house as the time neared. There's something odd that happened around that time that I can't bring to mind."

"Is there anyone else around town who might remember something more, like a neighbor? How about the rest of you? Anybody have anything to add, especially her last name?"

"How about you, Betty?" the woman said to a completely shriveled up woman. Vin thought she had to be nearing a hundred.

To his surprise, she was bright. "They had a hired girl, I remember that. Doubt she was kin, though."

"Why do you say that?"

"I only saw them at church and she acted, well, what can I say, well, different, that is, when she came. It seemed the mother, Ruth, and the girl seldom came to church together. Sorta made sense, I guess. They had the little boy when they arrived, and he was a dickens, never behaved."

"Hildie Liston might remember," a man with an oversized nose and frizzy hair said. "She lived on the next place past the Wessens'. To save them gas, Hildie'd have her husband stop and they'd give her a lift to town. We were on the same party line, but closer to town. When it rang two shorts and a long we knew it was for the Wessens. Everybody listened to everybody else's calls. They didn't get many other calls. My misses said it was hardly worth picking up the phone. It was always the same. 'Any reason you want to go to town. We're going in ten minutes.' Always the same. Sometimes yes, sometimes no."

"Where can I find this woman?" Vin asked.

"Down the street a couple of blocks on the other side. Can't miss it. Another nursing home. Lots of 'em in town."

Vin smiled and was about to thank them for their interest when the woman, Betty, interjected, "About that time there was talk . . . ."

"And talk was all it was, Betty," the man cut her off. He looked at Vin and continued, "What I'm saying is this is a small town and if everything was true that people talked about . . . well, you know, most of it's just gossip, it's the way them women pass the time. Nothin' to most of it."

Vin smiled again. "Yes. I understand. Thanks for your interest. I'll leave my name and phone number in case someone should recall any thing more."

The other home was three blocks down the street, not two, but Vin found it. And, he found Hildie. She was wearing a light dress with pink flowers on it, and getting around with a walker. She took it in stride. They were seated in a bright sitting room with a scattering of people. Two men were playing checkers. Vin introduced himself and told of his previous encounter.

"I'm hoping you can shed a little light on this," he said.

Looking at him nodding her head, he wasn't sure if it was a nod or a tremor of old age, she replied, "I don't see so well. Enough to get around, but not to read. The sound of your voice says there's more to it than an inheritance."

Vin smiled. "Not much gets past you, does it?"

She smiled in return. "I knew 'em. Didn't talk much. That winter there was a girl name of Margaret staying with them. Could have been related to Ruth 'cause there was a striking resemblance, but I doubt she was."

"Why not?"

"They was different, cut from a different piece of cloth. And, it wasn't the way she dressed or fixed her hair. Just, somethin' about her."

"Do you remember her last name. Without that, I can't get far. My parents mentioned Margaret from time to time but never her last name or even why she was there."

"Can't rightly recall. Seems it was an odd name, in a way. Ended with youth or something. No, 'muth', something 'muth.'" Then she stopped and looked at Vin. "Your mom and dad both dead?"

"My ma's still alive, but she doesn't want to talk about it. It's kind of the way she's always been. If she got it into her head she didn't want to discuss something, that was it. It could be anything from the neighbors to politics. That's why I'm here."

Hildie shifted in the padded armchair she occupied and grasped her walker as if to leave. Vin sensed something was troubling her, something about what he had moments before said.

"Did I say something wrong? I didn't mean to."

"Oh, it's not really that." She settled back in the chair again. "I'm a Catholic and we never read the Bible as much as them Protestants did, but I know it well enough to recall there's a line in it someplace saying to 'let the dead bury the dead.' What I mean is, Margaret would be near seventy now so what would she need with money? You said there wasn't so much. And, like I said at first, I don't think it's about money."

"You're right. I'll tell you. As far as I know there's no money at all. But, I thought if I told why I was really here everybody would think I was crazy. My whole life my mother told me I was born on Ash Wednesday, said it a hundred times. A while back, I found a chart that calculated Ash Wednesday for any year, and out of curiosity checked the year I was born. It turns out I was born eight days after Ash Wednesday. Ma flatly refuses to say a word about it. Since then, I've had a feeling something bad was going to happen, like a storm coming. That might sound nuts, but that's the truth. Can you tell me anything else?"

She didn't look at him, but there was deep sadness in her eyes, even the start of a tear. "If the storm's commin', I suppose it'll come. Maybe it'll wash us clean." With trembling arms, she raised herself and hobbled off.

Vin had the impression she was more bowed then when she came in, and the steps came more slowly. He too felt an added weight as he left. Something had happened in those few minutes. What it was, he couldn't put into words. On the sidewalk, he stopped and looked back, not that he intended to return, but that turning that way might help him understand what was bothering him. She knew something that was serious, or in her mind it was serious.

The sun was bright and warm. He'd be glad of the air conditioning in the car. In the driver's seat, he started the engine. In a minute, the AC was cooling the interior of the car, though it took longer for Vin to notice it. There was still a long list of nursing homes he intended to visit. Not only did he feel too fatigued to do another interview, but it seemed there'd be little else he'd learn. His thoughts returned to what Betty at the first place had started to say. Was it his imagination, or did everyone in the room become stiff as she started to speak. It was now clear that he had not imagined the reticence of the people in the room. They all knew more than they would say. What could they possibly be hiding? Then it hit him. It wasn't what they knew, but what they suspected. There had been a lot of gossip about what had happened to the Wessens during the storm, after the storm, and why they left.

They were in agreement that Carl and Ruth Wessen had operated a farm northwest of town for about a year, and Margaret lived with them for some of that time. They confirmed, or didn't dispute, the fact that he was born at home during a snowstorm. The only other things were that the farm failed, the bank took it, and they left. These were all things he had already known. They knew that Tim was a "dickens." He already knew that, too. The only new piece of information was that there was something they wouldn't talk about. It was something they may have convinced themselves was true, but there was no evidence to prove it.

Vincent saw a diner on Main Street, that is *The Original* Main Street, and went in for lunch. Having eaten he felt better, and started out to the "home place." It certainly had not been home for long. Most of the roads were paved now. Over the period of forty years improvements were bound to happen. He missed one turn, doubled back, and turned off at a gravel road. Two miles down the side road he saw it. The driveway leading to it was used by whomever worked the land. He saw immediately a shed had been repaired and was open on one side. It housed farm machinery that was still used. That accounted for the use and maintenance of the driveway.

He drove to the cluster of trees that marked the former homestead. Stopping the car, he turned off the engine, and opened the door. Standing up, he looked around. The sound of his door closing startled him. The air was still and hot. Later in the summer there'd be the song of cicadas to break the silence. Not now. Puffy white clouds swam in a sea of blue overhead. He could almost hear the footsteps of tired feet that had worked the land so long ago. They spent little of the product of their hands and sweat of the brows on themselves choosing instead to invest in their children, land, and homesteads. Now, we, the last generation, were squandering that wealth on cell phones and digital televisions.

To his left was a field of oats starting to head out. If he remembered correctly from his previous visit, there had been a lawn with apple trees beside the driveway. Beyond the trees spread a large garden with rhubarb plants on one side before the field started. To the right were what remained of the other buildings.

The house still stood, but barely. The porch was collapsing so he felt it would be dangerous to go inside. Walking around it, he was taken by how small it was. It was square, of course, the least wall for the most interior space. There was still a shred of rope hanging from the limb of an oak tree near the house. There had been a swing. He could almost hear children laughing as they played about. He was reminded of a poem he had read not long before.

Life on the Land

> Wind lapped waves in the brome,
> Land lashed by the rain.
> Sun bright and warm, still at the noon.
> Night with no moon, stars bright as gems,
> Bats overhead, night birds calling.
>
> Were we ever so young, so part of the earth?
> Our hearts full of hope, the future so bright?
>
> Now the homestead's gone back,
> Back to the wild.
> Summer breezes still stir
> Where we played with the kittens.
> Life on the land, lost and forgotten.
> I long to return to the place of my youth.
> My memories still young,
> Though, swept by the wind.

They had little by our standards, but he wondered if life had been so bad, especially in the summer. But, winter. The cold and snow could fight a man to death. With that thought, he turned his attention to the barn.

The tired old building was in the process of collapsing as it was left to rot in its throes of death. He walked, almost paced off, the indistinct overgrown path from the house to the barn. How was it possible to become lost in such a short distance? Was the storm really that bad, or did fatigue, worry, and perhaps hunger make it seem worse than it was? Why hadn't he asked his father more about what went on that winter? It seemed absurd that he would not have. It came to him that it was the reluctance, more of a wall, that had been erected around that time. Something had happened. Maybe, by objective standards, it had not been so bad. But being the ones to endure it made it far from objective. He could understand that.

After the attack on Pearl Harbor, the Japanese in the U.S. had been put in camps. In hindsight knowing how the war ended, one could make the argument that that was an over reaction. But, at the time, they didn't know what they faced, or how the war would end.

He had seen a movie about a court case where people in comfortable chairs, well fed, and in no danger sat in judgement of a man who, during a catastrophe, had taken the law into his own hands and managed to save the lives of some people, while allowing others to die. In Vin's mind he had always fought the very idea of that trial, because the jury knew how it ended. That's not the way of life. You are never certain what the next minute will bring. Maybe something terrible did happen here during that blizzard all those years ago.

Vin drove back to town not sure it had been a good idea to go to the farm. He looked at nostalgia the way he looked at alcohol, a little made him feel good, any more and he got a hang over. He was feeling hung over, at least psychologically, as he headed south on Main Street. Nearing the interchange with I-94, he saw a sign on the right for the local mortuary. A quarter mile later, about to enter the on-ramp headed east back to Minneapolis, he stopped. There was no one behind him. After a few seconds of indecision he made a U-turn and drove north, made a left, and in a couple of blocks saw the funeral home. A thirty-something woman greeted him as he entered.

"Sorry, sir, we don't have a viewing scheduled until four o'clock."

"I'm not here for a showing. My business might seem a little unusual."

She considered him without replying.

"I'm wondering if you were in business in nineteen fifty-three."

"Yes we were. However, since then we've moved, and the name has changed some. What is your interest?"

He thought he might as well continue on the original theme. "There's a matter of an inheritance, and I'm trying to locate a woman. It has occurred to me that the reason I can't track her beyond having been in Sauk Centre in the winter of that year is that she died here."

"The obvious place to look would be the bureau of vital statistics in the county seat, which for us is St. Cloud."

"I'm afraid that is not likely to be helpful. You see, though it may seem odd, I don't know her last name."

"Yes. That does complicate it a little."

"I know she was here the winter of nineteen fifty-three. Her first name was Margaret and she was in her late teens at the time. My idea is that there probably weren't many women that age who died in this town that winter. Do you still have records of that time?"

"We do, but it would take some work. I'd have to charge you."

"How much do you require?"

"I get requests like this now and then from people establishing their family histories, and charge fifty dollars. How soon do you need it, because if we get busy it may take a few weeks."

"A couple of weeks would be okay."

They went to an office and Vin wrote out his name, address and phone number, as well as what he knew about Margaret, even that Margaret might not be the right name. He noted that she should start with February and proceed as far as June if necessary. Vin handed her the money in cash along with the sheet of information. She gave him her business card.

"If you should find her, I'd appreciate all the information you have."

She nodded. "I'll copy the records, such as they are, and you'll have what we have."

As Vin merged with traffic on I-94 east, the old adage came to mind that a fool and his money were soon parted, only it didn't really seem that way. If she had died, it would seem odd. Maybe the old people had been reluctant to talk about it because they felt guilty for not helping a family in the community when they desperately needed a lift.

— 12 —

Camilla was surprised to see Paul home when she arrived at four-thirty. "Is there anything wrong, Paul? You're never home this early."

He was sitting on the living room sofa not looking at her. Looking a little closer, she could see he was upset. "Something is wrong, isn't it? Want to tell me about it? It can wait if you want, but sooner or later we'll have to talk about it."

He looked at her in something of a stupor. "Might as well. I got fired from my job on the campaign."

"Why? Did you make some mistakes?"

"An FBI guy came in this morning and told the campaign manager I had sent threatening letters to some big time members of congress, wouldn't say who. My boss said he couldn't have it appear as if there were illegal activities going on so that was it for me."

Camilla could see he was taking it hard and knew why. He was a loner and tended to avoid people. The first few days at the office were hard and they had talked about it. She had told him it would get better, and it had. This was his second full week and he was starting to like it. This would be a real set back.

"Did you write some letters?"

"Sure."

"Did you write them on the computer? I have to ask, were they threatening?"

"No to the computer, and no to the threatening. They were hand written. The other kids working on the campaign said that was the kind politicians paid the most attention to."

"It's too bad you don't have copies. If you did we might be able to figure out what you might have said that made them think you were threatening them."

Paul picked up a couple of sheets of paper from the coffee table. "Here are copies. I found a file folder of carbon paper in the file cabinet in my room. I'd never seen it before and wondered how well it would work. It's amazing how the pre-technological world got along. Anyway, they don't look threatening to me," he said as he handed them to her.

There was one to Representative Norma Holleran, and one to Senator Harry Rutlen. Both said the same thing.

Dear Representative Holleran:

Your intractable pro-abortion stand is wrong. You know that. You have the blood of millions of innocents on your hands. You must change because you have little time left, and hell is for eternity. Think about it. After you die there are no second chances, no changes. You suffer forever. You are a Catholic so you understand what I am saying.

Sincerely,

Paul Sanders

Camilla shuffled them looking at one and then the other. The penmanship left a little to be desired, but they were legible. There could be no mistaking the words. The letter was firm, but there was no way anyone could draw the conclusion that he intended physical or any other harm to either person. Certainly, they must receive a lot worse letters than this.

He was slouched over with his hands in his pockets. She couldn't help feeling empathy for him. He was suffering. She said, "I agree. If they feel threatened by these letters, they are too thin skinned to have the jobs they have. We'll talk to Vin about it this evening. Try not to worry. We'll figure it out."

She knew it was doubly bad because they had invited his parents and younger siblings for dinner on Sunday. It was sort of by mutual agreement so they could see how Paul was doing. She knew he would be asked for inside scoop on what happened in a national political campaign. Now it was spoiled.

Saturday morning, June 12

Vincent was having breakfast when Paul entered the kitchen. It was early, just seven o'clock, and Camilla was still sleeping. Paul knew the rules and put a pan on the stove to fry a couple of eggs. They had discussed Paul's situation the evening before and it seemed there was little else to be said about it.

"Paul, what do you say we go fly a model airplane this morning. It's a nice sunny, day with little wind. I want you to give it a try."

Vin had bought a radio controlled airplane kit for his boys when they were old enough to build it. The first one hadn't worked well since Vin had never flown an RC plane, and, as with everything else, there was a lot to learn. At the time, he didn't have the time nor the money to join a club, so they learned it by themselves. For the second plane, they bought a slow flying glider type plane with a motor on it. That worked better and all of them learned to fly it. They had located a park that had not been developed where there was an open space large enough. When his boys were in college there never seemed to be time, so it had fallen into disuse.

A couple of years before Vin took it out to the park and tried again. By that time, the county had put in paved trails to accommodate the increased use of the open space so flying there was not an option any more. There was too big a chance an errant plane might hit someone. He had spent time driving around the area and found some unused land a couple of miles away where nobody seemed to care. It was low land with the soil mostly peat. There was brush, tall grass and weeds but no open water. Some governmental agency had put in drainage ditches long before he had found it. This resulted in eighty acres of land with few trees, but lots of other vegetation.

"What's the point of my flying, I'll just crash it."

"Of course you will. But, where I go to fly it doesn't matter much. There's a lot of thick grass and brush, and if it does make it to the ground, the dirt is soft. I crash it all the time. Put on your oldest pants and shoes, because you'll get wet from the dew."

"I don't feel much like going."

"It'll get you out of the house and give you something new to concentrate on. It'll do you good."

"Yeah. Everything is supposed to do me good, like the campaign job. Except everything goes putz."

"Come on. It's a nice day, and I've got all the batteries charged up. I could use the company. Do me a big fat favor, how about that?"

"Jeez. Old people sure know how to get to me."

The Wessens lived on a corner lot. Their garage was detached and was accessed from the street that ran perpendicular to the front of the house. As Vin backed out of the garage, Alvin Freidmuth was watching. They had loaded the plane in the trunk while still in the garage so there was no indication of where they were going. Alvin thought there would be a chance Wessen did something on the weekends that would give him the opportunity he was looking for. He had spent a couple of days the week before and knew when Wessen left for work, and when he came home. The route he drove offered possibilities, but he hoped to find a better angle.

There were two people in the car, Wessen and another who didn't look like the wife. He followed them on to I-35W North. Some miles later they exited at Highway 23. Maybe they were going to walk in a park. Alvin was driving Blanche's minivan since it was less likely to be noticed than his bright red Mustang. A mile north on Highway 23, they turned west on Highway 14. Some distance further, they turned to the right going north. It looked like a business development area. He drove past so as not to give the appearance he was following them.

Returning, he slowed to a stop opposite the entrance. There was a sign proclaiming Wild Ridge Industrial Park. Fifty-five acres complete with utilities ready for your business. He drove in. There were a couple of buildings to the east of the street and one to the west. Each had paved parking lots. One building to the east had three cars parked by it. This was obviously a development from before the credit crunch. The streets were laid out with curbs and pavement. The investors had expected to fill it up fast and make gobs of money. Now, it waited. The road made a loop and he was headed back the way he had come when he stopped. There had not been a street leading out another way, and he had not seen Wessen. He lowered both front windows wondering where they had gone. A buzzing sound came from the right. He got out, looked over the roof of the van, and saw a small red and yellow model airplane rise into the air.

At the point where the plane first appeared from behind some brush, he knew he could not see them and they could not see him. He drove further and finally spotted Wessen's car parked behind the business to the west of the road. This was looking promising. He parked in the lot with the three cars in it. He had no worry of anyone seeing him because they all had dew on their windshields indicating they had been there all night. He felt good about how canny he was becoming in noticing the dew.

He locked his van, and walked to the street. No movement in sight as he looked both ways. What a perfect place. The sound of the plane got louder, and he was surprised to see it nearly overhead. He watched as it did a few less than smooth maneuvers after which it started to spiral down, still under full power. At fifty feet it pulled up, righted itself and proceeded in the general direction of the obviously none too professional pilot.

On the far side of the street, the undeveloped land started. He was shocked to encounter the heavy dew. After twenty steps, his shoes and pants up to his hips were soaked. Fifty yards later he stopped behind a ten-foot willow bush. Luckily, it was over seventy degrees already, so the wet clothing didn't cause any real discomfort. He could hear them talking. It seemed Wessen was teaching a younger man how to fly the plane. He felt he had to get close enough to see where they were standing. The buzzing stopped. He looked up and saw the plane glide as it was controlled from the ground. Actually, it was a pretty sight as the brightly colored plane caught the sun against a solid blue sky. It swished overhead as it headed for a landing not far from the two men.

Alvin waited for the motor to start again before moving further. As he shifted his weight, he stepped on a twig producing a sharp snap.

Immediately he heard the younger voice say, "What was that?"

"Probably a deer," the older one said. "There are dozens of them out here. I frequently flush several as I walk in to my flying place."

That was useful. First, there were deer that could be blamed for any inadvertent noise he would make. Second, the comment implied he always came to the same place to fly. With the plane in the air again, Alvin moved closer being careful as he placed each step. His clothing was not the best. He was wearing jeans, and a blue shirt. At least it wasn't white. When he was thirty yards away, he could see them, or parts of them through the foliage. He took note of the brush around them so he could locate the spot later. Then, he slowly moved away. He found a fully concealed place and sat down to wait for them to leave.

An hour and a half later he heard voices retreating. He back tracked to the brush near the street and watched them leave the parking lot. He nodded his head. This was it. Once again, he proceeded into the wild land. The dew was beginning to dry and the temperature was rising. By the time he found the place they had been, he was sweating profusely. There was a clearing in the bushes about fifty feet on a side that had shorter grass than the surrounding area. Once found, this was the logical place Wessen would come. From there Alvin looked at all the possible places he could use for his ambush, and selected three that were good, with one being by far the best. There was a twenty foot high broken off tree fifty feet from the best place so he had a guide to finding it. He even had the presence of mind to step off the distance from each shooting place to where they had stood. After that, he walked part of the way to the parking lot following their path in the grass. Most of the way they followed a deer trail, which made sense. Okay, he had it figured out.

As he crossed the street, Alvin was feeling smug. He wouldn't have to pay Marv's exorbitant rates who, after all, failed in his attempt. As he came in sight of his car, he was struck by what he saw. One of the cars with dew on the windows was gone. Someone had come to pick it up and obviously had seen his van. That was really dumb. Why hadn't he considered that possibility? Driving away, he thought about it. People aren't normally very observant. A couple of weeks ago, he wouldn't have even noticed that one of the cars was missing. If they had noticed it at all, they'd assume his minivan belonged to someone walking his dog in the area. It was okay.

Sunday afternoon, June 13

Vincent made his weekly visit to his mother. Occasionally, he picked her up and brought her out to the house for the day. She enjoyed that, but always let it be known that she didn't like to be there when there were a lot of other people around. She had always been that way. Relatives especially seemed to annoy her. He could understand Camilla's relatives in a way, they were strangers. It would have been nice if she tried to make friends with them, though. He smiled as he thought about it. She didn't discriminate. His whole life he remembered how she had never liked relatives, his father's or hers. Both sides had been against their marriage, and she never buried the hatchet. He couldn't complain because she had been a good mother.

"Hi Ma," he said as she opened the door. "How'd your week go?"

"Hello Vinny. You know, it was quiet as always. They repainted the stairwell and I sat out there for a while and watched the paint dry. That was the highlight, I'd say."

The comment about watching paint dry was one he and his brother would use now and then when they were bored. She'd say they should get off their backsides and amuse themselves. That's what she had done when she was their age.

When the conversation lagged as it normally did Vincent said, "Why were you so reticent to talk about my birth date last week? You surely remember what was going on then. It seems all mothers do."

She sat silently in her favorite chair for some time. Vincent assumed she was hoping he'd feel uncomfortable and start another subject. He sat with a neutral expression on his face and waited.

Finally, she said. "Oh, I suppose there's no problem in saying something about it now. You were born on Ash Wednesday as I always said. You remember that we spoke quite often about the terrible blizzard at the time. Your father had gone to the barn to do the evening milking and on his way back to the house became lost. It was only a fifty yards from the barn to the house. It was that bad. Eventually he ended up back at the barn. The second time he used the kerosene lantern to help find his way. I'm not sure how he did that because he could only see a few feet. I was frantic thinking I'd never see him again. When he finally arrived, he was nearly frozen to death."

This was one of the stories Vin had heard a hundred times.

"Anyway, you were born that night. For the next several days that whole part of the country was digging out. The wind had blown so hard that the snowdrifts were hard as ice. Carl could walk on them like a cement sidewalk. He fed the milk to the pigs for three days because he couldn't get out. Finally, he had to hale the township snowplow making a final pass along the road to have him plow the driveway. That took the last five dollars we had until the next cream check.

"We had learned that births that were not registered in a timely manner were subject to a fine. I'm not sure if that was true or not. But, the government back then was just as ugly as it is now, only with fewer laws it had fewer things to be ugly about. And, us being so poor, we wouldn't get a free pass. If a doctor got behind with registering births, the bureaucrats might look the other way, but not folks like us.

"I was sick. You, being a newborn, were hard to care for, and Carl was working day and night. When he finally found time to register your birth, he lied about the date. It was our little secret that we never intended to reveal. And, what difference would it make to anyone? Now, you know what you were never meant to know." The "I hope you're satisfied," hung thick in the air.

Although that was a plausible explanation, Vin didn't buy it. The things he had learned on his trip to Sauk Centre a couple of days before were still rattling around in his head. What he did now made him feel terrible, but he had to know. He mentioned he had to use the bathroom. With the door closed, he used a tweezers to take some hairs off her hairbrush on the shelf. He put them in a small plastic bag which he then zipped shut.

As he left her that Sunday afternoon, he felt like a criminal. That didn't change the fact that for the first time in his life he could understand what drove people who had been adopted as children to seek out their birth parents. It was obvious from her body language that there was more to it than she was saying.

— 13 —

Vin didn't go directly home after his visit with his mother. He had an idea about how he could put one part of the puzzle to rest. He made a detour to visit a friend, Henni Froom, who lived in Maplewood. He wasn't sure how his first name came to be since he was Japanese, second generation. They had met some years before, through his wife's work in pro-life. He pulled up to the curb and got out. He went around to the back where he expected to find him on the deck. Henni was alone with his poodle beside him.

The dog made a woof as Vin came around the corner of the house. Henni waved. "Vincent. There you are. I was wondering if you became lost. Come on and take a seat. Can I get you anything?"

"Hi Henni. Iced tea, Coke, anything not alcoholic. They're out like flies on a dead carcass trying to get DWIs. After all, it's summer."

"Yeah. Lots of nice fat fines, and even fatter overtime. Our finest at work."

Henni was of slight build, very Asian looking, and spoke with no hint of an accent. He was a microbiologist who worked at a lab that did employment drug testing, and more recently, DNA testing.

After a sip of ice tea, Vin produced the two plastic bags. "Well, here they are. The one with the 'M' on it is my mother's, and the one with 'S' is mine. I suppose you think this is crazy." Vin's statement was more for his benefit than his friend's because he did think it was a little over the edge.

Henni smiled. "I'll tell you that after the test. If they match, then I'll say you're crazy." They both laughed.

"Why on earth would you think you were adopted? Certainly, there are times when the birth parents have totally masked their identity, but the fact of the adoption is always available."

"Let's just say that it'll make me feel better when the test shows my mother is really my mother. It's a funny feeling I have. How's business?"

"Couldn't be better. With society in such a mess, with wide spread use of drugs, nobody getting married, and all the rest, everybody wants to know stuff about somebody else. I can't say I approve of the way things are, but it's great for business."

As they visited, Vin wrote a check for the testing fee. It was a beautiful evening, warm, and enough breeze to keep the bugs away, perfect for watching the twilight approach. As Vin took his leave, Henni said, "I'll let you know in a few days."

"Thanks."

Monday evening, 6:00, June 14, Washington

The five were in their places, and though it was the President's prerogative to speak first, they were all looking at Joab Feinstein. The President nodded indicating he should start.

"I've worked Holleran's phone calls and emails. It is almost certain that her brother launched a sniffer at her email address and learned the contents of the mails from Holleran to that professor as they were setting up the weekend in upstate New York. I doubt he was the man on site because he's a rather mousy guy. He probably hired someone to do it. A PI from Minneapolis rented a Ford Explorer at Dulles Airport on Thursday, and we located the vehicle getting off the toll road in the area of the cabin on Friday. It's circumstantial, but it fits."

The President broke in, "Why was he there? Any indication it was for Holleran's protection?"

Feinstein took in a deep breath and slowly let it out. "It's hard to say. We also learned that Holleran's father is still alive and worth upwards to a half billion. As we can see, barring any cockeyed fixations on the old man's part, the two of them would split the money. He's ninety-six, so it's not likely to be long. Maybe the son was simply trying to double his money. People have committed murder for a lot less than a quarter billion."

Sal Khurz indicated he wanted to get into the discussion. "What are we going to do about this? Nobody was hurt and there's no law against walking around in a forest in the middle of a thunderstorm. Still, nobody pulls crap like that and walks away."

Feinstein nodded. "It occurs to me that the son, his name is Alvin, and his PI are from Minneapolis which is attached at the hip with St. Paul the home of the Ellefson campaign. I have a notion we can combine your dirty tricks with my messy dirty tricks and solve several problems at once. I propose a car bomb to blow up an abortion clinic using Alvin as the driver. He does a Timothy McVeigh, parks it, and walks away. Only we're accidentally watching and tip off the police. He's associated with Holleran so that brings her down. Then we leave some not so subtle evidence that implies Ellefson, some of his workers, and a local pro-life organization were involved. I'm not sure right now if we'd have the bomb explode or not. If it exploded it would be a world news event. However, if not, it would be easier to make all the connections. The perpetrators would be careless about leaving incriminating evidence under the assumption it would be destroyed in the explosion. Right now, I'm leaning toward the big bang."

The President looked skeptical. "You sure that'd work? That's a lot of connections. Somebody might get suspicious that it was a bit too convenient."

"We can refine it as we go. The biggest thing is what we feed the media. If we don't mention Alvin is related to Holleran, that connection isn't made. We had a hard time finding that link ourselves. That's a closely guarded secret. Few in the media know it.

"Remember the murder of George Tiller in May of 2009 in Wichita, Kansas? He was a famous late term abortion provider. The killer, Scott Roeder, supposedly made several calls to someone at an organization called Operation Rescue to get directions to the Lutheran church where Tiller was at the time he was shot. Operation Rescue is a national pro-life organization, by the way. It didn't matter if those calls were made or not. An open and shut case of a slaying with a suspect in custody who confessed was turned into an FBI investigation. That's all it takes."

The President looked at the others. "Any disagreement to this plan?" There were none. "When will you be ready to act?"

"It'll take a couple of days to put the details of the plan together. Following that, the field work will take the better part of a week. I'll plan to have everything in place a week from this Friday, June 25. Any conflicts with that weekend?"

"None that we can't maneuver around with that amount of lead time. That sound okay?" the President asked looking at David Adams his chief of staff.

Adams was thinking about what was scheduled. "Nothing really important. I'll let you know for sure on Wednesday."

A few other items were discussed and they adjourned. Having the meetings at this time of day tended to keep them short as everyone wanted to get on with ending their busy days.

Tuesday morning, June 15, Minneapolis, Minnesota

Starting today and for the remainder of the week, Alvin dedicated mornings to his task. First, he purchased a deer hunting bow. The modern compound bows had always fascinated him with all the pulleys and strings. There were few shoppers in the first place he went so the clerk was happy to explain how they worked. It turned out that the object of the complicated reeving and leverage was to get a bow that required substantially less force to hold it at full draw than when partially drawn. It also meant that with less force required to hold the modern bow ready to shoot, there was less likelihood of upsetting the flight of the arrow by the release. With a standard bow, the more it was pulled the more force it required. This meant that at the very time that the hunter was trying to be steady as he aimed at the target, he was forced to exert the maximum effort to give the arrow its greatest speed.

After examining several models, he knew which one he wanted. He thanked his tutor and left. The young man was none too happy about this, but Alvin knew he didn't have anything else to do with his time. He'd buy it at a different store when it was busier, so he'd receive less attention.

The next items on the list were a lightweight camouflage suit that would fit over his street clothes, and some boots. After the mission, he liked to think of it that way because it gave him a good feeling, he'd dispose of the boots so any footprints could not be traced to him. In fact, he'd saw the bow and remaining arrows into small pieces, put them in a plastic bag along with the boots and suit, and dispose of all of it in a Dumpster someplace. After visiting the sporting goods departments in four stores, he had what he needed. Along the way, he bought a target board and some practice arrows. He had a dozen hunting arrows. Though, he knew he wouldn't need that many, he wanted some for practice shooting after he became good enough to hit the target board. One of the salesmen had mentioned it was good to actually shoot real arrows before the hunt because it wasn't quite the same as practice arrows.

Wednesday, Thursday, and Friday Alvin drove out to the north of town to the Carlos Avery Wildlife Management Area where he located a place to pull off the road, walk into the woods, and set up his target to practice. It was difficult at first. He was not in good physical shape, but his muscular physique permitted him to draw the bow and hold it well enough to aim. He paced off the distance he expected his shot to be. Having mastered hitting the target from that range, he experimented with other ranges. By Friday, he had it under control. Each day his arm muscles protested a little more to the unaccustomed use. If he remembered, he'd take a couple of aspirins for the sore muscles on Saturday.

The week had not started out productively for Paul. On Monday, he called some employment agencies looking for summer work. There was nothing. Too many people were looking for temporary work with the hope it would become permanent. Most employers felt the same. Summer work, where it was certain the employee would quit at a specific time to go back to school, was not even considered. Since he had started out the summer expecting to do volunteer work, he looked at pro-life organizations. Where Camellia volunteered they primarily counseled and helped pregnant girls, so that was not something Paul could help with. Not having a car full time made it harder than otherwise would have been. But, he located an organization that was loosely federated with a national group. It was close to a bus line where it would be about as hard to get to as the campaign office. Camellia let him use her car on Tuesday so he could go in and meet with them.

They seemed to hit it off and he started that day. The work was mundane, much as it had been at the campaign. In fact, one of the things they had him work on was comparing mailing lists to weed out the duplicates. He didn't mention his experience at the campaign in the hopes he could start over. The biggest thing he missed was the energy of the campaign, and Chad Gigsby. The people here were positive and hard working, though they were also a little jaded by the years they had invested in the struggle.

One of the ministries they undertook was providing volunteers to demonstrate in front of abortion clinics. The main one they frequented was the Midwest Headquarters of Planed Parenthood on Ford Parkway in St. Paul. The building held the administrative offices for a several state area as well as the "clinic" where the abortions were performed. The courts had in some states managed to convince judges that racketeering laws applied to pro-life demonstrators. It was about as silly an association as one could make, but nobody ever said the pro-abortion people were logical or fair. The judges were pro-abortion, and that was all that mattered. In Minnesota, they could picket on the sidewalk in front of the clinic and counsel those women going in for an abortion if they could get near them. When it was learned that there were demonstrators present "pro-abortion escorts" met the women in the parking lot and guided them into the building. It was all very civilized and murderous. It was reminiscent of knights of old. There was etiquette associated with combat between selected champions for each side. All very refined and humane, don't you see, after which one or the other of the knights ended up dead.

On Thursday, one of the other volunteers who had a car drove the two of them to the clinic for Paul's first day of being a public nuisance, as most of the population viewed it. Over the years, several abortion doctors had been converted and became pro-life activists. From their testimony, it was learned that if there were only one person demonstrating with a sign, even across the street, things just didn't go as well as if the street were vacant. This was what kept them at it. It was a thankless and boring job. One of the things that had surprised Paul was the suggestion that one of them carry a digital camera. Frequently efforts were made to antagonize the protesters into doing something that might be grounds for arrest. If there were an altercation, pictures of who it was and what was happening were most helpful in court.

On Friday he was updating information in a spread sheet program. It was contributions for the past month. He asked about how they backed up their data and was told they didn't have a specific procedure in place. Paul had seen how religiously the campaign manager, or someone he designated, backed up the data files on a flash drive each evening. The little thing was carried home every night. In case of a fire, vandalism, robbery, or simply a mistake by someone who erased a file, they had a back up. The computers could be replaced. It was the data that was valuable. Paul had the car that day, so he went out and bought a couple. He showed them how easy it was and it became a standard practice.

Friday evening, June 18

Vincent was not surprised to hear a car pull up on the tarmac by his garage as he assumed it would be Henni Froom. Henni had called earlier in the day and said he'd be in the neighborhood and would drop by with the DNA results. After all, Vin owed him a beer or other refreshment.

Coming around the garage from the patio where he'd been reading, he saw his assumption had been correct.

"Hi Henni," Vin said as his friend closed the car door. "Have a seat on the patio and I'll get a couple beers."

When Vin had returned, they settled down asking about one another's jobs and families. Then, Henni said, "I learned something odd. The hair sample from your mother had been done once before by the lab. We had it on file."

"I agree, that is odd," Vin said. "Would you know who had it done?"

"We hold information like that confidential. I suppose I can say it was requested by a professional investigation outfit in town."

"Nothing more?"

"I can't say. And, what would you know if I gave the name of the company. They are even more secretive than we are."

They sipped their beers and enjoyed the evening. "I guess that means you did conduct the test on the two samples I gave you."

Henni paused, and then said. "Yes we did. The results were not what you expected. The owners of the two samples are not related. That is, your mother is not your biological mother. I'm sorry if that's something of a shock. We did the test to the same standards as we would if it were a case of capital punishment. There is no mistake."

Vin took a longer pull on his beer, set it on the patio table and rubbed the palms of his hands together. "Yes. As it settles in to my mind, that will be more than odd, more of a shock. For now, I don't know what to make of it. She has always acted strangely in the case of relatives, especially hers."

The sound of a loud motorcycle passing on the street broke the silence as both men sat in thought.

Vin brightened a little. "She always seemed paranoid about people getting her personal information, like someone was after her. She was worried about identity theft before the term was invented. Maybe, some things happened to make her worry more than normal. She even mentioned DNA testing once.

"How about this? If something was particularly worrying her, she had it in her to snatch a hairbrush from someone else's room in the assisted living complex. That poor woman would think Alzheimer's had hit her with a vengeance as she turned her apartment upside down looking for the brush. Meanwhile, my mother puts this stolen brush in the bathroom where it is clearly visible, and keeps the brush or comb she uses out of sight. She'd do it, I'm sure of that. Both this other person and I took the bait exactly as she planned. The next time I see her, I'll subtly ask about whether strange people have been in her apartment recently."

"It leaves the question open as to who the other person was, the one who hired the PI," Henni interjected.

"That could be trouble, I suppose."

"I wouldn't worry too much. Since it was a PI outfit, it could be anything. Kids run away from home, and years later begin to wonder about their parents. In other cases, it's a matter of adoption. Most of the instances would be nothing to be concerned about. I suppose it wouldn't hurt to mention it to her, though."

"Yeah. It must be something like that. Somebody got the wrong person. That's why the tests are made, because people aren't sure."

— 14 —

Saturday, June 19

Paul was up with Vin making his breakfast and ready to go flying. The previous week Vin had grabbed the transmitter from Paul when he had gotten into trouble the first few times. On what turned out to be the last flight, Vin had left him on his own. Even though he was catching on fast, he finally drilled it in under power. The rubber bands used to hold the wing on had released and the fuselage buried itself six inches into the soft dirt breaking the prop but nothing else. Vin had done this himself at the beginning of his flying, so told Paul not to worry. The engine was so packed full of dirt that they quit for the day so they could clean it up at home in the basement. Today, as Vin had hoped, Paul was ready to re-deem himself. The enthusiasm was good to see.

Driving to the rear of the building where they parked, Vin noticed the flag out front was flapping a little. There was wind, of perhaps five to eight miles per hour from the south. Not as nice as having it totally calm, but acceptable. The previous week it had been under five miles an hour and from the north. The few white puffy clouds made the sky interesting.

On Saturday morning, Alvin watched the silver Taurus back out of the Wessen driveway. He started the Mustang and followed, staying a long way back. He knew where they were going, so there was no point in be-ing spotted. He could hardly keep from humming "Quarter billion, here I come," as he drove. Over the weekend, Blanche and he had, for the first time, seriously discussed what it would be like to have all that money. Alvin had deliberately low-balled Marv when they were planning the hit on Norma. Eugene had well over four hundred million. If he did the act, there was no need to give Marv ten percent. The taxes on the amount the

IRS would be able to find reduced his take to not less than a quarter billion, and he would end up with a lot more, he hoped.

They agreed to take out fifty million to spend. With the rest invested even at five percent, it would gross them ten million a year in interest. With a little caution, they decided they could live in that. Out of the first fifty, though, they'd buy a decent house, and a jet. Alvin had priced them and very nice slightly used ones were available for a couple million. They both really wanted their own, but agreed it was prudent to share one, at least until they got the hang of having serious money. Wow, it gave him a giddy tingling feeling just thinking about it. Imagine, deciding to hold back and *share* a jet. Tut, tut. Mustn't be an irresponsible spend thrift here. He couldn't help laughing.

Alvin watched with satisfaction as the silver car a half-mile ahead took the Highway 23 exit. He slowed down to let them open the distance. He exited in his turn. As he entered the business park, there was no sign of them. Driving past the building to the west he craned his neck and caught a glimpse of the car behind the building. Today, he parked to the side of the business with no cars in the lot. He oriented his car so it was more or less aimed at the street in case he had to make a hasty departure.

Now, he began the step by step plan he had worked out. He took the key out of the ignition, opened his door, pushed the door lock button, then the release trunk lid button. He got out, pocketed the key, and closed the door. In the trunk, he had the bow and arrows wrapped in the camouflage clothing. He looked in all directions and saw no one. Lifting out the weapon, he looked once again, and closed the trunk lid as quietly as possible. Across the parking lot, he looked both ways at the street and saw no movement. The buzz of the model engine caught his attention. It was going well.

Hurrying, but not running, across the road he entered the tall grass moving behind the first clump of brush. Out of his back pocket, he pulled the thin leather gloves he had worn in practice. Then, he carefully unwrapped the bow with its rack of arrows on it. He slipped the camouflage bottoms on with the elastic waistband. Then, over his head went the top. It had a hood that he raised. He strung the bow, gave it a quick once over, and set off.

Stealth was imperative as he cautiously made his way deeper into the wild land. The dew was nearly as heavy as the previous week, which he came to expect. He hadn't thought about it before, but he hoped he wouldn't spook any deer. That would give him away. But, it would not have made sense to come out early and drive away any deer, or would have it? It didn't matter, he hadn't. He was calm and in control. It surprised him how alert he was. The motor stopped so he lowered himself into the bushes and waited until it was started and the plane launched again.

As before, he could hear them talking. That was good. They were completely unaware of his presence. The motor started a little unsteadily, then peaked at a constant speed. He could tell it was launched by the change in intensity of the sound. Time to move again. He guided on the broken off tree until he was at his primary shooting position. They were both looking up as he slowly moved to where he could see them through the leaves.

What was this? They were standing on the opposite side of the clearing from last week. He had not taken into account that with the opposite wind direction, they had to launch in the opposite direction. He cautiously moved a little further to his left. By the time he moved enough to have a clear shot, there was another bush closer to them that blocked his shot. He hadn't expected this. Should he try for one of the alternate locations? As he considered it, those positions might be no better and the less moving around he did the better. He simply had not planned to have them at the new location. Slowly, he fell to one knee. Oh, look at that. From a kneeling position, there was an opening in the brush nearest him that gave a clear shot.

He picked an arrow off the rack and nocked it. He'd do Vin first. That was his main target anyway. And, he might be more apt to keep his head after the shooting started if he went for the boy first. Okay, show time. He drew the bow, felt it pass beyond the heavy pull zone and come to the fully drawn position. His muscles complained bitterly, with what felt like electric shocks going through his shoulder. Didn't matter! He bore it, brought the sight to bear and let fly. It was something of a surprise to feel the lower limb of the bow jolt his arm. There had been a dead branch in the grass that was struck by the bow as it snapped forward. This pitched down the arm that supported the bow. A second after the twang of the bow, he heard a clatter like a garbage can being overturned. The arrow had gone low and to the left hitting the pail in which Wessen carried the support equipment.

In a practiced fashion he plucked another arrow from the rack and nocked it. What the . . . both men were gone! Well, they were just a couple of suburbanites. They wouldn't know anything about getting away. He had the weapon, and he knew they weren't running. He considered what to do. After a second of indecision, he pulled the arrow fully back, stepped around his bush, and swept the bow around the clearing. Not a sound. There, he heard someone running through the grass behind a bush. Movement in a gap between bushes caught his attention as he heard the boy yelling for help. He gauged the distance just as the boy fell in the grass, lowering his aim, he let it go. His shoulder really hurt now. Shaking it off, he nocked another arrow.

Paul was at the controls as Vin watched. He was impressed at how quickly he was catching on. He almost felt envious seeing as it had taken him many times out, and a couple dozen crashes to get this good. The arrow banging into the pail made them both jerk. Paul started to ask why Vin had kicked the pail as he kept his attention fixed on the plane. Vin knew in an instant what had happened. A flashback to a time long in the past said it all. He grabbed Paul's arm and viciously pulled him around to the backside of the willow cluster and forced him on to his stomach. The transmitter Paul had been holding was lost in the bush as they moved. In the distance, the model motor could be heard winding up and the plane spiraled down to power itself into the dirt again. Vin clamped his hand over Paul's mouth. Then put his finger to his lips indicating no sound. He proceeded to furiously unlace his boots and slip them off. He knew he couldn't run with the heavy boots, and he anticipated he'd be running for his life. The two pair of wool socks would have to do.

Vin put his mouth to Paul's ear and barely whispered. "Someone tried to kill one of us with an bow and arrow. This is what you do. When I say so, you run thirty steps that way," he pointed to their rear, "then turn to your right for five steps, and yell 'Help! Help!' just two times. Immediately fall on the ground and crawl on all fours as fast as you can for ten yards. Then get up and run for the car randomly zigzagging as you go."

Vin put the keys in his hand. "Put 'em in your pocket. At the car get in and go as fast as you can behind the building and to the street on the far end. The cell phone is in the cup holder. Once at the main road call nine-one-one. Got it?"

Paul looked dazed.

"Good. Do it, now!" he said as emphatically as possible with a whisper. Vin jabbed his elbow painfully into Paul's ribs galvanizing him into action. He was up and running.

Paul was counting steps as he ran with a fury. Thirty, more or less, not sure, lost count twice. Turn right. Yeah, this way. Five big steps. "Help! Help!" Then fall. Now what? What's next? Something swished in front of him down in the sod. The colorful shaft and feathers of an arrow lodged inches from his face. Crawl! Now he remembered. Nobody ever crawled that fast. Bravo! A gold medal in the Olympics crawling competition. Must be ten yards by now. Up and running. Jink to the left, jog to the right, now right again a few steps, than left. The foliage tore at him. At one place he ran through a blackberry bush, and almost screamed in pain as the half inch thorns raked his thighs. Not far, now. He had the keys out by the time he got to the car. Unlocked the door, slammed it, key in ignition, motor running, in reverse, seat's too far back, no time. Accelerator down, rubber squealing, let off. Wow! Missed the Dumpster. Around the end of the building and on to the street. Out of the business park, down the road, and pulled over. The cell phone. Switch on, nine-one-one.

Vincent hadn't been in a situation like this for longer than he cared to remember, and had hoped he would never have to bring it to mind again. Whether he liked it or not, the battle to stay alive was joined. As Paul started to run, Vin used the noise to mask his movement to his right getting nearly to his destination. Now if Paul followed instructions, he'd be yelling for help to his left rear any second. Vincent slid on his belly the last few feet. It was possible to move very quietly if there were time, so he had to split the difference and make a little noise in exchange for faster progress. He remembered where the bucket had ended, on its side with the open top against the tall grass pointing roughly toward his present position.

Paul's cry for help came a little sooner than he would have liked, but he compensated. He heard the arrow released, permitting him to judge the location of the shooter. At the bucket he inched closer and retrieved a plastic bag with a roll of heavy nylon cord, and what amounted to a small grappling hook. In the area where they were flying, there were a couple clumps of six-inch diameter poplar trees. Model airplanes, like kites, being what they are, gravitate to trees. He used the hook to snag the branch holding the plane and break it off. These popular trees had small brittle branches. It had worked twice in the past, so the method had merit.

What he'd do now was place the hook on a bush and slide away to the side of it. It was risky but no option was without danger. The shooter had gone in pursuit of Paul for twenty yards and then given up. As he returned to the clearing Vin was ready. He gauged the distance of the man by the sound. This was on a level of perception few people would understand. With each step the man was crushing the two foot stalks of grass. This made a characteristic sound. A much quieter sound was made as the leaves of the grass brushed against one another. The effective difference between the louder and quieter sound determined the distance of the man making them. This was easier to hear at night when the sense of sight was inoperative. Closing his eyes, he let his whole being hear the sound. The training of those decades before was still there. He estimated the hunter at twenty feet away, far enough to make it work.

He gently pulled on the nylon rope. The hook broke the first stick to which it was attached with a snap. This got the man's attention. The hook now engaged the bush and Vincent shook it. Thawing! The arrow sliced into the bush. At that instant Vincent stood up and shouted, "Here!"

His assailant still had the hood of his camouflage suit up. That had been decisive in reducing his hearing enough for Vincent's movements to go unnoticed. The sharp word and the appearance of the man so close startled him so that he dropped the arrow he was about to nock. This was the plan. It was also the plan to get a good look at him.

After the single word, Vincent was off running with all his might. First, he dashed behind the willow clump where Paul and he had first taken refuge. From there, he ran straight away. He knew that each step of distance he could put between himself and the bow would drastically reduce its accuracy. He jumped over low clumps of brush, and zigged and zagged to one side or another. Behind one larger clump he deliberately fell and crawled to the side. Rising some yards away in the grass, he looked back. It was important to get up and be seen so the man would know he had not been hit. The man had followed a short distance, and obviously concluded he could not overtake a man who was literally running for his life.

Vincent directed his general direction to where he knew there was a culvert that made a ford of the ditch toward which he was running. Over the ditch he angled to his left so if the man were to follow he'd encounter the ditch, something not easily crossed.

The last Vincent saw of the man, he was running in the direction of the street as fast as Vin had been running away. Stopping he bent down and put his hands on his thighs as he struggled to catch his breath. If he had been certain the man had not had a gun, he could have taken him when he dropped the arrow. Since there were no shots as Vincent ran, it was likely he did not have one. Better to be alive than take the chance, though.

Vincent glanced at his watch. It was less than three minutes before he heard an engine winding up. In the gaps between bushes and buildings, he saw a red car flash past. It made a right on the main road a quarter mile away, and sped off to the west. Vincent started walking back. His left knee hurt from a twist it received during a zag causing him to limp. His feet were a little sore, but not as bad as he had expected.

Alvin was bounding through the grass and weeds toward his car. The boy had made his escape. He had heard the car tires squeal as he drove away. How long for the police to get here? No point in wondering. He had to leave the area as fast as possible. At the street, he didn't even bother to look both ways. He had his keys out and pressed the fob to unlock the doors and open the trunk. He threw in the bow, and slammed the lid. The engine came to life and he shifted gears leaving rubber on the road with each one. At the main road, he headed west. It was the route he had checked the week before. In a few miles, he encountered a stoplight at Lexington Avenue. The light was green, for through traffic, but he wanted to make a left, so he took a chance and did it on a red arrow. Two miles south and he was at another traffic light that was green. Now up the overpass and right onto 35W. On the interstate, he moved to the left lane and drove with traffic at seventy-five. It was likely he would get away clean. But, the job wasn't done.

Alvin drove in consternation. He figured that the bottom part of the bow had hit something hidden in the grass. That was the only explanation. It was nothing but bad luck that the arrow hit the pail. If it had been a clean miss, they might not even have noticed it, and he would have compensated on the second shot. The plan was good, he knew that. The location perfect. Maybe, gunshots would not have been heard. It was an awfully deserted place. Too late now. No point in second guessing himself.

Wessen was good, though. He had them both out of sight in a second. He used the kid to divert his attention while he rigged the decoy. The way he managed to snap the twig and shake the bush twenty feet from his actual location was not the work of an amateur. Wesson's sudden appearance and sharp yell startled him so bad he dropped the arrow, just as he knew it would. Well, next time, it would be on his turf. Then it was good bye, sucker.

— 15 —

The piece of real estate called Lino Lakes had only one police car on duty, as was the norm for Saturday morning. When Paul called nine-one-one, he did not know where he was. After some questions, he remembered they had taken the Highway 23 exit from 35W. From there, he described where he was. The on duty cop happened to be south of 35W about as far away a possible and still be in the town. It was seven minutes after Paul made the call that the patrol car drove into the business park.

Vincent, still without boots, was approaching the street and flagged him down. A well built man of about thirty with his blond hair cut short got out and asked, "You the guy that called in the attempted murder?"

Vincent responded, "No, he did," pointing to Paul who was pulling to a stop behind the patrol car. "But, we're together."

The officer gave his name as Jim Douglas, and after a short interchange he was satisfied the danger was gone, and called it in.

"You want to see where it happened?" Vincent asked.

"Darn right. What are you doing in stocking feet?"

"I wear hiking boots out here because they keep my feet dry with the wet grass. I knew I couldn't do much running in them, and I knew I'd be running for my life if I were lucky enough to live long enough to run."

As they walked to the clearing where they had been flying, Vin explained about the model airplane and why they like to fly in this place away from everything, and that he had permission from the business owner to park there. He also took the opportunity to pick up his boots and put them on.

The obvious thing was the arrow sticking in the bucket. Vin had a steel box containing a special regulated power supply he had designed and built that was used to start the glow engine. The arrow had pierced the plastic pail and made it most of the way through the steel enclosure.

"That's impressive," the officer said. "What makes you think he was deliberately shooting at you?"

"Because he tried two more times, that's how," Vincent retorted. "Beyond that, the arrow is nearly horizontal in the pail so it was shot at close range."

"Hmm. Yeah, but he missed by a lot. I hunt deer with a bow and this looks like he was only trying to scare you."

Vincent walked over to where he thought the shooter had been. Douglas followed. Vincent stood behind the brush just as Alvin had. Then, he bent down and saw the opening.

"See here. He couldn't get a shot at us standing up, so he knelt down." Vincent stooped and felt the ground. "If you carefully feel the ground you will notice the smooth indentations from his knees in the soft ground."

The officer did so and nodded. Vincent parted the dark green stalks of grass in front of the position and cleared the two-inch dead branch. It had clearly been scraped recently.

"He had to kneel down to get a clear shot. Then the lower limb of his bow hit that stick as it sprang forward, causing the shot to go low."

"That's pretty good." The officer said. "That could explain it. What about the other shots?"

They returned to where Paul was standing. "He shot once at Paul as he was running for the car. I don't suppose we'll be able to find that one."

Up to this point Paul hadn't said anything and was largely forgotten. Left with his own thoughts he dwelt on how closely he had escaped death. As the other two men turned their attention to him he was trembling all over, and appeared to be going into shock.

"I can find it," Paul blurted out.

Vin, seeing his state, went to him and said, "Slow down, Paul. Here, sit down a minute before you pass out." Vin used a piece of carpet to kneel on while he was starting the motor for the model plane. "Sit on the carpet piece, and stop breathing so fast. You're okay, but you have to slow down. Take slow deep breaths for a few minutes. Put your head on your knees and relax as completely as you can."

The great thing about being young is a person recovers fast. In less than five minutes his color was better as he slowly got to his knees and then stood up. "I's a shocker to think how close that was. I fell in the grass and didn't immediately start to crawl like Uncle Vin said. It missed my nose by an inch."

Paul walked slowly, to where he had been in the grass. It took a few minutes to orient himself but he soon found it. He was about to pick it up when Vincent said, "Don't. Leave it there."

Douglas said. "Why not pick it up? We want to see if it matches the one in the pail."

"Leave it a minute."

Vincent went to it, carefully uncovered it, and using his outstretched arm aligned it over the arrow. "Okay."

"What are you doing?" Douglas demanded.

"Checking the direction of flight. It came from nearly the center of the clearing where we were. It indicates there was only one shooter."

"Yeah, of course."

Back at the clearing, Vincent explained the decoy he had set up. In a few minutes, they recovered the third arrow in the bush that was shaken by Vincent's rope.

Douglas screwed around his mouth for a minute as if thinking and said, "Yes. I would say that guy was intent on killing you. From what you said, when you stood up you looked right at him. Did you recognize him?"

"No. Not even close, though I'd recognize him if I saw him again."

After a pause, Douglas said, "How about you telling me exactly what happened from the time the first arrow hit the pail so I get the chain of events straight."

Vincent nodded. "Paul was flying the plane, and I was watching. He was catching on fast. When the arrow hit the pail, it made a pronounced crunch as the arrow went into the steel battery box. Paul started to make a sarcastic remark that would have been something like I 'kicked the bucket,' isn't that right?" he said looking at Paul.

Paul nodded.

"I glanced down, saw the arrow, and assumed the worst. It hit with such force that it screamed lethality. I grabbed Paul's arm and, against his protest, pushed and shoved him behind this clump of willow brush forcing him down on the ground. I whispered to him what had happened. It must have been my action and the sound of my voice, because he didn't disagree.

"I told him to run thirty steps to the rear of us and then turn and run five steps yelling for help after which he was to fall in the grass and start to crawl as fast as he could."

"Wait. What made you come up with that sequence of actions for Paul?"

"First, I'm familiar with bows and arrows. When I was a kid, my dad gave me a bow and arrows for Christmas. We lived on a farm then so there was plenty of game to shoot at. The bow only had a thirty pound draw so was not strong enough for deer hunting, and it wasn't given to me for that. During my growing up years, I spent a lot of hours making arrows, shooting arrows, and looking for lost arrows. In my whole life, I only shot one squirrel and one rabbit with it. But, I learned that as distance increased the accuracy of a bow falls off dramatically. I read once that the vast majority of deer taken by bow are shot at ten yards or less. At that range it's hardly sport anymore.

"Anyway, I figured Paul could get thirty steps before the shooter had nocked another arrow and moved to a place where he could see him. This would put Paul out of the immediate kill range of the bow. Then, with Paul running at approximately right angles to the line of sight it would be a full deflection shot adding more uncertainty for the guy with the bow. I had him yell for help so the shooter would be sure to see him. Then with him crawling through the grass a hit would be most unlikely. You see, I needed a distraction."

"Hey." Paul said interrupting the narrative. "You used me as bait."

"Not bait, a distraction," Vin corrected. "As soon as Paul started running, I used the sound of his movements to mask my own as I crawled to where the bucket had fallen. When Paul yelled, the man saw him and gave his full attention to that direction. With Paul in the grass, the shooter let go another arrow and then had to wonder if he had hit his mark, so he took several steps toward him. As he did that, I took the rope I had removed from the pail, hooked it to the bush, and slid back to the position I had selected.

"When Paul got up after his crawl he was partially masked by that high wall of willows," Vincent said pointing, "so the man could not get off another decent shot, and Paul was opening the distance fast enough so as to make it futile, anyway. When the man returned to look for me, I first pulled the rope taught until it broke the dry stick I had put the hook on. As I said before, the snap got his attention, and then I shook the bush and he shot. Immediately, I stood up and shouted at him. It startled him to the point that he dropped his next arrow. Then I rushed behind the clump of willows and took off running with the goal to put as much distance between me and the bow as possible. He may have shot more times, but I didn't see any arrows.

"Paul in his haste to get away squealed the tires which was perfect, because it told the shooter one of us had for sure gotten away and would be summoning the police. Soon thereafter, you arrived."

Douglas was standing with his jaw almost hanging open in wonderment. "That is the most amazing tale of quick thinking I've ever heard. But, why didn't you start running when Paul did? It would seem that with two of you running in different directions it would have improved the odds."

"First of all, I wanted to get a good look at him, which I did when I stood up. I knew I wasn't aware of anyone who would want to kill me so that would likely be my only chance to try to figure it out. And, at first, I had it in mind to take him. When he dropped the arrow I might have, except that he was further away than I had expected, and if he had been carrying a gun, I wouldn't have made it. So, figuring the better part of valor was staying alive, I ran for my life."

"Impressive. Very impressive. You have specialized military training or something like that?"

Vincent chuckled. "Yes, of course. My number came up and is was drafted. I spent a tour in Viet Nam in the Quartermaster Corps. I can handle a pencil with the greatest facility. I can even twirl it in my fingers like a baton."

"Funny," Douglas said flatly. "That's not what I meant, and you know it."

"I know you didn't, but that's all I have to offer. I did a good job of moving all kinds of stuff from gas cans, to tents, to paper clips. No army can survive without the mass of stuff needed to keep it going."

"Okay. From your comments, I gather you don't have any ideas as to who it was, but I must ask you the direct question: do you know anybody who would want to kill you? Even someone who'd hire another to do it. Think hard."

Vincent shook his head. "I'll have to give it some thought. There's nobody that I have a feud with, or have sued, or similar things. There are no previous marriages of either my wife or myself. Our children are all grown and have careers of their own. The neighbors are fine. No fuss about them having loud parties late at night, barking dogs or anything like that. There's nothing at work where I'm trying to beat someone else out of a promotion or things of that sort. I'm drawing a total blank."

Douglas appeared to accept this. "But, it's unlikely this is a case of someone trying to kill at random. It rarely is. And, there seems to have been planning."

"Yeah," Paul said. "Remember last week we heard a stick snap in the brush over there someplace." He pointed in the direction of where the guy must have used for his approach. "You said it was a deer. But, today when we came in we startled some deer and they ran off through the grass and bushes like a heard of elephants snorting as they went. Last week we only heard that one, clear, snap. He was there, figuring out how to do it."

"You're saying he was stalking you," Douglas interjected.

Paul enthusiastically nodded his head. "Yeah. That's it."

Douglas rubbed his chin. Looking at Paul, he said, "And, what about you? Does anyone want to kill you?"

Vincent casually looked Paul's way trying not to reveal anything to the officer. Paul was looking a little glassy eyed. It was a stretch to think that whoever had caused him to be fired from the campaign would have done this.

Paul shrugged, and Vincent tried to catch his eye and shook his head slightly in the negative, but Paul didn't notice.

"I was volunteering for the summer on a political campaign. An FBI agent came in and told the campaign manager I had written threatening letters to members of congress. I was dismissed from the campaign an hour later. I didn't send threatening letters. That was made up. Why would somebody do that? Now, look at this. We could both be dead. What kind of ugly people are they?"

"You really think the two are connected?" Douglas asked incredulously.

"Why not? I've spent my entire life in a small town, not hurting a fly. I come to the city for the summer, try to do some volunteer work, and my life falls apart. I'm furious."

Vincent broke in. "I can hardly see there'd be a connection, either."

"Well," Douglas said, "you've done a pretty good job of convincing me someone tried to kill either or both of you. You don't have a clue, and the FBI is the big time. That seems like the logical place to start."

They gave Jim Douglas Fred Clements' name at the FBI, and he took the pail and arrows as evidence with the understanding the pail would be returned shortly. Vincent considered it unlikely he'd ever see it again in his lifetime. Douglas left. Vin and Paul found the radio transmitter in the bushes near where they had first fallen to the ground. It took a half-hour of searching the grass before they found the plane. It was painted bright red and yellow precisely to help in such an endeavor.

As they drove away from the Wild Ridge Business Park, Vincent said, "This is not meant to say you did anything wrong, but it might have been better if you hadn't mentioned the thing at the campaign office to that policeman."

"Why not? It's the only possible connection either of us can think of."

"That might be, but consider this. After we think about it, we might come up with some other explanation, and the campaign thing will only serve to muddy things. On the other hand, if we later came to the conclusion there might be a connection, we could have always called him and said that after thinking about it we came up with a possible connection. As it is, that option is no longer available to us."

Paul was silent, then said, "Yeah. I see what you mean."

"It always seems to me it's best to tell less rather than more when dealing with authorities of any kind. This is not really the same, but once I worked with someone who had been deposed as part of a lawsuit. He said that he learned real fast not to say one word more than necessary because the lawyers would tear apart anything he said in minute detail. It's the way things are these days. I don't see it'll be a problem, though. We'd probably have told him about the campaign at some point, anyway."

After they had driven for a while, Vin said, "Now that I think of it, I did the same thing you did, darn it."

"What do you mean?"

"I gave him too much detail. Remember he asked if I had specialized military training? While it was happening, I did the first thing that came to my mind."

"Now that you mention it, you did something I'd never have been able to do."

Vin laughed. "I grew up on a farm. When I was in high school, a friend and I went duck hunting together on weekends in the fall. We didn't have a duck boat, decoys, and all that stuff. So, we made sort of a standard tour of various potholes and sloughs in an area we came to know. Some days we'd walk twenty miles. We'd see the ducks from a far off, and would have to crawl through grass, mud and what have you to get close enough for a shot. We'd get a few now and then. But, we crawled a lot. It was best when where was wind so they couldn't hear us moving up. That's where I got the idea to have you run to disguise my sounds."

"Must have been a lot more fun when you were a kid, huh?"

"Not so much. We didn't have computer games and a lot of stuff that you have. It was just something we did to amuse ourselves. I, especially, hated to be bored."

When they returned home, Camilla was in the kitchen. Vin and Paul took the plane to the basement and came back upstairs. Setting around the kitchen table, they related what had happened.

"I thought you had been gone longer than normal. That's serious. Who could have done it?"

"My best guess is it was someone who owned the land, or was leasing it, something like that. It doesn't make a lot of sense, I know. Why not just tell us to get out of there and not come back."

"I thought you told the policeman you had permission to be there," Paul interjected.

"No. I have permission to park behind the building on weekends. That's what I told the cop. I don't know how much land goes with that business. I doubt that he owns all those acres of scrub land."

"You're right," Camilla said. "Even if the guy was furious about you being on his land, why didn't he call the cops and have them remove the trespassers."

Vin nodded. "The land is not posted for no trespassing, so even if the police did tell us to leave, they would have told the owner to make his intentions known by putting up signs. Without them who would know? It was innocent enough. It's not as if we were digging up black dirt and hauling it away or anything like that."

"That means," Paul said, "that trespassing and property ownership is probably not the reason. What else is there?"

"I wish I knew."

"It might bring us back to the connection with the campaign, and Paul's letters," Camilla said.

Vin shook his head. "I don't see how. In any case, Paul, do you know anybody on the campaign that you could call and see what the talk around the office has been? Norma Holleran was originally from Minneapolis, wasn't she? Does she have any relatives living here? Any information might help."

"Chad Gigsby would be the one to call. We were sort of friends. However, he's also the biggest gossip there. If I call him, the whole world will know it."

"I think you should do it. Don't say anything about what happened today. Ask what's new, and slip in that we'd like to know anything he can find about Holleran. That would make sense, because he knows the letters were why you were fired. We won't be flying model airplanes for a while, but still, we have to find out what happened."

"How about the police?" Camilla asked.

"They don't have anything to go on. Unless the perpetrator slips up and brags to the wrong person about it, I don't see what they can do."

Sunday evening, June 20

Vin arrived for his regular visit to his mother. He wasn't in the mood after what had happened the morning before. Certainly, he wasn't about to tell her about that.

"Hi Ma. How's been your week?"

"Mine's been fine, but you look a little frazzled. Something with the job?"

That was a blessing. The job was a good excuse for being out of sorts. With little to talk about, they often discussed the people at his place of employment.

"Yeah. That Lenny Olson's been at it again. His big mouth will get me dumped out of there yet. No matter what happens, my fault, his fault, or random things out of anyone's control, he gossips it around that it was my fault. I swear, if we had an earthquake, he'd have the word around that I caused it."

"Try to let it go. He'll get his just reward, though I wish it wouldn't be so hard on you."

"How have you been doing? Any new people in the building, any visitors, anything to liven up your life?'

He hoped that was general enough not to leave the impression that he was interested in visitors.

"Mrs. Hormoz died this week. It was somewhat sudden, though she had a bad heart. Not surprised she didn't wake up one morning, Tuesday I think it was. There was that woman around a few days ago. Guess it wasn't this week. She was selling cemetery plots. It was odd that she got in here. They always keep those people away unless we say they have an appointment. Then, we go to the party room to meet them. She was nice enough, not pushy. It turned out she had me confused with another woman in the adjoining building. Her children went to the same school as your boys did so we chatted a little.

"You're not worried about me, are you?"

"Oh, no. You seem to be capable of fending off the evils of our decomposing society."

She smiled. "Yes, I like to think I can. I've taken a few precautions. People can be so devious, you know. I like to think I can stay one step ahead of them."

Vin nodded. And, he thought, one step ahead of me, too.

— 16 —

Monday Morning, June 21

Jim Douglas picked up the phone as he set down his coffee mug. He had come in from patrol for a break. His desk was in the police section of the relatively new Lino Lakes city office building. He should have been off work today, but was filling in for one of the other officers who was attending to personal matters.

He leaned back and said, "Officer Douglas speaking."

"This is special agent Fred Clements at the FBI. I read the report you emailed me about the attempted murders on Saturday." There was a pause as Douglas head a long breath being let out. It was a classic bureaucratic technique of relaying displeasure. Finally the voice continued, "How can you be sure it wasn't some kid playing games, or that those two guys aren't pulling your chain?"

Douglas was rankled by the condescending manner of Clements. "First of all, that Wessen guy said the 'kid,' as you call him, the shooter, was over fifty years old, and that he was wearing a complete camouflage suit. That's in the report. I'll stand by my conclusion. Someone tried to kill either or both of them. And, it was only by the freak chance that the bow hit that concealed branch that at least one of them isn't dead. If you want to drive out, I'll show you the scene. My boss, the police chief, was skeptical, too. We drove out and I showed it to him. While he's withholding his final verdict, he's ninety-eight percent in agreement with me, now."

"But, that connection to the campaign is a stretch."

"Let me ask, why was Sanders let go from the campaign? They said something about letters."

"I was making a routine, and I mean routine, investigation because those politicians in Washington are such prima donnas. We have to do it when they make a complaint. I followed procedure. After a few calls I found where this Sanders was and went there to make routine inquiries. If the campaign manager decided to can him, there's nothing I could do about it. What do I care about the dumb kid? He shouldn't have written the letters."

"I don't know much about what you guys do, so don't think I'm trying to second guess you, but maybe there's more to it than that. Every time we in the public get a glimpse behind the scenes at Washington politics, it seems like such a vicious business. Whose campaign was he working on?"

"Walt Ellefson's."

"Oh boy. I think you stepped into something there."

"What does that mean?"

"I follow this kind of politics a little, because my wife follows it a lot so I know about that race. That House of Representatives seat has been held by a Democrat for decades. Now, Ellefson looks like he'll take it for the Republicans. This could have campaign sabotage written all over it."

"To the point of killing people?"

"That's why you're in the big city, and I'm in the boonies. I called it the way I saw it as far as it being an attempted homicide. I sent you the report because that's all either intended victim could come up with as a motive. Use it with discretion."

"In the report attached to your email, you suggest that Vincent Wessen had specialized military training. Talk to me about that."

"The biggest reason I said that was because instead of taking off running as fast as he could, he stuck around. That could easily have gotten him killed after he was home free due to the flub-up of the shooter. The kid got away, he could've, too."

"But, the reason he gave as you related in the report makes sense. If the shooter missed once, he'd be back to try again. It was in Wessen's interest to try to identify him so the perp could be apprehended."

"A member of the species *homo-suburbius* wouldn't do that. Someone had, a second before, tried to kill him. He'd have run like crazy. Anyway, he'll call for a copy of my report which I'll give him, sans my comments of course."

"Yeah. I agree with that."

"Please, keep me informed if you learn anything, will you? We'd like to close this case. It's not nice to have things like that going on in a quiet pastoral setting."

"You be sure to do the same."

Jim Douglas made a note after the call. His report had been received and read by the FBI. That's all he needed to know.

———————————

Fred Clements leaned back in his chair and ran his hands through his hair. It felt good to stretch his muscles. He'd worked out hard over the weekend, even ran into his old martial arts coach and they went a few rounds. He wasn't into that as much as he had been a few years ago, but his reflexes were still sharp. His mentor said as much. It made him feel good that he wasn't going to pot the way so many of his colleagues were.

Back to the situation. He pondered whether or not to forward the report to Jessie Lopez in D.C. That was the man who had sent the first request to him about the letters. Without investigating the scene in person, he had to take the word of those cops about the attempted murder. The police academies were doing a lot better at teaching investigative procedure in recent years. The victims were not from the same jurisdiction, so it was unlikely there was any local politics involved. All of this made him decide to accept the fact of the crime.

How about the connection to the campaign? He didn't like it, mainly because these things tended to get a life of their own, and it could come back and bite him. Yet, those pieces of ornery low life in Washington would stoop to something like this, of that he had no doubt, especially in a close race. He could mention it to his supervisor and let him decide. However, it didn't seem to warrant that. Finally, he decided to send an email to Lopez asking him to check with the big shots telling him to find out what hidden agenda might have prompted the first request about the letter. He'd mention that it had caused an eighteen year old volunteer to be fired from the campaign. Especially, he would ask him to delicately discern if they saw that particular political race in Minnesota as pivotal in some way. He'd attach the cop's report and comments simply as an explanation as to why he was making this request of him. In addition, he would emphasize that under no circumstances was it to be shown to the Senator or Speaker of the House.

Later that same Monday morning, Washington, D.C.

Jessie Lopez had been with the FBI for six years, the last two in the Washington office. It wasn't bad duty except for the unreasonably high cost of living, and he had a family. When he read the email and attachments from Clements, his first move was to print it and check with his supervisor. After all, this involved important people. His supervisor, in turn shot it up the chain another level. What Clements in Minneapolis had not thought of was this inquiry, in effect, accused two of the most powerful people in the country of two cases of attempted first degree murder. At the very least, it put them as accessories before the fact. That wasn't something one did lightly.

By noon, everything that could be raked together about the case was in a file that rested on the desk of the Director of the FBI, the top of that particular food chain. Only the Director of Central Intelligence trumped him. Along the way speculations about the possibility of tampering with a rival campaign was debated from several points of view.

Later in the day, gravity had exerted its influence and the case had tumbled back down that very same food chain. Jessie sat in front of the desk of his supervisor, Dick Doren. Doren was speaking with the appointment secretary of Norma Holleran. A meeting was set for an hour from then. After that call, an appointment was made with Senator Rutlen in his office at exactly the same time. This was intended to keep the two parties from comparing notes between meetings. Doren and Lopez would take Holleran, and two other agents would do Rutlen.

"Okay. All set," Doren said. "Let's see what shakes lose. I doubt this will go anywhere, but who knows."

This same morning, Paul was nearing the pro-life office where he had been working. He flipped an envelope into a mailbox as he walked past. It was another letter to Representative Holleran. He wanted her to know that he had been fired from the campaign for her ridiculous over reaction to his first letter. He was still steamed about it. Then, whatever was the meaning of the thing on Saturday, he intended to get her to back off. He involuntarily shrugged. That was, if she even saw either letter. Those people were so far above the world of normal people it was impossible to see how they could ever enact a just law, even if they wanted to, not that they ever had any such intention.

Monday Afternoon

The session had ended early this day so Holleran was in her office when the call from Agent Doren had come, and she had approved the time for the meeting. She suspected it would be a perfunctory report that they had checked out the letter. It should have been done with a less formal means of communication, but this was, after all, Washington. Everybody wanted to get face time with the powerful.

That the FBI agent, actually two to Norma's surprise, had arrived fifteen minutes early did not come as a surprise. She made them wait twenty minutes as a matter of precedent. Nobody got in early.

Norma looked at the business cards of the two men as they were ushered in. "Special Agents Doren and Lopez. We spoke some days ago, didn't we Agent Lopez?"

Jessie nodded.

"How can I be of service to you?"

Doren began. "We are here to follow up on the request you made of Special Agent Lopez to check on a letter you had received that you viewed as threatening. Since the letter came from Minnesota, we handed off the request to our Minneapolis office. Our agent there, by the name of Clements, found Paul Sanders, the sender of the letter, working as a volunteer for the summer on Walt Ellefson's campaign for the House of Representatives. Clements went to the campaign office of Walt Ellefson. In case you don't know, that's a hot race in Minnesota this year. That seat has been held by a Democrat for years, and Ellefson is the odds on favorite to win. Upon arriving at the campaign headquarters, Clements first talked to the campaign manager. Clements was somewhat surprised when the campaign manager said Sanders would be summarily dismissed from his job. The reason given was that they could not take the chance of even the slightest impropriety smearing the campaign. Our agent didn't consider it appropriate under the circumstances to talk to Sanders, so did not.

"A cursory check of Paul Sanders, who is eighteen years old, showed that he had graduated from an accredited high school as a home schooler. His SAT and ACT scores were in the ninety-eight percentile so the home schooling worked. He lives in a small out-state town were he was active in his church. He is registered to start at the University of Minnesota in the fall. He has no police record of any kind. Everyone we called who knew him said he was a quiet, studious young man everybody liked. The family is well known in the community."

Holleran was beginning to get a sick feeling in her stomach as she replied, "I'm very sorry about the young man getting discharged. But, you can hardly blame me for that. I didn't write the letter, he did. What else did you learn? I doubt there are two FBI agents sitting in my office to tell me a volunteer was found to be unsuitable."

"In that, you are correct Ms. Holleran. We are not here about that. After the quick background check of Sanders and the meeting at the campaign office, Clements dropped the matter. In hindsight, now that a couple of hundred people have read the letter, it doesn't seem very threatening. You surely must get letters more pointed than that all the time."

"What! Why would hundreds of people have read that letter? Don't you people have any sense or propriety or even any control of your cases! Can anybody read the hot gossip? What is going on?"

"We are here to try to find out what is going on Ms. Holleran. Paul Sanders was dismissed on a Friday. Eight days later, on Saturday, some-one tried to kill him along with his uncle. It was thoroughly investigated, and there is no question, it was attempted murder one."

Holleran's complexion had gone several shades lighter. When that happened, her makeup no longer made the smooth transition to the color to her natural skin causing her to have a painted look. She was unaware of this, though, as she tried desperately to connect what she had just heard with the attempt on her life. "Continue," she said. "I assume you have more."

"I will briefly describe the crime. The two men were in a secluded place with waist high grass and assorted brush and bushes. They were flying a radio controlled model airplane. They liked that place because it was away from other people and there was no danger of crashing the plane into someone or something. They had permission to be there. The attempt was made with a high powered bow and arrow of the kind used by deer hunters. Three arrows were recovered. They had three-bladed, razor sharp steel, arrowheads. In case you're wondering, no, this is not deer hunting season. Through an unanticipated mistake on the part of the shooter, the first arrow missed. Then, the quick thinking on the part of the older man and some fast running on the part of both, resulted in nei-ther of them being hit. They are fairly certain the perpetrator was there the weekend before, the day after Sanders was dismissed, setting up the hit.

"When asked, who might have had a reason to kill them, the older man said he had not the slightest idea. We checked him out. Not a park-ing ticket, house paid off, etc. Sanders, on the other hand, could think of someone in an instant—you and, or, Senator Rutlen. The kid is really mad. Not only was he unfairly, in his mind, fired from his job, he was nearly killed. When he was lying in the grass, an arrow missed his nose by an inch. He could start shouting that you attempted first degree murder on him. It's time to come clean about the letter. It's simply not that threatening. For your information, we have two other agents interviewing Senator Rutlen at this time. Also, for your information, this case as gone all the way up to the Director of the FBI and back down. That's why so many people have read the letter. Now, please, tell us about the letter?"

Holleran didn't break eye contact with Doren. It had to be politics, all of it, and she needed time to figure it out. Keeping an even voice she said, "This is Washington. The main product of this town is politics, someone trying to get the upper hand on someone else. It seems a little peculiar that a routine matter like this should go so far."

To this Doren replied, "I can't speak to why any of it happened. You came to us, we followed up, and that led to where we are now."

"How about this? I'll have to do a little checking. There might be more to the letter than even I suspected. Can you hold off any further action until tomorrow morning?"

Lopez was watching Doren as closely as Holleran was. This was clearly a country mile out of his league. There was no doubt she was a politician, a good one.

Doren answered, "Okay. We'll be back tomorrow morning at seven o'clock. Is that acceptable to you?"

She nodded. "Please, show yourselves out."

The two FBI agents where hardly out of her office when Norma Holleran was punching the number of Wally Stern's cell phone into her phone. To her immense relief, the phone was answered. "Wally, this is Norma. Please, don't hang up. I need to talk to you, and you are the only one I know who might have the answers. Please. It has to be tonight. Can you do it, please."

"Wow! Things must be bad. I haven't heard 'please' used so many times since, well, I don't think I ever have. I'm on my way home. I think it might be safe to have you come out to my house. My permit to buy a gun arrived late last week and I bought a nine-millimeter Ruger last Saturday. I haven't had a chance to shoot it yet, but I'll load it as soon as I arrive home. Maybe, I can get in some early practice shooting at the assassins waiting around outside. Come for supper. I'll shoot while you cook. How's that sound?"

"Wally. Please. Not now. I may be in serious trouble. If this doesn't let up, my head will split open. I've never known such pressure." In a small voice that was just audible she continued. "Thanks for the invitation. Is it possible you could have a little something ready to eat? I'll be there about seven."

"Okay. Seven it is."

— 17 —

A taxi dropped Norma off at the secluded residence of Wallace Stern only a few minutes after seven. He opened the door before she pressed the door bell button. "Come in. I'll have something on in a few minutes." As she came into the light, he said. You don't look so good." Then, with genuine concern he asked, "What happened?"

"It's the same business that occupied us the last time we were together. How this could be happening is beyond me. It's like someone else has taken control of the world, and nobody is in charge of anything, least of all me."

"Do you want a glass of wine?"

"Yes. It's nice of you to ask."

"Okay. The door is locked, and the gun is loaded," he said holding it up, "so tell me about it."

"You weren't kidding. You really bought a gun. I'm so bad off, that actually makes me feel good."

Wally was busy in the kitchen and she sat at a dinette chair fingering the stem on her wineglass. "After I got back from the cabin I had my staff look for letters like you said. There was only one that was even close. I thought about what I should do and I began to wonder if anyone else was having the same problem I was. Well, the next most visible pro-abortion Catholic in Washington is Senator Rutlen. I went to see him and showed him the letter. Just like that, he said he had received one, too. His had been odd enough that it didn't fit into any category of letters to answer so it sort of stood out. However, he had not had any of the mind control things that I had. He agreed with me that we should have the FBI look into this crazy guy."

Wally dished up a fried pork chop for each of them along with some buns and a small salad.

"This looks good. I'm sorry to put you out this way."

"It's okay. But, I'm sure you aren't to the high point of the story yet, are you? Save it and eat. You can continue later."

Twenty minutes later, Norma continued as Wally put together a desert. "The man who wrote the letters turned out to be an eighteen year old boy. Super clean. However, he had signed up to volunteer on a political campaign for the summer. It happens to be a hotly contested one where a Republican is likely to replace a long term Democrat. The FBI agent went to campaign headquarters and the first man he talked to was the campaign manager. The agent hardly had his ID out when the kid was told to get lost."

"So, it smacks of tampering with a federal campaign, is that it?'

"What are you putting together there?"

Wally smiled. "It's my version or strawberry shortcake. If you order that in a restaurant, they use sponge cake, and that's not right. I use cornbread. It's hard to even find a recipe for shortcake any more. Besides, I like cornbread so have what's left over for breakfast the next morning. They had fresh strawberries at the store yesterday, and they're just ripe enough today. Chop them up, not too much, put a little sugar on them, add some whipped cream out of the can, and there you are. It's quite good. Here you are," he said placing the dish in front of her. "Have at it."

As they ate, he asked if she had brought the letter with her. She produced a copy from her purse.

"You're right. This is very good shortcake."

He nodded in acknowledgement of her compliment, and laid out the letter on the table reading it several times as he ate.

Dear Representative Holleran:

Your intractable pro-abortion stand is wrong. You know that. You have the blood of millions of innocents on your hands. You must change because you have little time left, and hell is for eternity. Think about it. After you die there are no second chances, no changes. You suffer forever. You are a Catholic so you understand what I am saying.

Sincerely,

Paul Sanders

"That's a nice touch about the blood on your hands. If I had thought of it, I would have said to look for that, too. It's perfect, and I can see why there weren't any more like it. So, is the problem one of tampering with an election?"

"Partly. There's more. This afternoon two FBI agents were in my office asking me about the letter. This is what they told me. Sanders was fired on a Friday. Eight days later, on Saturday, the kid and his uncle are out flying a model airplane in a deserted brushy area, as I gather, and someone tried to kill both of them with a high powered bow and arrow. Somewhat miraculously, they both got away unhurt. They suspect the attacker was there the Saturday before, the day after Sanders was fired, setting up the murders. The older guy had no idea of who would want to kill him. But, the kid, who was still plenty put out about being fired from a volunteer job with no chance to defend himself, mentioned Senator Rutlen and me right away. The FBI guys insisted the letter wasn't threatening, certainly not enough to cause people to be killed. They are, therefore, assuming there is more to it than simply the letter. They are right, of course, as we both know."

"What did you tell them?"

"Not much. I told them it was politics, the stuff of life in Washington. We meet again tomorrow morning at seven. That's why I called you. This brings us to the connection with the person who tried to kill us. It's all too crazy. I know how the kid feels since that's how I feel. I'm sure it's the same with you. So, think hard. What's going on? It seems there must be some connection."

They finished their meal. Wally picked up the dishes, and put them in the dishwasher. Neither said anything. When Wally sat down again, he said, "I don't see that you can possibly tell them about my conjecture about the prayers."

"I didn't mention it, but I was told that Senator Rutlen was being questioned at the same time I was. That was obviously so we wouldn't compare notes between question sessions. When I first discussed this with him I told about your analysis of the situation, that Sanders was doing it through mental telepathy by means of prayers. He may relate that to the agents."

"That may make it tougher. If there's anything modern society, especially cops, don't want to hear it's that people are influenced by the spiritual. You could tell them about the attempt on us. That could get a bit sticky, though. Perhaps you could use your position to stave off any ill effects."

"What if they ask if I have any idea about who would have wanted to kill me?'

"Do what the other guy did. Say you don't know."

"Then, why didn't I come forward right after the shooting at the cabin. In fact, why didn't we call the sheriff the next morning when you discovered the holes in the wall? I know the cell phone worked; I turned mine on and got a signal. The sheriff knew where we were."

Wally didn't answer. Neither one said anything.

"Okay. Let's start at the beginning. Have you had any more cases of saying things that you didn't intend to say?"

"No."

"It does appear that with Sanders getting fired, he stopped praying for you. So, the thing that started all of this has, for the present, been solved."

"Fine. Only, now I have a worse problem."

"It reminds me of the story of the monkey's paw."

"What's that."

"A man of little means comes into possession of a withered monkey's paw that is said to be magical and would grant three wishes. He is reticent to use it, but his wife persuades him to wish for some money, not a lavish amount, but certainly enough to help them. A man comes to the door shortly after the wish was made. He most contritely says their son has been killed at the factory. The standard recompense in such as case is a sum of money exactly the same as the woman's wish. After the funeral, the woman, by means of much begging, convinces the man to wish for their son back. A few hours later, in the night, there is a knocking at the door. The woman is frantically unbolting the door knowing it is her son who is knocking. Just as the door starts to open, the man makes his third wish. When the door is opened there is no one there."

"What your little tale suggests is for every problem solved, a worse one will take its place?"

"I'm not saying that. I shouldn't have mentioned it, I suppose. Things happen and often there's no explanation. Sometimes, though, a diversion helps the mind to come up with solutions. It has occurred to me that in the morning you should make a very assertive point of saying that your new problem is entirely of the FBI's making. It was terribly inept of them to barge into a campaign office and start throwing around accusations. If the boy had not been fired, there would be no connection made of the attempted murders with you. Am is right?"

"That seems certain."

"In addition, even with the firing, there is still no evidence to link the crime in the bushes with you. There is only a peeved young man saying the first thing that popped into his head. The FBI should be reprimanded for such shallow investigation of a crime. It smacks of discrimination against politicians."

"What if they ask about the prayer connection to the letter?"

"Brush it off. Tell them to solve the bow and arrow case, and stop bothering you. That is, unless you want to report the attempt on us. I'm still not sure either way on that. Nothing more has happened since then."

"What you said will work with the FBI tomorrow. It still leaves me wondering about our case, though. Somebody went to a lot of trouble and expense to make some holes in the cabin that should have been in you, too. That did happen. We can't ignore it. It's getting so I'm afraid of every shadow. What if I make more antiabortion statements? I would expect to be killed if I did, and I'd be helpless to stop it."

"I've thought about it too. Being helpless is tough, isn't it? We all die sometime. The question is, have we been living in such a way that we accept it without fear? We all expect to have at least several weeks after our test results come back 'positive' to get ready. However, for many people such a preparation period isn't granted. Maybe, this is the time we have been given to get things in order. If you knew you would die twenty-four hours from now, what would you do?"

Norma's head was bent forward, eyes staring at the table before her. Wally shifted his chair scraping it on the floor. Her head shuddered. "I don't want to think about that. There are too many conflicts. Everything is a dilemma, my work, my beliefs, that shooting, life, death, tomorrow, time, time without end. How can a person be expected to cope with that?"

Wally got up and gently took her arm coaxing her to stand up. "Come on. I'll drive you back to your apartment."

Minneapolis

It was Monday evening in the middle of summer, and Alvin Freidmuth should have been enjoying it more. Normally, he and a few friends would do nine holes of golf in the evening or whatever else pleased them, and then have a late supper intermixed with beers and jokes. Due to his preoccupation with the matter of his inheritance, they were beginning to question whether he had taken up a romantic pursuit. His answer was he had to spend a lot of time with his aging father who wouldn't last much longer. The incident in the bushes with his bow and arrow had been conceived perfectly, and in his mind executed flawlessly, as well. The bow hitting that hidden branch was rotten bad luck.

As he left the diner he frequented that was only a mile from his house, he failed to notice the man who had been watching him all through his meal. The man flipped a twenty on his table to cover his food and followed Alvin out the door. To avoid door dings, Alvin invariable parked his Mustang at the very edge of the lot, the driver's side door near a hedge. He pressed the key fob to unlock the doors. As he bent to put his hand on the latch, he was grabbed on the left arm, and felt a solid object jab him in the back.

The voice from behind him said, "That's a gun in your back. Don't call out. Slowly drop to your knees." The voice was calm and cold as steel with an eastern accent.

They were both on their knees on the pavement hidden by the car. "We'll have a little chat right here."

Alvin tried to face the man and the gun in his back became more painful. "Don't do that. You will not see my face. If you try anything, I will hurt you. I am with a special unit of the ATF. Do you know what that is?"

"Alcohol, Tobacco, and Firearms."

"Good. We also have an active program to assist other governmental agencies find terrorists. We found you, right."

"What are you talking about?"

"You were behind the attempt to assassinate Norma Holleran, a highly placed government official."

Alvin tensed. How was it possible they could know? It didn't seem likely Marv would have ratted. He stood to gain tens of millions. It was unlikely they could have topped that offer.

As if in answer to his thoughts the voice said, "That was some sloppy use of sniffers on the Internet. You left tracks all over the place."

So, that was it. Marv wasn't as good as he let on. In his mind it seemed as though the whole world knew what he had done, but he wasn't going to admit anything. "You don't have any proof or you would have arrested me. You're out fishing, since you don't have a clue."

"Not true. Marv Wilson will pay for his part in it. For now, I'm going to make you an offer since you weren't the actual trigger man. Are you with me?"

"Whatever you say. You have the gun."

"Fine. We are inclined to over look certain infractions of the law for services rendered, that means rendered in the future, of course. I'll only ask once before you go to prison for a long time. What's the answer?"

"Keep talking. As I said, you're the one with the gun."

"Hence forth, I will be known as Raven. Any instructions from Raven will be executed exactly as stated. Do you agree? That's a yes or no, not you've got the gun. Which is it?"

"Yes."

"Very good. I will soon start contacting you by phone, letter, email, note left in your car, anything. Don't tell another person or the deal is off and you go to prison. Now, stay in this position for another two minutes without moving your head. The silencer on this gun is very silent. If you try to look, you will die."

Joab Feinstein left the parking lot of the diner, walked around the corner, and drove off in the dark blue rental car. It had gone as expected. People like mushy Alvin were easy to handle. Things were on schedule for a fine display of his craftsmanship a short few days hence. He and his "assistant" had arrived in town the evening before after the drive out from Virginia. The acquisition of equipment was proceeding satisfactorily. He'd spend tomorrow in Wisconsin finding the final ingredient for his masterpiece.

Tuesday morning, June 22

After returning from dinner with Wally the evening before, Norma had been more relaxed than in a long while, and had slept well. So well that it was five minutes after seven when she arrived at her office. The two G-men were there waiting. After ten minutes of checking messages from over night and reviewing her schedule for the day, she had the two agents ushered into her office.

No coffee or other courtesy was offered as she pointed to the chairs each was to occupy. Then she began. "I received a letter. You may think it nothing, but it wasn't directed at you either, was it? In my mind, I imagined a homicidal maniac that had been thrown out of an asylum because of budget cuts made by the previous administration. I expected your investigation to show something like that. Instead, you find an eighteen year old boy who has never been in trouble, and who certainly does not have the resources to harm the senator or myself. Fine. Mission accomplished. Report back and close the file. But, no. You have to go into a campaign headquarters throwing around accusations.

"It is a certain fact, is it not, that if that boy had not known that the FBI was checking into his letter writing habits, and especially if he had not been fired, that there would be no shred of a connection with the bow and arrow incident and me?"

Neither agent said anything hoping it was a rhetorical question. It wasn't.

"I asked you a question. Answer it."

Doren had expected this. Give a politician time to land on his or her feet, and either one will. "I see your point. A connection may not have been made."

"May not have been! Absolutely would not have been, and you know it!"

Doren had to go with what he had, though, he knew he had a weak hand. "Senator Rutlen mentioned you were having some sort of mind control performed on you. And, it had something to do with the letter. What do you have to say about that?"

"That has no bearing on our present situation. From what you said yesterday, I am in danger of having someone accuse me of trying to kill them. I am telling you, I did not. This is all the result of the bungling of a routine inquiry. If the media even gets a whiff of this, I'll see the head of your director rolling down Pennsylvania Avenue like a bowling ball, and your heads will be right behind it. Is that clear!"

Doren nodded.

"Good. I suggest you get to work solving the bow and arrow case. That was a shallow piece of work to use the testimony of a clearly upset, possibly terrified, boy who said the first thing that came into his mind. I'm not impressed. Now, I have a busy day. Please, see yourselves out."

When she was alone, she reached for her bottle of headache pills. If it hadn't been for those men, she might have made it through the day without one of those things. Various people had told her go to a doctor and have a check up. Whenever she had decided to do it, something came up and she put it off. Maybe during the August recess she'd find time.

— 18 —

Tuesday morning, June 22, Central Wisconsin

It simply wasn't going to go on. He had considered all the possibilities. Working with machines was what he did. Being a millwright by trade, it was something that came naturally. Having been raised on a farm, the variety of tasks from cutting wood, welding, and fixing everything from cars to tractors and machinery had trained him how to make things work and get things done.

Leaning back on his heals, he lowered the five pound cultivator shoe to the ground. There was no denying the fact that he had bought the wrong parts. These were for a larger machine. He let his frustration burn off as he rubbed his hands on his thighs. It was Dutch Tuley's nature to be a tad paranoid. That's what bothered him. Did the guy at the implement store on the north side of Madison make an honest mistake, or had he deliberately sold him something he couldn't use in the expectation of never seeing him again. It was probably the latter. The cultivator was old, and parts scarce. He had to admit that he had been too eager in his hopes that these were the parts he needed so he had not checked closely. Part of the blame was his. Part of the blame was *always* his.

He made the hundred and thirty mile trip to Madison expecting to find a job. With no economic expansion, companies were not adding production capacity, hence there was little work for millwrights. The ad in the paper had looked promising, and his call to the number listed was even more positive. The guy sounded like they couldn't find enough qualified men. In reality, the agency handling the hiring had ten openings. They found it was in their interest to be able to choose the ten from two hundred applicants rather than twenty. He'd been suckered. The positions had been filled before he even arrived. When he learned the score, he let the man have a piece of his mind. They nearly came to blows. That had cost him a day and a tank of gas—for nothing. The worst of it was the guy would never forget him, probably pass his name around town, too. Scratch Madison for future employment.

As he thought about it driving back, he knew that if he had been a woman he would have had a job, and the quota of ten positions would not have mattered. Several months before, a man at a placement agency had said that if a woman came in with his work record and references, he'd have work. I was a free shot for the head hunter, though, because there were no women with his credentials. He supposed it would have been much the same if he had been a minority, too. How long could the country stay afloat with rules like that?

The cultivator was even older than the ancient International Harvester tractor on which it was mounted. He could see the work around alternative. It would take some cutting, welding, and drilling, but it wasn't as if he had a choice. He had eighty acres of corn in the ground and the weeds were about to choke it. The last of his savings had gone into the gamble of getting a good crop, and a bigger gamble yet that prices would be up at the harvest. He had put up half of the money and the bank the other half. A good chunk of his money went for crop insurance with the bank as the beneficiary. It was good land and he had bought enough fertilizer, too much as it turned out, but he had scrimped on herbicide. His rate of application obviously had been below the threshold where it was effective. That lent the urgency to the cultivating. The first time through, it had not been effective which was why he needed the swept cultivator shoes, the ones that wouldn't fit.

The fix amounted to making a bracket for each shoe with two sets of holes in it. One set to match the cultivator and the other to match the shoe. Having found the piece of steel he needed on the scrap pile, he was required to cut it using his Lincoln arc welder set to the highest current using a large welding rod. The acetylene in his gas torch had run out months ago. With no money to spare, the tank remained empty.

Flipping back his welding helmet, Dutch caught sight of movement coming toward the open door of the shop where he worked. It was a lean man in his fifties, clean shaven, with a pointed chin. He hardly stood five-eight. His close cropped hair was streaked with gray.

Dutch was in his forties, hard and filled out with a strong, wide chin. His hair was black and too long. There never seemed time to get a haircut. Besides, that took ten bucks, and if he had that kind of money to spare, he'd rather buy a twelve pack than get his hair cut.

"Howdy," the man said.

Dutch nodded to the man, reached down, and flipped the switch on the front of the welder. With a bang, it shut off. He wasn't afraid of strangers, nor did he mind making a new acquaintance. It's just that this normally happened at a tavern as they were swapping hunting stories over a beer. He responded with, "Ya."

"You have a good start on your corn," the man said gazing at the field that began fifty yards from where they stood.

That statement put Dutch on guard. That cornfield looked like the worst one in the county, which it was. You could hardly tell where the rows were among the weeds. "I got a good germination rate," he replied. Figuring he might as well get to business he asked, "What can I do for you?"

"A man who comes to the point. I like that. At the feed store in town, they said you had some ammonium nitrate fertilizer you might be convinced to part with. I'm in the market."

"Yeah, I ordered too much. They refused to take it back. Can't say I blame them. They buy to order and only stock a ton of this and that to make up for when somebody runs short. After planting, there's less call for it. Thought I'd do a second side dressing application just before it gets too tall for the tractor. Even with that, I got more than I need, though,"

The man nodded. He clearly wasn't a farmer.

Dutch looked thoughtful for a time and then said, "The rest I kind of decided to save for next year. The money's spent, and I worked it out how to get along without it."

"But, you would see the wisdom of selling it if the price was right, don't you agree?"

Dutch had known that line was coming. They wrangled about the price and finally settled on more than twice what Tuley had paid for it.

"How much would you be wanting?"

"Enough to fill ten fifty-five gallon drums. Do you have enough for that?" the man asked.

The mention of putting high nitrogen fertilizer in barrels was a red flag. Dutch was thinking fast. "Don't rightly know. You hold on there a minute. I have to go to the house and get some stuff." He was walking away before the man could reply.

Five minutes later, Tuley was back with a tape measure, a calculator, and a pad of paper. He also had two cans of Pepsi that he held by the bottom in the palm of his left hand. Holding his hand out toward the man he said, "I was in the mood for a lift, and I know it tain't polite to drink alone," he said with a wink."

The small man took one of the cans and popped the top.

"Follow me," Tuley said.

He led the way to a shed where the planter was stored. He laid the things he was carrying on a board, and popped the top of his Pepsi, taking a long drink. He then climbed up on a wheel. "Ya see, at the start of planting when these fertilizers canisters are empty, I dump two fifty pound bags of fertilizer into each one. That fills it up to here," he pointed with his finger. Pulling out the blade of the tape measure, he determined the canister's diameter and depth. "So, fifteen inches in diameter, and twenty inches deep. Let's see." he tapped on the calculator. "Then two hundred thirty-one cubic inches per gallon, that's seven point six five gallons per bag, or seven bags per drum to fill 'em an inch or two from the top. That sound okay?"

The man nodded.

"You want seventy bags. I've got it."

The lean man looked surprised.

Tuley thought, just because I'm wearing overalls, and have dirt under my fingernails, doesn't mean I'm stupid.

"Who's going to fill the drums?"

"You."

"That'll cost you a couple of hundred more."

The man nodded again.

"Payment?"

"I happen to have cash. Would that be acceptable to you."

"That'll work. Got a time table?"

"I'll stop by in the morning about eight with a truck and the drums. Can you do it then?"

"I'll be here."

The man nodded and handed the almost full can of Pepsi to Tuley who cupped the palm of his hand and grasped the bottom. The small man got in his dark blue car, and drove off.

Tuley watched the dust drift away. It was noon so he went to the house. He made some sandwiches by slicing venison off a cold roast from the refrigerator. He liked it with a little mustard. He should have planted soybeans rather than corn, but with the demand for ethanol, the price of corn was high. This was the third year in a row for corn, and he had decided to plant beans next year. With beans, he wouldn't need as much nitrogen fertilizer because they were legumes and later in the summer they actually added nitrogen to the soil. This made it even more lucrative to get rid of the extra ammonium nitrate.

Half the farm was cultivated, and half was timber and marsh. That meant there were lots of deer, and deer loved corn. They ate some of his crop, but he got even as he ate a lot of them, year round. They all did. The game wardens knew what was going on. However, with the sport of deer hunting in decline the herd had to be kept in check. Even with that, if he had figured the herbicide right, he wouldn't be so pressed to cultivate, and could go fishing. The change of diet would be welcome.

Sipping his coffee between bites, he considered the deal he had made. He needed the money, but wondered if he needed it this badly. The little nerd was making a truck bomb, there was no hiding that. Tuley subscribed to a couple of periodicals from the white supremacist fringe. He didn't consider himself part of that bunch, but he liked to keep up to date on what they were saying. The purchaser had obviously gotten hold of a mailing list and found him. He had been laid off for nearly eighteen months, and the unemployment checks had stopped long ago. The guy knew he'd be receptive.

They, whoever they were, only had to pour a measured amount of fuel oil into each drum, about five gallons if he remembered right, let it age a little, then stuff a stick of dynamite into the resulting brew. There you had it, one big bomb. And, at thirty-five hundred pounds for just the fertilizer, that would rattle some windows.

At the first mention of fifty-five gallon drums, he should have said no. So, part of the blame was his. Part of the blame was *always* his. He had the sense to start distancing himself from the matter with the offer of the Pepsi to the buyer. As soon as the blue car was driving away, he had emptied the can. Now it sat on the shelf above the coat hooks behind the door with a box of shotgun shells in front of it. He had wiped it clean before leaving the house and had not touched it except for the top and bottom rims. He had a clear set of the man's prints.

As for loading the barrels, he'd use a new pair of gloves and never take them off until he was finished. After the guy left, he'd burn the empty bags and the gloves, maybe even burn his shirt and overalls, too. No telling what kind of contamination he could pick up from having been in contact with the drums. In the shed where he stored the fertilizer, he'd fill in the space of the missing bags at the bottom back of his pile.

He had some railroad ties out back. He's use them. The man at the feed store knew how much he had wanted to sell back, so the pile had to look that big in case anybody came around asking questions. He hated the very idea of involving any level of government, especially the FBI. He wished he hadn't become involved in this. What could he do, though, he needed the money. In addition, he wasn't so sure the guy would have taken no for an answer. His only advantage was his possession of the buyer's fingerprints.

The dark blue car was driven by Joab Feinstein. It might have seemed strange that someone in his position as confidant to the President would be engaged in activities such as these. In view of his history, it wasn't. Born in the U.S. he had spent much of his early life in the Middle East. Trained by the Mossad, he'd been in the messy dirty tricks business all his adult life. Many would call him a terrorist. He, not surprisingly, saw it differently.

This was going well. His comrade, the driver from the cabin incident in upstate New York, was acquiring the fifty-five gallon drums, some of them plastic, some steel. This bomb would explode in three stages, as did McVeigh's. A blasting cap would set off the intermediate explosive which would in turn cause the ammonium nitrate and fuel oil mixture to explode. For the intermediate step, he'd prefer to use Tovex Blastrite gel, a modern explosive used in mining and road building. Timothy McVeigh had used three hundred fifty pounds of it. However, it wasn't possible for him to get that any more than it was for McVeigh. If anything pointed to a high level conspiracy in the Oklahoma bombing it was the Tovex. It would have been easier for McVeigh to walk out of Fort Knox with three hundred fifty pounds of gold than for a nobody like him to come into the possession of three hundred fifty pounds of Tovex. Dynamite was less used these days due to the problem of the nitroglycerine weeping out of it with age and making it unstable. In any case, buying dynamite was as difficult as Tovex, so forget it.

The intermediate explosive he'd use was *Tannerite*. This was a binary explosive used primarily as a target for firearms practice. It exploded when impacted by a high powered rifle slug. For long range shooting, it made it possible for the rifleman to see when the target was hit by means of the explosion rather than having to walk a half-mile or more to the target each time.

Since caps were necessary for all explosives, they were the hardest to get. He and his helper had driven out from Maryland, and made a stop in Chicago, his old stomping grounds. There were people in Chicago he could trust who supplied the caps. Even with that, he did not plan to use them. Rather, he brought along a mechanism that used the signal from a cell phone to shoot a rifle bullet into the Tannerite.

They already had Dutch Tuley's name on the rental agreement for the truck . . . . Bam! Feinstein slammed his hand against the steering wheel. "That lousy bastard! The can of Pepsi. He got my fingerprints. He's a little too smart for his own good." Go back and get it? No. If he did it deliberately, and he had, it was hidden by now. "Okay, smart guy, we'll handle you," he said aloud

---

Dutch Tuley knew this was trouble, but he didn't panic. The guy would figure it out about the can of Pepsi. He put the fingerprinted can in an empty mayonnaise jar. A wadded up newspaper pressed down on the top of it would keep it from rattling around. After that, he screwed the cover on. Taking a shovel, he buried the jar in the woods behind the house. Returning to the house, he loaded his deer rifle and shotgun. That evening, he'd visit one of his buddies who lived six miles away. There was no getting away from it, he'd have to tell him about the deal, and get some help for the morning.

Tuesday noon, June 22

Needless to say, Randy Offit, the Director of the FBI was none to happy to learn of the simile the Speaker of the House of Representatives had used in his regard. It was catchy enough so that no matter what the security level of the case, it would be repeated until half of the people in the Bureau had heard it. If that many in the Bureau became aware of it, then all of Washington would know. For a year to come, someone at a reception would casually mention that he had been driving up Pennsylvania Avenue and noticed what appeared to be a bowling ball rolling their way. On closer inspection, it appeared to be someone's head. If the one retelling the story was a friend he'd break out in laughter and slap him on the shoulder, if not it would follow with a knowing stare—you're on your way out.

He didn't know who the klutz out in cow country was, but the reprimand would go down through channels so everyone in the chain of command would feel the sting of that man's incompetency.

That evening after Norma had returned to her apartment she had a call from Wally. "How'd it go this morning?"

"Like you suggested, I read them the riot act and they left."

"Okay. I hope not too savagely, though, because I've been thinking about what happened to us. I'd like to see it resolved as much as you do. See what you think of this. Type up the events at the cabin so as not to include unnecessary details. In a day or two, call the FBI back. Tell it to them the way you've laid it out. Or, maybe just give them the typed report. Whatever you decide. Say that you've been concerned about the incident, but didn't know what to make of it. Nobody was hurt. After thinking about it, and the bow and arrow incident, you thought the FBI should know, not that it seems possible the two are connected. Be sure to send me a copy of what you write because they'll be around to see me, too."

"What happened at the cabin has been wearing on me. I see people ready to kill me hiding in every shadow. The other day I was afraid to eat a sandwich that I had sent to my office thinking it had been poisoned. I'll write it up like you suggest, but I'm still a little afraid to call in the FBI. It's hard to explain. I'll think about it."

"I can't understand your reticence, but for now I'll have to trust your judgement. Try not to worry too much."

— 19 —

Wednesday, June 23, Central Wisconsin

By eight o'clock, Dutch had the cultivator fitted with the new shoes, and the International Harvester gassed up ready to hit the field. Of course, that would have to wait for the completion of a certain transaction. At eight-fifteen, a white box truck drove up with the little man driving. He appeared to be alone. That didn't surprise him. The road ran past the property a couple of hundred yards to the west of the buildings. The land between the house and the road was wooded. If the buyer had brought a friend, he would have dropped him off on the road to sneak through the trees and come up behind the house.

Dutch lifted his hand and motioned the driver to swing around and back up to the shed where he stored the fertilizer. This he did. The engine stopped and the man got out.

"Morning," Dutch said.

The man nodded. "Ready to start loading?"

"Yeah, as soon as we get the financial stuff out of the way."

"What, don't you trust me?" the lean man said with unmistakable mockery in his voice.

"Let's just say, it's common sense," Dutch replied. "If I cut open my sealed bags, they're lined with a moisture proof barrier you know, load your barrels, and you don't happen to have the money, I'm kind of out of luck, wouldn't you say?"

With a sweep of his hand, he withdrew an envelope from his back pocket. There followed a tense period where fifty dollar bills were meticulously passed, one at a time, from one hand to another, the latter being Dutch's.

At the conclusion of the operation, Dutch said, "That'll do."

The man unlatched the roll-up rear door of the truck and opened it. Dutch threw back the tarp covering the bags of fertilizer and starting carrying them to the truck and hefting them into the back. After twenty bags, he climbed into the truck and removed a lid from a barrel starting toward the front. When full, the drums would weigh more than three hundred fifty pounds, so any moving had to be done while they were empty. The very front of the cargo space had something covered with a heavy black plastic sheet. The smell was unmistakable; the plastic covered containers of fuel oil.

Dutch paced himself so he could complete the job without a rest period. Each bag was laid on the cover of a neighboring barrel with the end hanging over the open one. He cut it with a box cutter and let the white crystalline material fall into it. He was on his last barrel and nothing had happened to interrupt his labor. This was good, but it caused him to worry.

———————————

At seven o'clock Danny, Dutch's friend, had parked by a lake a half mile away and walked through the woods to the farmstead. Wearing his deer hunting camouflage suit, and carrying his rifle, he settled down among some bushes to wait. A little after eight, there was a rustle in the leaves to his right. It might be a deer, but then, maybe not. Not a deer! The man was at home in the woods and was doing a stealthy job of his approach. Might have had special commando training in one branch of the service or another, Danny thought. He carried a rifle, probably a thirty-thirty, something that could be purchased in any sporting goods store. He let him come, moving only his eyeballs. When he was fifteen feet to his right front, he said in a subdued, but clear voice, "Freeze where your are. No sound."

The man did as he was told.

"Throw the gun to your right, now."

With a casual toss the gun landed with a crunch in the dry leaves. By this time, Danny was standing several feet behind him.

"Any sound or false move and this thirty-aught-six with two hundred grain hollow point will pop your head like a melon. Indicate you understand by moving your head."

The man nodded.

"Good. Now, drop to your knees. Clasp your hands behind your head. Fall on your face." The man was following instructions. He knew enough to live to fight another day.

"Very slowly stretch your right arm out perpendicular to your body. Good. Slide to the right. A little more. Stop. Place our hand on that rock. Got it? Good. Turn your face the other way. You know what's coming, so don't fight it."

Danny cautiously approached the man keeping his rifle aimed at him.

"I have the safety off, my finger on the trigger, and the muzzle aimed at you. Just which part, you don't know."

He placed his boot on the man's forearm and raised his full weight on it. The bone snapped. The man let out a short gasp. Danny stepped back.

"Okay. All done. Get up on your knees and turn to face me, slowly."

This done, Danny could see the pistol behind his belt.

"Two fingers only and slowly, remove the pistol and toss it to your left."

Another thump in the leaves.

"Stand up and turn around. Let your right arm hang at your side, with the left, clasp the back of your neck. Walk forward. Don't forget, no safety, finger on trigger, rather pissed."

As Dutch filled the last barrel, the little guy was getting nervous. He wasn't twitching or anything like that. He was too professional. It was his shifting position as if looking for someone, or a sign, that gave it way. With the final bag was dumped, Dutch put the lid on followed by the clamping ring. The bolt slipped through the ferrules and he used the ratchet provided to turn the bolt pulling the ring tight.

Dutch had watched the movements of his buyer every chance he had. No weapon was obvious. It was too hot to wear any kind of jacket without being conspicuous. His shirt was tight against his back, and an ankle holster would have shown. He jumped down from the truck and pulled the rear door down and latched it. He said, "Looks like that about does it."

The man frowned.

Off to their right a voice said, "Yo, Dutch."

They both turned. Two men approached. Dutch made a point of staying to the side and behind the other man.

"Wa' 'cha doin' in these parts, Hank?"

By agreement, Dutch would call Danny, Hank. Since the buyer would know Dutch's name, but not Danny's, there was no point in giving away Danny's name.

"Was out tracking the cougar that took a couple of my young stock. Came across this feller wandering around in the woods with a broken arm. No tellin' folks. Doesn't say much, neither."

Looks were exchanged. No need for words in such a case.

Dutch turned to his buyer, "Say, you look like the Good Samaritan type, how about you giving him a lift into town where he can get that arm looked after?"

"Yeah. Suppose it'd be no trouble." He made a twitch with his hand and the man with the broken arm went to the passenger side of the truck cab. The truck started and drove away.

"You think that guy from the woods would have killed me?"

"Yeah, probably would have. Can't say I like your new friends, Dutch."

"Can't say I do, either."

Driving away, Feinstein said to his partner, "You're a great help. What am I supposed to do with you? I have a notion to pop you and dump you in the woods. He got the rifle and your nine-millimeter, I see. I planned to use the rifle to detonate the Tannerite. It was purchased for cash at a Texas gun show two years ago. It was clean. Now I have to use detonating caps the residue of which can be traced easier than a gun."

Flavian Cutter, Flave for short, replied, "Not such a good idea for you to pop me, not for you or for me. The army has my prints on file, and you said that guy has yours. They'd find me eventually and put it together. Get me patched up with a cast on this arm, and I'm good to go." He knew Feinstein was inclined to kill him because of the arm so he had to remain useful. He was surprised at the professionalism of the man called Hank. "You said these were some country bumpkins. That guy had special training."

"Excuses won't help!" Feinstein snapped back. He was indeed inclined to put the incompetent boob out of his misery. But, this was the US of A. If his operatives started disappearing on jobs he'd be out of helpers. Americans! They were so soft. He pressed a speed dial on his cell phone as he drove.

"Yeah. This is Joab. I need the name of a discrete doctor in the Minneapolis area who can take care of a broken arm. Yeah. Just a minute, gotta pull over." As soon as he was stopped, he removed a notebook and pen from his shirt pocket. "Go ahead. Okay, we'll find him."

After a half-hour of driving silently, Flave was rocking back and forth slowly as he tried to cradle his arm. "This thing is really starting to hurt."

"Yeah. Next time be more careful. Nothing like pain to drive home a lesson. The schedule is shot because of you. Later today we have to come back and handle that guy assuming we can make it in time. He won't sit on that evidence for long. How could you have let that happen?"

Cutter was in no position to argue, or offer comment.

Feinstein wasn't one to let unexpected setbacks stop him. He considered the possibility of calling a couple of helpers from Chicago who'd have to drive up during the night. After some thought, he decided against it. It was the old problem with security. Years ago in a Mossad class on security a wary old man who had done it all and survived a long life in the business had used this example. Standing by a blackboard holding a piece of chalk he said, "Assume you have a secret. You tell John, that's one. He made a one on the blackboard. Then you tell Ben and the instructor made a second one beside the first. Finally, you tell Judith as he drew a third one beside the first two. You see," he concluded, "there are now a hundred and eleven people who know the secret." It was too true to be ignored. They'd get by with what they had even if he had to do more of the work than he liked.

He was pleased that they had all the makings for the bomb in the truck. He had picked up the two hundred pounds of Tannerite in Virginia and hauled it out with them in the white panel van. It had been transferred to this truck yesterday. It still required mixing, a messy job intended for Cutter, but he'd be able to handle it. There was enough fuel oil in five gallon cans in the back, too. The fertilizer had been the next to the last item. It was intended that Tuley be the last item. If it would have been necessary to kill him, they would have. But, the better alternative was to bind and gag him to be left in the cab of the truck when the bomb went off setting the blame clearly on the white supremacist fringe.

Their base of operations was a warehouse, a kind of maxi-storage. He had leased a walled off double bay twenty feet wide by sixty feet long with a furnished office and bathroom. The panel van they'd driven out from the east coast was there, as was the blue car he had rented in Minneapolis. That's where he was now headed with the truck to prepare the bomb.

They switched to the blue car at the warehouse and set off to find the doctor. The address was easy enough to find, however the doctor was out of town until the morning. Back at the warehouse, Feinstein found the makings to splint Flave's arm and make a crude sling. This wasn't going well. He had planned to be back at Dutch's farm by nightfall. Now, Cutter's condition was worsening. He had a fever and the Tylenol he was force feeding him was only partially effective. They were forced to hole up in their motel room for the night.

Wednesday morning, June 23

Fred Clements didn't know what to make of his summons to the office of the director of the Minneapolis division of the FBI. That division included several Midwest states. It might be to receive a commendation for one or the cases he had closed recently. Why not? He worked hard and got results. As he entered, the expression on the man's face was not in keeping with that of an award ceremony.

A half-hour later Fred Clements departed from the same office, his tail feathers still smoking. He had stood riveted to the floor accepting the invective tirade until his mind was numb. The specter of the director's head rolling down the street like a bowling ball was derision at it's best. It was the only bright spot in the whole thing. He had been prompted to chuckle at this, but knew he didn't dare. To avoid laughing, he clenched his teeth together until it seemed like his eyes would pop out. With the onslaught past, he walked, almost marched, shoulders back and face expressionless to his cubical. He still had his job, but there were some thinly veiled threats that his employment status could change dramatically at any moment. Okay, he thought. Time to find out what's going on. There were some wolves out there about to have their sheep's clothing ripped off.

He had been uneasy about accepting the report of that cop in Lino Lakes. That fool in D.C. making such a big thing about it was water over the dam. He had to get to the scene and straighten this out.

At eight-thirty, Clements drove up to the city offices in Lino Lakes. It was a calm sunny morning of seventy-five with promise of a hot day. As he entered the police offices, the first person he saw was a well built man of thirty with short blond hair. His nametag said Douglas. Looking him in the eye he said, "Clements, FBI."

Douglas instinctively thrust out his right hand and said, "You got here fast. Traffic must have been lighter than normal in downtown Minneapolis at this hour."

Clements took the offered hand nonchalantly, wondering what this guy would know about traffic in downtown. "Ready to review the scene?"

"Do you want to see the evidence before we go?"

"Let's go out there first."

"Your call. You want to ride with me or follow?"

"I'll follow."

"Good enough. Let's go."

It being a workday, the parking lot was nearly full behind the business where Wessen had parked. There were no windows on the back of the building, and if no one had seen them drive past the offices on the end, their presence would go unnoticed. Clements parked beside Douglas and came over to him carrying a digital camera.

So, where'd it happen?"

"Out there," Douglas said pointing. At the same time, he started into the shoulder high grass and cattails at the edge of the parking lot. Douglas had changed into old shoes and a uniform that was due to go to the cleaners as soon as he learned Cements was on his way. Clements was wearing dress slacks and a sports coat.

Ten steps into the foliage, Clements said. "What's this. This grass is soaking wet."

"Of course. I was glad you decided to come out in the morning. It's the same time of day as the shooting so you can see the crime scene as it actually was. Come on, it isn't so bad after a ways."

By the time they arrived at the clearing in the willow bushes, both men were soaked up to the waist, and their garments above the belt were damp. Clements looked at his shoes that had a nice shine when he had left home in the morning. Now, he could feel water squishing between his toes.

"Okay. Here's the way it was," Douglas began. Clements followed him through the sequence of events as related by Wessen and Sanders. The rope Wessen had used to shake the bush had been left in place. They found a spare propeller that had fallen out of the bucket when it was overturned by the first arrow.

Clements had his hand on his jaw as he looked about the clearing pondering what was supposed to have happened. It was a lot different from the scenes he normally investigated—all bushy and wet. The lush vegetation was exuding moisture at a high rate making the humidity in the closed space uncomfortable. The relentless sun didn't help. He wished he had worn something on his head. He slipped his sport coat off since his shirt was becoming wet with perspiration.

"What about back there?" Clements said pointing. "Was there any indication of a path in the grass where the alleged perpetrator came in and ran out?"

Douglas nodded. "There was."

"Whose idea was it to check on that?"

Douglas looked askance at Clements. "Well. I was the one who suggested we see what we could find. When we found a likely trail in the grass, Wessen ran beside it. From the way the dew was brushed off the grass by Wessen, it was obvious that was where the guy had passed. Why did you ask whose idea it was to check it?"

"What makes you think this wasn't a setup by Wessen and the kid? They could have done all of this. Neither of them were hurt. It's all circumstantial."

"I'll admit, Wessen was pretty cool about the whole thing, but the kid wasn't. He was shook up. To think Wessen sneaked way over behind that bush, picked up the bow and arrows he had previously hidden there, and shot the pail while the kid was flying the plane is pushing credulity a lot. Sanders said it wasn't a second between hearing the pail tip over and Wessen pulling him behind the bush. To be a setup, they would both have had to be in on it, and the kid wasn't. I'll swear in court to that. I've been at crime and accident scenes enough times to know how people act. The kid was surprised, shocked, and scared. I was afraid he'd go into shock at one point. Nobody's that good an actor."

"Maybe. What's your explanation?"

Douglas was not aware of the brouhaha in Washington or he might not have been so forthcoming. "I hunt deer with a bow, not here, up north. You might be surprised at how territorial these guys get about their hunting spots. Wessen said he had been coming out here off and on for years to fly his plane even before they started developing this area. If he had been out here in the fall and spoiled somebody's hunting a couple of Saturdays, they'd be plenty mad. I see it as a hunter wanting to scare him off, and getting a little carried away."

Clements had been taking pictures from various angles. As he put the camera into its case, Douglas said, "Anything else?"

"No. That should do it."

"Are you coming back to the office to see the evidence?"

"Don't see any reason to do that. I suggest you start looking at this as a setup by those guys. This doesn't feel right, none of it."

Driving away, Clements was starting to hate Wessen more with each minute. He had ruined a good pair of shoes, and the slacks and coat would have to go to the cleaners. Besides that, there was the need to redeem himself with the Bureau. Wessen was into something, he was sure of that. If he pressed him, the guy would make a mistake. It only took once. Then, they'd admit he had been right to handle the kid at the campaign office the way he had. When he returned to the office, Clements intended to make a report to the effect that it was his opinion the whole incident had been staged to embarrass the two in Congress who had received the letters. It couldn't do any harm, and it might stir things up. He'd make a point of saying it was his assumption so if things changed he'd be in the clear.

Sal Khurz sat at his dirty tricks desk in his dirty tricks office. He couldn't claim sixteen hundred Pennsylvania Avenue as his actual address, but it was within walking distance. He resided in one of the myriad government buildings among the innumerable civil servants doing an endless variety of menial jobs all at the behest of the President. To the occupants of this rodent colony their jobs were far from menial. If you were to ask any one of them, they would tell you the future of the United States, in some way, hinged on their being at their duty station faithfully frittering away the day doing things. Not meaningless random things, mind you, but those specific things that it was their purpose in life to do. However, taken as a whole, all of the specific things took on the appearance of, in fact the reality of, Brownian movement, the finest example of random motion observed in nature. The dirty tricks of Sal Khurz were far from random, though they were carefully crafted to appear that way to the general public. If you were inclined to question the veracity of that statement, you had only to ask him.

It was nearing lunch time when the dirty tricks secretary brought an envelope to the office of Mr. Khurz. Sorry. Poor choice of words. She wasn't a secretary. In other venues, she would be an administrative assistant. However, this being Washington, she was a managerial aide. And, to be totally honest, Mr. Khurz held the position of Special Assistant to the President on Political Affairs, that is, dirty tricks. In the envelope was a copy of the report that Mr. Clements, special agent for the FBI in

Minneapolis, had forwarded to Washington less than an hour before. The bow and arrow case, as it had become known, was rather sensitive and anything relating to it was flagged and immediately sent to the White House for review. As we have seen, the term White House encompassed something more than a single building.

It was with some delight that Khurz read the report. Now, they were getting someplace. He'd have his managerial aide craft the news story he would leak to the Minneapolis media. It would be a perfect first salvo to take out Ellefson, and lead to the successful initiation of the larger operation.

— 20 —

Wednesday evening, June 23

Alvin and Marv were having beers and burgers in the sports bar again. The main event of the evening hadn't started yet, but the place was filling up. The decibel level was nearing the threshold of pain. It was a good place to have a serious discussion. They were in a corner at a small table where none of the screens were at a good viewing angle. That was okay with them, they weren't watching.

Alvin had no intention of telling Marv about his aborted attempt to get Wessen with the bow and arrow. Who knew when the police might start to pressure Marv about the thing in New York? What he didn't know he couldn't tell. What he had learned from the latest couple of downloads from Eugene's office convinced him that his hunch had been right about Wessen.

With no one appearing to take an interest in the two men, Alvin leaned over to Marv, "I listened to the recording you downloaded last evening. In the afternoon, that old bugger called his lawyer and told him to make up the will so the Wessen dude gets most of the money. Can you believe it?"

"I can believe anything. How you want to handle it?" he asked with his penchant of leaving out the verb.

"He has to go. I'll do it, but I need a gun, a three-fifty-seven, or something like that with a silencer."

"Not a good combination. It's nearly impossible to adequately silence a revolver, and three-fifty-sevens only come in revolvers. I'd suggest a nine-millimeter pistol. That'll have plenty of punch, and the ammo is very common."

"Fine. Whatever you say. But, I want one with no history, and one you won't feel bad about losing. I like the thing they did back east with your equipment. I wish we had something like that here."

"Nothing that fancy, but I'll handle it. When you want it?"

"As soon as possible. I scoped the guy out this week. I know how to do it."

"Don't you ever work?"

"That's none of your business as long as you're getting paid, which you are. But, yes I do. I sell securities for people's retirement accounts. I can work as much or as little as I want, within reason. My wife has a regular job that pays the rent. She agrees it's worth a little loss of my income for such a big prize. I don't tell her what we're doing, and she doesn't ask."

"Okay. We'll meet tomorrow morning like we did last time in the morning. Say, six-thirty. I'll have it."

"Wait. There's another thing. Can you get me one of those tracking gadgets like you used on your trip to New York? Ah, while you're at it, can you get me two of the things that you put on cars and have them work with one tracking screen?"

"Sure. Don't see why not. You planning to track their cars?"

"Yeah. I can't take any chances of him taking different routes to and from work, and even switching cars. He took his wife's car one of the days while I was figuring this out."

"Can do. How you fixing to get the trackers on their cars. Prowling about parking lots at work places is risky. People know who's supposed to be there. It's different in store parking lots. How much do they shop?"

"I see your point. What do you suggest?"

"What's the access to their garage like?"

"The cars enter from the street on the side of the house. It's a corner lot, and a detached garage."

"That's not bad. I'll also bring you a garage door code breaker. It shoots codes at the garage door opener until one connects. If it's not too new, it'll work. The latest models have enhanced protection in the codes, and the breakers aren't up to it yet. Go late at night. After you have the code, the machine loads it on to a remote. Then park a block away and walk up. You only have to open it a couple of feet to get in. The small door probably has a lock that can be opened from the inside. Leave that way. Be sure to bring along a small flashlight so you can see what you're doing. The front grill is usually the best."

"Okay. Thanks."

"Don't thank me. The bill will be in the mail, as they say."

They finished their second beer and left as the game was starting. Others quickly commandeered the table.

That same evening, June 23

Special Agent Fred Clements knew he'd have to rattle Wessen to get him to slip. To this end he was visiting him at home in the evening as he was relaxing. The door chime could be heard in the house. After no response, he pressed it again. Were these people who refused to answer the door? From his own experience, he knew it was normally someone selling something he didn't need. Well he'd wait them out. After the fourth no answer he decided to let the whole neighborhood know.

He pounded his fist on the door and shouted, "Police. Open up."

The man who finally opened the door was Wessen. Clements recognized him from his DMV photo. The face was not happy. This was intended. It was working well.

"Clements from the FBI. Can I come in?"

He didn't say it like a question. He reached for the latch on the screen door and started to open it.

The door was instantly snatched out of his hand, closed and the lever snapped to lock it. They glowered at one another through the screen. Clements maintained eye contact without saying anything to let the tension build.

Finally Vincent said, "Don't see why. Show the ID or beat it."

If confrontational was what Clements was after, he had it.

"Do you know who I am?"

"Yeah. Freddie Clements."

The use of the diminutive form of his name angered Clements, though he didn't show it.

"I'm here to talk to you about the game you played out in the brush in Lino Lakes. Either here or downtown, makes no difference to me."

"So, you want to talk about it, talk."

"I think you set the whole thing up to get even for your, son is it, this Paul, being dismissed from Walt Ellefson's political campaign. You, in effect, accused the Speaker of the House of Representatives and the leading member of the U.S. Senate of attempted murder. That's serious business, buddy."

"He's not my son. He's my nephew. Can't seem to get anything straight, can you?"

Frequently changing subjects was a proven way to get people to reveal things they were hiding. "That was very clever the way you staged that. You have specialized military training, don't you?"

Vincent regarded him for a few seconds. "I assume you accessed my military records, though you may have missed that too seeing as you got my relationship to the boy wrong. If you did, you know I had the standard basic training, fired expert with an M-14 rifle, which isn't that hard if you do what they tell you to do. I spent the rest of my tour in Viet Nam in the Quartermaster Corps filling out forms."

"I've seen your record. It's not all there, though, is it? You had other training that was off the books, so to speak."

"Now you're really guessing. Sort of desperate, are we? They must have really slapped you around for your ninny performance at the campaign office."

Change the subject again. "Why'd the kid send the threatening letters to those high ranking members of Congress?"

"They weren't threatening. Have you read them?"

There was the slightest twitch on the part of Clements. Vin saw it.

"You haven't even read the letter, have you? All of this. Doing what you did so Paul would be dismissed from the campaign. Then coming here to throw silly accusations around without a shred of data to back them up, and you haven't even read the letters. You pretend to be working the case, but you only have one ore in the water."

Clements was about to retort, but was cut off.

"You'd better leave. You're making a fool of yourself. I will report to your superiors that you are now inventing a nonexistent military record for me. Better take some time off. You're losing it."

Vin closed the door, none to gently.

As Clements drove away, he thought the meeting had not gone as well as it might have, but his main goal had been accomplished. The purpose was to upset him. Wessen wouldn't sleep well tonight. And, he wasn't done with him yet.

Thursday morning, June 24, Minneapolis

As radio alarms went off and people went to their front step to get the morning paper, they were met with an unexpected headline.

Ellefson Campaign in Trouble

Members of the Walt Ellefson campaign in the fourth congressional district appear to have become over zealous in their efforts to unseat their rival, a long time incumbent Democrat. Our investigative team has learned that a member of the campaign staff sent threatening letters to high ranking members of congress, Norma Holleran, the Speaker of the House of Representatives, and Senator Harry Rutlen, ranking member of the Senate. The FBI, upon inquiring into the matter, discovered the writer of the letters was a young man of eighteen who had no intention of bring harm to either member of Congress. When contacted, Holleran's office said the investigation was something that is routinely done in cases like that. There the matter would have ended, but it didn't.

Ellefson's staff immediately fired the staff member who sent the threatening letters with no further investigation into the matter. Presumably, the matter would have ended at that point, except it didn't.

Eight days later, last Saturday morning, local police were called to the scene of an attempted homicide in a brushy area north of the metro. It is alleged a man for unknown reasons tried to kill the young man who had been fired from Ellefson's campaign, and his uncle, with a high power bow and arrow. The two men were flying a radio controlled model airplane at the time. Miraculously, neither man was injured. When asked if either of them knew of anyone who might want to kill them, the younger man immediately mentioned the incident of his letter and subsequent firing from the campaign. He blamed the Speaker of the House and the Senator because in his opinion the letter was not threatening but that they were using their power to exact revenge.

That allegation, in effect, accused senior members of Congress of attempted first degree murder which brought the FBI into the case at a new level. Anonymous sources tell us that the FBI agent who further investigated the case is of the opinion that the whole bow and arrow incident was staged to embarrass the Speaker and the Senator. What everyone is asking is did the Ellefson campaign encourage young impressionable staff members to send untoward letters to opposition members of Congress? And then when these members of Congress responded, as it was their right to do, did the campaign further suggest the staging of the attempted murder incident?

Vincent Wessen awoke to music from a radio on the nightstand a few inches from his ear. That seldom disturbed his wife, Camilla. She had another radio set for a half-hour later, six o'clock, and it was tuned to the top of the hour news. Getting the news first thing upon waking was more than he could handle.

Vin was completing his breakfast when Camellia entered the kitchen. He had already shaved, and would be leaving in a few minutes. This was her normal rising time on those days when she went into the office, though they seldom crossed paths.

"Turn on the radio," she blurted out. "They've got the story about you and Paul and the bow and arrow shooting as the lead story."

Vin snapped on the radio and went to the living room where he flicked the remote at the TV. The radio story was over, but one of the channels had talking heads discussing it.

"No names," Vin said as he stood ten feet from the television. "As long as it remains anonymous, we'll be all right, at least for a while. How can this be happening? Who could be doing this? If my name gets mentioned, I could lose my job."

He paced the living room rubbing his forehead. "What do they mean, fabricated . . . ," he paused. "Oh! That lousy FBI dork that was here last night. He was berating me about how it was all made up. He leaked it! What can that stupid FBI hope to gain? They got Paul fired. Now, there're after me. What purpose could that serve other than being mean just for the fun of it? Is that what all the power they have over people turns them into?"

Camilla could see Vin's consternation. Beyond that, she was worried about his job, too. He was of an age where he'd never get another job with full benefits. "Are you going to work?" she asked. "What if they start giving names during the day?"

Vin took a deep breath. "Yeah. I have to go to work today, and I'm behind schedule. There are some time critical items I have to take care of. Might have to start taking vacation if this madness doesn't stop, though. I have to decide what to do if things change." He kissed her on the cheek, grabbed his lunch from the refrigerator, and set off.

Washington, D.C., June 24

Norma Holleran had already heard the story by the time she arrived at her office. This was a political town, and this was politics at it's best, worst, most extreme, what ever you'd call it. Donna was waiting for her when she arrived. Their gazes met.

"What do you think?" Donna blurted out. "I mean about the Ellefson campaign, the bow and arrow."

"I don't like it. This is being stage managed by that brood of vipers the President keeps in his hip pocket. Yes, we want to hang onto the House seat that Ellefson's after, but this could really blow up."

She spent the next hour lost in the mountain of things that needed to be done, though it was hard to concentrate. Her mind kept returning to that news story. It was so patently false. How could the people be so easily led without asking questions? There was no foundation for the story. As soon as anyone tried to dig into it, other sensational non-news would take the headlines and it would disappear. But, the damage would have been done. It was good that they had not mentioned names. That could come next to keep interest in the story if it were necessary. What about the innocent victims?

With a jolt she sat up. What was she thinking? That technique was what the left always used. That's how they managed to keep abortion, global warming, welfare, gay rights, and all the other liberal agenda items alive. They managed the news. She knew it because she was part of it. What was special about this instance to make her think something was wrong? A growing pain filled her mind. It was because she was personally involved in this instance. The conservatives had always been thought of as irrelevant nonentities, like dust that accumulated on your furniture. The dust, like the opposition, was there, and would always frustrate you by its persistent reappearance. Nevertheless, just as there was no morality associated with dusting, there had been no morality connected with disposing of those whose views differed from yours. Since the cabin incident, she had a growing sense that it was happening to her, as if she were a piece of dust. And, she didn't like it.

The tone on her intercom distracted her thoughts. She had to leave for a short meeting before the morning session started.

As she arose, she for the first time, gave serious consideration to not running for reelection. Would the President and his minions even allow her not to run? Stopping briefly, she popped a pill for her headache.

— 21 —

Central Wisconsin, Thursday, June 24

Dutch Tuley hadn't slept well as his mind thrashed about trying to figure out what to do. He had his loaded deer rifle under the blanket with him all night. Even standing it against the wall beside the bed seemed too far away. He was up at first light and cultivated for four hours before coming in for breakfast. He had remembered the license number of the truck so he'd start there. After eating, it was ten o'clock so he called his sister in Superior, Wisconsin who worked in a law office.

"Hi, sis, it's Dutch."

"Dutch. You know I told you not to call me at work. Is this important?"

"Yeah. It's big time important. I think I stumbled onto something where a lot of innocent people could die. It's complicated, and I have to ask you to say nothing to anyone. I need some information."

There was a pause. "Are you there?"

"Yes. What are you into, Dutch?"

"I was in the wrong place at the wrong time, that's all. I need you to look up the plate number for a truck. Please, can you do that?"

"Can't you call the police?"

"I'm not in the best standing with the locals. Mostly, I don't have enough evidence for anyone to believe me. I need the name and address of whomever owns the truck. And, I need it now."

"Do you want me to call you back?"

"No. I'll hang on. You can do that, I know you can. Go on line to the DMV. Here's the plate number . . . ."

Dutch listened for tire sounds on the driveway, and the sound of anything else. There was a steady wind blowing that would mask the sounds of anyone on foot. He could hear her clicking on her computer. There was a lull in the typing.

"I'll have to pay my boss for this. It'll come up on the monthly bill."

"I'll make good on it if I live long enough."

"Okay. Here it is. M and Y Rentals. I've got the rest, you want it?"

"Sure. I've got a pen."

She gave him the address in St. Paul and the phone number. He thanked her and hung up.

Dutch paced the kitchen wondering what to do. At least the truck was a rental, it wasn't stolen. He wondered who rented it. That could lead somewhere. After a few more minutes of indecision he called the number his sister gave him.

"Tuley! Bet I know why you're calling. The answer is no. You can't extend the time of the rental."

A shudder went through him. They had rented the truck in his name. It was even worse than if it had been stolen. He'd be linked to the whole thing. "Wait a minute," Dutch said. "How'd you know it was me?"

"Caller ID, of course. You got the special rate because you wanted it for less than a week. You must have it back by noon on Saturday. I have it reserved for another customer to pick up at one o'clock. I told you that. Sorry, no extension."

"That's not why I'm calling."

"Something wrong with the truck? It's practically new."

If the guy would only stop talking so I could say something, Dutch thought.

"No. No. Stop talking and listen to me," Dutch interrupted. "Somebody rented the truck in my name and will use it for a truck bomb. Listen to me or you won't have to worry about the next customer, there'll be no truck."

"How do I know you didn't rent it?" He wasn't talking so much now.

"Describe the guy who rented it."

"Normal looking white guy, probably works out, certainly not fat. Light brown hair, blue eyes, six feet or so, had a scar on his chin."

"That's not me." Dutch knew that was the man Danny found in the woods. "When did he rent it?"

"Mid morning on Monday."

"I was in a different city at that time and have a solid alibi." That made a big difference. The man he had almost punched out at the employment office would remember him.

"So, how do you know about a bomb?"

"I work a farm in central Wisconsin. I bought too much ammonium nitrate fertilizer this spring. Not being in the best financial shape, I asked around trying to sell it. They must have asked around too and found me. We made a deal and when they came to pick it up, they paid me extra to dump the bags into fifty-five gallon drums in the back of that rental truck. There was more stuff covered with black plastic. It smelled of fuel oil in the truck. Anybody been using that truck to haul fuel oil?"

"That'd be illegal with that vehicle. I wouldn't allow it."

"No kidding. Ever heard of an ANFO bomb?"

"No."

"That's there you mix ammonium nitrate fertilizer and fuel oil and set it off with a stick of dynamite. I sold them almost two tons of fertilizer. There'll only be confetti size pieces of your truck left. You know how the government keeps talking about a war on terrorism? They'll call it an act of war so your insurance won't cover it."

That last about war had popped into Dutch's mind as he was talking. It was a nice touch, he thought. The guy on the phone would have incentive to find the truck.

"I'll come after you. My records show you rented the danged truck? You get it back on time."

Dutch paused. He'd have to get the police involved. From there, it was only a stone's throw to the FBI. "Call the police and maybe the FBI. Tell them what I told you."

"Why didn't you do that?"

"Hey, I'm a single white guy who lives in the sticks and owns a deer rifle. They'd come out and arrest me on general principles and consider the job done. You're a businessman. You live in the neighborhood, so to speak. You pay taxes. They like taxes. They'll listen to you."

"Never heard it put that way, but you're right. I'll do it. But, they'll have to know about you."

"I know. If they send the FBI out to see me, tell them to send at most two guys, and in a government vehicle. The buyers had planned to kill me after I loaded the fertilizer for them. Well, they didn't, but I'm watching my back side, know what I mean?"

"If I call back, will you be there?"

"I'll be around, but not by the phone. What's your name in case I have to call you?"

"Ask for Mac."

"Okay, Mac. I hope you can make them take it seriously. I'm scared to death."

"I'll try. Oh, don't forget, Tuley. If I don't get the truck back I'll sic my lawyers on you and when they get done you not only won't have an alibi, I'll own everything you do, right down to your underwear, got it hayseed?"

The line went dead.

After he hung up, Dutch admitted for the first time, he was more frightened than he had ever been in his life. They'd be back, and the FBI would be here. And, he pounded his fist on the table, that skunk, Mac, would take his farm in payment if the truck were lost.

He didn't know who he feared the most. The only reason he was still alive was the buyer had more important things to do. Or, maybe they'd let him live and leave so much evidence that there was no way he could dig himself out. Above all else, he had to find the truck. The remark about hayseed was not about to go unanswered, either.

There was still about eight hours of cultivating to be done. He wondered if it would be safe. Someone could hide in the woods at the far end of the field and pick him off. The man with the broken arm wouldn't do it, and the other guy would be busy—he hoped. The FBI would likely arrive some time in the afternoon. He had about decided to do some cultivating, and then remembered what he had read about the FBI in the publications. He had to prepare for them and for the eventuality that certain other people paid him a return visit.

For the next half-hour, he wandered around the house, barn, and sheds trying to imagine what an enemy would do. The FBI, he hadn't quite classified them as an enemy yet, would drive a car up to the house. If they failed to follow his instructions, and they would, they'd also have some guys come through the woods to the west and north of the house. The barn was eighty yards to the east of the house. To the south of the barn was a cattle pen. He had sold his stock expecting to find work so it was unused. The south fence of the pen ran two hundred feet from the barn. Weeds and grass had grown up in the pen, and especially along the fence. He'd lie in wait along this south fence.

Having served in the First Gulf War, he had received the normal army training with emphasis on escape and evasion. He finished near the top of his class. The part of it that had taken his imagination were the instructions on how to disappear into the landscape, how to hide in plain sight. Along the south fence, dried stalks from the previous year's tall weeds were lying on the ground. He'd burrow under them at the end of the pen that faced the house. That way, he could watch through the west fence and see the house, the rest of the buildings, and the woods to the north.

With his deer rifle loaded and at hand he worked himself into position. His training worked well for him. He knew he was perfectly concealed. He had thinned the weeds and grass in front of his position so they looked natural, but still gave him an adequate view of the farmstead.

As he relaxed, he realized he felt safe for the first time since the thin guy had arrived to buy the fertilizer. The air was warm with the sun bright. He was shaded by the new growth of weeds along the fence row, and the earth was cool. After fifteen minutes he rested his forehead on his arm and fell asleep.

Washington, D.C., June 24

After the morning session, Norma returned to her office looking haggard. Seeing this, Donna was apprehensive as she handed an envelope to her. "We found this in the morning fan mail. Another one of those letters. As you asked, we didn't open it."

Norma smiled slightly. "Why not? Today's as good as any other day for that to show up. I doubt it can be anything new. More of the same repent or die stuff. But, thanks for keeping it out of the run of the mill."

In her office, Norma looked at the letter for a couple of minutes as she sipped coffee. Finely she slit it open and read it.

Dear Representative Holleran:

What are you doing? You got me fired from my campaign job, and then you sent an assassin to kill my uncle and me. He used a powerful bow and arrows with heads each having three razor sharp steel blades. That is an insane retaliation for a simple letter. This is out of hand and I want it stopped!

You have been targeted. Is that because you are too blood thirsty for even your liberal friends? Remember hell. I'm trying to save you from eternity.

Sincerely,

Paul Sanders

It took a minute for things to make sense. Was he saying he knew about the attempt on her life at the cabin? It sounded like it. He certainly knew about the bow and arrow shooting. His description of the arrowheads was exactly the same as the FBI agent had used. That left little doubt the incident happened the way Sanders and his uncle had reported it. Somebody had attempted to kill her, and the same with them. From the first, she had found it hard to imagine the story about the bow and arrow shooting being fabricated. It was too absurd. And, the postmark showed the letter had been sent before the news story had appeared.

Leaning back in her chair, she closed her eyes. With relief, she realized how lucky it was they had not reported the attempt on her. With no injuries, no deaths, no evidence as a vehicle license number, the whole thing she and Wally had experienced could be leaked as a made up incident, too. It would look like she was going off the deep end. She could imagine how Sanders must be feeling.

How he could know about what had happened at the cabin was puzzling. She read the letter again. Could that sentence be interpreted to mean she was targeted by the Republicans with an all out effort to unseat her? No. They'd tried that before. Her district was all fruits and nuts. If every conservative turned out and voted twice, she'd still win, hands down. It had to have something to do with the cabin. Someone was out there trying to kill people, and she was one of those on the wrong end. The only odd thing was their lack of success, as if some real bumbling fools had become involved into the assassination game. For a second, no longer than that, the thought crossed her mind that Alvin, her brother, fit that description perfectly.

She let out a long breath. It was time to face something that had been dodging in and out of her mind for days. She had to call Sanders and find out what was going on. That meant a call to Mr. Helpful, Wally. As the phone rang, she was bothered by the way she had come to depend on him in recent weeks. Being dependent was not part . . . .

"Hello."

"Hi. Wally, this is Norma."

"World falling apart again?" It was said with a trace of humor.

"Let's say the cracks are getting a little wider. I received another letter. Same guy. It was postmarked before that ugly story in Minnesota came out. It's worded a little strangely, but he implies he knows about our incident. You want to see it?"

"Of course, I'd like to see it. Is there any reason, though?"

"I'm thinking I should call him if I knew his phone number, and had someplace to call from."

"Ya got an extra fifty bucks? I'll go on line and get the phone number for the address on the last letter. Then I'll buy a non-contract cell phone and meet you. I could pick you up at eight. Eat something so we can go to a park for the call."

"Thanks. That'll be fine. At eight."

The slamming of a car door jolted Dutch awake. A car had stopped ten yards from the house. It was two-ten. The car was a common silver color, not at all government looking. The man from the passenger side was standing beside it with his hand under his sport coat. His head snapped in quick movements taking in the scene. After five minutes, he tapped on the car's roof. The second man emerged. After a hesitation, they began walking to the door, one ten feet behind the other.

Dutch could see by their actions that they really assumed he was the terrorist. If he was, why had he gone to the pains of telling them who he was, where he lived, and what he planned to do? The mindset of those people that the only bad people are white men was astounding. One of them had reached the door and knocked. After several more tires he shouted, "FBI." Well, that's who they said they were. They probably were government from the sleuthy way they behaved. True terrorists would have stormed the house.

Failing at the door, they wandered around the farmyard. He had made sure the doors to the sheds and barn were standing partly open. Covering each other, they made a search of each building. After fifteen minutes they returned to the car and partly sat on the front fender. One said, "We'll give him another twenty minutes," after which they discussed batting averages for the Twins baseball team.

Ten minutes later, Dutch was about to reveal himself, when movement beside one of the sheds caught his eye. Alerted, he scanned the area in his field of view more carefully. Sure enough, he spotted another one. They seemed genetically incapable of following instructions. After the twenty minutes, one of the men by the car yelled, "Okay, guys. He's a no show." Using a hand radio, he made a call. A few minutes later a black Suburban drove into the yard. The sounds of footsteps to his right rear cause him to freeze. A man was walking through the pen. In all, four men emerged, all wearing jackets with large FBI letters on the back.

Counting the driver of the Suburban, seven men had been dispatched to "talk" to him.

Feinstein had Cutter at the doctor's office at nine as directed the day before. With the x-rays, setting the bone and fitting a cast, it was after eleven thirty when they left. They paid in cash as the doctor had expected. His clientele normally did. Cutter had been given a shot of morphine and antibiotics shortly after they arrived. By now, he wasn't feeling any pain. Feinstein stopped for fast food and they set off for Wisconsin. Cutter ate a burger and in fifteen minutes was asleep. His arm had kept him awake all the previous night.

Twenty miles from the farm, Feinstein was shaking his companion. "Come on. Time to earn your keep."

"Yeah, sure. Most have dozed off."

"Whatever. Your turn to drive. We're close enough that I need a driver that looks like he might belong here. If we see anybody, I'll slip down out of sight."

Feinstein pulled to the shoulder and stopped. Cutter unsteadily walked around the vehicle to the driver's side. The morphine was starting to wear off. The arm ached, but not so bad that he couldn't drive. A mile from Dutch's farm, Feinstein unlatched his seat belt and slid down on the floor.

"If it looks clear, drop me off, go down the road a half-mile and turn around. Stop at the same place where I get out."

A half-mile from the farm Cutter said, "There's a black vehicle that appears to be stopped on the road about where I'd be letting you off." He slowed, pulled over to the left lane and passed. A man partly shielded by brush had a black jacket with FBI in big letters on the back. Once past, he speeded up as if this were an everyday occurrence.

"You didn't stop."

"Course not. There was a guy wearing an FBI jacket by the black Suburban."

Two miles past the farm Feinstein pulled himself back into his seat. "From what you saw, we know where we stand. We have to assume the farmer remembered the truck's license plate, and that he is now, either willingly or unwillingly, giving them the plate number, the pop can with my prints on it, and the guns with your prints. He may have even remembered the plate number of this car." They drove in silence for ten minutes.

"We can hope this car is clean because I see no alternative to driving this back to St. Paul. If we make it, we'll have to leave it in the warehouse and get another one. It's a sure bet they took the plate as we drove past them." More silence. "We'll need another truck, one that looks nothing like the one we have. Maybe a big pickup. When we get back to the motel, I'll go on line and see what there is."

"You mind taking a turn at driving? Arm's hurting and I don't want to take a chance on hitting anything. I'll take one of those pills the doc gave me."

———————————

Dutch gave them two and a half hours to return to their lair and then called the Minneapolis office of the FBI.

"Who's calling?"

He knew they had caller ID but said, "Dutch Tuley."

"What is the purpose of your call?"

"Mention truck bomb. That'll get their attention."

Five seconds later a man's voice came on the line, none to pleasantly. "This Tuley?"

"Yeah. Who's this?"

"Nicholas Calloway, director of the FBI for Minnesota and Wisconsin. I sent a couple of guys all the way out there to talk to you and you took it into your head not to be home."

"Listen up, Nick! First of all, I am not the enemy! And, you just lied to me. You didn't send two men, you sent seven. You couldn't care less how many people get killed, do you? All you want is to drag a white guy into jail with a hundred reporters watching and cameras flashing. I have fingerprints of two of the guys. Fingerprints, I might add, that you would now have in your possession if you weren't such an ass."

"Okay. Calm down. I wasn't the one who ordered the truck full of backup. Can I send someone back out now to get the evidence?"

"No. Be here at eight tomorrow morning. Send the two guys who were discussing Twins batting averages. I had a lot of time to observe them so I'll know who they are. Tell them to park in exactly the same place. Can you do that?"

"You were there listening to them the whole time and didn't show yourself? We're losing time!"

"Tell that to the stupid fool what ordered the assault on me. Don't forget, you didn't see me today, and you won't see me tomorrow. If I see anybody prowling about my place, I'll shoot first, ask later. I'm scared to death. If the terrorists come back, I'm dead. That means you'll never find the evidence I have." After a pause, "You would have arrested me, wouldn't you?"

"Those were my orders."

"You guys are so dumb. If you had me in jail, and your town blew up, how could I have done it? I repeat, I am not the enemy. You are looking for somebody else, and the leader of the bad guys is not white! And, don't go brain dead on me and think that necessarily means he's black. Get that through you thick skulls. Eight o'clock tomorrow. Two guys!" Dutch hung up.

— 22 —

Thursday afternoon, June 24

At one-thirty, Alvin began his second operation against Vincent Wessen. He carried a black computer bag out of the house with him. In it was the gun supplied by Marv. The first thing he had to do was go to the place where his wife worked. They lived in the southwest part of Minneapolis, west of the lakes. She worked in St. Louis Park doing something or other in a real-estate office. It was entirely an inside position so he knew she would not be out on calls. He also knew she parked in a lot that could not be seen by anyone in her office.

Arriving at the parking lot, he spotted her minivan and parked a couple of rows away. The back of the building had no windows, which was okay with him. He drove the vehicle away, and headed toward Minnetonka on I-394 west. During the previous week he had learned Wessen worked in the northern part of Minnetonka. His route home took him to the freeway entrance to 394 eastbound toward downtown Minneapolis where he probably made the connection to I-94 headed north or through the Lowry Tunnel to connect to 35W. That wasn't important, as long as he could pick him up getting onto 394. As the time approached he entered the on-ramp, pulled to the side and waited.

Alvin hadn't had a chance to put the tracker on Wessen's car. If he went a different route today, he'd miss him. In that case, he'd put the tracker on tonight.

Vincent was keeping his eye on the small clock on his desk as it approached three o'clock. This, he always did because if he left work even fifteen minutes after three, it could take him an extra thirty minutes to get home. Rush hour ramped up at a startling rate in those few minutes.

Three was the earliest he was allowed to leave. It didn't bother him that he left that early because he was at work well before the start time required by that departure schedule. Working for a company that had flex-time was a blessing to him. Being an early riser was not in his genes like some people but forced upon him by the commute. Living in Arden Hills and working in Minnetonka meant he had a twenty-mile drive that nearly crossed the center of Minneapolis. The good thing was that there were a dozen routes from which he could choose, all within a mile or two of the same distance.

Leaving the AB Equipment Company office building, he was struck by the intense heat for this early in the year. This was August weather. It was forecast to hit a hundred today. He waved at the other half dozen employees who shared his dislike for inching along in traffic. At times, they'd laugh about the spectacle of some hapless person being trampled as they single mindedly made their way out of the employee entrance to their cars. They came in together and left together with each having what amounted to an assigned parking place since they all arrived at such predictable times.

Out of the parking lot, Vincent decided to go the I-394 route again today. He rarely used that freeway coming in to work, but the last few weeks it had proven to be a good bet for going home in light of summer road construction on most of his other routes. He'd get on 394 by the Ridgedale Shopping Center, take it into the city going against the heavy traffic. There he'd make the connection to I-94 in a spaghetti junction near downtown. Where I-94 intersected I-694 he'd go east, again, against the heavy traffic, and be home in twenty-five minutes without a single stoplight after getting on 394.

Being a Thursday in June, the traffic on I-394 was moderately heavy. However, Vincent expected no problems as long as some klutz didn't cause an accident. What he did not notice was a maroon minivan following him on to the freeway as he passed the metering light now blinking yellow. Here the freeway was three lanes with the left most lane being the "diamond lane." That was the car pool lane for vehicles with two or more occupants, enforced only in the morning. In the evening heading into the city, it was open for anybody to use. He shifted to the center lane.

After several miles, the three lanes necked down to two lanes where the diamond lane ended on the left at a liftable barricade. Here the diamond lane became two lanes that were pay-for-use lanes in the morning.

That meant they were open to traffic headed into the city in the morning and visa versa in the afternoon but users had to have a remotely read device in their car to pay for the use. Car pools were free. It was frequently a little nerve racking as one approached this neck down because cars would race up the diamond lane trying to pass as many vehicles as possible before the merge to the right. This caused the cars in the center lane to hit the brakes to avoid an accident.

Vincent was what one might call a moderately aggressive driver so at times he duked it out with a would-be merging driver. Today he saw a minivan coming up fast in the diamond lane at well over the speed limit. Vincent pressed down on the accelerator a little, though he was already five miles over the speed limit. It became clear that he would not have had to speed up to prevent a conflict. The maroon vehicle would never have been able to pass him in any case. At the last second, the minivan was forced to brake hard and pull in behind Vincent. Immediately Vincent switched a lane to the right so the guy who was in such a hurry could get past him. There was no point in irritating him. But, the minivan did not accelerate as he had expected. Well, who knew what was going on in that driver's head? Maybe he was on his cell phone and was ignorant of the merge as he came to it.

Concentrating on the other traffic, he noticed that in an effort to get past some merging traffic on the right he was going over sixty-five. Police constantly patrolled this stretch of road so he immediately stabbed his foot on the brake.

Vincent had forgotten about the minivan until he saw the hood on his left out of the corner of his eye. The vehicle was heaving up and down in a short stretch of road where Vincent knew the pavement had been uneven since the freeway was built. At that instant, he heard two bangs in rapid succession as something hit his left knee. At first, he thought he had a blowout or his tire had kicked up some debris on the road causing it to impact the underside of his car. Concentrating on the operation of his car to determine if there were any damage, he hardly noticed the maroon minivan accelerating past him, though he later recalled that it had the passenger's side window open.

With his car handling normally, the first thing to enter Vincent's mind was that the minivan driver had completed his phone call and was making up for lost time. His attention was drawn to a warm draft on his midsection. He glanced down to see a hole in the door just above the armrest. It wasn't registering yet. The minivan now changed lanes and was directly in front of him. Without knowing why, he glanced to the right and there was a hole in that door too. Now it connected. Someone from the maroon minivan had shot at him. He also saw the broken glass where one bullet had passed through the windows. He slowed down to fifty-five. The van pulled to the left lane, then started falling back to compensate for Vin's slower speed. He's staying with me, Vincent thought. He sees he failed and will try again. Vin instinctively pulled to the left to stay behind the van.

Due to the freeway tangle as I-394 terminated at the downtown area the far right lane exited, the next one curved right into the Lowry Tunnel, the next lane to the left curved down and under to emerge onto I-94 going north. The far left lane exited to downtown streets. His nemesis switched a lane to the right. Vincent stayed behind him. They were nearing the Lowry Tunnel exit. There were a couple of hundred yards where the lane headed to the tunnel and the one on its left ran parallel with a solid "do not cross" white line between them. Vincent saw an opening, instinctively put on his right turn signal, and started to cross the solid white for the tunnel. He didn't want to go that route, but anything would do to get away from that nutcase. At the last minute the minivan driver saw his intention and did the same. Vincent pulled back to the left and with that his assailant was headed for the tunnel and he was on his way to 94 north.

As Vincent merged into traffic on I-94, his breathing started to return to normal. What was that all about? Could that driver have been so upset about the merge at the neck down that he actually took a couple of shots at him? But, it wasn't even close to being a conflict. He had heard of freeway shootings. Wow! That was intense. As he replayed the incident in his mind, he could see the vehicle bouncing up and down at the time of the shot. The driver had not anticipated the uneven roadway or Vincent would likely be dead. It also explained why he pulled ahead of him because if he had shot accurately, there would have been a massive car pile up. The way he attempted to stay with him into the tunnel meant he intended to try again.

Glancing at the hole in his door, he saw that the bullet penetrated just high enough to pass over his thighs and grazed the center armrest. By chance, his hands were on the upper part of the steering wheel at the time of the shot or he might have lost both elbows. A second shot had hit the window immediately behind his head and continued on out the other side. The holes appeared positively huge.

Vincent's mind was hopping about. Three lucky breaks in close succession, the uneven road, his hands high up on the wheel, and their separation at the tunnel, what were the chances? The bad news was he could remember almost nothing about the other vehicle. He hadn't had the presence of mind to look at the plate number. No bumper stickers, dents, or anything unusual registered. It was a dark red or maroon minivan. He decided that after he arrived home and had a chance to settle down, he'd go on line and look at minivans in the hopes he would find some make he'd recognize.

After a period of driving in which he watched every other car like a hawk, especially those behind him, he was stopped with a closed garage door in front of him. He punched the button on the remote clipped to the sun visor and the door opened. Inside, with the door closed, he got out and inspected the car. Two bullets, and the slugs had passed out of the right side of the car, so no ballistic check was possible. The two lanes on his right must have been free of cars at the time of the shooting.

It wouldn't leave him. That neck-down on the freeway wasn't even close. Did he really expect me to slam on my brakes and risk an accident just so he could be one car further down the road? That was insane. Welcome to the valley of the insane. But, what possible other motive? Could someone at work be willing to go to this extreme to speed along his retirement that was still several years in the future?

It was over a hundred degrees in the garage and sweat ran down his face. In the house he started the air conditioner and took a drink of water. Vincent's wife wouldn't be home for another hour, so, as was his routine, he changed and started exercising with his weights followed by a run on the treadmill. After his shower, he paced the living room as he considered calling the police. There was no question he had to do that. Or, did he? The bow and arrow shooting suddenly came to mind. All this time he had blocked that out. This was the second attempt on his life in a couple of weeks! The circumstances could not have been more different, with the exception that both times he had not been hit.

No. It was not possible that the shooting today was meant only to frighten him. Either shot could easily have killed him. If he called the police, they'd ask the same thing the cop in Lino Lakes did, do you have any enemies?

Oh! He stopped and slapped his head. Only the evening before that FBI agent had been around accusing him of fabricating the bow and arrow shooting. Once again, no injuries, no witnesses. And, here there wasn't even any evidence. They'd accuse him of putting a heavy chunk of wood on the far side of the car to absorb the slugs and shooting the holes in it himself.

He returned to the basic problem. This was a serious matter, a homicide not quite realized, in fact two. With no injuries or deaths, no license number, there'd be no interest. The only possibilities he could come up with were either this was a case of mistaken identity, or it was someone he had encountered in the past who took offense to something he said or did. Now, mentally unbalanced, this person blamed him for all his woes in life. That didn't fit. Who drives a conservative fairly new minivan and is at the same time homicidal. It couldn't be for Vin's money. He didn't have any to speak of. Though he loved his wife dearly, one woman was all he could even imagine having in his life. It wasn't some sort of love feud.

As for someone at work, that was really the Twilight Zone. There was not a single one of his colleagues he could call a friend, and in fact, most of them didn't like him. He had always suspected it was because most of them were a little dim-witted and not a little lazy. Since he worked as hard as he humanly could to do the best possible job, it left many of them harboring resentments toward him. It also left virtually no time for gossiping around the water cooler so they probably saw him as aloof, making him the subject of their nattering. He had even discovered that in the present laid back, indolent American society there was an epithet for people like him. He was an over-achiever, truly disgusting, you see. Why can't he take life a little easier, chill-out? There were, of course, as in any random collection of people, a few others like himself who truly applied themselves and kept the company afloat.

This wasn't helping. He began pondering the altercation again. By the time the driver realized Vin wasn't going to die and cause an accident he tried to fall back for another try. If it hadn't been for that quirk of fate that neither of them saw coming where the two lanes split, he would have gotten his second try. Vin signaled to switch lanes, the van switched lanes accordingly, and then Vin didn't do as he had indicated. That simple, life and death. However, if he were ready for a second try on the freeway, what would stop him from another try someplace else?

The sound of the back door opening meant Camilla was home, unless his attacker was stalking him into his own home and had taken the trouble to get a key for the back door. She dropped her handbag on the chest in the living room and said, "What happened to your car? The hole on the passenger side door and the windows?"

He parked on the left in the garage and she on the right and of course, the splayed out sheet metal would be noticeable, as was the splintered glass. "Oh, nothing really. Just the exit wounds for the bullets that went through the car. You might as well sit down and I'll tell you about it."

She listened attentively for as long as it took to tell what there was to say. "Have you called the police?"

"Not yet. I'm still thinking about it."

"Well, if you don't, I will. This guy has to be found. That madman could be out there right now waiting for dark and then breaking into the house and kill us both."

"Let's think about it for a little before we do anything rash. If he intended to break in and kill us both, why did he try for only me on the freeway today? I see now that he was after me with the bow and arrow, not Paul. In addition, if he were going to kill us in the house he would have done that first rather than after he put us on our guard. No matter what, we'll be sleeping with loaded guns at hand tonight. I don't think we have any worry on that score, though."

"But, the police. We have to call them."

"Think about it. If I had the license number, they'd have the owner's name in a blink. Then we might get someplace. But, I have nothing. Don't forget the FBI agent last night. He was already accusing me of faking the first shooting." He paused thinking. Then asked, "Do you plan to use your car tomorrow?"

"Tomorrow's not my day to go in. Paul would normally use it, but he can take the bus again."

"I'll have take your car to work. I can't drive mine the way it is. Look how quickly you saw it. If anyone asks I'll say mine needs some work on the brakes. Remember last winter I had that antilock brake sensor go bad? I can say that's what happened with all the details anyone cares to listen to. Most of those guys at work don't do their own repairs so there'll be little interest. I'll buy some body putty and paint and fix up the outside of the car over the weekend. You can call around and find where I can get replacement windows."

"I don't like it. Shouldn't you be staying home?"

"I don't like it, either. The alternative is to cower in the basement for the rest of my life. It seems to me that the best thing is to play dumb. Make him think he missed completely. Now that I think about it, the windows in the maroon minivan were heavily tinted, and the one on the front passenger's side was all the way down. I think I would have seen a person in the passenger's seat if there were one. That means, the guy had to drive and shoot. His car was bobbing up and down due to the uneven road which required more than the normal attention to driving, so he could think the shots went in front of the windshield and hit nothing. I hit my brakes a little at about that time since I saw I was doing sixty-five in a fifty-five zone."

After supper, Camilla insisted Vin call the police. Then they wrangled about who to call. They could call the state highway patrol because it happened on a state highway. Or, they could call the Minneapolis police because it happened in Minneapolis. Or, they could call the Arden Hills police because that's where they lived. It seemed to him Minneapolis was the place because it happened in that jurisdiction. After the call, he put the phone down in disbelief. Wow! That was a non-starter. "What, no bodies, not even blood? Half the cars in North Minneapolis have bullet holes in them. Get real. Go on line and download the 'shooting incident' form and fill it out."

When he had the form on his computer, he realized how little information he actually had. He entered what there was so it would be on file. He printed a copy of the form for himself. It had a computer generated case number so he had something to reference in the future.

— 23 —

Washington, D.C. 8:30 p.m., June 24

From the parking lot at the park Wally Stern had chosen, they had a view of the sunset. The disk of the sun was not evident having succumbed to the haze in the northwest.

"Are phone numbers listed on the Internet?" Norma asked.

"The normal white pages are. To use that you need the full name of the person subscribing to the phone. I had to pay to match a number to an address. It's not so much, so don't worry about it. Here's the phone, and on this sticky note is the number. You're armed and dangerous. Your show."

"I've been thinking all afternoon about what I'll say. It seems silly, really."

Arden Hills, Minnesota

"Paul! Phone call." Camilla's voice was a little shrill. Things were tense as they discussed what had happened to Vin on the freeway. The phone ringing added to the irritation.

Paul had an extension in his bedroom. There was a small desk and a table with a computer. The silicone chips in the computer were a few generations old, but it worked well enough for what he needed. He had been told briefly about what had happened to Vincent.

"Hello."

"Is this Paul Sanders?"

"Yes. Who's this?"

There was a pause. "When I tell you who I am you might not at first believe me. But, I think I can convince you who I am." There was hesitation in the woman's voice.

"Well, okay then, tell me who you are."

"I am Norma Holleran, the Speaker of the House of Representatives in Washington."

"This is some kind of joke, right? Someone from the campaign office."

"No. It is not a joke. In fact, it is very serious. You wrote me two letters. The first I received sixteen days ago. I turned over a copy of that one to the FBI so there are many people who've seen it. The second one I received today. I had that one handed to me by a staff member unopened so no one has seen it except you and me. Let me read it to you."

After having read the letter, she said, "Is there anyone else who knew about the letter that could be making this call?"

"How'd you know where to call me? My phone number wasn't in the letter. I still think this is a gag."

"Is there anyone else who could have read this letter to you? It's not as if someone could have hacked into you're computer and stolen it because it's hand written."

"You could be someone from Holleran's office whose job it is to randomly call people who disagree with her to make threats to silence opposition to abortion. How do I know you're not somebody like that?"

"Let's take it a step further. You've been praying for me, haven't you?"

There was a long pause. "Well? Nothing to say? You prayed that I'd say something that you would call pro-life. Isn't that true? Moreover, you remember the sensation in the press when I made that remark at the college on the evening of June first. That was the exact time you prayed for me, wasn't it? You sound like a smart guy. You put it together, didn't you? And, you did it two more times, too. Nobody else knows about the other two times. Tell me I'm wrong."

There was another pause. Finally, Paul said, "So, if you believe all of that, why are you calling me? If you are such a firm believer in prayer, it doesn't make sense that you would hold the views you do. This conversation is making no sense at all."

"But, you do not deny that you prayed two more times for the same reason."

"I'm not going to continue with any more of this."

"Please, don't hang up yet. I have something more to say. Okay?

"So, say it."

"What if, just what if, because of that statement I made at the college, someone tried to kill me. That's just 'what if' remember. If they had succeeded, you would have been a party to murder. Let me ask you this, in your value system does the end justify the means?"

"No, it never does."

"Good. We agree that for you the end does not justify the means."

"But, that's true for everyone."

"You may choose to believe that, but a lot of other people don't. This now gets really nasty. You see, I know what you believe. If you truly believe it, then I am using your beliefs, beliefs that I do not hold, against you. For me the end *does* justify the means. Therefore, you must stop doing what you are doing or the next time the supposed attack on my life, just supposed, mind you, might succeed, and you will have directly caused a murder. For you that would be a mortal sin, so stop it!"

"Your belief system is a mess. That's not the way prayer works. If my prayer was effective for you, and it seems it was, my prayer was what prevented you from being murdered. If you had been murdered, though, it would have been your evil beliefs and actions that caused it. You decided to run with that ugly crowd, so don't dump on me."

"We'll leave that subject. I have a very important question to ask you. Are you still there?"

"Go ahead and ask."

"You say in the second letter that I have been targeted. What did you mean by that?"

That was something Paul had picked up at the campaign office. He believed it because other rumors had turned out to be true more often than not. Now he didn't know what to say. In addition, through the whole call, Paul felt something ominous, like evil spirits skulking about his room. After a few seconds, he replied, "This call has gone on too long. If you want an answer to that, come to town and meet with me. I don't understand it, but something's wrong."

"All right. I'll call you in the morning to set it up. Do we have an understanding?"

"I'm going to end this call." Paul placed the phone in its cradle.

Paul sat only a minute after which he opened his door. He didn't want to be alone. Camilla and Vin were still discussing what to do about the freeway shooting when Paul sulked into the room, his hands thrust in his pockets and plopped on the sofa.

They both looked at him but it was Camilla who spoke. "What's the matter with you? Was it something about that phone call?'

He nodded. "Yeah. It was the call. Guess who it was?"

They both looked at him because they could see he wanted to tell them.

"It was the Speaker of the House of Representatives in Washington."

"It was a prank," Vin said. "It had to be."

"I don't know," Paul replied shaking his head. "You see, I mailed her another letter on Monday. I suppose quite a few people have seen the first one by now. But, she said the second one had been delivered to her unopened today. Whoever it was had the letter. Why wouldn't it be her?"

"I don't know. What did you say in the letter?"

"Told her we were almost killed by this guy with a bow and arrow and that this was getting out of hand. Why is a stupid letter causing so many problems? When I sent it, this thing hadn't hit the news yet."

Camilla leaned forward as she spoke. "It's odd, I'll say that. Don't worry, though. I'd recommend you don't send any more letters. That should end it."

"I don't know. She wanted to go on about some more stuff. I was getting a funny feeling, like my skin was crawling, so I said if she wanted to discuss it further to come to town so we could meet. I don't know why I said that, but she agreed. I almost dropped over. She'll call me in the morning and set it up."

There were deep breaths all around. Vin spoke, "She's from the San Francisco area, so if she were headed home this weekend, it wouldn't be hard to make a stop for an hour or so in the Twin Cities. She has an Air Force jet all to herself."

Vin's problem was forgotten for the moment. "Can you tell us why she would want to stop here and meet with you?"

Paul wouldn't look at either one of them. "It's one of those things that could be random chance, or caused. I don't know which, but the odds are it wasn't random. I think it's possible she's having sort of a spiritual crisis. It might even be that she's having a change of heart on all of those liberal issues, especially abortion."

"There's more to it than that," Camilla interrupted. "You'd better tell us about it."

Paul told the whole story including the fact that Holleran had figured it out that he was the one who had prayed for her. Neither one had anything to say. It was too crazy to be made up.

"How about the meeting? From what you said, I'm pretty sure she'll be here to see you. There's an Air Force Reserve station at the airport. It's a fair guess that's where she'll bring her plane. I'd say meet her outside away from buildings."

Vin went to a kitchen cupboard for a metro street map. They gathered around the kitchen table. "Minnehaha Falls Park is only a few miles from the airport. How about meeting there? We'll both drive down. Tell her to take a taxi to the park. There won't be many people arriving that way. We can drop her off at the airport afterwards." He looked at Camilla. "You want to come?"

"I'd rather stay home so if the meeting goes wrong I'll be here to do something. It all seems totally surreal."

Central Wisconsin, Friday, June 25

The dew was heavy with no wind, the sky clear. Dutch, wearing his deer hunting cammies, had been in the woods behind his house since dawn. He thought about how good it would be to get his life back to normal, if that were possible. It had been almost completely dark when he had taken up his position in the bushes. Three hours of waiting had left him edgy. It wasn't that his vigil was entirely unpleasant. As the morning arrived, a couple of gray squirrels made him the center of attraction for several minutes until they came to the conclusion he wasn't dangerous and went about their business. Three ruffed grouse on the wing sped past weaving among the branches, an aeronautical feat unimaginable even with the application of modern technology.

It was nearly eight when he heard tires on the gravel driveway. That would be the FBI boys if they had learned enough to follow instructions.

Dutch slipped along a row of long untrimmed lilac bushes on the south side of the house. The car was the same, and it was parked in the same place. Two doors opened, two men emerged. They were the same two from the day before. They looked around and then leaned against the front fender, backs to him. He watched them for several minutes. From thirty yards away he said, "You can walk this way."

The sound of his voice caused them to jerk slightly, their heads swiveling around. Their hands instinctively went under their light coats.

"No. Hands empty and in full view. Come now, make it quick."

In seconds, Dutch had them behind the house and examined their credentials. "Tom Holden, and Gerald Ranklen. Fine, Tom and Gerry. Suppose I'm not the first one to make that observation. Wouldn't surprise me if your bosses were Dick and Jane. Okay. I'll assume for the present that you two are really from the FBI, not that it means I'm not in the presence of enemies. That was a nasty trick coming out here yesterday to arrest me. On what grounds? A phone call from someone who'd never seen me?"

He saw only blank faces. Being careful to remain beyond arm's length from them, and with his rifle pointed in their general direction he said, "Don't wonder that you don't answer."

Pointing at a shovel leaning against the back of the house he said, "You, Tom, take that shovel and we'll find the evidence."

As they walked the hundred yards into the woods Dutch told them his alibi for when the white truck had been rented. They listened without comment. Arriving at his destination he kicked back some leaves and pointed. "Start digging there. Be careful because this one is in a glass mayonnaise jar. You don't want to break it."

After a few shovels of dirt, he told him to get on his knees and scoop the rest of the dirt out by hand. In a minute, he had the jar. "That Pepsi can has the prints of the small guy. Now, that way," he indicated with the barrel of his gun.

With more digging, they retrieved a nine-millimeter pistol in a zip top plastic bag. "That piece of evidence was donated by the henchman who now has a broken right forearm. Nice clean break so it should heal well assuming he availed himself of medical care. Wouldn't surprise me if he didn't. He might not want to show his Blue Cross Insurance card. People might start asking questions."

Gerry looked him in the eye, "You have a mean streak in you, don't you?"

"Actually no. Trying to stay a live is all. I hate to be used. The bad guys used me, then the FBI tried to use me. It would be nice to find someone who actually wanted to solve this."

"If you were in our custody, we could protect you. Seeing as that's not likely, what are you planning to do?"

"First, finish my cultivating before the weeds destroy my crop. I haven't thought much past that."

They didn't talk as they made their way to the car, there being nothing more to say. Gerry opened the driver's side door as Dutch said, "Drive carefully, and don't come back. The gun will be loaded at all times."

The yellow dust wafted off the driveway. That was done. Dutch was tired, but decided to do as he had said, finish the cultivating. Even if they did shoot him, he didn't want to see the field of corn go to waste. He was that kind of guy. Maybe through the hours of sitting on the tractor he'd think of something.

Arden Hills, Minnesota

The phone rang at a quarter to seven. Camilla answered it. It was for Paul. He took it in his bedroom.

"Hello."

"Is this Paul?"

"Yes."

"This is Norma Holleran. I'm serious, I will meet with you. Will you agree to that?"

"My uncle thought you were serious even if I didn't. I'm not going to buy a plane ticket and come to Washington."

"That won't be necessary. I plan to go home to my district this evening, and could divert a little and stop in Minneapolis. I do that sometimes."

"You do? What do you care about this place?"

"I'm from there, and some of my family is still there. When I land the plane goes to the Air Force Reserve terminal at the main airport."

"That's what uncle Vin said you'd do. So, since you are following his plan anyway, you might as well continue. Take a taxi to the Minnehaha Falls Park. It isn't far. Ask to be let off in the parking lot near the falls. We'll be there. Afterwards, we'll drive you back."

"Your uncle is good at figuring things out. All right, we have some things to discuss. Expect me between seven-thirty and eight. Eternity will be on the list."

— 24 —

It was Friday afternoon and Vincent Wessen was coming back from the shop when he chanced to see his boss, the vice-president of engineering, approaching him. As they met the other man said, "Vin, what's going on? A just talked to a guy from the FBI. Asked a lot of questions about you."

"Did you get his name?"

"Yeah. Clement or something like that."

"Is he still here?"

"Might be. He asked for the names of a couple of people that worked with you so he could interview them. What could I do? I gave him what he wanted."

Vincent thanked him and continued walking. He was sure Clements would be talking to a couple of guys in his group who worked on the same machinery as he did. He slowed as he approached his cubicle. The walls of the cubes were four and a half feet high. It was supposed to give the area an open feeling. He always hated the low walls because it made sure none of the sounds around him were attenuated. For the first time, he was grateful for them. There was Fred Clements in his cubicle and he appeared to be going through Vin's desk. The dirty piece of crap, Vin thought. He held back, though, stopping by a copy machine slowly making a few unnecessary copies as he kept an eye on the man.

After five minutes, Clements finished with his poking around and walked to the main aisle where Vincent appeared intent on collating copies making sure his back was to him and his head lowered. Clements passed taking no notice of him. After he passed, Vin followed. Beside the door of a meeting room, Vincent grabbed Clements' ear with his right hand. The head followed the ear and clunked against the door. At the same time, Vin placed his right foot beside Clements' causing him to lose his balance. There was no latch on the door so they fell into the room. The end of the heavy meeting table was only a few feet beyond the door, a little to the right. Vincent was well aware of this since the table was a little too long for the room, and the room a bit too wide for the table. This was commented on in almost every meeting held there.

Vincent pulled Clements past him being sure he could not regain his footing. Immediately Vin brought his left hand over and pressed it against the back of Clements' head. With the weight of both men now falling forward into the room, Vincent directed Clements' head so it connected with the two-inch thick edge of the table, crushing his nose.

It happened that a woman in a blue pants suit was sitting at the end of the table a short distance to the right of the door working at a laptop computer. She raised her hands instinctively to ward off the onslaught as she cried out. Vincent stopped his forward motion by placing his hand on the edge of the table. Clements rolled to the floor to the left reaching for his gun in his shoulder holster as he did. Vincent, seeing what was coming, grabbed the left arm of the woman and bodily threw her on Clements. Instantly Vincent launched himself onto the smooth tabletop, sliding past Clements so as to be beyond his head. He flipped himself off the table over the low backed chairs and landed on his hands and knees facing the top of Clements' head.

The woman clawed at Clements' face as he tried to extract himself from the banshee. Thankfully, from Vincent's point of view, the door had a closer so it swung shut of it's own accord. That muffled the woman's squeaks and grunts from those outside the room.

Clements had seen Vincent slide off the table and was bringing his gun over his head to get a shot at him. Vincent saw the move coming and grabbed the gun barrel, now at an awkward angle for Clements, making his grip on it less firm. With the gun in his possession, Vincent brought it down to smash it into the forehead of Clements. At the moment of impact, Clements shifted his head and the butt of the gun landed in the left eye. The second attempt delivered a solid blow to the forehead. Clements went limp.

The woman struggled up, and Vincent looked into flaming eyes. She was about to let go a tirade when Vincent grabbed her hair and slapped her supporting arm away. She landed on top of Clements' unmoving body. Using the hair, he slowly turned her head so she could see him.

"Sorry about the fuss, lady. But, this is serious."

She struggled, but was held firm. "You will pay for this you monster. I had the use of this room for the rest of the afternoon, and no one was to disturb me! What do you think you're doing! You can't throw people around like they were your property."

"Sorry again, but something unexpected came up." He pulled harder on the hair squeezing it together in the back so her eyes became slanted. "Listen to me carefully. If I release you and you run out of here screaming and hollering, call the police, and things like that, you–will–be–dead –today! If his man doesn't do it, his buddies will! Take your over-fed feminist push-men-around chromosomes and park them. Don't fight this. You can't win. Now, did you understand what I said?"

The woman was conflicted, Vincent could tell that. She wanted to even the score so badly she ached inside. Yet, the intensity of the man's voice was hard to resist.

"Did you understand?"

Hesitantly, she replied, "Yes."

"Good. I will release you and you can get up. Leave the room. In a half-hour you can come back. Did you get that?"

She nodded. Vincent slowly released his grip on her hair. She stood up, straighten her clothing, and was about to leave the room when Vincent said, "Please, slide that bottle of water beside your computer over to me, will you?"

To his surprise, she did it and didn't sneer at him. The door closed, of itself, behind her.

Clements groaned. Vincent knew he was in deep trouble. What could he do? He looked at the gun in his right hand, a nine-millimeter something or other. He'd have to give it back to the guy, but when he did he'd be shot, no doubt about that. It had all happened so fast. Worst of all, at any moment someone could look into the room. He had to disable the gun. It occurred to him to remove all the bullets, but the guy probably had more clips in his car and would be back to even the score. In horror, the thought he had been blocking made its way into his consciousness. He knew what to do, though it would be dangerous. He proceeded to pull the slide back and ejected a round. He placed it on the tabletop, slug up, and pressed the barrel over the lead as far as it would go, then tapped it lightly in as far as it would go. After that, he took the gun in both hands and laid the brass cartridge against the edge of the tabletop and pressed down. The brass casing fell off spilling the gunpowder on the carpet. He put he empty casing in his pocket. Now, he pounded the end of the gun on the bottom side of the tabletop until the slug was driven in flush with the end of the barrel.

This meant Clements had no weapon, and neither did he. Looking around, Vincent saw what was left of a fruit plate that remained from a luncheon meeting. It had a foot long two-pronged fork laying on it used to serve the fruit pieces. He grabbed it.

Okay, now to the bag of dirt on the floor. The guy had shown he was quick and in terrific physical shape. Better not to take and chances. He reached over and undid the man's belt, pulled it out, and put it around his wrists as tightly as he could pull it. He then wrapped the lose end around to knot it.

Time for the main event. Vincent poured water on his face and slapped his cheek. The man opened his remaining good eye. The blood from his battered nose had mostly clotted as he breathed through his mouth. "You awake?"

There was deep malice in the eye as he made a quick move to bring his legs up and put a lock around Vincent's neck. Vin jabbed the fork into Clements' groin. The motion of the legs continued from the momentum for a few inches, and then reversed. The legs fell heavily on the floor. Clements had labored breathing.

"Settle down Slick," Vincent said. "It'll only get worse."

He tugged at his hands and realized they were bound. "You'll pay for this!"

"I've been paying. Right now, I want to know what's going on. Twice in the last couple of weeks, someone has tried to kill me, and only by a freak chance, he failed. He won't fail the third time. I'm so far out on borrowed time that anything you could do to me would only come after I'm dead. And, you happen to the personage that connects it, so talk to me!"

"Twice? I only know about the guy with the bow and arrow."

"Well, you people should get together. Yesterday, someone drove past me on the freeway and blew a few holes in my car missing me by a fraction."

"I never heard about that."

"You mean, all the harassment was only over the one time? Coming to my house and terrorizing me, and then coming here to get me fired like you did Paul, and to top it off, snooping in my desk. You are really low, you puke. I have a mind to stab out your other eye." He was holding the fork above the eye.

"Hold on. Nothing rash."

"I want you to take a message. At the rate things are going, I'll be dead in a day or two. I will do anything and everything I can to prevent that. That means, Slick, I will kill on sight. Got that? Anybody even comes close to me, he's dead. Got it! You seem to be the only common thread. It started by you getting Paul Sanders fired from the campaign. It's been nothing but hell ever since. I want it stopped! And, if I ever see you or even think you've been around, I will get you. Is that quite clear?"

Clements had much the same expression as the woman of a few minutes before. He wanted a piece of Vincent so bad he could taste it. Yet, there was caution in the face, too.

Vincent twisted Clements' already sore right ear. "Is that clear?"

He tried to nod.

"Say it!"

"Yes."

"Good. Don't even think about forgetting. You still have all your body parts, more or less. If we ever meet again, that will no longer be true."

Vin reached over to a tray on the table and took a small pile of paper napkins. "Now, we are going to walk out together and go to your car. I will unbind your hands. You take some napkins and put them on your nose. Nasty nosebleed you have there. I will have your gun in your back. Remember, I have nothing to lose, and someone who has nothing to lose is dangerous and reckless. You comprehend that?"

"Yes."

"Good. Up you get, now!"

Vincent stood back as Clements struggled to get up. He leaned heavily against the table, then shuffled slowly toward the door. Vincent was behind him with the gun, jabbing him in the back with it at random times. Clements was unaware of the slug in the end of the barrel. They turned to the right and made it the twenty feet to the employee entrance. In a few minutes, they were at the visitor parking lot.

Vincent had the keys and pushed the lock button on the fob and noted the car that clicked as the doors unlocked. He opened the driver's side door and let Clements get in. He waited until he had his seat belt on.

"Okay. Here are the keys, and here's the gun. Notice I rammed something into the barrel. If you shoot it, it'll blow up in your face. Don't forget, take a message!"

"You bastard!"

"Get the hell out of my sight."

Vincent walked to the front of the car stepping up on a two-foot retaining wall so Clements couldn't back over him. Clements saw the evasive action and glared. He backed out and drove away.

Vincent was immediately back in action. He went to his desk and pulled open the bottom drawer. He kept a handful of clean shop rags there in case he discovered grease on his hands when he returned from the shop. Immediately he went to the conference room. Using the remainder of the water in the bottle he wiped a few smears of blood off the table and then attacked the carpet. It helped it was a reddish brown. With things cleaned up, he straighten the chairs and glanced around the room. He went to the water cooler and refilled the bottle to the level it had been when the woman gave it to him. Back in the room he straightened out the woman's effects as best he could remember them. He opened the door a crack, and seeing no one was taking an interest, proceeded to the shop where he disposed of the rags.

Upon his return, he had to walk past the conference room. The woman was at that time returning. She looked at him and asked, "Well, have you finished with your meeting?" It wasn't really a question, more of a sneer.

"Meeting?" he responded.

"Yeah. The one with the guy on the floor in there."

"I'm sorry. You must be mistaken. I haven't been in that room today."

She snorted and opened the door expecting to see a debris field left by demonic mayhem. To her surprise, there was not the slightest thing out of place. She turned to see the man walking away. It didn't seem possible.

Clements drove to the emergency entrance of the hospital a few miles away. It was faster than calling 911, and he didn't want to have a ruckus near the company where that man worked. He had met his match, and then some. Two hours later his supervisor had been to the hospital, debriefed him and was back in his office. He was on the phone with someone in the D.C. office.

"I'm sending you something over night. It's too late to use UPS Red, or anything like that, but you'll have it in the morning, I'll see to that. As soon as I get it into the computer, I'll send the report of my debrief of Clements to you."

"What are you sending?"

"I don't want to prejudice you, so take a good look at it, solicit any other input you think you need, and get back to me as fast as you can. That's all I'll say for now. I have a funny feeling about this."

It was only a half-hour to quitting time when Vincent had returned to his desk. At first he felt a sense of elation, though that soon faded. He hadn't accomplished anything the rest of the day. Now, he was in the basement where he built model airplanes talking to Paul. For the time being, he didn't want to dump the events of the day on Camilla. The two attempts on his life were pushing her to the limit as it was. But, he felt he had to tell someone so there would be a record of what had happened with Clements should a third attempt on his life be successful.

He was saying, "I should never have poked that slug up the barrel of the gun the wrong way. That could come back to haunt me."

Paul had a questioning expression so he continued. "If the bullet had gone off while I was tapping it on the table, it could have killed me, to say nothing of the results if the gun had accidentally been fired."

Paul sat for a few seconds seemingly satisfied and then asked, "Do you think he managed to get you fired, too?"

"Don't know. If the woman keeps her mouth shut, I might make it. It depends on how hard she looked for evidence in the conference room. I didn't have time to do a really thorough job of cleaning up. There must have been something I missed. Certainly a forensics lab would find plenty of evidence of what went on."

"How about Clements. He sure deserved what you gave him, but are they going to sit still for that?"

"I know what you're saying. That's unlikely. Quite frankly, I'm a little surprised they haven't been here already. Anyway, another night with no sleep. Sorry to have burdened you with this."

"No problem. Now, it's my turn. I, or we, have a meeting with 'The Speaker' in the park this evening. She's headed home as you guessed she might be and will stop here on the way. It's all set up like you said. She'll take a taxi to the park."

Vin was beyond caring. Could it get any worse?

— 25 —

Vin and Paul left the house at six-thirty with Paul driving. "Ever been to this park," Vin asked.

"Nope. You?"

"Nope. All we have is this aerial photograph I downloaded from the park's website. We'll stop at the parking lot near the falls. Try to find a place on the east end, but the best would be to park between two other cars. If there are parking meters you feed it. Then saunter away. There are a lot of trees in the area. I'll slump down out of sight in the car for a few minutes until you're away."

Paul had Camilla's cell phone, and Vin had his. "Put your phone on vibrate. If I see anything wrong, I'll call. Expect short statements."

Vincent knew it carried some risk, but he brought along the same lightweight jacket he had worn to the flying field the first time. Camilla had an identical one and Paul would wear it. They were dark blue with a white banner slanting across the back. They had purchased them while staying at a resort some years ago. Vin's plan was to have two the same in the park to cause confusion. They also wore dark shirts.

"Remember, if anything happens, as soon as you can inconspicuously do it, slip off the jacket. Turn it inside out and put it back on if you have time. Otherwise, rely on your dark shirt. We'll be there early so carry the jacket as we look around. When you see the taxi drive up, put it on. I'll try to keep you in sight."

The parking lot didn't have parking meters but went one better. There was a tall yellow robot with its feet stuck in concrete. It's purpose was to dispense parking slips after having been jollied along with dollar bills that it happily inhaled, seventy-five cents per hour. Paul fed it three dollars and got his slip. He returned and placed it on the dashboard as instructed. After that, he started toward the pavilion a seventy-five yards away. The falls were a short distance beyond the building.

A few minutes later Vin exited the car and angled to the left. They met some fifty yards from the car near the bandstand. Further on was a fountain, really more of a multi-tiered bird bath, in the center of concentric rings of paving stones, flowers, paving stones, and more flowers. To the west of the fountain one could look over the wooded ravine and see Minnehaha Falls. The stream flowed to the south of the bluff on the left where they stood. Twenty yards to the east of the fountain, stone steps descended into the ravine twisting and turning with many intermediate landings. The pair made a quick descent of the long steps to the bottom of the bluff. The aerial photographs gave no indication of land elevation. It made sense now. At the bottom, the stream passed at the south end of a grass covered valley. Fifty yards directly across the open area the land rose again to where the photo showed more parking areas.

At the top of the steps again Vin said, "I suggest this. After you get together with her, walk toward this fountain. There are light posts so the place will be illuminated, and there are benches. There should be enough people about to make a shooting unlikely. In case of something odd happening, go down the steps, across the valley and up to that other parking area. I'll pick you up there. That'll be Plan B. I recommend that if you sit down, don't stay in one place for more than a few minutes."

Paul nodded. He made no objections to the effect that all of the precautions were unnecessary. Enough had happened to make him realize the wisdom of being prepared.

Alvin was home in his study watching a ball game. Every ten minutes he made a call to the tracking device on the car belonging to Wessen's wife. Less often, he called Wessen's car. He knew there were a couple of bullet holes in that one so didn't expect him to be driving it for a few days.

The setup on the freeway had been perfect. That short section of uneven road had come at exactly the wrong time. He remembered the sight of his out stretched arm silhouetted against the open window as it bobbed around. From what followed, he had to admit Wesson had not been hit, or at least not seriously. But, it was real close. No point in dwelling on that. It was obvious that with all the switching lanes, Wessen had not managed to get his plate number or the police would have been around to question him. Except for the momentary glance Wessen had of him out in the bushes, he was still anonymous.

There was a time-out in the game so the channel went to a commercial. Alvin pressed the speed dial for the tracking device on the wife's car. It was moving south on I-35W. The game was forgotten. He checked the other car. It was still in the garage. After ten minutes, he called the first car again. The transmitting time of the devices on the target vehicles was limited by their small batteries. Marv had warned him not to leave the transponder on continuously except in critical circumstances. He was now on Hiawatha Avenue, Highway 55, headed to the airport. It was unlikely he'd be leaving town on a Friday evening, but he could be going to meet someone. An airport parking ramp wouldn't be the worst place to meet up with him. It was worth a try.

Alvin put on a lightweight jacket to conceal the gun, took the tracking display and left for his car. On the street he pulled to the curb and tried the tracker again. Wessen was stopped at Minnehaha Park a few miles north of the airport. That was perfect. He'd drive west a couple of miles to Highway 100 south. From 100, he'd take the Crosstown freeway to Hiawatha. He could be there in twenty minutes.

It would have taken twenty minutes on a good day. This wasn't one of those. There was perpetual construction on the Crosstown which he had forgotten about. That, when combined with Friday evening traffic, slowed things down. He would have made better time using city streets. Yet, every time he checked, the car was still at the park. He had taken his Mustang thinking he could make better time. At five minutes to eight Alvin was driving into the parking area from the exit end so missed the sign warning of fines for not paying a parking fee. It wouldn't have mattered in any case. He'd rather pay the fine than be seen buying a ticket. He parked immediately. The lack of sports cars was evident. Should have taken the van, he thought. The parking area was separated into two sections divided by a narrow median with bushes growing in it. The tracking device showed his location and that of the target at the same place. The sun was setting and the lights in the lot and along the park trails had come on. Standing up and closing his door, he spotted the target car parked beyond the median.

With their plan laid out Vin and Paul separated. Paul moved toward the pavilion and loitered in an area where he could see the entrance on the west end of the parking lot. Vin took up station to the east of the parking area. He sat down with his back to a tree and pretended to be reading a paper back book. The light was becoming dim for that, but he wasn't reading anyway. At ten to eight a taxi appeared. An elderly woman emerged. Vin wasn't close enough to recognize her, but Paul was. He slipped on his jacket as he approached her.

Ms. Holleran?"

"Yes. Paul?"

"Yes, that's me."

"I'm sorry to do this, but do you have some identification? I'm a little unsure of this."

"I understand. Everyone would recognize you."

In a corner of the parking lot under a light Paul took out his wallet and showed her his driver's license. She nodded.

"We should walk a little," Paul said. Crossing some grass, they came to a paved trail leading to the pavilion where there were a dozen people in sight.

"Let's stay away from the people, not too far, only enough so I'm not recognized. You understand that, don't you?"

"Yes."

"Are you here alone."

"No. My Uncle Vincent is about keeping an eye on us. There was another attempt on his life yesterday so we're being cautious. He was alone that time so we're assuming the assassin was after him rather than me the first time. Someone tried to kill you too, didn't they?"

She drew in a short quick breath and looked at him. "Yes."

"No matter how much we differ in our outlook on life, I don't wish you to come to a violent end."

"That's kind of you to say that." They angled off the path through the trees, the leaves lightly crunching under their feet. It was a beautiful stand of white oaks with all the underbrush cut away. The failing light made it nearly dark with daylight visible beyond the trees.

"If you knew the meaning of that statement, you might not think it was so kind."

"Why not?"

"We'll get to it."

They neared the fountain that was deserted except of a man with a dog. Paul didn't like it, thinking it could be a disguise. He directed them to the west of the fountain where there was an overlook for viewing the falls. There had been ample rain causing a small torrent to plunge over the precipice. To change the mood he recited a few lines.

Gitche Manito, the mighty,
The creator of the nations,
Looked upon them with compassion,
With paternal love and pity;
"I am weary of your quarrels,
Weary of your wars and bloodshed,
Weary of your prayers for vengeance,
Of your wranglings and dissensions;
All your strength is in your union,
All your danger is in discord;
Therefore be at peace henceforward,
And as brothers live together."

"Is that a poem?"

"That's from the *Song of Hiawatha* by Longfellow. It's a book length poem about heroes, love, and pain. It's the American equivalent of Homer's *The Iliad*, or Tension's *Idols the King*. Since I knew we'd be coming here, I took the time to look it up and memorized a few lines. Hiawatha was born of the beautiful Wenonah. Deserted by Hiawatha's father, the West Wind, Wenonah soon died of loneliness. It was Nokomis, the grandmother, who raised Hiawatha. Minnehaha was the wife of Hiawatha.

"Ever seen the falls before? You said you were from here?"

"No. I never have. It was nice of you to memorize those lines, and they speak to important issues. However, we have some business to attend to, and I suggest we get started. Have you been saying prayers for me again?"

"Have you been saying unlikely things?"

"Not really. At times, I've felt moved in ways I didn't like, though."

"Like coming here to see me?"

"That could be one."

"That might have been the result of a prayer. You see, I've been praying for your metanoia."

"Is that something where you take a pain pill or do they operate?"

Paul smiled. "It has nothing to do with a medical condition. I guess you're unfamiliar with the word. It means total conversion. Normally people think of conversion as changing one's religious views, accepting a new faith. Metanoia is a complete turning around of all aspects of your life.

For you, it means not only coming back into full union with the Catholic Church, but repudiating all of you liberal views such as abortion, euthanasia, homosexuality, premarital sex, the welfare state, all of it."

"Not that I necessarily agree with what you're saying, but all of the items you enumerated seem to fit a category except for the welfare state."

"We should keep moving," Paul said. "I had planned to sit on a bench by the fountain, but there aren't enough people. The lone man with the dog looked a little suspicious."

Paul couldn't help noticing her intense concentration so he tried to provide an answer. "The welfare state is really the safety net. There are no safety nets in life or in death. And, that's the problem with it. When you die, depending on how you have lived, you go to heaven or to hell. On the way to hell there's no safety net. You go there and you stay there. That means, having so-called safety nets for failures in your life teaches you to think there will always be one, even after death. On the other hand, if in this life you learn to take responsibility for your failures, you'll have that attitude with respect to your afterlife, too."

"That's actually quite profound. Where do you get this stuff."

"I was home schooled and my parents made sure there was always plenty of good reading material around."

"But, I think that faith and religion deal with spiritual things. The things in this world are in a different category. You can keep them in different compartments of your mind, in a manner of speaking. The two aren't related."

"Uncle Vin, his wife and I were discussing how you could hold the political and social views you do and still think you're a Catholic. Aunt Camilla mentioned the 'two truths' doctrine. This idea says that what is true in philosophy and science may be false in theology, and visa versa. She said that idea appeared in the thirteenth century and was condemned and thoroughly trashed by Thomas Aquinas. It is refuted by observing that God is the source of all truth. He reveals religious truths directly, and He permits us to determine natural truths through natural reason. But, God is the source of both, so there can be no contradictions, no separate compartments. The pernicious thing about two-truths is that once it is applied to science and philosophy, people immediately apply it to morality. They excuse cheating, lying, stealing, artificial contraception, abortion, and every other sin and perversion by seeing them as separate from religion just as you said. As we've seen, that's not true."

With continuous glances in all directions, Paul was trying to spot trouble. He hadn't seen anything out of the ordinary, though it would be nice if he could locate Uncle Vin. That in itself didn't bother him too much because he had come to accept the fact that the guy was good at whatever it was that kept a man alive in dangerous situations.

"Paul, why did you say in your letter that I had been targeted?"

"I heard it at the campaign office. There were dozens of rumors and the odd thing was that so many of them eventually came to light as being true. For example, they knew you were looking for my letter. Of course, they didn't know it was from me yet. That changed when the goon from the FBI came to the office."

Holleran stiffened but didn't say anything. Could her staff be so infiltrated?

"Have you heard any rumors recently?"

"Nope. I called one of the guys that I was friends with on the campaign the other day. It's not the same. I'm not one of them anymore. I really liked that, you know. Where I am now isn't the same."

"What are you doing?"

"I'd rather not say. What I'd like to know is who released the story to the press about the bow and arrow shooting. So far, there haven't been any names. But, if they do mention us, Uncle Vincent will probably be fired, and I will have my life screwed up. Neither of us are very happy about that. Any comments?"

They had turned from the view of the falls, and were skirting to the south of the fountain. "Did you have anything to do with that?" Paul persisted.

"No. I was as surprised as you were. It didn't make me look good either. It sounds like something planted to defuse Ellefson's campaign. There are people actively engaged in things like that during every election. It's not connected directly to the Democratic Party, but generally they know about it."

Their steps had taken them to the east of the fountain. The man with the dog had strolled away.

"Paul, why have you been so insistent on mentioning eternity in your letters? You even suggested saving me from eternity. I don't understand."

Paul grimaced. Holleran assumed it was because of her question, but it was from the vibration of the cell phone in his pocket.

Paul and Norma Holleran were out of Vincent's sight. He didn't like it. However, he couldn't watch the parking lot and them, too. The fountain area was beyond the trees and the pavilion. Only one car had arrived after the taxi. It disgorged a female jogger wearing tights. She slapped a card on the dashboard, a season ticket. Torn, he had decided to move toward the fountain when he glimpsed a flash of bright red entering the lot from the exit end. Alerted, he stepped partially behind a tree. A man stood up as the sound of a door closing reached him. He was wearing a baseball cap. In the failing light, it made it impossible to see his face, though he was too far away to have made a positive identification even in full daylight.

The man casually passed Vin's car stopping momentarily to look at the parking slip on the dashboard. The expiration time was printed in large numbers so park police could easily see which cars to ticket with a fine. He started toward the pavilion where food and beverages were served, nonalcoholic drinks, of course. Vin slipped on his windbreaker and followed staying among the trees fifty yards to the left. The man held a brisk pace, as if on a mission. He completely circled the building and paused in indecision on the south side. Proceeding forward, he stopped at the three foot stone wall where he could see the falls. To his right, a bridge crossed the creek above the falls. Another trail led along the top of the bluff on this side. Earlier, he and Paul had discovered stone steps leading down to Minnehaha Creek on this side so people could descend to the bottom of the gorge and look up at the falls. At the bottom of the steps was a bridge across the creek leading to more steps up the far side of the ravine.

After a moment the man started in the direction of the bridge above the falls. He was practically running. Vin moved up to the wall. On the far side, he saw the man start down the steps. Trees obscured most of the steps but here and there he caught sight of his man. Now, he was on the bridge below and heading Vin's way moving fast. Vin had located Paul and Holleran to his left, and watched the situation unfold. When the man started up the long steps on his side, Vincent had to move back to the northeast of the fountain. Predictably, the man appeared at the top of the steps, and after a pause, started to the east. Fifty yards from the fountain he stopped. Paul had his back to the man and the unique design on the jacket was clearly visible.

— 26 —

Alvin spotted Wessen's car as soon as he was out of his. He glanced about trying to determine if anyone was taking an interest in him. Why would they? After all, a shinny bright red Mustang zipping into the parking lot from the wrong end happened all the time. Casually, as if about to start an evening stroll in the park, he walked between two cars, one of which happened to be Vin's, and spotted the slip of paper on the dashboard through the windshield. Hesitating, he understood immediately about the parking fees. Wessen had paid to stay until nine-fifteen, and it was now eight-ten. It wasn't a bad setup in the reduced light, except his time was limited by the encroaching dusk. After dark, it was unlikely he'd be able to find him. He didn't bother to think of a plausible reason for Wessen to be here, and that it could be a trap.

He proceeded around the pavilion noticing that the attendants were preparing to close for the evening. Stopping on the south side only an instant, he started toward the wall. The falls were before him and a bridge to his right. Crossing the bridge, he could hear the falls on his left. On the far side of the creek, the path led to the top of steps leading down to the foot of the falls. Speed was essential so he descended somewhat rashly knowing he could come upon Wessen at any moment. The steps turned one way, then another. At one point, there was a dead end with a wrought iron railing that gave a view of the falls. Reaching the bottom, he had seen no one. The bridge below the falls stretched before him. Thinking only of being the hunter, he trotted across the bridge. To his left was another dead end with yet another view of the falls. The falls looked as it had in the numerous pictures he had seen over his life. To the right, the path led to the bottom of the steps. He took them two at a time.

At the top, he had to pause to catch his breath. Having never been at the park, he failed to realize that it covered over a hundred sixty acres. However, having found Wessen's car he assumed he wouldn't be far from it. Starting off again, the path rounded a bend to the right. Coming in view of a fountain, he saw two figures. He stopped abruptly, so much so that it might have attracted attention. As unbelievable as it seemed, one of them had his back to Alvin and was wearing a jacket he recognized, dark blue, with the white banner slanting across the back. It was Wessen. He had worn it the first time he was out flying airplanes. Alvin was west of the fountain and two hundred feet from Wessen who seemed to be talking to a woman. The only other person in sight was a man with a leashed dog walking off to his left.

Bearing to the right of the path, he approached more slowly near the low stone wall at the edge of the bluff. The limbs of trees arching over him reduced the light so it was unlikely either of the two near the fountain had seen him. Except that they were moving away from the fountain in the opposite direction. His thought was that Wessen had taken up a casual conversation with a stranger and would soon go about his business alone.

Paul had been absent-mindedly resting his hand on the cell phone in his jacket pocket. When it vibrated, he immediately withdrew it and flipped it open.

"Yes."

"Plan B. Do it now. He's just on the other side of the fountain from you." The call ended.

Holleran could see something was wrong as Paul snapped his head in the direction of the fountain. He saw nothing out of the ordinary, which in itself was unsettling. He had to assume that Vin, from a different vantage point, saw what was coming.

"We have to take evasive action. This way, quickly," Paul said taking her arm.

He led her to the top of the steps, a few yards away, and they started down. She was wearing a beige linen jacket over a matching blouse. It was too light. He shucked off his windbreaker pulling it inside out and threw it over her shoulders.

"Your clothing is too light."

They were making their way down much too slowly for Paul's satisfaction. "Please hurry if you can."

They reached the first landing where the steps turned forty-five degrees to the left. After that, it was thirty steps to the next turn ninety degrees to the right. As they completed the second turn, first one ping, and then another chipped the stone wall on the right. One bullet ricocheted with the characteristic whine for a dozen feet before imbedding itself in a tree.

"Were those shots?" Holleran asked.

"I'm sure they were."

Clutching the hand railing on the left, she was moving faster. Down and down some more. Finally, a hundred and thirty steps after they started, they were at the bottom. They were off at a slow trot across the open area with security lights some distance off to the left. There was no avoiding the grassy area, though from his experience in the bushes, Paul led her in a zig zag pattern. Into the trees at the far side they stopped and looked back. There was no sign of anyone following. There was still enough light to be certain of that.

"I think we're okay for now," Paul said. "If we get up this hill, and all else works as we planned, Uncle Vin will be on top to pick us up."

"Who shot at us?"

"That's the big question. The only hint we have is he owns a bright red sports car and a maroon minivan, assuming it's the same person all the time. Are you all right?"

"For now. My feet will be sore again."

There were several trails on this slope since it was more gentle than the nearly sheer cliffs in the area of the falls. They started up.

Vin made the call and pocketed the phone. He was pleased to see Paul act exactly as planned. The shadowy figure moved up fast as soon as they disappeared down the steps always glancing around. He stopped and raised what had to be a gun. At his distance, he wasn't sure, but it sounded like two pops.

While the man was intent on moving up to Holleran and Paul, Vin stationed himself to the north. With the sound of the shots, Vin faked a loud sneeze, turned, and started jogging toward the bandstand. The man looked in the direction of the sound, and saw the logo on the windbreaker. As soon as he was under the trees, Vin intended to run to the car. Before he made it to the trees, he felt a sting on the inner side of his upper right arm. He sprinted for the trees with the bandstand on his left. It was a blur as he dodged this way and that trying to keep tree trunks between him and where he thought the gun was. He wanted to take the windbreaker off, but he was pressing his arm against his body to stop the bleeding.

He had the keys in hand as he arrived at the car, and pressed the button to unlock it. He slipped in, had it running, and was backing out when a figure appeared from the trees. There were no more cars to the left of him. The man seemed as intent on getting to his car as shooting Vin. Maybe he thought it would be too risky to do it here under the lights. Vin punched it down closing in on the man. The little engine didn't have enough power to squeal the tires, but the sound of the engine revving caused the man to look at Vin for a second before he was forced to dive for the grass. It was only an instant, but if he had to say, it was the same man as at the flying field.

Vin was out of the parking lot and headed east caring nothing about speed limits. He slowed at a stop sign and turned right at a sign pointing to the Wabun Picnic Area. The road split, and split again. Each time he stayed to the right assuming that would be closer to the place Holleran and Paul would appear. He was moving too fast, had to slow, though he knew the red car would be on him in a minute.

There was a lone car parked and no sign of movement as he slowed to a crawl. There, on the right, coming out of bushes. It was them, the one thing going right. He stopped and unlocked the doors, lowering the right side windows.

"In the back!"

Paul opened the door for Holleran and they piled in. Paul's foot was hardly off the pavement and Vin was moving. Vin fumbled with his seat belt. "Buckle up!"

He was off wishing he had his car with its larger engine. His was a Taurus, and Camilla had a Sable with the small engine. It would have to do.

"Either of you hurt?"

"My feet are a mess. Going to have blisters again."

"I mean shot!"

"No," Paul answered. "We were shot at a couple of times. How about you? You hit?"

"Once. Not bad. If you see a red sports car, get your heads down."

He was out of the parking area nearing a stop sign where going straight ahead would lead to 46th Street. West on that and he'd intersect with Hiawatha Avenue. Shortly before the stop sign, he saw the red car coming toward him.

"That's him." Vin burned through the stop getting a salute from another driver, then left at the red light between cars and was moving faster than he should.

"Ms. Holleran, I'd like you to meet my Uncle Vin."

"Pleased, I'm sure. Do you always live like this?"

"Only since I became associated with you. Paul, I got a glimpse of the guy, and I'm pretty sure he's the same one as at the flying field. Ms. Holleran, who do you know in this town? Anybody you can think of? There must be some connection."

They had blown through another red light and were approaching Hiawatha. Vin pulled to the left lane and stopped at the red. At an opening, he floored it making the left. This thing was so gutless. How'd Camilla stand it?

Holleran hadn't answered as he was accelerating, switching from one lane to another. "Who do you know?" Vin demanded.

"There's only my father and my brother."

"The brother's name—I've got to know. It must be someone he knows."

After a pause, "Alvin."

"Does he drive a red sports car?"

No answer.

"You could have been killed, and the same for me. Does he?"

"I don't know what he drives."

The winking colored lights in the rearview mirror add to the festivities.

"We picked up a cop. We're only a mile or two from the Air National Guard station at the airport."

The siren sounded behind them.

"Pull over. I can handle them. I have immunity."

Vin pulled over. "Watch for the red car."

The policeman came up to the side of Vin's car. Paul was watching out the rear window.

"There he goes, turned off at the last stop light behind us," Paul said.

When Alvin saw the jacket disappear down the steps, he was pleased. Having only moments ago come up such a course, he knew what to expect. However, the ones he came up were different in that they were nearly a straight run. Here, they angled off in a new direction at each landing. By the time he could see down, Paul had peeled off the jacket. What Alvin saw was a dark shadow rounding the corner. He shot twice. The sneeze to his left startled him as the specter of being caught made him pause. There was the jacket fifty yards away. The guy must have jumped the wall on the left side of the steps and exited out of the brushy area beside the paved trail.

The bugger was crafty and quick. He raised the gun for a shot. Wessen lurched and broke into a dead run. He was angling to the left toward the bandstand. It was hard to see for a second shot because a steel light post fifteen feet high was nearly between him and his man. With the light on, it produced a glare. Again he shot and immediately heard a metallic ping. The light went out. He had hit the light post and severed the wire inside. Another shot was pointless since the jacket was under the trees in the dim light and weaving constantly while running at full speed. Alvin was encumbered by having to keep the gun under his jacket as he ran. He could not chance anyone seeing him chasing the other man with a drawn weapon, especially as he neared the parking lot. Wessen had backed his car and floored it as Alvin was running to his car. He dove back the way he had come losing the grip on his gun as he landed. He found it, but the search cost him precious seconds.

In his Mustang, he sped in the direction Wessen had gone. He spotted him emerging from the picnic area as he was headed in the other direction. Turning around he followed, and was a block behind when Wessen made the left on red onto Hiawatha Avenue. It was green when he got there. Two blocks later he saw the patrol car light up. That was it. Alvin turned right at the next light and was gone. Wessen had been hit, it wasn't serious because he kept running. He still had not had a good look at Alvin's face and it would not have been possible to get his plate number.

Holleran lowered the back window. "Officer, please look at my identification."

"Stay out of it. My business is with the driver."

"No it's not. It is with me. I am Norma M. Holleran, Speaker of the House of Representative in Washington. Look here."

She held out an identification folder larger than the normal driver's license.

"This is official business, and you're interfering. That man was acting under my instructions. We are headed to the Air Force station at the airport where my personal Air Force jet is waiting. We can sort it out there."

He looked at the identification, and at the face. He hesitated, then returned the identification.

"Okay." He turned his attention to Vin. "I'll follow you. Nothing funny. That was some terrible driving back there."

"Yes sir."

Vin started moving. "How do I get you to your plane?"

"Stay on Hiawatha past the intersection with the Crosstown. It's on the right. I'll tell you when we're there."

"Ms. Holleran, please handle it so I don't have to get out of the car. If they see the blood, it'll all come out and hit the papers that there was an assassination attempt on you. I don't know about you, but my job won't survive that. Can you do that? And please, warn the cops off me. He will have called in my plate number as it is."

"I'll do what I can."

"By the way. What does the 'M' in your name stand for?"

"I don't tell that to people."

"Come on. I'm bleeding. You owe me something."

"Well, you did a good job, I'll have to say that. It's Margaret. Now you know. Don't tell anyone, will you?"

"My lips are sealed."

She turned to Paul. "We didn't finish our conversation. There's eternity left, and what was it that I wouldn't like if I knew?"

"Neither subject can be handled with a sound bite. We'll have to leave it for next time, unless you want me to send you another letter."

"Not that! I'll call you, that good enough?"

"Sure."

They arrived at a guardhouse and Holleran had the window open again with her ID out.

"Good evening Madam Speaker," the guard in desert camouflage uniform said. "We have a guide car waiting."

Vin had his window down. The guard said, "Follow that Air Force car."

Vin nodded.

At their destination, an Air Force Lieutenant Colonel opened the door for Holleran. The policeman had been allowed to tag along. The Colonel and Holleran talked with the police officer. After a short three way discussion, the police officer approached Vin's window.

"When we leave here, you can go. Watch the red lights. You understand?"

"Yes sir."

The guide car led them to the gate.

Driving back on Hiawatha Avenue Vin said, "I'm glad that's over. I hope I don't have to go to a doctor with this arm. It's starting to hurt." He pulled over. "You drive."

With Paul driving he asked, "Did you have a nice discussion?"

"I guess. She's a typical liberal, all conflicted. They make a good show of it, but they're all a mess. It's clear she isn't as sure of her liberal beliefs as she wants everybody to think."

"At least we learned a few things. She's from here and has a brother named Alvin and a father, both presumably living in town."

"And, her middle name is Margaret," Paul added.

"Yeah. Not much, but it's a start."

— 27 —

Saturday morning, June 26

Nick Calloway hated to come to the office on a weekend. He was a strong believer in the proposition that if you didn't waste time and stayed focused during the week you'd keep up with the work. The worst of it was, he wasn't even sure this was necessary other than the fact that he had little choice but to stop by the hospital to see how Fred Clements was doing. It was just that these two cases coming up at the same time gave him a gut feeling they were related. It went beyond timing. The whole thing with the Ellefson campaign, Sanders, and Wessen had exploded in their faces. The threat of a truck bomb seemed insane enough to fit the pattern.

He called the forensics technician on duty to see about the progress of the fingerprints they had received from Tuley.

"Yeah, Jorgan. This is Calloway. Anything on those fingerprints, the ones from the farmer in Wisconsin?"

"We made a good match off the gun. They belong to Flavian Cutter, ex-Navy SEAL. We had a problem with the ones from the Pepsi can. They matched, but there had to be a mistake. I was told to take some more samples off the can and sent them on. They're running them again in Washington now. Due to the error, there's interest in Washington. It'll be an hour or so."

"So, who's the man from the can?"

"It's Joab Feinstein. What can I say?"

Neither name meant anything to Calloway. "Okay. I'm leaving the office to check on my man in the hospital. You have my cell number. Call me when you hear something."

"Will do."

About to hang up he said, "Wait a minute. Give me the spelling of those names, will you?" He thought it was possible Clements would recognize them.

Two steps from his desk Calloway stopped and returned. Remaining standing, he flipped his note pad back to where he had Tuley's number and punched in the numbers.

"Yeah?"

"This is Nick Calloway from the FBI in Minneapolis."

"Now what? Coming out to arrest me? Again?"

"No. I said I wouldn't do that. There's no evidence that says I should or even could."

"Yeah, but if your boss said to arrest me, you would. No need to answer that. We both know the answer. Why are you calling?"

"We received the results from the finger prints. I want to give you some names and see if you recognize them, okay?"

Dutch immediately sat at the kitchen table and grabbed a pencil. There was an advertising flyer handy to write on. "Let's hear them."

"Flavian Cutter."

"You say Flavian? What kind of name is that?" Dutch was clarifying that he heard the name right and at the same time was making sure he had enough time to jot them down.

"I don't know what kind of name it is. From that I guess you don't know him."

"Yep. I don't. Who's next."

"Joab Feinstein."

"Another odd one. As in j-o-a-b?"

"Yes."

" Never heard of him either. Any more?"

Calloway paused. It was a long shot, but he saw nothing to lose. Yeah. One more. Ever hear of Vincent Wessen?"

"That with an e-n or an o-n?"

"With an e-n. You know him?"

"Knew a Wesson with an o-n a few years back. Can't recall that his first name was Vincent, though. None of them click as recent. Come to think of it, neither of the guys that were here gave even a first name."

"Well, if you think of anything call me. You have my office phone and my cell number, right?"

"Yeah. Any word on the truck they rented in my name?"

There had been no effort to find the truck. Did the country dude think the truck was the only thing on the list of things to do? "We're working it, but no progress yet. Something will break. I'll let you know." He didn't say that Tuley would likely be the last one to know, but why get into that?

Fred Clements was resting after a tough night. Nick Calloway, being his supervisor, had to stay abreast of his condition lest the big boss called. Walking from the parking ramp to the hospital, Vincent Wessen became more than a case file to him, it was evolving into a burning grudge as he thought out the best way to destroy that cowboy. The nurse gave him an update on Clements' condition including the fact that he was sedated. Calloway sat in the chair beside the bed. He knew Clements tended to be a bit aggressive at times. In fact, he had been reprimanded only six months before on that account. Still, this was unacceptable. While mulling over his options, his cell phone buzzed and he answered it thinking it was the technician with further results on the fingerprints. Instead, it was the call he had not expected until Monday from his colleague in D.C., Dick Doren.

"Your package arrived this morning as you promised. It certainly seemed odd. I took it around to a couple of guys that are good at that sort of thing. You were right to send it to me. This is serious. What I say now is from the top. Back way off from Wessen. Forget what happened. Your man was in a bar room fight. He never went to the place where Wessen works. Hope that Wessen isn't fired from his job like Sanders was, or all hell will break lose. Clements was off the reservation in more ways than one. You and your office are temporarily off that whole case until we get some things sorted out here in Washington. Did you get all that? You'll be getting official notice of that within the hour. This is a heads up for you."

"Wow! What happened?"

"It's a tangled web. We'll discuss it down the road unless it becomes slapped with secrecy. Between us, don't believe any of that BS from Wessen about how he could be dead any day. He could have killed both guys that made an attempt on him if he had had a mind to. Why he didn't is the question being asked here. We're looking at ways to keep utility vans out of his neighborhood until we get this under control. Anyway, those are your orders. We'll be back soon, I hope, so you can start working on the case again. But, hold off completely for now."

"Understood. Wait. What was that about utility vans?"

"In your debriefing report Clements reported that Wessen said he'd kill on sight, not shoot on sight, kill. He might think the guys in a cable van are the FBI staking him out. If he did, zap, they're dead."

"Who is that guy?"

"Don't ask."

"The President will see you now," the secretary said.

Three men were ushered into the Oval Office to see the President coming from behind the desk. The Director of Central Intelligence, the DCI, the President knew from his regular briefings from him. The director of the FBI he knew even better. He was from the Chicago gang, brought in at the behest of his chief of staff. The Brigadier General he had never met before.

"Sir, this is General Sandy Gillby. He heads up the various special forces units of the army, the Green Berets, Rangers, and similar units. We're here to have him brief you on an unusual situation that has come up."

"I have ten minutes, can you do it in that time?"

"Yes, sir. Sandy, I'll let you give the background," the DCI said.

The General began, "During the Viet Nam War, a variety of special forces units were used for unique missions. Some of these were the Ranger squads who went into the jungle to kill or capture Vietcong for intelligence purposes. There were even a few units called shadow companies that were on the books, but were not where the records said they were. Instead, they were in places where they were not supposed to be, like Cambodia. Sometimes they did things that were quasi illegal. All of these units were made up of volunteers. Of these there was a small group that was, for lack of a better term, a shadow of a shadow, or shadow-shadow units. These were totally off the books. They were specially trained to do specific missions. And, their code of honor was that they never failed. Sometimes, not a single man returned, but they never failed to accomplish their mission.

"What concerns us is how these men were recruited. Everyone who goes into the army, then as now, takes a battery of tests to determine skills, intelligence, psychological stability, to name a few. Someone got the bight idea to see what those that volunteered for special forces had in common on their tests. The data from that analysis was distilled down to a set of traits, a template. Then they applied the template to everyone else in the army. The computers of the time were nothing like ours, but good enough for that. Those they found who compared favorably to the template were approached and more often than not they were willing to change jobs and be a part of some special operation or other. Of course, no system is perfect, and many of the volunteers washed out of the training. However, there was still enough for these teams. Here I must stress that many of the men who completed the training were more than special, prodigies would be more accurate. We all have our strengths and weaknesses. It's simply a fact that there are a few who have an overdose of what could be called warrior genes.

"The men who made up the shadow-shadow groups were left administratively in their original units. That is, the morning report, the form each company fills out every day showing the location if each member of the unit, showed them present, but no one knew where they were."

"Wait," the President interjected. "If someone isn't at his job, people would surely notice."

"That's true. However, this is common. A brigade might want a marching brass band. There is no band in the table of organization. So, the word goes out that anyone who can play a musical instrument is to come forward. Those selected for the band are listed as special duty on the company roster to which they are officially assigned. Some infantry squad is a man short, but that's it. The only difference with these shadow-shadow guys is they were not listed as being on special duty. They were listed as present. Everybody in the army follows orders from privates to generals, so if the company commander was told to list him as present, he did.

"These shadow-shadow squads were very good. But, finally they became too good. There came a time when a division staff was seen as screwing with one of their missions, so two colonels from the staff were found dead. People knew who had done it, but nobody was about to arrest these guys. So, the units were decommissioned. The men went back to their old units. Some of them were actually of solid enough physiological makeup to fit back in without missing a beat. Others didn't do so well. Some are in military prisons, many are dead. However, some are still out there. You see, there is no way of knowing who they are because all of the military records show them at the only job they supposedly held during their entire tour of duty.

"There is another possibility that I must mention. Some men who possessed the traits matching the template did not agree to be a part of a shadow unit. However, they are in the population and have that natural ability to think quickly and act precisely to survive in unanticipated and dangerous situations."

"I follow that. What's your point?"

The General handed the President a nine-millimeter pistol. "See the bullet jammed in the end of the barrel the wrong way? It strongly indicates the man who is the subject of this meeting by the name of Vincent Wessen did not pass up the offer to be in a shadow-shadow unit. That's a trademark of those men. It says that they were so good they thought guns were for weenies. That doesn't mean that they wouldn't use guns and weren't expert marksmen. From this and other evidence, we think one of these men has surfaced."

The director of the FBI, Randy Offit, continued the tale. "He seems to be connected to the incident when Norma Holleran made that odd pro-life remark a few weeks ago, and how you had her in here to give her a right proper dressing down about it." He paused and glanced at his watch. "If we are to stay on your schedule I must keep this short so we don't have time to explain how that is connected to this man. Suffice it to say one thing led to another, and two attempts were made on the life of this shadow man. We don't know who did it.

"Yesterday the Minneapolis agent assigned to the case, being a little over zealous, went to interview the man's boss where he worked. While there, he had a chance meeting with the shadow man which was not a good thing. We are pretty sure our agent will live. He may never regain even partial use of his left eye. We may not have to amputate his right ear. After extensive re-constructive surgery, his nose will look something like it did the day before. And, with luck he may not have to have any of his privates amputated."

"Don't you bother to teach your agents martial arts. How old is this shadow guy?"

"The guy is in his late fifties, the agent is in this thirties, in superb condition, and practices martial arts as a hobby. He's an expert. Yet, he didn't lay a hand on him. That's how good the older man is."

"Why do I want to know any of this. Can't you handle it?"

"The point is this. The two attempts on him were not successful. That makes sense. However, the perpetrators in both cases seem to be still alive or we would have found some bodies. That does not make sense unless he is trying to find out who gave the orders. Because of the altercation at his work place, he now appears to blame the FBI for his cover being blown. That makes the trail lead in the direction of the federal government. And, well, you are at the top of that chain of command.

"He might think you are the one who ordered the hits on him. If he were to act on that belief, he would kill you. There is nothing the Secret Service could do to prevent it, unless you want to spend the entire rest of your term in office in this building. Remember, these guys never fail in their missions, even if not a one of them comes back alive. That's why it matters to you. We are pulling out all the stops to get a handle on this. But, if you are in any way connected to what happened to this man to make him surface, we'd be most appreciative of knowing how. Right about now, we could use a little help."

"This one man has the entire federal government running scared? I don't believe it."

"There's no question we could kill him. However, a lot of people, innocent or not, would die before we got him. We need to find out who's trying to kill him."

"I was angry with Holleran, I admit that. It was politics, though. Her remark sent the wrong message to the other side. In addition, it diverted the media's attention from what I wanted to do for the good of the country. That's all. This is Washington. That goes on all the time, you know that."

"Yes, sir. Due to his assault on our FBI agent, we feel he's too big a menace to be left at large. As I mentioned, we are not inclined to take the direct approach and arrest him. It would be far better if he were drawn into a criminal plot and killed as a result of it. If you agree to that, we'll set something up."

"Agreed, as long as I'm not involved."

"Of course, sir."

The DCI left immediately while General Sandy Gillby followed the FBI director to the office of the President's chief of staff, David Adams. When the door was closed, Adams looked at the General and said,

"Charlie, you make such a handsome general that I do believe you missed your calling. Did he buy it?"

"Every word," responded Randy Offit. "With the DCI there, we had a good witness that he agreed to a covert operation on U.S. soil with the intent of killing a U.S. citizen. That'll keep him in line."

Charlie Divner, an all around special duties man, flipped his general's hat on a chair and sat in another. "Who dredged up that shadow-shadow story. It was good, just far out enough to be believable."

Adams was grinning. "Seth Goldman and I hatched that. I agree, it is pretty good, and on short notice, too. It isn't all fiction, though. We aren't that inventive. There was scuttlebutt, stories, even a few facts that support the idea. The generals on the ground were desperately trying to win that thing in Viet Nam and were willing to try just about anything. Meanwhile, the suits in Washington were goofing around with global politics, body counts, and everything but winning the war. The odd thing is it fits the story of Wessen so well, we started to wonder who he is, after all. Doing what he did to Clements took a lot of savvy."

"Well, who is he, then?" Divner asked.

"We haven't found anything yet, but it's Saturday. We'll need some time."

Looking at Divner, he continued. "Don't lose the soldier suit, Charlie. You may need it again. We paid a lot getting you into that on a Saturday morning."

— 28 —

While the Director of the FBI was in the meeting with the President, Nick Calloway was called by Jorgan the forensics technician. The fingerprints from the Pepsi can had been verified. He immediately called the two other agents now working the cases, Tom Holder and Gerald Ranklen, and told them to meet him at his office. He was in on Saturday and misery loves company. Besides, this was important. While he had been warned off the Wessen case, nothing had been said about the alleged truck bomb case even though he personally thought they might be connected.

With the three of them in Calloway's office Nick began, "Talk to me. The match of the prints has been double checked. The prints on the pistol might be explainable. They belong to Flavian Cutter, ex-Navy SEAL. Who knows what these guys do for employment after they get out? Their training doesn't exactly match what's needed to be the manager of a furniture store. But, how does this guy in central Wisconsin get a Pepsi can with Joab Feinstein's fingerprints on it? We also did an analysis of the remaining few drops of Pepsi that were still liquid. The can was opened within the last few days. This indicates the man was at Tuley's farm."

"So, what's the concern?" asked Holder.

"Don't you get it? Joab Feinstein is one of the President's inner circle of advisors."

"Oh! That Feinstein. What would you expect? If you look at that man's resume you'll find he was trained by the Mossad and spent most of his life as a terrorist. Our fearless leader brought him to Washington, cleaned him up, and put a suit on him, which my ma would say was like putting a saddle on a sow. That aside, he was obviously out at Tuley's farm buying ammonium nitrate fertilizer to make an ANFO bomb like Tuley suspected. Unless, of course, the President has decided to go green and plant grass on the roof of the White House."

"Sarcasm won't help. I can't pick up the phone, call the President's unlisted number, and tell him to call off his dogs. What brings him to this part of the country? What possible reason?"

Ranklen spoke for the first time. "Maybe it's connected with the bow and arrow shooting and Ellefson's campaign?" The bow and arrow incident was known to everyone in the local Bureau. It was becoming a part of FBI lore somewhere between a UFO sighting and a Jolly Jingle ice-cream truck that sold drugs to kids. And, the connection was exactly what Calloway had been thinking earlier. "That whole business seems to be connected to Washington. Maybe the bow and arrow was the first step and they are about to ratchet up the action."

"You think Feinstein did the bow and arrow?"

"No. But maybe Cutter did."

Calloway pondered this for a few moments. "As far out as that sounds, you might have something. But, think about it. Every time we've run something up the chain of command, the response has made things worse. The order to arrest Tuley was terrible. He was being an honest citizen trying to help." Calloway shook his head as his earlier conversation with Jorgan came to mind. "It'll get worse again. When the match was first made to Feinstein, they assumed it was a mistake because of who it was. Our guy had to take more prints and sent them along. With confirmation, the hornet's nest will really be buzzing. Expect the cover-up to start at any time."

Nothing was said. They were thinking out the possibilities. Finally Calloway asked, "Could he really make an ANFO bomb? Timothy McVeigh used Tovex to set off his ANFO. Since then that's become even more regulated than it had been before."

"There's always Tannerite," Ranklen said. "That's a binary explosive used as targets by sportsmen. When struck by a rifle bullet it explodes. A couple of years ago a man put a hundred pounds of it in the back of his old dump truck down by Red Wing, Minnesota. He shot into it from three hundred yards away. It demolished the truck. Several miles away at the Prairie Island nuclear power plant, the seismic sensors thought they detected an earthquake and shut down the reactors. Anybody can buy that stuff because until the two ingredients are mixed, they are not classified as an explosive. I'd guess that twenty or thirty pounds would do the trick."

"Oh. That makes me feel real fuzzy inside," Calloway said. "We're in a tough spot. If we say Feinstein is in the Midwest buying the makings for a truck bomb, and he turns out to be rambling around the White House we really look stupid. If we say nothing and a federal building becomes rubble with a hundred people in it, we're in worse trouble."

"Wait a minute," Holder said. "We happen to be in probably the most visible federal building in town. Time for some field work, I'd say."

"Point taken. We have until Monday before we might have to bring in the higher-ups. What can we do locally?"

The two men before Calloway did not know about the latest information on Wessen. Based on the remarks from Doren in Washington, he decided he couldn't mention it for the present. However, without including Wessen it left them with few clues other than the rental truck. He wished he had not asked Tuley if he recognized the names, though it seemed unlikely it would be a problem.

"You two, find the man at the truck rental place who handled the box truck rental. It's in Tuley's name. Take along photos of Tuley, Feinstein, and Cutter. Take along a dozen photos, you know the drill. If you can find Tuley, see if he can identify our two friends from out east. Also, check out Tuley's alibi for the time the truck was rented. I still find it difficult to believe a man like Joab Feinstein would be doing this."

"I have another one," Holder said. "While we were all out at Tuley's place on Thursday, a dark blue car came by. Nothing special about it, but one of the guys took the plate. Turn's out it's a rental by someone who doesn't exist. I've also checked with the hospitals for anyone coming in with a broken arm. Nothing. But, if he went to some small town clinic or hospital we might not have heard."

Calloway nodded. "We could put out the word to the car rentals to watch for the name that doesn't exist. But, if they needed another car, they'd use another fake ID, so forget it. Sorry for the weekend work, but it comes with the job. Call me if you find anything."

Vin's wife, Camilla, had bandaged her husband's arm as well as she could without sutures the night before. It had been a project since the wound was in an odd location being on the inside of his upper arm. He jerked from the pain each time she did any thing, and she kept telling him to be still or she'd never get any were. They managed. It would take longer to heal and leave a scar, but barring an infection, it would be all right. It was mid-morning before Camilla and Vincent stirred after Friday evening's ordeal. Vin and Paul were seated at the dinette table as Camilla cleared away the dishes from a late breakfast.

Paul had been up earlier and done some searching on the Internet. As Camilla busied herself Paul said, "I searched the web for Alvin Holleran and there's nothing that was useful for us. We still don't have much information. I wonder if Norma Holleran was ever married. The bio on her website doesn't say one way on the other. You'd think some tabloid or investigative reporter would have dug up information about her early life. But, no. Prior to her graduating from Burkeley there's nothing. It's odd when you think about it. Such an important person with no childhood."

"How about parents?" Camilla asked.

"It mentions Eugene and Laletta. But Eugene Holleran doesn't show up in the white pages of the phone book or on line."

"Maybe they're both dead."

"She said she had family here," Vin replied. "Alvin, a brother, and her father. If both parents were dead, I don't think she would have said it that way. She didn't mention a mother."

They were discussing what could be happening when Camilla said looking at Vin, "I doubt this has any bearing on Holleran, but a letter came for you a few days ago. With all the madness, I didn't want it to get swept up with the junk mail and thrown out so I put it on top of the refrigerator."

Vin retrieved the envelope and saw it was from the mortuary in Sauk Centre. "This might be interesting," he said as he slit it open. The other two watched in anticipation as he read the two sheets of paper.

"Well?" Camilla asked.

Vin didn't respond as he searched first one page, then the other again and again. Finally, he said in deliberate words, "It's a hand written note from the woman at the mortuary and a photo copy of a death certificate. It answers questions, but asks more."

Unable to restrain herself further, Camilla reached for the sheets of paper. He relinquished the note.

"This is a death certificate for Margaret Norma Freidmuth," he continued. It says she died of complications from the flu while staying at the Carl Wessen farm. That leaves no question that this is the right Margaret. It also says she was an orphan and, get this, she died on the same day I was born in rural Sauk Centre, Minnesota." They sat in stunned silence wondering what this could mean.

Camilla asked, "How old was she?"

"Her date of birth is given as January twenty-eighth, nineteen thirty-six, so she would have been seventeen in nineteen fifty-three."

"Don't know if this means anything," Paul interjected, "but Norma Holleran is seventy-four. Let's see, that means she was born in . . . yeah, nineteen thirty-six, the same year."

"Do you remember what day of the year she was born?" Camilla asked.

"I don't think it gave a birth date, only her age."

Vin was still staring at the death certificate looking perplexed.

"What is it," Camilla asked.

"It's curious about the names. Paul, you remember that when I asked Holleran what her middle initial 'M' stood for she said she didn't tell people that. But when I pressed she said it was Margaret."

"Yeah. And she asked you not to tell anyone."

Vin nodded. "It was almost as if she was pleading with me. Now look here. Her name is Norma Margaret, and this girl is Margaret Norma. Margaret died as an orphan at the age of seventeen. I wonder if that was the secret the old people in Sauk Centre were hiding. There was something suspicious, even wrong, with the death of this Margaret. They gossiped about it and put together a fact here and there. Now, they have a gut feel for a story that is most unusual, one they'd just as soon not talk to outsiders about."

They hadn't noticed that Paul has slipped away. He returned with the phone books for Minneapolis and St. Paul. "Look up that last name of Freidmuth in the white pages he said sliding one of the books over to Vin. How's it spelled?"

Vin gave the spelling and opened the Minneapolis book.

Paul was first. "Here in St. Paul, Eugene Freidmuth. That's the only one."

"I'll be darned," Vin said. "In Minneapolis is Alvin Freidmuth, and wife Blanche."

Paul was talking over his shoulder as he left the room. "Wonder if either of them is famous. I'm going on the web."

As Paul pushed the bits in and out of the computer, Vin and Camilla reexamined the sheets of paper. Vin said, "The woman says she searched from January to July and this was the only death she could find that matched what I gave her. If another sick person named Margaret had been taken to the St. Cloud hospital and died there, she might not know about it. That is, if the mortuary from another town handled the burial."

"Yes. But, I doubt two young women, both named Margaret, would have died in that area in a few month's time. She must be the one your mother mentioned. Wonder what she'd say if you showed her this death certificate?"

"I don't see that I can. It would be like accusing her of something."

"Hey. Come back here and see what I found," came the elevated voice of Paul from a back room.

Vin looked at Camilla with a startled almost concerned expression.

As they entered Paul's bedroom he pointed at the monitor. "Look. Eugene Freidmuth, age ninety-six. If Holleran is seventy-three her father would be at least that old. And, he's really rich. There are tons of postings about him. They mostly deal with philanthropic gifts to charities, the arts, stuff like that. He's a 'who's who' in the Twin Cities."

"Keep looking. I think that inkjet printer on the table by the computer still works. Print pages that look important."

Vin and Camilla returned to the living room. Vin sat in a winged rocking chair and put his feet up on the ottoman. "I don't feel so good," he said. "Add it up. I've had three attempts made on my life, one of them where the woman who is arguably the third most important person in the country could have been killed, too. All of this seems to have started when Paul sent a letter to the same woman. Now we learn the man who is probably her father and her brother both live in this city. The father is very rich which means power. She has power too, but of a different kind. The two combined could make an awesome thing. And, I hate to say it, this woman appears to have some strange connection to my birth."

"That's grasping at straws," Camilla said in an unusually stern voice.

"It's not all connected yet, I'll admit that. But, it'll eventually come together. I know it!"

Vincent didn't give voice to his next thought. Something else bothered him. Who beside himself had tried to do a DNA match with his mother? And, what did she know to make her take the evasive action of leaving someone else's hairbrush in her bathroom? Beyond that, it seemed certain she would know something, maybe all, of what happened in that little house on that day in February, nineteen fifty-three.

Joab Feinstein paced the smooth concrete floor of the warehouse space he had rented. Cutter was in the passenger seat of the white panel van asleep. When he took a pain pill, it was lights out for him. When it wore off, he wandered around moaning. That was about to stop one way or the other. Being the end of June it was hot in the closed space and a body would start to smell in no time. He was nearing the point of putting up with a stench rather that the man.

He located a place where he could rent a Ford F-350 pickup with dual rear wheels on Monday. He insisted on the availability of a soft top canvas camper shell. They would have to transfer the fifty-five gallon drums of fertilizer from the box truck to the pickup. Then it was necessary to add the fuel oil to the fertilizer and place the Tannerite in a cavity among the barrels. That meant there could be no topper on the pickup while they worked, but the load had to be covered once they were done. The canvas top was also advantageous because with a cell phone bomb trigger, there would be no interference with the signal.

Worst of all, he was torn about whether or not two hundred pounds of Tannerite would be enough. McVeigh had used three hundred and fifty pounds of Tovex. From what he had read, the experts agreed that had been over kill. But, still . . . .

Earlier in the day, he rented another car with yet another false ID. He had one ID left for the pickup. He'd prefer to use Tuley's ID for that, but had to assume the authorities were watching for it. Time to get started.

He opened the door to the van and shook Cutter. "Come on! We have work to do and you can't sleep all day. You have to stay awake and pull your weight. Got it?"

Cutter opened his eyes and nodded. "I'm awake. Wha-da-ya need?"

"Come on, out of the truck, walk around, get your circulation going. Okay. I made up a shopping list of the stuff we're likely to need. You take the van and get the bigger stuff. You taking this in?"

Joab could see this wasn't going well. He stepped over to their pile of supplies, ripped open a twelve pack and returned with a can of warm soda. He popped the top and said, "Here, bottoms up."

Cutter emptied it in one draught. His eyes snapped open. "Wow! What's in that stuff?"

"Caffeine—five times the maximum daily allowable per spoonful. It's a real favorite with teenagers. Never leave home without it. Listen up. The Tannerite still needs mixing, and I'm told it has to be a good job. So, buy a tub like they use for mixing mortar, a hoe, a kitchen scale, and a scoop. We'll mix it in twenty pound batches and put it in plastic waste-basket bags. We also need some type of dolly or cart to move those four hundred pound drums from the truck to the pickup, as well as some planks or something to bridge between the two vehicles. Remember, you pay for all of it in cash. Keep a running total in your head so you don't spend more than a couple of hundred dollars in any one store. It'll add up fast."

"Ah . . . sounds good, but I need money. The few twenties in my pocket won't cover it."

Feinstein looked uneasily at Cutter as if deciding what to do. The cash was in his money belt and he was pondering the ramifications of whether or not to reveal this to his compatriot. If he went to the office or the john to retrieve the money, it would signal that he had a stash there and didn't trust him, which he didn't. If he opened his shirt where he stood the packets of money could provide a severe temptation. He concluded that either way Cutter would know about a mother lode. Having decided, he opened his shirt, zipped open one of the pouches and produced twenty fifties which he handed to Cutter.

"After I get the pickup on Monday, I think we'd better stay out of sight. That means, we'll sleep here. I'll pick up some sleeping pads, sleeping bags, a cook stove, stuff like that, and plenty of food. We should be ready to go a-bombin' by Wednesday morning."

Feinstein laid out a map of the city on the hood of the car. He had marked the locations of the stores most likely to have what they needed. Cutter was on his way at eleven-thirty.

— 29 —

Dutch Tuley was headed south on interstate I-35. He had driven to Superior, Wisconsin where his sister lived. After some discussion, and his having to tell her more than he wanted, she relented and agreed to exchange his pickup for her car. It was the part about his telling the FBI everything he knew that made her come around. He promised to return the car with a full tank of gas. In Forest Lake he neared the split where I-35 became 35E and 35W. Taking 35E was the obvious route for his primary mission which was to find Mac at the truck rental place and convince him he had not rented the box truck. However, if he took 35W he'd go past the Mills Fleet Farm at Lexington Avenue. It would add a few miles, but not much. He needed some 30-30 cartridges for his deer rifle. He'd stopped there before and found the prices better than in the small towns around him.

In the Fleet Farm store, he resisted the temptation of stopping at the gun counter. He had extra money in his pocket from the fertilizer, but that would have to last. Coming out, he was behind a man with his arm in a cast. Odd, he thought. There's a man with high hopes of his arm healing because with the bad arm he wasn't about to use most of the stuff in the cart. The man stopped at the back of a white panel van. Dutch was thinking it would be neighborly to offer assistance. Then, he saw the man's face from the side. Could it be! Dutch turned his back and made for his sister's car. He started up and advanced a parking row where he stopped in sight of the man fumbling with his purchases. With the rear doors of the van open he could see it contained a couple of fans, extension cords, a cordless screw driver, all kinds of stuff still in the boxes. It was as if he had been robbed and was replacing his tools.

When Danny had marched the man out of the woods, Dutch had a good look at him. However, his attention was on the buyer of the fertilizer thinking he'd try something. From what he could remember, the size was right, and the face was as he recalled. He'd be an identical twin if not that man himself. He remembered a faint vertical scar on his chin. The distance was too far to see that. The broken right arm was expected if he was the one.

The van backed out, and Dutch followed it onto Lexington Avenue getting the plate number as he did. It was out of state but the state wasn't readable. All interest in the truck rental was forgotten. There was plenty of traffic so he stayed two cars behind. The white van went over the freeway and on to the southbound entry lane to 35W. Dutch followed. He was sure this was the man, and he had his box truck. Go, buddy, go. Lead papa to the hideout.

The van driver was being mister clean having set the speed control at exactly seventy miles per hour, the posted speed limit. If he had to switch lanes to pass a slow moving car, he signaled, then pulled back to the right lane after passing so the eighty mile per hour traffic could pass him. In less than ten miles, they were down to sixty, south of the I-694 interchange. From the middle lane, he switched into the right. Three cars back, Dutch did the same. Nearing County Road C, the driver of the white van signaled and took the exit ramp. The light was green at a cross street where they took a left. At County Road C, the light was red. The van came to a stop. As it did there was a left green arrow and it went left.

Dutch was concerned because there was little traffic on County C as it went under the freeway. Past the freeway the van crossed the intersection on the yellow light, but Dutch was stopped as it went red. He lost the van as it disappeared in a left turn. Moving again, Dutch wondered if he should press his luck. If the man had been suspicious of being followed, and the following car made this turn after all the others, he'd know it. Dutch decided not to risk being spotted. However, driving past the street where the van turned off, it was not in sight. Either, the driver had sped off greatly exceeding the speed limit, or more likely, had stayed to his conservative driving habits until he reached his destination less than a quarter mile off County Road C.

Dutch continued on until he found a fast food place and ordered lunch. Slowly munching his food, he wondered what would happen if he called the FBI with the information. If they took the case seriously, they could search the area where the white van had disappeared and find them along with his truck. That was the question. Were they taking it seriously? That man Calloway said they would have arrested him at the farm. Dutch was sure the only reason they hadn't tried the second day was because he had in effect threatened to shoot them. Maybe they considered him a crank trying to waste their time. As he thought about it, that seemed the most likely.

Sniping at the remaining French fries, he pulled out the names written on the border of the flyer. They could be anybody. Calloway didn't say they were the ones matching the fingerprints. He saw a payphone and phonebooks and went to them. The only one of the three listed was Wessen. He wrote the address further along on the margin of the advertiser. What would happen if he paid him a visit? First, he thought, see what kind of place it is. Why not?"

After the late breakfast and the revelations from the mortuary, Vin and Paul decided to let it rest and get to work on the car. Camilla had, the day before, bought the rear door windows, and Vin now returned with body putty, paint, and sandpaper for the holes in the doors. Paul had one door apart and the shattered glass removed.

"Of all the places to shoot holes in a car, those windows are about the easiest to repair," Vin remarked. "The damage from that shot will truly look like new when we're done. I hope we can do as well with the doors. Those are small areas so if we're careful it won't show."

Vin inspected the work Paul had done. "Have you ever worked on cars before?"

"Not at all. My dad isn't inclined that way. Being a real-estate agent in a small town, he saw it as a form of advertising to take his car to the various garages in the area. Some were better than others, but he put up with it for the sake of business."

"Yeah. A small town is a different world, isn't it? In that respect, I like the city. You know, I've been thinking, isn't it odd that the assassin knew we'd be at Minnehaha Park? Either he has our phones bugged, or he put something on our cars so he knows where they are."

They finished replacing the glass in the right rear door. Paul remarked. "I suppose it wouldn't be that hard to track the cars. They have cell phones that parents give their out-of-control kids that tell them where they are at all times. Of course, it assumes the kids keep the phones with them rather than drop them off at a friend's house before they go out to do mischief. The phones use the Global Positioning System."

Vin left the replacement of the inside door panels to Paul and started going over Camilla's car. He knew for sure the shooter had tracked that one. He assumed it would be on the outside attached to a plastic piece. The main areas would be the front bumper and grill and the back bumper. It took ten minutes and the use of a mirror but he found it.

"Look at this, Paul. Behind one of the slats of the front grill was this small device attached with peal off adhesive." He held up his trophy. In less than five minutes, he found a similar one on his car.

"That answers the question of how he knew where we were. We still don't know *why* he was at the park, or if it was the same man the other two times. I wonder if it would be better to leave them on or take them off."

"Why wouldn't you take them off?"

"Taking them off would work for the weekend, but I'll have to go to work on Monday. If the two cars are seen as permanently parked in the garage, he'll know we found them. I'm afraid that might force him to attack the house some night and kill us all."

"Can't you go to the police? You've been shot and that thing is evidence."

"We've been over that. What would I tell them? That we were taking a stroll in Minnehaha Park in the late evening when I was shot? Moments later I was stopped by a cop for reckless driving. But, don't worry, we were only escaping an assassin with the Speaker of the House of Representatives in the back seat? Not only wouldn't they believe me, they'd drag me in for psychiatric evaluation. Don't forget, Holleran fixed it so I didn't get that ticket. We'll leave the transponder off when we go to church tomorrow. But, I'll have to put it back on Monday when I go to work."

Camilla stepped into the garage. "Could I convince one of you to mow the lawn. It's looking pretty ragged."

"I will," Paul said.

"Thanks for the offer, but I could use a workout," Vin replied. "You have the pattern now so the other door should go faster."

Vin started on the front lawn and was methodically pushing along thinking of random things. Sometimes, he became angry, ready to tear somebody's head off if he only knew whose head that was. Other times he was glancing around expecting to see someone taking aim at him. The car pulling to the curb annoyed him at first, then something close to panic took root. With effort, he brushed off the thought. Probably for the house across the street. But then, why not make a one eighty and park on that side? What the heck, it was a public street, so he was entitled. The driver didn't walk across the street, but came his way, a little uncertainly. As Vin approached the concrete walk that ran from the curb to the front step, the man raised his hand in greeting. Vin stopped and raised his hand thereby releasing the safety bar that caused the motor to stop. He hated it when it did that. Well, it was stopped.

"Are you Vincent Wessen?" the man asked.

Vin eyed his closely. "I don't know you, do I?"

He shook his head. "I'm Dutch Tuley. I farm in central Wisconsin. This morning a guy from the FBI asked if I knew a Vincent Wessen, spelled with an e-n. Is that you?"

Cautiously, Vin replied, "Yes. May I ask the nature of your visit and how the FBI becomes involved?"

Vin could see the man was becoming nervous. "It's a nutty story. It looks like some guys may be making a truck bomb. They bought the ammonium nitrate fertilizer from me and would have killed me after I loaded it for them if I hadn't taken certain precautions. Have funny things been happening to you? There must be some reason why the guy at the FBI would ask if I knew you. He asked three names and I didn't know any of them. You were the only one in the phone book."

Vin didn't respond in any way. This was unexpected, but it could be a thread to answer his problem. If he could get information without giving too much it was worth a try.

"I will leave if this is all wrong. I'm not even sure why I came."

"No. Stay a minute. Might as well come around to the patio so we can sit. I have had occasion to, shall we say, interface with that particular bureau of the federal government recently."

Vin stepped into the garage and said, "Paul, come out here. You might as well hear this, too."

Tuley was right behind Vin and saw the broken glass and the exit hole in the right door. "I see somebody is unhappy with you. That looks ugly."

"Let's hear what you have," Vin said.

Dutch related it as it happened. Even to the chance encounter with the white van in the parking lot.

Vin asked, "Is it reasonable that they could make a for-real bomb out of that?"

Dutch nodded as he answered. "Very much so. That's what Timothy McVeigh used in Oklahoma City."

"I don't see that I can be of any help. My case seems completely un-related. Some guy is trying to shoot me for reasons I cannot imagine. I got a good look at his face the first time, but didn't recognize him. Other than that, he drives a bright red sports car. I doubt he's a professional or I'd be dead."

"I was wondering, it might be asking a lot, but could you drive me into the industrial area where the white van disappeared? I'm afraid the guy might have seen me following him and would recognize my car. There was no doubt about the intent of the man in the woods that Danny stopped. They *are* killers."

"Which makes me feel, oh so, inclined to go near them."

"Guess I shouldn't have said that, huh?"

"Let me see an ID."

Dutch complied.

"Paul. How about finishing the lawn, and then doing what more you can on the car. We'll have to finish Sunday."

The place where Dutch had last seen the van was five miles from Vin's house. They drove slowly. The streets were on a grid. They tried them all. With the massive over building during the real-estate bubble, there were several with "For Lease" signs on them.

"I don't like it," Dutch said. "There are too many places." None of them had any vehicles standing outside.

"My suggestion is to come back Monday," was all that Vin could offer. "There are so many buildings and streets, I doubt your car would stand out. This is probably a pretty busy area during the work week."

Back at the house, Dutch thanked Vin and, driving his sister's car, headed back to Wisconsin. Vin and Paul returned to the garage and continued work on the car.

6:00 p.m., Washington, D.C.

The group of five, minus one, Joab Feinstein, were assembled in the secure meeting room. It was unusual, but other commitments had made the Friday meeting impossible. The President began, "What's this I heard about our missing member? The FBI director called me a couple of hours after the briefing on the shadow-shadow man. That's bizarre in itself. Is that true that his fingerprints associate him with the making of a truck bomb? We were discussing a couple of sticks of dynamite at an abortion clinic and implicating the Ellefson campaign and maybe some pro-lifers with it."

Sal Khruz replied. "I haven't been able to get an answer to that. He hasn't called in. A BlackBerry message from him, always cryptic, said he had experienced a setback and was recovering. The planned date of today is set back to Wednesday. The FBI said his fingerprints connected him to the purchase of ammonium nitrate fertilizer that could be used for a truck bomb. I'm going on the assumption that he's planning to make it look like that was the intent, but that some white supremacists flubbed up and it was a dud."

The chief of staff, David Adams, asked, "How are the finger prints even possible. Was he asleep? We can't have screw ups like that."

"The FBI report I saw said the farmer offered him a can of Pepsi. It was a hot humid day. The farmer must have suspected something because the can has only our guy's prints on it. My concern is that most of his experience was in other countries. In the U.S., he worked in Chicago where the police were working with him to fix little things like that. The local FBI in Minneapolis might actually try to solve the case."

Seth Goldman, the National Security Advisor, lifted his finger indication he wanted to be recognized. "If the farmer actually was clever enough to understand what the fertilizer would be used for, and set it up so he got the prints, he's what we could call a problem. He could make up a story and go to the media. He already has the FBI, and I might add, us involved. My thought is we should take him out of circulation."

The others nodded and the President said, "Do it as soon as possible without making it look like world war three is about to start. We must maintain a credible detachment from this. Agreed?"

The three others nodded their assent. Khruz added, "So far there isn't much to worry about. A single piece of evidence like the fingerprints can be handled. Things like that always happen. It's only when a chain of evidence begins to point to certain individuals that it becomes dangerous. Joab's too professional to let that happen."

— 30 —

Monday morning, June 28

It was totally dark, though, without the cloud cover there would have been the first signs of dawn to the northeast. Dutch Tuley turned out of the driveway onto the narrow paved road running past his place. He hardly looked for other traffic because rush hour traffic hadn't started yet. Here, rush hour meant five cars an hour. He didn't exceed the fifty-five speed limit for his own safety. The deer would be rousing and even at this speed he'd be hard pressed to avoid a deer on the road. At least he would likely survive the collision.

A car appeared above a rise some distance ahead. The high beams of the approaching vehicle were annoying as Tuley went to low beam. The jerk never did go to low beam as he sped past. It was a heavy vehicle as evidenced by the bow wave that rocked his car, and it was driven by a city slicker who cared nothing about deer crashes. On a hunch, Dutch reduced his speed as he followed the vehicle in the rearview mirror. It was nearing the vanishing point when the red flare of brake lights appeared at about the location of his driveway. At that moment he was over the rise and increased speed. It was the feds again, he knew it.

The normal route to the Twin Cities was to head southwest and intersect Interstate I-94. He decided to angle to the northwest and cross into Minnesota at Taylors Falls. That road would lead to I-35 and then branch to 35W and on to Roseville. It occurred to him the real rush hour would be starting as he approached the metro and this was probably the best route, anyway.

It was six-twenty as he took the exit for County Road C. There was enough traffic to be inconspicuous. He made the turn where he had last seen the white van. Coming to a stop sign, the street went ahead or to the right. To the left was a drive between two warehouses. He turned left. In the rear, most of the bays had loading docks, a few with eighteen wheelers backed up to them. He took another left. At the end of the second building were two bays with no loading dock. These were meant to have trucks driven into them. Those would be the most likely. On the end of this building a small pickup was backed into a parking space with dew on the windshield. He backed in beside it and slid down in his seat. From here, he could see behind four large warehouse buildings. The street to his right was visible for a short distance. Across that street, was the entry to the rear of more industrial buildings. None were more than ten years old. This whole area had been built up during the real-estate bubble.

Vincent's hands were pouring a cup of coffee but his mind was miles away. He normally didn't have time to brew coffee in the morning, but he was up early and needed the caffeine to stay awake. What would the day bring? The doctrine of divine providence said that God permits evil, but that good always comes from it. If saying his prayers with a fervor previously unknown to him was a good result, then he had to admit God's plan was working. If a good night's sleep was part of the plan, it assuredly was not working. The only silver lining was that it would be over soon. If that crazy man didn't kill him, he'd die of exhaustion. At the moment, solving the problem wasn't even part of his thinking. He simply existed.

He physically shook so much at the sound of the phone ringing that he spilled coffee on the floor. Of all the . . . . Who could be calling at this hour? He grabbed the extension in the kitchen lest it awaken everybody in the house. "Yeah, who's calling?" There was irritation in his voice, and he didn't care.

"This is Minna Simons, Norma Holleran's private assistant. Is this Vincent Wessen?"

What now? was the first thought to enter Vin's fevered brain.

"Yes. It's early in the morning, and I'm tired. Sorry if I was abrupt."

"That's not a problem. Ms. Holleran told me about the incident Friday evening. She was deeply upset at having put you through that. You were wounded, am I correct?"

"Yes, but worst luck, it looks like I'll live. May I ask why you're calling?"

"I'm afraid, I'm calling with bad news, and that I'll be asking you to aid her once again. Last evening as she was arriving at Andrews she was suddenly taken quite ill. I won't go into it now, but we are preparing a press release for an hour from now. She has a terminal condition, and has a great desire to speak with your nephew, and you too if you'll come, before she dies. It seems some things were left unsaid in the park on Friday."

Vin plunked down on a dinette chair. "I don't want to be the one to refuse a dying request, but I'd have to take vacation, not to mention the expense of the plane ticket, two actually. I refuse to let Paul go into that D.C. snake pit alone, especially after what's been happening to us over the past few weeks. How long does she have?"

"As far as how long, we don't know. They're doing all the tests they can."

"Yeah. It's interesting that she conveniently exempted herself from the national health care bill she forced through the house for everybody else. I'm inclined to tell her to take a pain pill and call it good. What have I gotten out of it but a bullet hole in my arm, and I can't even go to a doctor. Nice going, Madam Speaker." He was becoming agitated, something he prided himself in not doing on the phone. Irate customers loved it when they could rile him.

"I can't speak for her record, though I understand there are legions of people who don't like what she did on health care. I have been her private assistant for over twenty years. I can say this with perfect honestly, your nephew has had a more profound effect on her than anyone since her college days. If she had met someone like Paul decades ago, the world might be a different place. I can only ask that you come."

There was a pause. Vin was thinking that he never used all of his vacation anyway, and money wasn't everything.

"Please, excuse my lack of matters. I'm distraught, too," Minna continued. "She will send her Air Force jet to get you and return you home. She asked me to be on the plane and escort you the whole way. There'll be no checkpoints, no press. I know how to avoid that. I think it would be advisable to plan for overnight. There are times when she's perfectly lucid, but other times when the drugs put her out."

Paul came sleepily from his room having be aroused by the ringing of the phone extension in his room, and then the intense words of his uncle. He raised his eyebrows questioningly.

"Hold on a minute. Paul's here. I'll ask him."

Vin put his hand over the mouthpiece of the phone. "It's Holleran's assistant. The Speaker has taken seriously ill and is not expected to live.

She wants to finish her conversation with you. She'll send her plane. I said I'd have to come along if you agreed. That's okay with them. What do you think? I know it's sudden."

Paul was wide eyed. "Sure, I guess. It can't be any more dangerous in D.C. than it is here. Wonder if the plane will crash."

Vin spoke into the phone. "He wants to know if the plane will crash?"

"Tell him that I'll be betting my life that it doesn't."

"She says she'll be coming on the plane, and she's betting her life it won't."

"Okay. As long as she's on it."

"We have a deal. When will you arrive? I suppose at the same place where we dropped her off, is that right?"

"Yes, it is. I've made preliminary arrangements. If nothing changes, it will take a little more than three hours. May I assume you'll be at this phone for the next couple of hours?"

"Yes. I'll be here. You'll have to arrange something so we can get past the guard at the National Guard base."

"I've done it all many times, don't worry. You'll be required to show a picture ID at the gate. That's all."

Vin hung up the phone and supported his forehead with his hands. "Boy, if that doesn't take all."

"Are you going to leave the GPS transponder on the car?"

Vin thought a minute. "I suppose so. If he tries to shoot me again, might as well get it over with. Maybe he has a job to go to or something. By now, I'm sure he's not a professional. If he sees us show up at the National Guard base again it could spook him, like we're recruiting some serious help."

"That's a nice fantasy Uncle Vin, but more likely he'd think you're helping to restore one of those old war birds at the museum they have there. He'd think that's a good place to lay in wait."

"Thanks for bursting my bubble, but I suppose you're right. It doesn't change anything, though. We have to leave it on. I don't want him coming here."

By eight-thirty, Dutch had decided he was out of luck. Either the bombers were long gone, they were not stirring, or he had the wrong place. A large pickup with dual rear wheels on the street caught his eye. It took a left behind the buildings across the street. It's an odd thing about large personal vehicles, pickups and SUVs especially. Unless you're beside them, it's hard to tell their actual size. But, dual rear wheels screams big vehicle. The back was covered with an easily removable canvas topper. Again, this was something that was seen at times, but not common. His curiosity aroused, Dutch started up and followed. Interestingly the dualies didn't stop at any of the buildings on the block but proceeded across the next street. He followed. At the street, Dutch could see the pickup had slowed and was angling away from the building. It stopped and started to back toward the building when it became masked by the trailer of an eighteen wheeler.

Before he knew what he was doing, Dutch was slouched down in the car driving toward the pickup. Here too, the two end bays had a ramp up to them for driving in. One glance was all he intended to permit himself. The pickup was backed in and the door was rolling down as he passed. All that was visible were the grill and bumper of the pickup. The driver of the pickup was not visible to Dutch, and even if he had been looking Dutch's way, the door was probably too far down for the driver to have recognized him, though, he couldn't be sure. At the very least, he might have seen Dutch's car driving past at that exact moment. He'd think it could be a coincidence, but paranoid people seldom put much stock in coincidences. Dutch glanced ahead and realized this was a dead end. There was ample room so he did a one-eighty without stopping. By this time, the door had reached the pavement. Dutch drove out the way he had come in.

At County Road C he turned left, and at the stoplight left again. This was a four lane divided highway. He approached the second stoplight as the left turn arrow went to green. He took left. Unconsciously, he was heading to the area of Wessen's house. He was running, running scared. There was too much happening. The big vehicle careening down the country road in the dark and hitting the brakes at his place had to mean the FBI. He couldn't go home for a while. He drove for a mile, watching for a tail. Then he noticed that odd intersection. They were coming the other way, but that's where Wessen had turned. He did the same and a few blocks later stopped at the now oddly familiar house.

He went to the door and rang the bell. Eventually the woman answered. He had met her briefly the few days before.

"Hello. I'm Dutch Tuley. I was here last Saturday. Is you husband home?"

If he had a job, and being able to afford this tidy place said he did, it meant he was at work.

"Yes," was the cautious reply. "I do remember you. No, Vin isn't home." They were speaking through the screen door.

"How about the young man?"

"No. What is it you want?"

"Did your husband tell you anything about what we discussed? We even went out together."

"Yes he did. You look frightened. What's the matter?"

"If he told you about me you know there are people who are putting together a truck bomb. I believe I found where they are. But, they might have seen me. I need a place to get out of sight. Could I drive my car up by your garage so it's off the street and wait on your patio until I decide what to do?"

"If you know all this, why don't you go to the police?"

"Because as I was leaving my farm this morning I missed by a minute a large vehicle that turned into my driveway. It was the FBI coming to arrest me. You see, I sold the bombers the fertilizer they'll use for the bomb. It wasn't as if I had a choice. I met with the FBI once and if they come to talk they drive a compact. This was a load of guys."

Camilla was hesitant. He looked harmless, but don't they all? Yet, the FBI in their association with both Paul and Vin was anything but pleasant. She understood his concern. "Okay. Drive around back. We'll talk there."

When they were on the patio, Dutch said, "I need to call the FBI and tell them what I know. Where is a place that I can find a payphone? In that direction," he said pointing away from the direction he had come."

Camilla told him.

"I may think of some things to do, but I need a place to stay tonight. Could I sleep in your garage? If I go to a motel, I'll be forced to use a credit card to guarantee the room against damage even if I pay cash. If I do that, they'll find me. That's all I ask. Those FBI guys aren't real smart, and can't wait to jail a white guy for attempted terrorism."

Camilla nodded. "When you're here, park on the left of the garage apron. Vin will be home and we'll decide how to handle it. I can't let you in the house, you understand."

"No disagreement there. I need some time to figure. Think I'll sit tight for an hour and then go to make a call to the feds. It's not that I want to help them, but I don't want innocent people getting hurt."

Returning to he house, Camilla locked the doors as much from fear of the authorities as the man out back.

When Dutch called, he got the voice mail of Calloway. He harangued him about attempting to arrest him again. He told him about the changed vehicle, but not where they were. If he turned out to be mistaken, people would be hassled, and he would be blamed for wasting the FBI's time, again, filing a false report, or something. Why was this being so hard? They obviously took the threat seriously or they wouldn't have made three trips out to his farm. Why were they only interested in him, why weren't they trying to find the bad guys?

— 31 —

At eight forty, Vin and Paul arrived at the gate. After showing their driver's licenses the guide car immediately led them to where Vin was to leave his car. Fifteen minutes later the sleek Lear Jet taxied up. The door opened, they boarded, and were off. The morning rush of departures was over so they took off immediately.

Minna Simmons introduced herself as they entered. At cruising altitude, she produced some soft drinks and snacks.

She was saying, "When I left her, she was awake and expressed her appreciation that you had consented to come. It's such a shock for me, you know. All these years with her, I know her so well. I should have noticed something." It was clear that Simmons was unburdening herself. "For several years, she's been having headaches. The pain relievers became stronger, but not that much. What seems to have happened is the cancer was spreading through her body and the headache pills were masking it. She'd complain about one pain and then another. We're both getting older every day. I have my problems, too. So, we'd complain a little, and joke a little about replacing pain remedies with a youth potion. The press will go crazy, as will the President. The next most likely Speaker is much more conservative."

With that, she fell silent. Both Vin and Paul could see it was the end of Minna's life as much as her boss's, her friend's. They left things that way for some minutes. The hum of the engines, the hiss of the air slipping past the plane, the gentle motions, all of it together was a little hypnotic.

Minna spoke as she stared out the window. "It's such a shame that she has to suffer this way. Why can't we simply die? These old bodies of ours wear out and everything hurts. Then toward the end we stupidly cling to life when there's no reason to live. She'll never go back to the House, never take her position again. Why prolong it?"

Paul couldn't help but enter the conversation at this point. "That's the wrong way to look at it. I read a book on this recently, and I might not have all the answers, but here are some. First of all everybody suffers. There has never been a single person who has lived without experiencing pain. True, it seems that some people have a lot more pain than others. I don't know about that. In the final analysis, maybe God sends every person the same amount, and it's bunched up in different places in each life. Who knows?"

Paul waited to see if Minna was accepting what he had to say. She was attentive so he continued. "With that as a starting point, the question is this. How do we look at this inevitable part of life? Someone once said, 'Anyone who dies without having suffered, experiences an unprovided death.' When Fr. Benedict Groeschel was visiting Terence Cardinal Cooke as he was in great pain dying of cancer he asked, 'How's it going?' The Cardinal replied, 'Great for a man who's dying of cancer.' Later in the conversation Cardinal Cooke referred to his final suffering as 'this grace filled time.'"

"It's hard to think of it that way when you see her condition," Minna replied. "Either she's awake and in enormous pain, or scarcely conscious from the drugs. I suspect you haven't suffered much."

"That part is true. But, I see the value in getting my mind straight about it while I have my health and can rationally consider it. Today people consider it a blessing if someone they know goes from the bloom of health to death, preferably in their sleep, or in a second. They think it's so nice that they didn't suffer. However, it isn't necessarily nice at all. We need the time when we know death is coming to let all our worldly worries go and concentrate on what's coming.

"The example is given of someone in a doctor's office receiving the news, 'Your tests are positive.' You learn you have at most six months to live. You leave the office and find yourself on a sidewalk. A man rushes past because he's late for an appointment. A driver is honking his horn to make someone move out of his way. None of it matters to you because for you the world is ending. Suddenly the obnoxious coworker you have to put up with has less meaning, not only because you won't be around much longer, but because there are more important things to think about. You have to get your life in order—spiritually. Eternity is close at hand.

"It has been said that what our grandfathers could do in an afternoon will probably take us six months because of the miracles of modern medicine. It is possible that that is not an accident. The world is evil today in ways not imagined in the past. Maybe we are given more time to suffer before death because we have a lot more to atone for. Take this simple example. Years ago, a person might harbor resentments toward his neighbor. But, he was restrained in how overtly he displayed his displeasure because something might happen and he'd need his neighbor. Today we all expect that if we need assistance we'll call nine-one-one and some total strangers will arrive who are trained and paid to give assistance. They will be nice to us too because that's part of the package. We don't have to care about receiving help from our neighbors.

"Make no mistake, the health care plan Ms. Holleran championed will above all limit medical care in the final sickness. The excuse was to save money. They possibly also saw it as a mercy to save people from suffering. But, just as surely, they did not want them to have 'that grace filled time' in which to repent. Those legislators have sold their souls to the devil, and they want to keep as many people as possible from repenting. If misery loves company, eternal misery is fanatical about it—let's all go to hell together."

Vin broke in, "Paul, that's enough. She gets the picture."

Minna looked at Vin with appreciation in her eyes. Vin commented on the nice plane to which she shrugged and said it hadn't always been this way. For most of their time together it was a scramble to get the cheapest tickets while counting their frequent flyer miles.

Vin leaned back in the comfortable seat and stretched his legs. It occurred to him that if a person was forced to travel a lot, this was the way to do it. More than that, he was thinking about his situation. Where could the connection lie? Here he was moving with the rich and powerful at the same time his life was threatened, and he came upon this seemingly unrelated thing about Margaret.

Finally Vin said, "I suppose you know her life story pretty well, don't you?"

She smiled. "Yes. We are very close. It wasn't that way at first, but after ten years, you know, we became best friends."

"I don't want to pry, but she was married once, wasn't she?"

There was the slightest guardedness in her reply. "Why would you ask that?"

Vin wondered if he should proceed, then thought he had to. That man was still after him. "Well, let me ask another question. Is her maiden name Freidmuth?"

Minna's mouth fell open. "Now! What would give you that idea? I dare say."

The response was more than Vin had expected. "It's not such a big thing. She said she has a brother named Alvin as well as her father living in the Twin Cities. And, there is an Alvin Freidmuth living in Minneapolis, and an Eugene Freidmuth in St. Paul."

"Yes. But, she didn't give the last name. She never would."

"That's true. She didn't."

"How did you guess?" Her tone was that of someone in pain.

"Don't worry. I can keep a secret. What I'm about to say next may upset you so be prepared. It's just that I must get some answers. Someone has tried to kill me three times and I have no leads. The time in the park with Ms. Holleran was only the most recent. I have no idea how this could connect, but it's all I have."

She was bewildered by Vin's intensity. "Well. Go ahead and say it."

"I've located Margaret."

Minna's expression was a mixture of "I don't know what you're talking about," and "I'm afraid to hear what comes next."

"I mean Margaret Norma. It's a strange coincidence that Ms. Holleran's name is Norma Margaret."

The expression now was entirely that of "I'm afraid of what I'll hear next."

"I'm guessing she would be either a sister or half sister to Ms. Holleran."

Minna closed her eyes. She pulled a handkerchief from her pocket and dabbed at her eyes. There was unmistakable sound of sobs. Vin could see he had assumed correctly. Yet, what did it matter? How was this going to make any difference?

The White House

Randy Offit was shown into the spacious well lit room that was unoccupied. "The President will be with you in a minute," he was told.

Before he could sit, the door on his right opened, a Secret Service man entered followed by the President. "Offit," he said extending his hand. "I didn't know you were over here. I hope it's short because I'm on my way out. Call ahead, if you need time, you know that."

"Yes, sir. This is by way of information. Two days ago we spoke of those shadow-shadow units. You recall?"

"Yes. You, that general and the DCI. What is it?"

"We've been alerted the person who was the subject of that meeting is on his way to Washington. We've informed the Secret Service so you'll be seeing additional security for a while."

The President gaped in a double take. "So quietly apprehend him at the airport and tell him to take his business elsewhere. We don't care where, just not here. Is that so hard?"

"It sort of is, sir. He'll be landing at Andrews in less than an hour, in an Air Force jet. He has clearance, and will be met by a car from Holleran's staff. We don't know what to make of it."

"That's another of my problems, politics, how to influence the election of her successor. What's his motive, mission, whatever? Why's he coming to this town?"

"As much as we've managed to learn, it's to confer with Holleran. Might be she's planning to influence the election of her successor, too. Why wouldn't she? And, however she did it, she managed to get some good help."

The President rubbed his mouth in an agitated gesture. "Keep track of him. I want to know where he is every minute. Now, I'm running behind schedule." That statement was a non-statement, because in his lack of concern for others, he was always late.

———————————

Vincent was forced to admit to himself that Minna Simmons knew her way around Washington, and the press. The car was nondescript, but the driver knew the streets and avoided traffic. From time to time she'd press a speed dial on her cell phone and say one or two words. They were dropped off at a door of a large building without another person in sight. The door was unlocked, though it seemed that she locked it after they were in. The elevator they used was obviously for staff since its location was anything but obvious. On the fifth floor they emerged and walked a long corridor to a room with more than the usual number of people in the hall. A uniformed guard nodded at Minna.

"They're with me," she said. That was good enough. The door was opened and they entered.

Norma Holleran was awake and recognized them immediately. "Thank you for coming."

"It was hard to refuse the VIP treatment," Vin replied. "Ms. Simmons has been very gracious and accommodating. I should say thank you. I hope it will have been worth the trouble."

There were two women in white uniforms attending to the Speaker. "I wonder," she said addressing them. "These are close friends. Could we have some privacy for a while?"

"We'll watch your signs on the monitors at the main station. If something goes out of bounds, we'll break in."

"Yes, of course." They left.

The door was still closing when Minna leaned over the bed and whispered in a voice that Vin and Paul could hear, "Vincent has found Margaret."

Holleran's eyes became wide. They fixed on Minna, her trusted friend, to be sure she was serious. She was. Then to Vin. "Come closer," she said to him. "Is that true?"

"Yes I believe it is."

"What do you mean, you believe. Doesn't she know who she is?"

"It's not like that." He paused. "You see, she can't say. She's dead. I'm sorry."

Holleran's expression relaxed. "I see. Was it recently?"

"No. She died in nineteen fifty-three at the age of seventeen. She was in a small central Minnesota town of Sauk Centre. Do you know of it?"

"Yes, I do. *Main Street*. I read that book in high school. Sinclair Louis. But, how do you know this?"

"I went to the mortuary there and they still had her death certificate on file. You see there is a strange connection between you and me, or rather Margaret and me. Margaret died on the same day I was born, and in the same house. Do you know anything about that?"

Norma closed her eyes and grimaced. They opened again. "The pain is coming back. I have short periods of relative comfort, then the pain. Sometimes the medicine completely knocks me out. I may not have much time left and we have a lot to do. This information is more than I could handle when I was well. Now, it's confusing."

Minna grasped Vin's upper right arm to nudge him to the side. He snatched it away. "Please! Not that arm. That's really sore."

"Oh." Holleran said. "Is that the bullet wound from Saturday?"

"Yes. It still hurts a lot. Of course, I couldn't go to a doctor with it. It would have meant disclosing the whole episode at the park."

"Minna. While I'm still awake, I must insist that he be seen by a doctor while he's here. And, keep it quiet. Can you do that?"

"Certainly. You know I can."

"Good. Thank you. About Margaret. I don't know what to say. I know my father spent a considerable amount of money trying to find her. She wasn't to be found. I suppose this explains why."

"That's not the big difficulty," Vin replied. "It seems you are the same age as Margaret would be if she were alive. I doubt you were twins. Is that true?"

"Minna, I'm getting worse so I can't continue this. Vincent, come back when I'm better, will you? In addition, I must talk to Paul. You said in the car you could keep a secret." She clamped her teeth and squeezed her eyes shout. After ten seconds, she opened them again. "Is that still true?"

"Yes, it is."

"Minna, on the flight back, tell them the secret."

"All of it?"

"Yes. Now, tell the nurses to come back."

Paul was taken down the hall to what was a waiting room for the myriad people who wanted access to the Speaker. It kept some of them out of the hallway. Minna took Vincent to another floor. He waited in an examining room while Ms. Simmons spoke with a doctor in the adjoining room. When they came in, Minna said, "He'll take care of the arm. When he's finished, return to where we left Paul. You can't be wandering around. This is a secure facility."

Vin noticed the doctor of about eighteen was wearing military rank. As he removed his shirts, he inquired, "This is what hospital?"

"Walter Reed Army Medical Center. You don't know where you are?"

"Nobody said and I didn't ask. It's been that sort of day."

With the bandage off the doctor said. "What a mess. The doctor that did that to you should be thrown out of the profession."

"Hey. You're putting down on my wife. It's a bullet wound so I couldn't go to a doctor. They are required to report things like that."

"Have you had any antibiotics?"

"Of course not."

The doctor stopped what he was doing and went into the next room. He returned with a syringe. "Better use the left arm. The right one's not so good. What got you into a gun fight, anyway?"

"Not a gun fight. The other man was the only one with a gun. But, I'm thinking about changing that. I was saving the life of a very important person. Hint, hint. I hope you can keep your mouth shut. You can sew this up without a helper, I hope. The fewer people who know about this the better, okay?"

"Sure."

A half-hour later the job was done. The doctor rustled around in some drawers until he came up with a handful of foil packages of antibiotic capsules. "In twelve hours, no, I guess you can wait until tomorrow morning, take two of these, then one every twelve hours. Don't forget, and use them all."

"Yeah. Got it. And, thanks. You do a lot of these bullet things, do you?"

"Nope. That's my first one."

Wait until you're nineteen and I'll bet that'll change, Vin thought.

At five o'clock that afternoon, they were shown into Holleran's room again. She was awake, but seemed to have aged even from their visit a few hours before.

She looked at Paul, "What can you tell me about eternity. Could the rest of you leave for a few minutes? I'd like this to be between the two of us."

She could see the deference Paul showed for his uncle, and wanted him to feel free to say what he had a mind to say.

When they were alone, he began. "A couple of years ago when I was ill with a high fever, I had a dream, really a nightmare, I suppose. It was more than that, though. Do you know what a spiritual locution is?"

"No."

"That's when God speaks directly to your mind. You don't see images, nor hear voices. But, it is totally clear that God contacted you directly. It is indelibly impressed on your soul. You can't forget it even if you try. When I awoke, shaking and perspiring, out of bed on my knees on the floor with my head touching the carpet, I was begging God not to be dead, begging for another chance. The power, the awful reality of eternity and the granite hard certainty that once dead there were no more chances would not be swept away. In a moment, it was clear that hell was not what one should fear. It was eternity. It scarcely matters what torments hell might bring, even a minor annoyance that lasts without end is the definition of hell. In this life, everyone can see that no matter how painful, how humiliating things become, there is always the escape of death. Death is the final solution. But, after death, there are no more escapes. Your condition is final. The decisions you make in life add up to the total of eternity. A finite number of finite decisions added up to infinity. In normal mathematics that's impossible. In the calculus of God, it is a fact.

"At times, I have tried to revisit the experience. To hold the concept of eternity, as I know it to be, in my mind for more than a fleeting moment is impossible. It is as if the thought were to be held in my mind for a whole second it would drive me insane. A finite mind cannot hold an infinite object. The truly terrifying part of it is that we are all created for infinity. As small and weak as we are, we are driven toward the infinite with no escape possible. It all seems in some way unfair. The prizes of either the bliss of heaven or the defeat of hell are too great. We are not up to the task. But, don't forget, God is more than willing to give us the help we need, all we have to do is ask for it.

"Keep in mind that God is infinitely just and infinitely merciful. The difference between His justice and His mercy is this. His justice will happen, no matter what you do. There's no point in praying for His justice. You'll get that. But, if you expect to receive his mercy, you must ask for it. Only by humbly asking the mercy of God can you possibly hope to gain heaven. In addition, part of asking for mercy is repenting of your sins. That, and doing your level best to make amends for the damage your sins have done to others."

Holleran was hardly blinking as Paul spoke. At this point she said, "Please tell me you plan to be a preacher. Where have you been all my life? As Minna will tell you, my life started off pretty rocky. Where do I go from here?"

"You are nominally a Catholic. Call a priest and make a good confession. Let it all out, hold nothing back. Get it in your liberal head that you are almost out of time. Then, do the penance he gives you. If it's a light one, do more. It would save you a ton of purgatory if you'd come out and disclaim the liberal agenda, especially abortion. As your penance, you might not have to do that explicitly. But if you don't, how can you be sure you are really sorry for your sins? No sorrow, no forgiveness, no heaven, and hell for eternity. It's not worth the gamble."

"I don't know if I can do that. It would be as if I hadn't lived. My life would amount to nothing."

"What can I say. I can't force you to repent. Neither can a priest. That's where the rubber meets the road. There's no out-sourcing that function."

After a pause she asked, "There's one more thing. In the park you said that apart from eternity there was something else you had to say that I wouldn't want to hear either. What was that?"

Paul smiled. "In for a penny, in for a pound, is that it? It was only that you should be grateful if you are permitted to suffer intensely before you die. It's part of God's mercy. It's meant to break the hardness of your heart so you repent. You had a lot to do with the national health care bill that passed in the house. You all but legislated that as soon as an old person starts to feel pain, they'll be killed. This is what could be called your grace filled time. Don't think that being 'grace filled' means it will be pleasant. The opposite is the truth. The approach of death with its pain is an important part of life; it prepares you for eternity. In addition, it won't be only physical pain. You'll be stricken with fear, anger, humiliation, blasphemous thoughts, a sense that God has abandoned you, and more."

"I've encountered some of that all ready. As for repenting, I'll try."

"You don't get it, do you? It's too late for feeble efforts. *What does it profit a man if he gains the whole world, but suffers the loss of his soul?* I didn't make that up! Why should you care about your legacy or any stupid thing like that? This is the crack of doom for you; your part of the human struggle is ending. Get with the program. Make it right. Denounce your evil ways."

He paused wondering if any of what he said was registering. "Start with humility. We are all called to break through our shells of egotism. It is said that every person experiences two great maturings in life. The first is when you are young. You pass from a state of dependence to one of independence. That requires the virtue of courage. The second, the hardest, comes in old age when you revert from a state of independence back to one of dependence. That requires the virtue of humility. Old age and approaching death help you get ready to face your final judgement. There are no proud people in heaven."

Tears rolled down her cheeks. "It's not that easy."

"Of course it's not." In a milder voice, he continued, "You know, people are strange. No one would ever think they could get up from a couch where they've been sitting watching TV, eating junk food, with no exercise for years, and expect to win the Olympic hundred meter dash. Yet, that's what they expect to do with eternity. As the moment of death approaches, they expect to repent and go to heaven. But, that's when the devil will be the strongest. What makes you think that without the slightest amount of training, you'll be able to win the hundred meter dash against the devil?" He shook his head. "I'll call the others."

They left the hospital at six o'clock. By seven, they were airborne.

Twin Cities, 5:00 p.m.

Joab Feinstein was feeling satisfied with himself. With no thanks to his helper, he had managed to transfer the heavy barrels of fertilizer from the box truck to the pickup without dropping one or crushing any fingers. The fertilizer soaked up exactly the amount of fuel oil that the directions had said. Mixing the Tannerite had been time consuming, but he was satisfied he had done it correctly. There was still plenty to do. The main thing was to deliver his last messages to his buddy, Alvin. While he was gone, he'd have Cutter vacuum the entire place and then start packing. He intended that they would leave nothing in the bay. As far as he knew, there was not a single person who knew what they had done here. When the lease was up, the owner would find the place empty and clean, especially clean of fingerprints.

In the early morning he would follow Cutter as he took the blue car to another part of the city, where he'd park it, and then Joab would drive him back to their warehouse. They'd do the same with the other rental car. He would have done that with the box truck, except it might have alerted Cutter to what he had in mind. As far as Cutter knew, the plan was that he'd deliver the bomb truck to a shopping center parking lot. He'd watch from a distance as Alvin and Wessen arrived. When they were on their way, Cutter would drive Alvin's car back to within a few miles of the warehouse where Joab would pick him up. After that, they'd leave. He'd drive the white van, and Cutter the box truck. On the eastern side of the metro, they'd abandon the box truck and be on their way. On the drive back to Virginia, they'd dump a few bags of garbage and what not at a truck stop here, a restaurant there.

— 32 —

Monday evening, June 28

At cruising altitude Minna Simmons said, "Would you like a glass of wine. I think I'll be having one."

Vin nodded. "That would be nice."

Paul declined.

Seated again, Minna re-clasped her seat belt and began, "We never talked about revealing her secret. Other than her father, there probably isn't anyone alive who knows it. There was never a reason to tell her brother. I doubt even her mother was told the whole thing. Officially, Norma is seventy-four years old, but her biological age is only seventy. That's awfully young to be on the edge of death, don't you think?"

"Yes. I suppose it is. It's all tied up with divine providence and our own free wills. How that works is a mystery. Though it may seem young to us, in God's plan, it's exactly the right age for her to be dying."

"You people seem to have a keener sense of mortality than most people. Why is that?"

"I wouldn't have thought of it that way. It's only a matter of accepting why we're here, and living your life accordingly. Everything passes away. Why is that such a hard idea to grasp? We all see it every day, yet it's almost universally ignored. But, I think this chatter is keeping us from our appointed task. It seemed as if Ms. Holleran wanted us to hear her story. She may even have intended that we would publish it one day as a set of extenuating circumstances that would account for her public life. However, we have to hear the story before we can decide."

Minna looked as if she might cry as she began. "We managed to hide it so well, it's like a work of art will be destroyed by revealing it. Anyway, let it be done with. It started the summer after her third year of college. Her real name is Claire."

"Daddy, Daddy, please can I go? Rita's going, and we'll stay together. Nothing will happen. We only want to help those people."

Eugene Freidmuth had been having a running argument with Claire
for the past couple of days. She wanted to go to the South and participate
in the freedom rides to help end segregation. She had ended her junior
year of college a few days before and several students that she chummed
around with were making the trip. All the students were from the Catholic high school she had attended. That school had a graduating class of
seventy so they were a closely knit group.

In February of nineteen sixty, four black college students sat down in
a segregated Woolworth's lunch counter in Greensboro, North Carolina,
and refused to leave. They were allowed to stay at the counter but were
refused service. The major media picked up the story and soon that
means of protest spread throughout the South. In mid-April of the same
year, some young black activists went on to form the Student Non-
Violent Coordinating Committee, SNCC, in Raleigh, N.C. It was primarily a place for young blacks to become involved in the civil rights
movement. Soon after its founding, white activists were allowed to join
with them in protests and demonstrations.

Now in nineteen sixty-one the Supreme Court ruled that all buses and
railroads as well as the terminals and associated facilities must be integrated. The freedom rides were made to test compliance of the new ruling in the southern states. Mississippi and Alabama were the states where
the freedom riders were meeting the most resistance with Jackson, Mississippi as the focal point. In May, hundreds had been arrested and many
more beaten by Southern whites who objected to the coming changes.
This was where the group of students was headed.

"I don't think you should go. That's a volatile situation with a lot of
violence already. So far, the riders have only been beaten, but that could
change for the worse very fast. What do you think your mother would
say?"

"She's against everything. Besides, she's in Europe, and I'll be home
before she's back. Please, can I go?"

"When do you have to know?"

"Noon tomorrow. They leave the day after tomorrow."

"If I were to agree, it would be that you could go down there and see
what's going on, be a part of the street scene, so to speak. You could

learn a lot by just watching. But, absolutely no riding the buses, none of this letting yourself be arrested to make a point. Is that clear?"

"Well, I'm not sure what will happen. Maybe not becoming involved at all won't be possible."

"I don't care. That's the condition. If you don't agree and go anyway, it'll be an act of defiance, and you'll end up with no college tuition."

He could see the pout coming on. She was trying her darnedest to handle him, and coming close to succeeding.

"I'm not trying to be mean. It's that there are people who lie awake at night thinking of ways to use naïve people like you. You've led a sheltered life, and that's a wild situation down there. What do you say, agreement?"

She brightened up. "Okay. Thank you Daddy." She kissed him on the cheek and pranced off to pack.

Eugene knew he was a soft touch. He found it hard to refuse her anything. She was so bright and energetic with a measure of wildness. Alvin her brother, now only eight, was more introverted. Though a good student, he had a bit of a wild streak, too. They got it from their mother. At times, he wondered why he had married her. A large part of the reason was his longing to find again the happiness he and his first wife had shared. It was crazy, he knew, to ever expect he could have that again. They were so in love and it lasted only three years. His second wife was advancing in her career just when women were starting to make headway into the previously all male bastions of corporate America. He wondered at times if she had been promoted to her position precisely because of the travel. She was away from home three-quarters of the time. What sane person, man or woman, wanted that?

The students left at six on the appointed morning. There were seven of them in the extended window van. Besides one couple who were more in love with each other than the adventure, there were three unattached boys and two similarly unattached girls, Claire, and Rita. Their destination was Jackson, Mississippi. All of them were from the Highland Park area of St. Paul, an upper class neighborhood. Therefore, means was no problem. They didn't bother with camping along the way or any of the hippie stuff. They stayed in motels, usually the ones with the biggest and brightest signs. With no pressing schedule, they would arrive in Jackson on the evening of the third day.

Claire had jet black hair that she kept cut short. Her balanced features were rather ordinary looking except for large brown eyes, and lips that were a little over sized. It was the range of expressions that showed instantly the sweep of moods of the complex person behind the face that caught everybody's attention, even at first glance. She had been on the swimming team in high school and still swam three times a week. Therefore, her five-seven frame was in good physical condition.

Rita also had dark hair, with a tinge of red in it. She was five-six and fine boned. Her chin protruded slightly more than normal beneath a small mouth and light blue eyes. While she was more of a hellion by nature than Claire, she had a sense of balance that kept her from doing things that could get her into trouble. It was she who coaxed Claire to come on the trip because it wasn't something Claire would normally do.

Before leaving St. Paul, they had each purchased a blond wig. It was something they had talked about for years. Was it true that blondes had more fun? Here was a chance to test it. They had appeared the morning after their first stop on the way down wearing the wigs. There were the expected guffaws and kidding by the guys, but it wasn't long before it was accepted. It was important for the girls so they could get used to their alternate personalities before arriving at their destination.

On the trip down, they saw segregation for the first time in their lives. The lunch counter sit-ins that had started the year before had by no means integrated all the lunch counters in the South. Where there was a drinking fountain, there were two, one for whites, one for coloreds. As they checked into the hotel in Jackson, Mississippi, they were casually asked why they were in town because the desk clerk, white, suspected why they were there. They said they would visit friends. At that point, the two girls were brunettes. When they joined the protests the next morning, they'd be blondes.

It was a fact that having whites as part of the demonstrations was a mixed blessing for the blacks. In most respects, this was a black issue about blacks. It was essentially their fight. Counting whites among their number had its beneficial side, though. It showed that not all whites were bigots. It took some of the pressure off the blacks to have whites fighting whites. It was also good publicity. Segregation in the South was the most overt so this was the place that made for the best news. There was plenty of segregation in northern cities like Chicago or Detroit, but it was more subtle.

The freedom rides, as far as the actual riding went, had blacks buying bus tickets and sitting in the front of buses rather than the back. The actual demonstrations were in the cities especially in and around the terminals.

In most cases the signs indicating separate drinking fountains, windows to buy tickets, terminal lunch counters, and washrooms had been removed. That was done in response to the U.S. Supreme Court's ruling in the case of Boynton v. Virginia, December nineteen-sixty, which stated that all terminals and the facilities associated with interstate bus and train travel must be integrated. The integration of the trains and buses themselves had been required by a nineteen forty-six Supreme Court case. The overall goal of the rides was to test compliance with the Court's ruling, and to publicize the point that it was not being fairly applied. It was to the bus terminal in Jackson, Mississippi that Claire and Rita went on the following morning.

The Minnesota contingent, of which Claire was a part, agreed to separate in groups of two and three and not acknowledge one another unless the situation warranted it. Some of them bought bus tickets and rode to neighboring cities like Birmingham or Montgomery, Alabama. Once there, they bought return tickets on buses with freedom riders. Claire, good to her word, stayed in Jackson. Rita had no choice but to stay with her since they had agreed to stay together.

When they arrived at the terminal, there were a couple of dozen people standing about. Claire and Rita entered by the main door as if for the business of buying a bus ticket. Inside it was crowded. They immediately noticed a peculiar musky smell that wasn't body odor. It was the first time either had been in an enclosed space with blacks. Eventually they'd learn it was from the way the blacks did their hair. For now, it was part of their steep learning curve. They were in a world apart from anything of their experience. It might have been darkest Africa. The deep southern accents of the blacks with a lot of local slang thrown in made it seem as if they were speaking a foreign language.

Claire leaned over to Rita and whispered, "Okay, we're here. What do we do?"

"I don't know. Stand around and wait, I guess."

As time passed, more people entered the terminal, mostly white. It appeared something was going to happen as a few black men, a little older then they were, went around passing out small slips of paper to the other blacks. They stopped and had a short discussion with several of the black men.

Rita and Claire picked out the two boards hanging between the ticket counters, one with arrivals and the other with departures. The bus from Montgomery, Alabama, was due at ten-twenty, in fifteen minutes.

They made their way out to the street again. The crowd had swelled to hundreds. Earlier, there had been mostly blacks. Now, there were more whites than blacks, all young and well built. Several carried clubs somewhat concealed, but not so much as to leave the impression they were unarmed. The police were in evidence, though not as many as the girls thought were needed.

The terminal was of the type where the busses drove around to the back of the building and angle parked at a curb under an awning so the passengers could disembark and embark under a roof in case of rain. This was to the benefit of the baggage handlers as well. When the bus arrived at where it would have turned off the main street to the terminal, the crowd was heavy and not moving. These were mostly whites. Most passengers would not get out on the street because they would have to go in and claim their baggage, anyway.

Claire and Rita stepped on a small planter located at the curb that formed the base of a street light. It had seen better days and had the remains of a few sickly plants in it. Mostly it had become a repository of gum wrappers and cigarette buts. However, it served its civic duty this day by placing the two girls high enough to have a commanding view of events.

With the bus stopped, there were a few whites from the front of the bus who decided to get out and return later for their luggage to avoid the mayhem that was brewing. This opened the bus door, the whites who wanted to get out, did, and others immediately surged into the bus. The front-sitting blacks were dragged off and beaten with clubs. Belatedly, the police stepped in and separated the warring factions. The whites slipped away and the blacks were arrested.

After the bus eased its way around the building, Claire said, "Did I see that right? Those backs, even that girl, were beaten until they were bleeding."

Rita responded, "Yeah. And, it was the blacks who were arrested. No wonder these people are mad. To spend your whole life knowing the police won't lift a finger to help you must be like living in hell. They had no weapons, and didn't even try to fight back. Still, *they* were arrested."

"There were a couple of whites with them, did you see that? They were called 'nigger lovers' and beaten, too, even arrested. Whose side is anyone on?"

The object of the freedom rides, lunch counter sit-ins, and other disruptions was passive resistance. The members of these groups were carefully selected and trained. It was not a spur of the moment thing. It took a special sort of person not to lash back when being kicked, beaten, arrested, thrown in jail, and forced to work on chain gangs. They refused bail, thereby causing the political jurisdiction to spend the money of their incarceration. Few of the whites understood that it was not the individuals doing the beating who were the targets of the resistance, but the system of thought that produced them. That would take generations to change. Of course, publicity was a big part of the movement, and there was plenty of that.

After the arrests, the crowd started to disperse. Both sides, the blacks and the whites, knew in advance which busses would have freedom riders. Apparently, no more were scheduled for the morning. Rita had gone into the terminal to use the restroom when a young man was suddenly standing beside Claire. Without looking at her he said in a voice that was unlikely to be heard by others, "That was something almost beyond belief, wasn't it?"

She turned to see a young man about her own height. His appearance was so average that he'd blend in with any group of people. His hair was dark brown, not short, not long. His face was precisely well balanced, not handsome, not ugly, no glasses, darkish eyes. His clothing was clean, not crisp, not saggy, seemed to fit well. He was disarming in his comfortableness.

"Almost? It *was* beyond belief. It's as if the world suddenly became turned inside out. The police ignored the criminals, and arrested the victims."

"Wayne," he said extending his hand.

She took it and said, "Claire."

Looking more closely at her sudden companion, Claire was hard pressed to categorize him. He appeared about her age, certainly not an athlete, not sickly looking.

He spoke again. "You can see that the authorities feel they are above reproach; they answer to no one but their own beliefs and prejudices. They have become the enemy. Is there anyone left to stop them?" Answering his own question, he continued, "I doubt there is. We can expect only despotism in our future, and we have long lives ahead of us."

Claire stared straight ahead as she tried to summon up a rebuttal to what Wayne had said. The best she could do was to answer that this had been a mistake of some kind, that this was not the norm. About to speak her thoughts, there was no one there. What an odd guy.

Through the day, other busses arrived. There were angry whites about, but the vehicles managed to inch along arriving at the rear loading area. That space was relatively less congested. It seemed the freedom riders were the targets. If they were not present, it went better. It was a fact that the preponderance of all bus riders in the south were, and always had been, black. If simply being a black bus rider were to become a crime, there would be no busses for anyone.

Back in their hotel room, Rita and Claire discussed what they had seen during the day. It was worse than they had any reason to believe. The news coverage of it was wholly inadequate. The country at large was being kept ignorant of the situation. A short time before, on May 14, a Greyhound bus had been burned outside Anniston, Alabama. That was a big news story with the plume of black smoke rising from the smashed up vehicle. The story about the black riders being beaten was almost a footnote.

Their room came with a small television set. The national news ignored the day's events in Jackson entirely, and there was only a passing reference to it on the local news. They found it fascinating that the arrival of a bus with freedom riders on it the next day was mentioned twice during the newscast. It was as if the TV stations were going out of their way to alert the whites when to be ready.

The next day both young women were at the bus depot by eight-thirty. Though, the bus wasn't due until nine-thirty there was a crowd forming. As the arrival time neared, there was an announcement that the bus had been delayed for an hour. They were outside and did not hear it, but it didn't take long for the word to pass among those gathered about. Few blacks were in evidence. Ten-thirty came and went. The day was warm, which was particularly noticeable to the Minnesotans. The milling became more pronounced with a raised voice now and then. It was nearing noon and Rita had gone inside looking for a water fountain. It was hot outside and stifling inside. Due to the number of people about, it was a difficult jostling route to the fountain. There had been buzz among the white men that the bus had entered the city.

With Rita gone, Claire moved to the planter they had used the day before to get a better view. A voice beside her said, "Another hot day."

Turning her head, she saw the young man of the day before. He had spoken without looking at her.

"Oh, hi. Wayne, isn't it?"

"Yes."

Claire stepped up on the planter and looked intently down the street. "There it is, coming this way." She stepped down and continued. "How do those people do it? I mean, let themselves get beaten up and make no effort to resist."

"Can't say I know. By the way," he said holding up a couple of opened bottles of Coca-Cola, "you wouldn't want one of these would you? My friend sent me to buy some, and when I came back he was gone. I'd hate to let it go to waste especially on a day like this."

Nothing had ever looked so good to Claire. The condensation was dripping off the cold bottles. "It'd be wrong to let it go to waste," she said with a big smile.

"That settles it. We're in agreement, you get it."

He handed her one bottle and tipped the other up and took a long drink. She did the same. Almost immediately she wanted to say "Yuck." There was an off flavor to the Coke. "This doesn't taste right," she said looking at Wayne.

"I noticed that at first, too. They must use a slightly different formulation in the south. Different people, different tastes, I guess." He drank again. She took a sip.

For some reason, the soda had not cooled her nor slaked her thirst. She felt hotter and thirstier than before. Without giving it another thought, she drained the bottle. Wow, the sun was hot. Almost at once it seemed she might be getting sunstroke. The blond wig was starting to cause her scalp to itch.

"Can you see if the bus is making any headway?" Wayne asked.

Claire stepped up on the planter holding onto the lamppost to keep her balance. It didn't occur to her why he didn't simply step up and look for himself.

"Yep," she said with a slight carnival tone to her voice. "Less than a block to go. The people are all over the street, and not a cop in sight."

She stepped down. "Boy, it's hot. Think I'll sit a minute." She sat on the edge of the planter bent over with her hands on her thighs.

"I see it now." Wayne said. "This is going to be ugly. A lot of white guys have clubs and iron pipes. There goes a brick at a window. It cracked it, but didn't go through. If you want to see it, you'd better get in position."

She stood up and the world swam about her. However it happened, the bus door was open. Whites rushed in dragging the blacks off. Her eyes watered, and her head spun. What was wrong?

"Not a cop in sight today," Wayne harangued. "They'll kill them for sure. Not a living soul who cares, nobody to put a stop to it."

She stepped down almost falling. Screams, curses, and epithets were shouted as people cried out in pain.

Wayne had a solid grip on Claire's arm. His mouth was close to her ear. "You are the only one who can stop it. You must. There in the planter is a gun. Stand up on it holding onto the lamppost the way you were. Shoot over their heads. It will make everyone stop until the police arrive. You must do it now!"

Without knowing how it happened, the gun was in her hand, and he was boosting her up on the planter. She closed her eyes and pulled the trigger. The discharge was deafening, yet she pulled the trigger again, and again. By the fourth shot, the sharp report cleared her head. What was happening, what was she doing? The crowd was instantly silent as everyone fell to the ground. That quick, all eyes were on her. A sudden feeling came over her as if she were naked in public. The gun was dropped and she was off the pedestal running. In seconds, she was out of the mass of people. The street corner beckoned. After the turn at the corner of a building, the sidewalk was all but deserted.

What was this, the concrete was twisting as if it were made of gelatin riding on a windy lake. The breeze from her running felt good, invigorating her. If the ground beneath her feet would only lie still . . . how had she come to be in the middle of a street? Oh yes, angling across it. The hissing in her ears drowned out all other sound, even that from squealing tires of cars maneuvering to avoid her. Across now, the trees shaded the walk. It was cool, almost cold. Without warning an intersection appeared. She crossed on to another block, still running. Another street appeared which she crossed charging on. An alley appeared, and summoned her to it. As she turned she looked back. Someone was at the street corner a long way off pointing to her. In the narrow passageway, the horror of capture became overwhelming. After ten steps she noticed a tight hedge on her right. She stopped only a second and on hands and knees, began to squeeze between the branches. She felt her wig being dragged off leaving her head cool. The twigs scratched and gouged her back. On the far side of the barrier, her only thought was to squeeze part way back and retrieve the hairpiece.

Panting, hardly able to see, she looked up to see the bared teeth of a positively huge brown dog, the low growling sound coming from deep within its throat. The hissing sound was either less, or the growling was loud. In either case, there was no mistaking the sound of the animal. But, the dog was out of proportion, with its head now overly flat and wide, and then morphing into a head that was narrow and tall as if unseen hands were massaging a lump of marshmallow.

She patted the ground and said, "Nice doggie." The dog cocked its head. She whined in shear terror expecting to be mauled in a second. It whined in return. She held out a limp hand. It cautiously sniffed it. Her hand felt along its misshapen head until she could pat him and scratch behind his ears. A low playful ruff accompanied by a wagging tail allowed her to sense she had made a friend.

"Nice doggie. I need a place to hide." Crawling toward a misshapen gingerbread house, the back of the dog loping along side her was a full hand higher than she was. The presence of dishes for water and food, led her to believe this was the dog's domicile. A few times she stroked the animal's back that seemed content with its new companion. The noise in her head cleared for a moment letting in the sounds of raised and excited voices not far away. It seemed not to be a party or festival. Could they be searching for someone, a lost child, maybe? A moment later, she was left wondering why she was here other than to have the fine big dog as her friend. Mostly it was a dark corner to hide away in that she craved. The entry to the dog's house was out of proportion like everything else in this *Alice in Wonderland* world. The dog seemed to fret as she was about to enter, but she softly said a few words while scratching his head. He relented, she entered, and he lapped at the water in the brown dish, after which he laid in front of the doorway.

There was room to lie down if she bent her knees. Closing her eyes, the world seemed to tip one way and then another in an all together pleasant cadence. There was no thought about this being an abnormal state. The world was simply a fine place where things tipped and swayed and everything was made of rubber.

The voices drew closer. The confusion was giving way to determined orders.

"I'm a policeman, and will search these premises for the fugitive. She can't have gotten far!"

"Ah sorry Mis-ta Po-lice man. She taint in da back, no sa. Dat's Mis-ta Robert E. Lee's yard. Na body dun go in thare, less da Mas-tar round ta shush him, an' he's in 'Lanta ta day."

"She could have slipped into the dog's house. It's big enough."

The big animal had approached the gate where the policeman stood. It paced a few feet back from the gate growling and baring its fangs.

"Nice dog. I'll have a quick look in there, okay?"

"No sa," the woman said.

"Well, I have to."

He opened the gate, put one foot in, and in a movement too fast to see the dog had his pant leg in his teeth.

"Mis-ta Lee! Back yourself off!"

The fierce growling and tearing didn't stop. The Man hopped back on his free leg while grasping the gate and the latch post. Finally pulling himself through the gate, he closed it so only his foot extended into the forbidden space. The mouth opened and he jerked his foot back, lost his balance, and fell on his back. The woman snapped the gate closed and latched it.

"No sa. Nobody in dare. Mis-ta Lee see ta dat."

Visibly shaken, the police officer stood up, and slapped the dust and bits of dried grass from his uniform. Drawing himself up after the humiliating incident, he said, "If we don't locate her soon, we'll have to subdue the dog," pausing, "one way or another!" Looking about, he saw no one had been watching the inelegant proceedings. Pulling his self respect back into shape, he became less caustic. "If you see anything at all suspicious, you are to call the police immediately."

"Yes sa."

Claire, curled up in the doghouse, heard and understood most of the exchange, while slipping in and out of consciousness. Her grasp on lucidity slipped away when the immediate danger passed. Her sleep was troubled by dreams of a world where things were not connected in a normal way.

— 33 —

Rita stepped out of the terminal to see everyone on the ground, blacks and whites alike. The conflict of the day had been temporarily put aside in the common desire to stay alive. The first to stir were some people near the bus. They were whites helping what seemed to be an injured white. That was different in that the blacks had never struck back. In only seconds more, the crowd was up and yelling in confusion. The words "gun shots" were repeated. To her surprise, there were suddenly dozens of police around the bus. They seemed to pour out of every alley and store. A path was cleared to the fallen man with the white toughs being pushed around as badly as the blacks. An ambulance pulled to a stop, and in seconds the injured man was loaded and it sped off, lights flashing and siren blaring.

Other police were now in the area where Rita and Claire had been standing. Here again, people were pushed back. A black man was saying, "That white girl made the shots. The one with the fluffy white hair." He pointed in the planter. Rita watched as a police officer lifted up a handgun with a pencil through the trigger guard. Others were saying that she ran down the street. A large white officer said in a commanding voice. "We will find her. All of you go about your business and let the police do their work." And, what business is that? Rita thought.

Several police were already running in the direction the malfeasant had gone. The bus driver had used the few moments of confusion to make his turn and drive to the embarkation dock in the back.

Becoming conscious of herself, Rita realized others would have seen her with Claire. To add to the problem was her wig. If she were identified and found to be in what amounted to a disguise, it would suggest they had conspired to shoot someone, and escape by means of altering their appearance. Crossing the street, she walked as casually as possible in the direction of their hotel, which was in the same direction Claire had initially run.

In her room, she removed her wig and changed clothes. She'd inconspicuously dispose of the wig someplace away from the hotel. Out on the sidewalk, she started toward the bus terminal on the opposite side of the street, hoping to see Claire coming her way. As she had emerged from the terminal and the description was given, her reaction was to assume something had happened to make it look like Claire was the guilty party. Now, she'd see her bouncing down the street in her exuberant way to meet Rita and laugh about the crazy thing that had happened to her. No. Someone appeared to have been shot. That wasn't funny in anyone's book. In any case, it could not have been Chair who had fired the shots. It would all be straightened out.

Approaching the terminal, she slacked her pace. Scanning the area for Claire, she saw the crowd had dispersed and it looked like a normal day except for a cop across the street in front of the terminal stopping people and questioning them. She continued on. There was no trouble determining where the police thought Claire had gone from the location of the police cars. She went into a small restaurant and ordered a late lunch. It was impossible not to overhear the gossip. It seemed there was a Federal Marshall riding under cover on the bus, and he was the one who had been struck by a bullet. That explained the events around the bus, and the frantic search for whomever shot him. The talk was that it was a blond white girl who had done it. Several people attested to that.

The rest of the afternoon, Rita wandered the neighborhood staying well clear of the police. Around five, she returned to the hotel thinking Claire would have returned. There was no sign that she had been there. In the evening, she went out again. Using a route that would make it look like she was coming into the downtown area, she came down the street where Claire had last been seen. Seeing the alley, she hesitated, then entered it. The police were not in evidence. She stopped after a short distance and couldn't help thinking her friend had either been kidnapped and hauled away or apprehended by the police and was now in the deepest jail cell in the world. Leaning against a low wall, she began to sob.

Claire awoke with a pounding headache and disoriented. It was pitch dark. Then she opened her eyes—not completely dark. To her relief, the dim light that outlined the door to her hideout was made up of straight lines. She raised up on hands and knees and peered from the opening. A large mass outside the portal stirred as well. Oh, yeah. The big dog. His name was Robert E. Lee. That much she remembered. As her head came to the opening, a tongue as large as a dishtowel swiped across her face. She extended her hand and he sniffed it.

"Hi, Mister Lee," she whispered.

The dog whined a little, and she scratched his head. Another lick. This was getting sloppy, but the better part of survival in a case like this was not to offend her host.

The sun had set, and dusk was settling in. Still on all fours, she made her way to the thick hedge through which she had come. It was a struggle, but taking her time, and being sober, she managed to traverse the barrier without adding to her scratches. Her clothing was dark which was good in the gathering gloom. Swatting off bits of dried leaves, and straightening her clothing, she became aware of where she was. The alley. That much came back. Why she was there, did not. She froze at the sound of a cough followed by sobs. The timbre of the voice was familiar. She uncertainly moved toward the sound as a figure took shape. A stone scraped under her foot.

"Oh!" was the short reply. It was Rita.

"Rita?"

"Claire?"

"Yes." They ran to each other hugging as they met.

In two minutes, they had given the outline of what each knew.

"That guy put LSD in the Coke," Rita said. "I've heard people talk about parties where it was used. We can worry about that later. We have to get you out of town, and fast."

"How? Won't they be looking for me?"

"Yeah. We have to get on Highway 51 headed up to Memphis, and hitch a ride."

"Won't that be dangerous?"

"Like we have a choice? Besides, there're two of us."

They set off, and in an hour were at a truck stop. They both used the restroom, and Rita bought a few candy bars. Claire was ravenous. Standing in the shadows away from the entrance, they saw a man in his thirties walk to a car. Rita approached him. He agreed to take them as far as Winona that was half way to Memphis. They both got in, Rita in the front, Claire in the back. With the engine running, a second man arrived.

"Got a couple of passengers, Len. Hop in back."

The girls were sickened with fear as the car sped off into the night. The road signs indicated Highway 51, they were heading in the right direction, and the men were largely behaving themselves. After a half-hour as they were in the small town of West, the driver said, "Sorry, got to pull over and make a pit stop." With that, he took a right. Any filling stations where they might have stopped were closed for the night. Driving out of town the better part of a mile, they stopped at what appeared to be an unofficial park where people came to drink, and do such things that were not done in the light of day. Moonlight glistened off water in front of the car.

The driver, Curly, said, "You gals might as well stretch your legs too. This here's the Big Black River. Nice on a night like tonight, ain't it?"

It wasn't as if the girls had any choice in the matter as they were yanked out. It was all too clear what the men had in mind. Curly had Rita on the ground in less than a minute. She was struggling and getting nowhere.

"Ah, come on, how 'bout a kiss for big ol' Curly?"

Two seconds later there was a deep throated yell, followed by a thump and crack. "Little witch, nearly bit my lip off!"

Len, who had started pawing Claire, stopped. "Easy there, buddy."

"Hey, settle down! I didn't hit that hard. Thrashing around like a chicken with its head cut off taint goen to do no good . . . . Come on . . . . There, that's better."

"Curly, that's going on over there?"

"Oh for the love of . . . . Look here, this can't be."

"What?"

"It can't be!"

"What!"

"Durned little toad got a broken neck."

"Can't be." There was the beginning of fear in the remark.

"Sure as I'm sittin' here. That was the pop ya heard."

Claire was forgotten as Len rushed over to Curly.

After some rummaging around in the moon light Len said, "Sure as the devils own wrath. She's dead. We'll have to throw her in the river and hightail it out of here." After a pause, "Oops. The other one. What we gonna do with her. Got to get her, that's for sure."

Claire was running for her life for the second time that day. Len was tall and slim and gave chase. The roadway from the river was loose sand making the running hard, and he was gaining on her. When he was five steps behind, she bolted to the left into the bushes not knowing what to expect. She was soon slopping around in knee deep water.

"Not that way," Len said in a hushed shout. "That's the back water. Them cottonmouths'll get ya for sure."

After ten yards she stopped and discovered there was no pursuit. The splashing about had made it so she didn't understand the warning from Len. She was in woods heavy enough that there was little help from the moon. Moving as silently as possible she waded on trying not to trip on submerged roots. Finally, encountering higher ground she was glad to be out of the water. Not knowing what would be about, she pulled herself up into a tree, climbing ten feet up. The air was still with a dank clammy feeling. Frogs croaked, and a myriad of other wild sounds pressed in upon her.

The two men must have left, though, she had not heard the car. She felt it would be dangerous to try to find the road not knowing which way to go in the dark. It should only be a short distance to safety, but if she guessed wrong, she could become helplessly lost, or worse yet, fall into deep water, become tangled in roots, and drown. With that in mind, there was no alternative to staying in the tree until dawn. It had to have been after ten when they turned off the main road. That made it close to eleven now. It would be a long five or six hours until she'd have enough light to see where she was.

The horror of it all crushed in upon her. Rita was dead; there was no doubt of that. What would happen now? She had to get home and let her dad help. He'd know what to do. That was what kept her perched on that limb through the night, that and the fear of the unknown all around. In time, she made out pinches of light from the moon as it slowly made its way across the sky to open places in the leaves overhead. The sounds were everywhere. Some far away and others terrifyingly near.

Time passed like an eternity. After what seemed like a hundred hours, the faint gray of dawn began. It lightened gradually to reveal thick fog which for Claire was no better than the dark. She heard a vehicle. The sound came from the wrong direction by her reckoning. It stopped and a door opened and slammed. A man, elderly from the sound, talked to a dog. A rustle of breeze moved the tree tops.

By full daylight, the swamp had acquired its day time personality, the light wind dissipating the fog. She looked down trying to make out the ground to discover she had climbed higher than she imagined. Her tree was on a hump of ground fifteen yards long and five wide. Each time she looked down to plan her descent, she saw an unusual shape on the lower branches, but took little interest in it. She had lowered herself to the branch beneath her when her interest shifted dramatically to the odd growth on the tree. It had moved. Following the complete outline with her eyes, she recognized it. A large snake with a fat body was twisting its way up from one branch to another.

Claire froze, almost in terror, but not quite. She broke off a dead branch, snapping off the twigs. With it, she poked at the snake. With each jab, it opened its mouth that was a light pink inside. She tried for its head, once hitting its mouth with the sharp end of the stick. Finally, dislodged, it fell with a thump on the dead leaves. Looking all around for others and watching where she put each hand and each foot, she descended to the ground.

The snake had wondered off some distance from the tree as she started into the water in the direction of the sounds. After five minutes, she was coming to what looked like the bank up to the road when she spotted another snake swimming toward her from the right. Scarcely able to keep from screaming, she scampered through some bushes on the bank dreading the thought of coming upon another one. Nothing had ever looked so good as the sandy tracks leading from the river.

She paused to consider her position. During the long night, her thoughts had been primarily on surviving the swamp. Now, she had to think about how she would get home without ending up in a southern jail. She still had several hundred dollars in her pocket. Immediately, she removed two twenties and a ten from the other bills and put them in a separate pocket. A bus ran from Jackson to Memphis on Highway 51. It might be a problem if she tried to get on a bus in the little town they had driven through the night before. She needed a larger town.

Where she stood, she could not see the man at the river, but the hundred-fifty foot wide river was visible. A lazy current carried debris along here and there. She proceeded cautiously to the bend and saw an old truck pointed toward the river parked about where the men must have stopped the night before. He was dumping fishing gear in the back as if getting ready to leave. She advanced toward him.

The man was wearing blue bib overhauls and a tattered black hat. He looked to be seventy and his face hadn't kept company with a razor for a week. The stub of a cigar hung from the left of his mouth.

He looked up with a start having glimpsed movement. "Well, who have we here?"

Claire smiled. "A traveler who's a little lost."

"In a place like this, I'd say more than a little."

"Yeah, maybe a lot lost. It's not a long story. I was visiting my cousin in Memphis. She had friends in Winona up the road from here, and insisted we drive down to see them. They were putting together a party, and we, or rather *she* couldn't refuse. For whatever reason we ended up here. There was booze and some drugs, I guess. I had a couple of beers and had to attend to nature's call, lost my way, and fell into the swamp until now. That's it."

"Didn't they look for you?"

"My cousin's a little dippy and had been hitting the hard stuff more than was good for anybody. None of the rest knew me. Is suspect they pulled out not realizing they were one short."

"Couldn't you hear them talking and walk to them?"

"The sounds of the others seemed to be coming from every direction so I didn't know which way to go in the dark."

"How'd ya survive the snakes?"

"I climbed a tree until first light. Saw a couple of big fat ones this morning, but used a stick to keep 'em back."

"They're cottonmouths and poisonous. You're a survivor—tough little gal."

"You wouldn't be headed north on Highway 51, would you?"

The dog sniffed Claire's feet, possibly smelling the big dog, Mr. Lee, on her while the man contemplated the situation. "Suppose I could take you as far a Winona. Hadn't planned to go that far, but need a few things in town, so guess I could. Some dog hair on the seat, but you're not wearin' Sunday best, so's it probably won't matter."

"I could use some cleaning up, I'll admit that. Besides, I seem to get along with dogs."

He put the rest of the gear in the back, opened the driver's side door and said, "In, Patch." The dog leapt in tail wagging. The name fit as the dog was black except for a light gray patch on his back.

In Winona, Claire bought a burger at a chain fast food place, and used the restroom to clean up the best she could. In the downtown area was a Woolworth's store where she bought a few clothes. By the time she arrived at the bus station, she discovered the next bus was leaving for Memphis in fifteen minutes. Luckily, there were no freedom riders, and no demonstrations. After all, she was headed north.

In St. Louis, she could go either to Chicago or Kansas City. The bus for Kansas City left first so that's the way she went. From there, it was true north to Minneapolis.

She slept a lot during the bus ride, and when awake mostly pretended to sleep so a seatmate wouldn't take up a conversation with her. Arriving at dusk in downtown Minneapolis, she took a taxi to within a half-mile of where she lived.

The house looked better than a castle. She was home, home at last. Around back, the door was usually unlocked this time of day and it was today. There was a light from her father's study.

"Daddy, I'm home."

There was a pause followed by a scramble of movement. He swept out of the door with his hand on the doorjamb as a pivot. The light was still good enough for recognition.

"Claire! You're alive!"

She ran to him and he wrapped his arms around her. She sobbed.

"Come. Sit down. Are you all right?"

She nodded wiping away tears.

"The news. They identified Rita's body today. They pulled it from a river, what was it?"

"The Big Black, Daddy."

"What happened? They thought you might have been drowned too, but couldn't find a body. And, in Jackson. They matched the prints on a gun from those found in your hotel room. Did you really shoot that Federal Marshal? The FBI was even here asking if I'd seen you." He paused holding Claire's hands. "What am I doing? Tell me what happened, all of it."

She relayed the story from departing St. Paul to returning.

Eugene fixed a meal while Claire showered. After she had eaten, they discussed their options.

"It's a life changing event, isn't it?" he said

"I guess it is. They'll be after me for that marshal, won't they? It won't matter that I was stoned out of my mind on LSD. Did they say how bad the man was hurt?"

"In critical condition. It's bad. But, that's not the worst. While he's still alive, Rita's dead, and you're the prime suspect. You were together and she would be able to testify against you. They'd never find the two guys even if they tried, and that's doubtful."

"But, if they thought I was dead along with Rita, could I be someone else, take a new identity?" She paused a minute. "By the way, when does Mom get home? Does she know?"

"She'll be home tomorrow. She knows something's wrong, but no details. No point in stirring her up while she's in Europe."

"Yeah. What about a new identity? I absolutely don't want to spend time in a southern prison. The way those cops stood by as the blacks were beaten unconscious was more than you can imagine. Those are savage people. And, me a northern white kid sticking my nose in their business, and worst of all shooting one of their finest, they'd send me to the deepest dungeon on earth." She sobbed, "I'll probably be blamed for Rita's death, too. If I have to disappear forever, I'll do it."

"I understand how you feel. There may be a way for you to only partially disappear. It'll take a few days of checking. Meanwhile, you stay in the guestroom on the lower level. We'll keep the place looking like you're not here and above all, you must stay out of sight. Never go outside, in fact don't even walk past a window. I'll tell the maid not to come for the next week."

———————————

Minna Simmons finished her glass of wine, set the glass down, and continued. "You know what happened to Margaret, but they didn't. She seemed to have fallen off the face of the earth. Eugene was doing pretty well by that time so could afford to hire private investigators. They checked every kind of public record, Social Security, passport applications, driver's licenses in all the states, even the IRS. She didn't show up as anyone's spouse. They even did the best they could with criminal records. They didn't have her fingerprints, so there was nothing they could trace that way. You must remember, there were no computer files like there are today. All the checking required someone to pull up and read paper records.

"After a week they decided, she had either died, taken a completely new name, or gone to a foreign country illegally. That cleared the way for Claire to use Margaret's birth certificate. For her name, she reversed the first and middle. If anyone asked, she's say she once had a teacher with the name Margaret, and had hated her, so refused to be called by that name.

"Her parents put her on a train for San Francisco where she would begin at Berkley in the fall. She found a place to live near campus and as luck, or desperation, would have it, she 'fell in love' and was married before she had to matriculate for the fall quarter. With the marriage certificate, she managed to transfer her college credits from St. Paul with no questions so they all showed up on the Berkley transcript of Norma Holleran. That meant all of her college records were under her married name. Our free love society started in and around Berkley as much as anywhere. Nobody cared what marriage you were or were not in at any particular time. The marriage didn't last, not surprisingly, and she never married again. As she became more prominent, she arranged to quietly 'adjust' her early college records and other key documents associated with her life prior to Berkley. Claire Freidmuth remains to this day in the state of 'missing, presumed dead.'"

Minna had a melancholy expression as she finished. "That's the secret. I do hope you'll treat it with respect. I know you disagree with most of the views she's held during her professional life. But, there's a person there, too."

"What happened to the Federal Marshall," Paul asked.

"He was disabled and lived for four or five years before dying from complications of his wound. There is no statute of limitations on murder, you know."

Vin was tossing things around in his mind. "Did anyone ever identify the guy called Wayne?"

"Other than Claire, no one knew he was there. And, she was in no position to tell. We spoke of that at times. In all social upheavals there are third parties trying to use the circumstances to further their own ends.

"Don't forget that we might not have a country if the French fleet hadn't been lying off the coast of Yorktown in October of seventeen eighty-one. Did they do that because they liked the American colonists so much? Hardly. They were there because they wanted to spoil England's party in America. England was their enemy in Europe.

"Suffice it to say, Wayne was there to further destabilize the situation. He could have been from any number of fringe groups, but he wasn't. He was too well trained, his presence too well planned. We came to understand what he was, but that's beyond the secret, and I feel no obligation to reveal it."

— 34 —

Immediately after the incident in the parking lot outside the diner where the guy calling himself Raven shoved a gun in his back, Alvin Freidmuth began to wonder if it had been a prank. Then, the next morning, messages started coming usually hidden someplace around the outside of his house. He'd receive a brief text message telling him where to look. The most recent message had been cryptic, but clear, and really disgusting. He was to drive to three small businesses and dig through their trash, going Dumpster diving if necessary, to recover discarded papers with letterhead. It was so dumb. The first was a place that helped pregnant women not have abortions. In his opinion, that was as nonessential a function as it was possible to imagine. Who could possibly care one way or another? He was gratified that they used a garbage can. And, there were no food leavings to stink and stick to everything. That one went fast. The second shared the refuse removal with an entire building. There he had to go diving. It was so demeaning. Here he was looking for pro-life documents as well.

At the third, there was trouble. This was a campaign headquarters. The Dumpster was mainly filled with shredded paper. He wallowed about in small bits of paper for twenty minutes before he found two pieces of letterhead with coffee rings on them. There having been no need to shred these, they were thrown away intact. The orders had been for not less than five documents from each place, but this was going to have to do. As he searched for what he needed, the thought of revenge crossed his mind, but the memory of the gun in his back made him cautious.

After two hours, he had what he needed and hated to sit in his car the way he reeked. It was good he had leather upholstery that would clean up easier than cloth fabric. Following the directions he drove five miles and dropped the plastic bag with his booty in it by a bench in a park. It was one in the morning.

Tuesday morning, June 29

Dutch was up early having slept on foam pads in Wessen's garage. He washed up in the men's room at a McDonalds and shaved with the old electric he brought along. After that, he was off to the place where he might find his truck. Though, he had not been the one to sign for it, he remembered the threat of having a bunch of fat lawyers taking everything he owned. In his mind, the mission to find the truck had become identical to that of keeping his farm.

The temptation was great to walk up to the truck bay, pound on the door, and demand that his truck be returned. He had sense enough to realize that would be counter productive as it would end in his being dead, at which point the issue of keeping his farm or not would scarcely matter. He had spent time the previous afternoon watching the place. The bays with loading docks were moderately busy and people were about. Nothing happened at the end bays.

After some unproductive hours of watching he decided to ask around. At nine-thirty he drove into the rear area of the loading docks with purpose and parked with other cars. He walked to the closed doors of the end bays. Each had three small windows in it. Brown paper had been used to cover them from the inside. Next, he went to the steps leading to the small door beside some of the loading docks. It was propped open and several of the doors to the loading docks were open to allow the warm humid air to circulate. There was an office in the corner with a small air conditioner extending into the warehouse. He entered.

The heavyset man pecking at a computer keyboard looked up. He had four days growth on his cheeks and an unkempt beard. His stomach was like a watermelon in his lap.

"Yeah?" he said looking up.

"I was told to come to the bay at the north end of this building where I'd pick up a white box truck for a run to North Dakota. I've knocked at all the doors and nobody answers. The address is right and the layout looks like I was told, a couple of drive-in bays beside several loading docks. Are the end bays part of your operation?"

"Nope. Never have been. They're leased out separately."

"Well, then, have you seen anybody coming and going, have they come in here to use the john, anything like that?"

"Nope. Those bays have their own john. That space is normally for storage. Little traffic."

"Anybody else around who might have seen anything? I sure need that gig. That's my bread for the week."

"Ask Kim, the little guy out there on the forklift. He might have seen something."

"Well, thanks a lot, sure do appreciate it."

Kim was Asian and of slight build. His skill in handling the forklift was apparent. When asked, he thought he had seen a white box truck a few days ago, but couldn't be sure it went into either of the end bays. He hadn't seen the big pickup. That information helped a little. The dualies pickup did back into there, and if there was even a chance of a white one, it was strong evidence it was the right place. It's just that there was nothing he could do about it.

Vincent Wessen slept late. After getting home at eleven the night before, he and Camilla had stayed up later still discussing his day. Since he had not known when he would be back, he made arrangements to take vacation this day as well. With the time off work, he intended to type into his computer as much of Holleran's story as he could remember while it was still fresh in his mind. After that, he'd have Paul read it and make comments where he left parts out. The story would make a terrific piece of fiction.

Dutch had bedded down in the garage with his car pulled in to the empty stall left by Vin's car. Vin left his car outside thinking they'd talk in the morning. When Vin checked, Dutch was gone leaving a thank you note on the workbench in the garage.

Tuesday evening

The day away from work had not helped Vincent the way he had hoped it would. By nightfall, he was restless and irritable. He was about to call it a day and go to bed when he remembered the next day was collection day in the neighborhood for garbage and recycling. Both services were coming earlier each time and a few weeks back he had put his stuff out too late. In the hot summer, two week old garbage was noticeable a block away. The clouds had moved in making it nearly dark. No matter, he could have done it blind folded. After setting out the recycling tub, he pulled out the wheeled trash container. Plodding through his chores, his mind was turned inward. The outrageous events and revelations seemed unreal as if they were happening to someone else. If he had been more conscious of the world around him he might have noticed the figure in black tucked into the lilac bushes near the back of his lot.

––––––––––––––––

Alvin had received a call from his father Monday morning saying his sister was in the hospital with cancer. If he hadn't been under the thumb of the man calling himself Raven, he might have gone to Washington. He called twice and after an extensive run around learned little more than his father had relayed to him. He recalled she had always complained inordinately about her health. If it wasn't her head aching, it was her feet hurting, and everything in between. So, under the circumstances, he decided to continue following instructions and stay out of prison.

A phone call at six had consisted of three words, "Your welcome mat." The guy wasn't much of a talker. Immediately, he went to the front door and opened it looking for anyone on the sidewalk, or across the street. As usual, nothing. Under the mat were three envelopes which he picked up, replaced the mat, closed and locked the door. In his study, he considered them. One was labeled "Open now." Another said "Open as instructed." The third had one word on it "Wessen." It didn't take a rocket scientist for him to see that he was now in the business of delivering messages, too.

He slit open the "Open now" envelope. The note said the other two envelopes contained instructions for tomorrow, Wednesday. That he was not to open his until seven o'clock in the morning. He was to deliver the other to Wessen yet this evening and was further instructed to leave it on his patio in a flowerpot. He was to call Wessen, phone number included, at six-fifteen in the morning to inform Wessen where to find it and that Wessen was to follow the instructions under pain of death. Nothing new about the sanction.

Alvin watched Vincent go about his duties planning to wait until he returned to the house before depositing the envelope. Of a sudden, an odd sensation came over him. He was tired of being used as a thing. It was time he gave some grief, too. Plus, this was Wessen. If it were not for this man, his senile old man would be leaving his millions to him, not this jerk. There was the added consternation that if he had not acted too soon on the information about his sister, that thug from the ATF wouldn't be on his back. This would be the perfect time to nail the guy with his silenced Hi Point nine-millimeter. The ATF guy could go to blazes. One shot would insure his claim to the piles of inheritance, too much to count. Prepared to shoot, he paused. That would be too kind to Wessen. He had to be made to sweat. The urge to inflict pain washed over him. Let him know there was no way out, that he was totally under his power. Total power, life and death power. He could feel the demon taking control and did nothing to stop it.

He advanced quickly behind Wessen who was shambling along lost in thought. He pressed the muzzle of the silencer in Wessen's back and said in a whispered voice imitating as closely as possible the tone of the man called Raven.

"Don't move."

Wessen stopped and said in a conversational tone, "For crying out loud, what now?" He slowly raised his hands to shoulder height as he spoke. At the same time, he bent his right knee putting his weight on the ball of the foot. He did it to the right foot under the assumption his attacker was right handed. The fact that the pressure of the barrel in his back was a little off center to the right added credibility to his supposition. In addition, probabilities favored that because only twelve percent of the people were left-handed.

Using his right foot as a pivot he thrust off with his left foot swinging around dropping his right hand to the point the pressure in his back had placed the gun. His hand landed on the barrel, grasped it, and continued the downward motion wrenching the gun out of the hand holding it. The gun did not discharge as Alvin had not removed the safety.

Alvin was so surprised Vin had only to step back leveling the gun at him as he did. In a more desperate situation, Vin's continued attack was to plant the left foot shifting the weight to it, cocking the right leg and, with the foot turned horizontally, thrusting at the assailant's right knee. However, anyone unschooled enough so as to make the blunder of actually pressing the barrel of a gun into a person's back, seldom required a follow on attack.

"Now you are the one who is not to move," Wessen said. "And, I have flipped the safety to the unsafe position. I have no desire to kill you, but you will not escape. Do you understand?"

"Yeah."

"Slowly move with me staying the same distance away keeping your hands at shoulder height."

Vincent backed to the small door on the side of the garage, opened the door, and flipped on the light. As he stepped back he said, "Walk to the door and into the garage. Any quick move and I'll put you down. Nice silencer."

When they were both in the garage, Vincent closed the door and told Alvin to turn around. When he did, it was a shock.

"You're the guy with the bow and arrow! What the heck are you doing here? I don't get it. Why didn't you just shoot me and get it over with? Do you think this is a game like the guys that shoot paint balls?"

There were more than six feet from the front of the cars and the shelves along the wall. In this space was a step stool, and a bench stool by the workbench.

"Can I put my hands down? I don't even have a pocket knife."

Vin nodded. "Don't even think of taking a step toward me. I've been shot at enough. Toss your wallet, here, on the floor at my feet."

Alvin complied.

Vin kept the gun pointed at Alvin as he picked it up. There were a dozen credit cards, receipts from everything, a few pictures, in other words typical. Finally, he had the driver's license. He almost laughed.

"I don't believe it. Alvin Freidmuth. Son of Eugene, the rich guy, and brother to Norma Holleran, the powerful one. Except, she's not likely to be powerful for long, is she?"

"You know an awful lot of stuff."

"More than you can imagine, but not enough. You are going to talk to me."

"Suppose I might as well, but first, how did you know I had not released the safety on the gun. If I had put the safety off, I would have killed you."

"No, you would not have killed me. What you did was strictly unprofessional. By pressing the muzzle of the gun in my back, you told me exactly where it was. Then, it is humanly impossible for you to see me move, realize you must pull the trigger, and pull it before I have turned enough to be out of the line of fire. Even in full daylight when you know that is exactly what I will do, you can't react fast enough. Sometime when you're fooling around with your pals, not drinking, and being absolutely sure the gun is not loaded, try it. You'll see. Enough of that. Why the bow and arrow, and if I guess correctly the other two attempts, and tonight? Tonight's the stumper. You had me, so why not?"

"Can I sit down on this stepstool?"

Vin nodded, and did the same on the workbench stool.

"I'm not getting into reasons, motive, so to speak. Suffice it to say, I did try to kill you with the bow and arrow. As you could see, it wasn't as great a threat to you as it would have been by someone with more skill. I spent a week practicing, and would have made it if the bow hadn't hit the stick in the grass."

"That's pretty scummy of you. You just admitted you tried to murder me, and I assume Paul, as well. That's murder one. In addition, you're the one who shot at me, didn't you? More murder one. Lucky you're such a bad shot. You're really a piece of garbage, you know that?"

"Calling me names isn't going to help at this point."

"So, things have changed? You only poke highly illegal silenced nine-millimeters in people's backs now? Oh, I'm so relieved."

"As a matter of fact, yes, things have changed. I did something that the feds took offense at and they threatened to throw me in prison for a long time if I didn't play ball with them. The guy said he was with the ATF but he could have made that up. He had a gun in my back. I didn't even see his face. And, he had me on my knees so I doubt your trick would have worked, even if I were as expertly trained as you obviously are."

"What'd you do?"

"It was all in the family. I hacked into my sister's emails. Such a fuss. You'd think I was gunning for the President or something."

"That's pretty naughty. Then what?"

Here Alvin, as was his wont, saw no point in being honest so began to fabricate things where it suited his purposes. "I don't think this ATF guy even knew about the bow and arrow incident, but he told me to get a silenced gun, which I did, the one you're holding, and he'd send me messages telling me what I had to do to redeem myself. I was to make attempts on your life, but under no circumstances was I to kill you, or even wound you. I'm not that bad a shot! Anyway, you were needed for something else. It was as if they wanted to make you crazy so you'd do something they could hang on you, maybe put you in a position like they have me."

"So, why did you wound me, you puke?"

"I *did* hit you then, in the park. I was afraid I had. Sorry about that. Luckily, my second shot hit the steel light post. It went right through and cut a wire because the light went out. They'll think the neighborhood is going to pot. Is it bad, I mean your wound?"

"I don't believe this. Yeah, it's kind of bad, but I managed to get patched up. How about the car, you do that too?"

"Yeah. Boy, that wavy road really put me off my target. I could've killed you."

"No dinosaur dip, Darwin!"

"You're kind of a lucky guy, ya know that?" After a pause, "I'm thinking they, whoever they are, must be ticked off with you. You do something you shouldn't have to rile 'em up?"

"That's a long story. Briefly, an over zealous FBI agent was poking around where my nephew was working and managed to get him fired. The same agent became involved with your bow and arrow case. He came to the house and accused me of inventing the whole story. Later, he was at my place of employment trying to get me fired, too. I ran into him, forced him into a conference room. I almost pulled his ear off and smashed his nose against a table. There was a woman in a tight pants suit using the room at the time. As the FBI guy was drawing his gun, I threw the woman on him. She almost scratched his face off. I managed to slide along the tabletop and get past his head. While he was struggling with the banshee, I got his gun and pounded him in the eye. He'll probably lose it. Along the way, I stabbed him in the balls with a long pickle fork. I supposed he's somewhat perturbed with me."

Alvin laughed. "That's pretty naughty, too." Becoming somber he continued, "In fact, you've manage to top anything I've been able to do. I'm becoming resentful."

"Don't go into the dumper on me. Why are you here at all tonight, if not to kill me?"

"More messages from *them*." He pulled the envelope with "Wessen" on it from his pack pocket. "I was to leave this in a flower pot on your patio and call you in the morning telling you to read the message. I have one to read in the morning, too."

"Well? Have you read yours?"

"Of course not. I follow instructions. I'm not going to prison."

"Hey, booby. You're never going to prison. You'll be dead first. Do you have your letter on you?"

"Yeah, as a matter of fact, I do." Alvin reached in his shirt pocket and produced the folded envelope.

"Open it."

Alvin tore it open and scowled as he read. "Another one of those dumb things to do. Wish I could figure out what's going on."

Vin held the gun level at Alvin. "Hand me the letter for me. Nothing funny, understand?"

Alvin nodded and extended his hand from his position seated on the stepstool. Vin stepped forward and snatched the envelope, immediately stepping back again.

"I'm going to lay the gun down on the workbench and open the letter. A mine-millimeter slug does a lot of damage so don't move."

Alvin nodded.

Vin slit the letter open with his finger. The message instructed him to drive south on 35W from County Road E2 at exactly eight forty-five the following morning. He was to have his cell phone in his hand. He would receive a call and be told where to go.

Vin had Alvin read his which was the same except for a different starting point. They sat in silence for a long time. Finally, Alvin said, "It's getting late. What are you planning to do? You seem to be better at this than I am."

Drawing a deep breath, Vin replied, "This guy isn't from the ATF or anything like that. He's a terrorist. Don't ask how I know, but he's building a truck bomb like the one Timothy McVeigh used in the Oklahoma bombing. For some reason, the government is indirectly involved. I assume that because we're involved. Who but the government would know about our respective transgressions? We will be directed to the truck and told to drive it to the place they want."

"McVeigh got away before it blew up, didn't he? Sure he did. I remember that."

"There's a big difference with this. It was McVeigh's show. He could walk away if that's what he wanted. I don't think they intend that we'll walk away."

"Let's call the police right now."

"Yeah. And, the first thing we can do is poke a silenced nine-millimeter in their back. The government is involved, didn't you hear me? Why else would they pick us? From their point of view, we're expendable criminals. Why bother with a trial when what they want is revenge. But, it's more than that. We're both white males. It's not politically correct to think of Arabs or Moslems or any other minority as anything but the finest of upstanding people, and certainly misunderstood by us white people. Am I right?"

"When you're right, you're right. What do we do?"

"I don't know. They obviously know where we both live. If we fail to follow instructions they'll kill us, and our families, probably with torture all around. In case you haven't noticed, the government is out of control. Do I have to spell it out?"

"You might have to. I don't see it that way."

"Start by looking at what they're doing with us. Does this look like the rule by law, that the legislators, judges, police, FBI, the President are public servants doing the will of the people? I'm sure you remember, we had a close senate election in this state. The Republican won. They recounted ten times until the Democrat won then they stopped, still not having counted all of the votes. They even admitted they didn't count them all. Does that sound like the rule by law? It's the tyranny of those in power over the rest of us. I could go on all night, but what's the point? Suffice it to say, I'm looking at a Democrat who is finally getting what he's been voting for all his life. I, on the other hand, am being screwed."

Vin paused. "You drive a red sports car, right?"

"Yeah."

"You know what I drive. I'll see you in the morning. Don't be late. It's going to be quite a party. Now get out of here. Wait! On the off chance that we actually do walk away from the bomb, it will only be to have us identified as the bombers. Nice trick, either blown to a mist or hung as terrorists. Anyway, put a baseball cap or other floppy hat under your shirt so it doesn't show when you come tomorrow. As we leave the truck we want something to pull down to hide our faces. Be sure you have a couple of handkerchiefs so we can wipe off fingerprints." He paused. "Got another idea. Wear two shirts. The outer one gaudy so it's easily recognizable. As soon as we're away from the truck, we'll pull off the outer ones. How's that?"

"You *are* good at this. What line of work are you in?"

"It doesn't matter. Get moving. No. Wait one more minute. What do you do when you're not trying to kill me?"

"I sell investments for people nearing retirement. They're good, too, only lost half as much as the Dow Jones during that mess in two thousand eight. Do I get my gun back?"

"How about I give you one bullet back, right between the eyes?"

"I guess that means no."

After Alvin left, Vin went into the house and called Camilla and Paul. By this time, they could see the pieces start falling into place. They agreed it had started two places. The first was Paul's prayer and subsequent letter to Holleran. The second had to have something to do with Alvin and his father's money, or the simple fact that he was Holleran's brother. Unless Alvin actually revealed his motive for trying to kill them with the bow and arrow, they couldn't do any better than that. Vin related that he seemed rational enough, though he was typical of many Americans who had not been forced to make his own life. Things had been too good growing up, leaving him like millions of others as adult dependents knowing they would never be able to do as well as their parents.

Paul volunteered to follow Vin as he left for the rendezvous in the morning. Vin rejected it because if they saw him, they'd probably kill them all. They also agreed that anyone putting all of this into motion would not accept the interference of law enforcement without severe retaliation to them. Even quietly going to the local police and laying it all out wouldn't help. They'd immediately go into police think mode and notify the FBI and every other federal agency in the book. These in turn, would gladly sacrifice Vin and Alvin if they thought by doing so they could prevent the bomb from going off in a crowded place. There seemed to be no case where fewer innocent people would be at risk than Vin and Alvin, and Alvin's innocence was questionable. They were stuck with hoping something would present itself as the events unfolded.

— 35 —

Wednesday morning, June 30

At exactly eight forty-five, Vincent Wessen sped down the on-ramp to 35W. Thirty seconds after he merged with heavy traffic, his cell phone beeped.

"This Wessen on 35W south bound?"

"Yes."

"Good. Stay with the program and this will all be painlessly over in no time. Deviate and you die, as well as your family. Get into the left lane and exit straight ahead as the freeway curves to the right. Take a left at the first stoplight. I will stop talking but don't turn off your phone. Do you understand?"

"Yes."

With that, Vin heard music from a local station. The terrorist was keeping a transmission going so the cell phone company wouldn't automatically terminate the call. At this time, he was calling Alvin, he was sure of that.

After he made the left, the voice was back. "At the third stoplight you will see a parking lot to the right front across the street. You will pull up beside a pickup with dual rear tires. Leave your car unlocked with the keys on the floor. Don't be late. Reply."

"Understood."

The parking lot was for Har Mar Mall. He spotted the pickup while he was on Snelling Avenue waiting to make a left turn. Alvin was already there standing beside his car. As Vin drove up beside the red Mustang, he saw Alvin close his cell phone and throw it into the back seat. The guy was psychologically unable to disobey an order. Vin's phone was smaller so he pretended to throw it in, but didn't. Vin wanted Alvin to drive so he walked to the passenger side. He was wearing thin beige gloves he had borrowed from Camilla. They were tight and only went part way on, but they did the job. With the doors closed, a cell phone attached to the dash started to chime. Vin pressed the answer button.

"Welcome gentlemen. I will now state the rules. If any of the rules are violated, you will pay dearly. There is to be no talking to one another. You don't know each other, but that doesn't matter for the small job I have for you. You will not switch off this cell phone. If I hear the slightest sound that is not anticipated, you will pay. Every few minutes I will ask each of you to respond to me with the words, 'I am here'. By now, I recognize your individual voices. If either one is gone, you pay. Answer as I have stated, driver first."

They both answered.

"I am somewhat surprised at the driver. But, it is well. No street names will be stated, so pay attention. On your right is a street. Go to it and head in the direction the vehicle is now pointed. Answer."

After their response the voice continued, "There is a GPS transponder on your vehicle so I will know where you are to within three feet at all times. No deviation will be tolerated. Answer."

They drove south on Snelling Avenue. It was one of the few streets that went in a straight line south all the way through St. Paul, and down the Mississippi River bluffs. As they drove, Vin could tell by the way the engine labored accelerating from a stop that it was heavily loaded.

After a few blocks, they were directed to take a left on Larpenteur Avenue.

Vin searched around for anything that might help with their plight. Protruding between the back of his seat, and the seat itself was the corner of a sheet of paper. He pulled it out being careful not to tear it. He recognized the letterhead as that of the place where Camilla volunteered. It seemed to be a totally innocent, fund raising document. Its presence in this venue could only mean the perpetrators were making a connection between this truck and that pro-life organization. Without thinking, he snapped open the glove box. Immediately there was a response on the cell phone.

"I heard a sound? Both respond, driver first."

They responded. "What was that snap sound!"

Vin held up his hand to Alvin as he answered. "In extending my left hand to adjust the air conditioning, my wedding ring hit the gear shift lever. You wanted to make us sweat, well we are . . . ."

"Enough chatter."

Vin leaned forward and looked into the glove box. There were more papers, some nicely folded, others bent at odd angles as if rammed in hurriedly. Slipping some out he saw more of the same, at least a half dozen. A few were from the pro-life organization where Paul volunteered. A couple were from the Ellefson campaign. The telephone number in the heading was circled on a couple, and on others were crude hand drawn maps.

As they drove they were given instructions to turn south on Dale Street and some miles later west on University Avenue. When they intersected Snelling Avenue, they were directed south again. Vin could see that it was a strange detour that consumed time, and little else.

———————

At eight-thirty that morning Feinstein and Cutter had the warehouse bays they had rented cleaned up. All of the boxes, tools, and trash were packed into the white van. When it was ready Feinstein said to Cutter, "I've decided a slight change is needed in the plan. Having two of them in the truck could be a problem. That was ordered from above, and there is nothing we can do about it. With only one, he'd have to be occupied with driving and I'd be able to see if he stopped or deviated. But with two, I'm uneasy. What I want you to do is follow in the Mustang a minute after they leave. I'll detour them so you can get in front. Here's a map. Notice that they'll be leaving the bomb in a Dairy Queen parking lot. I want you to park a couple of hundred yards up the street, just west of Howell Avenue with the car facing east. Walk to the DQ and order something. Stand in a place where you can see the vehicles entering, but are not obvious yourself. When you see them drive in, and verify they are both in the truck, call me. After the call, start walking to the car. Don't hurry or you'll draw attention to yourself. I'll give you enough time."

Cutter was not happy with this turn of events but saw little opportunity to refuse it. Feinstein would be tracking the truck so he'd know precisely the time it arrived. If his call didn't confirm it at exactly the same time, he'd know he had not followed orders. There might even be a spotter Cutter knew nothing about who would independently verify everything. He was under scrutiny for his failure at Tuley's farm, and knew the slightest suspicion as to his loyalty would mean he would be permanently removed from his present employment.

At eight forty-five Cutter parked the pickup with dual rear tires in the Har Mar Mall parking lot. He loitered by a store pretending to be waiting for it to open at nine o'clock. A few minutes later he saw the red Mustang arrive, and a minute later the Taurus. The schedule was working perfectly. A minute later the truck drove away, and he went to the Mustang. Small compensation, but it was a great car. He left the car where he had been instructed, and entered the DQ. He was finishing his hamburger when the truck arrived. They were both in it so he pressed the speed dial.

"The truck just arrived, and they're both in it."

"Good. See that they park it to the west next to the fence."

This was more than he had been told he'd have to do. He was on the sidewalk as the truck stopped. "Exactly as you said." He terminated the call before there could be any more delays and walked up the hill toward the Mustang.

Vincent collected every page he could find with a letterhead that could implicate an innocent organization and stuffed them in his shirt. He even slipped off his seat and searched the floor. Where Snelling Avenue crossed Ford Parkway, they were ordered to turn left. Vin began to wonder if they were after the Ford plant near the river.

Approaching Howell, their master was back. "Past this street there is a familiar food establishment on the left, turn in there, go around it and park parallel to the fence on the west near the brick building. That is where you will leave the vehicle. Respond."

They both did.

As they crossed Howell, Alvin punched Vin in the upper arm. Vin was irritated as he turned to see Alvin mouth the words "My car," as he pointed.

Vin nodded.

All the way, Vin had been wiping everything they could have touched. Alvin grasped the steering wheel with one handkerchief and held another in his left hand to be used to shift into park and turn off the engine. With the truck stopped, Vin said, "We're here."

There was no response from the cell phone other than static that sounded almost like clattering. Alvin looked transfixed at the cell phone. Vin pushed him and mouthed "Go" as he pointed to the left. They both had to exit by the driver's door because they were so close against the chain link fence. They ran toward the street. At the sidewalk, Vin saw a man and a woman, both young, carrying picket signs. He rushed up and asked, "What place is this?"

"Planned Parenthood," was the response.

Things fell into place. He grabbed the guy by the arm and pulled him to where he could see the truck. "Call the police and tell them that truck probably has a thousand pound bomb in it. Then, get as far away as you can. I have to catch the guys who left it. Call now!"

For the third morning, Dutch Tuley was sitting in his sister's car, watching the warehouse area where he had seen the pickup with dual rear wheels. He parked at various places, so as not to become obvious. During the day, he drove around the other buildings in the area where he had seen the white van disappear on Saturday.

He was beginning to harbor a sick feeling that he'd never find his box truck. Making good on the truck would take more than he had. He wasn't the only farmer in Wisconsin, or any other state for that matter, who was in trouble. Each farm foreclosure put another one on the market. The large corporate farms would have been happy to buy them as fast as they appeared, except credit was impossible to get. That resulted in most sales being cash transactions, which in turn meant to sell a farm, the price had to be sinfully low. It also caused the mortgage value to be equally depressed.

Today he parked across the street from the set of warehouses where the pickup had backed in. Being a man of action, waiting was hard. He decided if nothing happened today, he'd be forced to return home and let the chips fall where they may. He'd been away from the farm longer than he liked with the FBI prowling about and all the rest that had been happening. Having closed his eyes for a few seconds to rest them, he opened them and there was the pickup coming toward him. It was low on its shock absorbers showing it was heavily loaded. He wasn't close enough to make out the driver as it turned onto the street but decided against following it. He wanted what was still in the warehouse, or at least, he hoped was there.

After a half-hour with nothing happening, he drove around to the other end of the warehouse. Due to the dead end behind the warehouses, he'd park on the street. From there he could step over the galvanized steel guardrail and be a few steps from the end of the building. It seemed there had to be some small thing he had missed on his previous walk around that would tell him if this was the right place. Carefully walking along the windowless end of the warehouse complex, he saw security lights high on the wall, but no cameras. The grass was mowed as one would expect. There were recessed sprinkling heads on the border of the lot, a perfectly maintained property.

On the lawn, aligned with the rear of the building were some six-foot shrubs. Beyond them, he heard a man's voice. Hope immediately arose inside him. It might be someone from building maintenance or possibly a real-estate agent showing the property to a potential leaser. If he could see inside the building, he'd know if he were wasting his time.

With Cutter on his way, Joab Feinstein was feeling upbeat. There had been snags, but as was his mettle, he had persevered to the end, or what was nearing the end. There were still a number of cell phone calls to make. The one drawback with his rented space was that the high metal content of the building made cell phone reception poor at best. He had allowed for this as he put his tracking display and four cell phones into a shallow box. He opened the rear door four feet and trailing an electrical extension cord, ducked out. The place he selected was to the left with his back against some shrubs. He switched on the display and carefully laid the cell phones in the box, each labeled as to its function. The cloudy sky made the display on the vehicle tracker easily readable and kept the temperature in check.

The first call informed him that Cutter had arrived at the shopping center. At the same time, he began making calls on two other phones holding one in each hand. Finally, another call from Cutter informed him that both Freidmuth and Wessen had arrived. Step one was complete.

Selecting another speed dial number, he rang the cab of the truck. It was answered. From there, he gave directions as needed watching their progress on the tracking display. They seemed to be making painfully slow progress, though when he timed the third leg of their detour, it was nearly identical to how long it had taken him as he verified the route a couple of days before. His nerves were getting a little ragged.

With Cutter helping little with the actual work, he was tired and his muscles ached. No matter, it would soon be over. When it was, he'd drive the box truck a half-mile away, walk back, and be off. It would be close, but he'd make it. The authorities would take an hour to get organized, and even then, there was no reason they'd be looking in this neighborhood.

At last, they neared their destination. Immediately, the other cell phone vibrated. It was Cutter. "Good. Watch that they park up against the chin link fence, I'll hold on."

"Yep. That's where they are." The call ended.

Still holding the phone with the call to the truck cab in his left hand, his heart skipped a beat. Show time. Palming the cell phone that he had not touched so far he was about to press the speed dial for the only number stored on the phone when his eye caught movement to the left.

Dutch was finding it hard to believe what he was hearing. From this end of the calls it was unmistakable that the guy was directing the truck, now loaded with the bomb, to its destination. The voice was hushed as he spoke directly and with precision into the cell phones but he recognized the voice. Dutch's movement were soundless on the supple, well watered grass. Stooped to stay behind the bushes, he moved to his left to come around the far end. The phone calls continued. It sounded like there was even a spotter at the scene to verify the truck was parked exactly as planned. As he peered past the end shrub, he saw the man. His movement caught the man's attention who turned toward him. The recognition both ways was instantaneous.

The man sprang to his feet the device on his lap falling to the grass. Still grasping the phone, he dashed to the door. After a second for things to register, Dutch was after him. The door was coming down. He dove and rolled under it coming up only to get a shoe in the face. He grunted and let it slide off. The man was looking at Dutch in quick glances intent on the cell phone. The detonation call, it had to be. Dutch had no time to be clever or cautious as he threw himself at the man. A quick dodge to the side almost worked but Dutch had his arm out-stretched and caught a fist full of shirt. He landed hard but sent the man sprawling. The cell phone clattered to the floor sliding under the front bumper of a truck and disappeared into the shadows. The man was up on his feet and hands, knees off the floor, scooting for the truck. Dutch spun after him. At the last second he grabbed the man's foot. Bracing his upper arms and chest against the bumper, he pulled. The man had fastened his hands onto the under carriage. Dutch pulled harder. He was, if anything, the stronger of the two. The grasp was released all at once and Dutch fell backwards on the concrete.

The small man flew at him. Dutch lifted a knee and deflected part of the assault, though a hand grabbed his hair. Writhing, Dutch gained purchase with the toes of his rubber soled shoes and pumped his legs as they slid across the floor. They stopped at the wall. Dutch managed to grasp a finger, and twisted it savagely backward, hearing cartilage grind and snap.

The pain enraged his opponent to the point of throwing Dutch off with a punch to the eye. Looking through watering eyes, he saw a blur making for the truck again. He was under it and Dutch dove head first nicking his skull on the bottom of the bumper. They were side by side. Knowing about the sore finger, Dutch tried to capitalize on it to disable the man. The problem was, he lay with his back to Dutch. Under the truck, the man's small size was an advantage. Reaching over he caught the wrist of the good hand. Bracing his other hand on his back, he pulled. The man spun over and landed another jab in Dutch's eye with the bad hand. His opponent cried out in pain as the blow landed.

By this time, they were nearly out from under the truck at the side. Dutch could hardly see as he was up on his hands and knees, the hand with the broken finger clasped in his right hand. Bracing a foot on the rear of the front wheel, he pulled. The man came out, and was instantly up. Dutch swept his arm around and latched on to an ankle. This dropped him. Nearly insane with rage, Dutch pulled his adversary away from the truck and began swinging him around in a circle moving toward the wall as he did. With the final revolution, he was close enough to the wall to make contact. There was a thump and the crack of another broken bone. The body was limp.

Dutch released the foot, standing back breathing hard. His eyes were clearing, though he'd have two black eyes come morning. He wasn't finished. Walking to the door he pressed the button to open it a foot, and pulled on the extension cord. The tracking display trailed in with it. He wrapped the cord around the man, knotting it frequently. He used all fifty feet of cord. Sitting back on his heels he let out a long breath as it registered that the truck they had been fighting under was *his* truck. He remembered the plate. It was right.

Worry about the man later. Walking around the back he unlatched and opened the roll-up a few feet. It was clean as new. In the cab, the key was in the ignition. It started. He slipped out and opened the main door, drove out, stopped, returned to close it and drove away. From studying a street map on Saturday, he knew the location of the rental place. He was going to get his farm back. Though, bruised and hurting, he was feeling good.

— 36 —

Alvin was running for his car as he turned his head to see Vin talking to someone on the sidewalk. It was incomprehensible that Wessen would do that.

He yelled, "Come on!"

Vin saw him and sprinted his way. In a short distance, he was ahead of Alvin. He saw a man with his arm in a cast and remembered what Tuley had said about breaking a man's arm. Whether he was connected with what was going on or not didn't matter. What mattered was finding Alvin's car and getting out of there.

The man heard the rapidly approaching steps behind him, glanced back, and started to run. The cast unbalanced the rhythmic motions of the man's arms interfering with his speed. He was holding car keys in his left hand. Ten yards from the Mustang Vin was closing and knew from the sound of the doors unlocking that this was the man Tuley had mentioned. From behind, Vin pushed the man who bounced off the door, lost his footing, and fell letting the keys clatter to the pavement. As he scrambled he rolled onto the cast letting out a short cry.

Alvin arrived and swept up the keys. Alvin was in the car with the engine running as Vin slipped into the passenger seat letting the forward acceleration of the car swing the door closed a half-second after his foot was in.

"Planned to leave me behind, did you, scum bag?"

Alvin glared at him. "You made it. Stop whining."

Police sirens could be heard. Vin lowered his window. They seemed to be coming from all directions.

"Go to the parking lot so I can get my car."

"Why should I?"

Vin paused as something occurred to him. "Because, dummy, we are each other's alibi. Got that? We have to work out something. And, drive carefully. This place is about to fill up with emergency vehicles of all kinds."

Suddenly Vin clasped his hands on the sides of his head, rocked back and forth, letting out a low keening sound punctuated at times by a few words. They were stopped at a red light on Fairview Avenue.

"Why me, God? No." More soft sounds. "He's such and jerk . . . . You can't expect this of me . . . ."

"Who you talking to?"

Vin snapped his face toward Alvin. "This is a private conversation, so butt out, okay!"

"Ah . . . sure."

Vin went back to keening. "Yeah, I know . . . child of God . . . yeah. Okay, you win, you always do. But . . . it's so galling! Cheez!"

Vin shook his head slowly. As the light greened, and Alvin sped off he said, "North on Snelling!"

"Back to the shopping center? I don't think that's such a good idea. Sort of back to the scene of the crime."

"That's a risk we'll have to take. Listen. Do you have any of the brochures, forms, and stuff you use to sell your . . . whatever?"

"Sure. I always have a box of stuff in the trunk. I know I'm a good salesman, but you want to buy a retirement investment at a time like this?"

"That's exactly what I want to do. We have to get to my house and be sitting at the kitchen table like we were at it all morning deciding on an investment, with papers strewn about, pads of paper with columns of numbers, calculators, you know how it goes."

"Yeah, that's not bad. It'll be the perfect cover. Besides, while I've been out trying to kill you, I've gotten behind on sales. I could use a commission about now."

"You disgusting low life! Don't you ever think about anyone but yourself?"

"Well, not normally, never saw any reason to. But now, I'm thinking about you, too, sort of indirectly."

They finally made the turn on to Snelling. The traffic was moderate but it didn't help. At the first traffic light, a fire truck came across the intersection on a cross street and fouled up the light cycle with its emergency control of the lights.

"How so?" Vin asked.

"We agree, the feds know about transgressions we have both made. However, mine are in secret, while yours are very much out in the open. If they have the slightest suspicion of you, they will eventually want to know what you were doing this morning."

"I doubt you've told me the full story about your misdeeds. It was a lot more than hacking a few emails. But, yes, that means this has to be the best act of all time. Remember, if it ever comes to having to tell under oath what I did this morning, I will not perjure myself. That means you go down, too."

"What's this? You'd go to prison for the rest of your life rather than tell a little lie?"

"Little lies don't bother me too much. Like if I have to deceive some cops into believing we were at the kitchen table since eight-thirty, I can live with that. Perjury under oath is a whole different thing. I know, in this society most people wouldn't bat an eye at perjuring themselves. I won't, it's a mortal sin, even comes as one of the Ten Commandments."

"You really make life hard on yourself, don't you. No wonder you're so surly."

When they were moving again, Vin remarked, "That's funny, I haven't heard an explosion. Maybe it was all for show."

Every time they heard another emergency vehicle they both looked to see if they were the object of attention. Finally, they approached the shopping mall. "Pull over and drop me off at the curb. Then go to my house, park in the front and collect your stuff. Meet me in the back."

Joab Feinstein opened his eyes. They focused on the ceiling of the warehouse. Waves of nausea wafted over him as he closed his eyes again. Conscious of the ceiling again, he knew he had blacked out for an indeterminate time. He rolled on to his side and bent his knees seeing the extension cord wrapped around him. Struggle was pointless until he regained more strength. The cell phone, where was the phone? Moving his legs, he pivoted around until he saw it, ten feet away, exactly where it had come to a rest under the truck. During the fight, he had never quite managed to grasp it.

Slowly he began to roll over again and again. A collarbone was broken along with the finger. After every turn, he had to rest and let the pain subside the little it would. At last, he was inches away from his goal. His hands were bound in front of him. Tuley had been in a rush and not done as good a job as he seemed able to do. Wiggling one way and another, he rolled to the phone so his hands would land on it. He clasped it and rolled on his back. He had to rest as he closed his eyes. He opened them and realized more time had elapsed. He pressed the on button and then the speed dial button. If there was no signal, he knew he would have lost. The phone chirped indicating the signal was too weak.

Rolling onto his side he bent at the waist and looked at the display. The no signal sign was blinking. Squirming, he rotated so his body faced the opposite direction. There he had it. He pressed the speed dial being careful not to change the orientation of the instrument. It indicated the connection was made, just as fast, it was lost again. The redial message appeared. He didn't bother. The trigger cell phone on the truck was set to vibrate mode so with the connection made the little vibrate motor was engaged. Except that the motor had been disconnected and the detonator connected in its place. He wasn't sure, but suspected if he were alert, he'd be able to hear the explosion even in the warehouse. The Planned Parenthood clinic was about five miles away. It would take the sound thirty seconds to reach him. It was difficult, but he tried not to close his eyes lest he pass out again as he slowly counted off the seconds. There it was, the solid, unmistakable whomp. Done. He closed his eyes.

Dutch pulled up to the rental office and sprang from the truck, then realized that had been a mistake. His knee hurt fiercely from one of his falls on the concrete floor. He limped to the rental office. A man sat in an old oak swivel chair by a desk shoved up against the wall on his right.

"Are you Mac?"

"Yeah. Who are you?'

"Tuley. I came to return your truck. Come with me and we'll inspect it."

"Oh. I remember you from the FBI pictures. Yeah. Well, I don't see that . . . ."

Dutch grasped his upper right arm and said. "You will come and inspect it, then we settle up, and I'm outta here."

He almost dragged the out of shape man from his chair. Dutch escorted him around the truck. At the rear, he opened it and said. "See? Clean," and closed it again. At the driver's door he opened it and said, "Clean again. No damage. Now, the contract."

The contract had been in the glove box and Dutch pulled it out of his shirt pocket. Through the whole inspection, his grasp on Mac's arm had not lessened. In the office, he said. "Pull out your copy of the contract."

"But," Mac tried to protest."

"But nothing. Get it."

This he did.

"Okay it was due back Saturday noon, and paid up until then. Right?'

"Yes. You don't seem to understand."

"So, how much more do I owe?"

Seeing there was no point in arguing, he said. "I don't charge for Sunday." This wasn't true, but he wanted the additional charges to be as little as possible. "So, to noon today you owe for three more days. That's sixty dollars a day, one eighty. With taxes say two hundred."

"Mark that on the form. Also write the time and date of return, that there was no damage and paid in full."

Dutch pealed out two hundred dollars of the fertilizer money and dropped it on the desk. He snatched the receipt, duly noted and signed.

"If you send your lawyers after me, or any police show up, I'll hunt you with a gun. Got that? That's not a threat, that's a promise!"

"Yeah, sure."

Dutch jerked him up by the arm again. "I have one more thing for you." With that, he hit him hard in the solar plexus with his right fist. Mac flew back landing on his venerable age-old oak chair causing it to fly into dozens of splinters. The man looked back in bewilderment.

"That's for calling me a hayseed!"

"But," Mac said to the back of the man as he exited the office, "the FBI said you were not responsible for the truck. They checked your alibi." It did no good, the man was gone.

Dutch stalked out, walking fast even with the sore knee. He was shaking his head as he started north on the sidewalk. Under his breath he said, "Ya gotta do something about that temper, Tuley."

In a half mile, he was on a main drag and managed to flag down a taxi. He had the driver drop him off a couple of blocks from the warehouse. The area was still serene as he entered his sister's car and lowered the windows to cool the interior. A block from the junction with 35W he saw a gas station. He intended to stop and call Calloway at the FBI to give him the location of the warehouse where he left the man tied up. Then, he heard the muffled boom. Oh boy, he thought. The guy in the warehouse set it off. He'd read in his publications how the FBI could track the location of any cell phone call by means of the relay towers. They'd find where the detonation call originated. He turned north on I-35 to Superior, exchanged his sister's car for his pickup, and headed back to the country. You can have the city, who ever you are.

Flavian Cutter was on his feet as the Mustang sped away. He had a thirty-eight snub nose but it was pointless to shoot. It would bring attention to him and if he disabled the car, he still wouldn't have transportation. He set off at a brisk pace headed away from where the bomb was parked. The throbbing in his arm was back. The bones had been shifted as he had been slammed into the car.

Twenty steps ahead a man of about forty approached a tan car parked along the street. The unlocking of the doors was made clear by the characteristic click. The man settled into the driver's seat and started the engine. As he put on his seatbelt, Cutter opened the passenger side door and slid in beside him holding the snub-nose in his left hand.

"I need a ride and don't have time to be pleasant about it."

"If you want the car, take it. I don't want to be shot," the startled driver replied.

"I want you to drive because I don't want your car abandoned in the area where you drop me off. It's only five or six miles. Now move!"

The man did as instructed. Transferring the gun to the right hand was awkward, but effective. From his shirt pocket he pulled out a roll of bills and with some difficulty pulled off four fifties. On County Road C, he had the driver stop a half block from the street that led to the warehouse.

Leaving the money on the seat as he exited, he said, "Be smart. Take the money, spend it, and forget this ever happened."

He approached the warehouse from the street and unlocked the personnel door. Feinstein was on the floor not moving. Examining him he found no pulse. Dead! He had to move.

Cutter rolled the body over and removed the money belt tied around the waist under his shirt. After that, he did the best he could to make it look like the body had not been disturbed. He started the white van, ran to open the roll-up door, backed out, stopped, and closed the door. From there he was on his way. He was sweating profusely. His arm hurt, and the fear of being stopped sent his heart into high gear. With luck he'd make it out of the metro before he was stopped, or if stopped, before the authorities knew what they were looking for.

— 37 —

As Vin exited the freeway near his house, he realized he had to make a detour. There was no alternative. Then it came, like a distant sonic boom. They had set it off after all, though the delay puzzled him.

Two miles out of his way he jerked to a stop in a parking lot, jumped out and ran into the doughnut shop. Three minutes later with a bag of mixed doughnuts in hand, he was off again. He pushed his speed to ten over the posted, hoping not to be stopped. He pressed the garage door button a fifty yards up the street so the door was open. He drove in and dashed to the back step of the house as the garage door closed. Alvin was waiting for him. "Did you hear it?"

"That thump. You mean that was it? It went off after all?"

"Yes. I wonder how many were killed." Inside, Vin yelled, "Camilla!" She was home today and Paul had taken her car.

"Yes. I'm here. There's no need to yell."

"Yes there is." He made introductions, "Camilla, Alvin. Alvin, Camilla. We were the ones who delivered the bomb. Did you hear the whomp sound?"

"Oh. That was it?"

"Yeah, I think so. Here's what we have to do. Alvin, lay your stuff out on the kitchen table. Camilla, start a pot of coffee. Then chuck three of the doughnuts down the disposal as fast as it'll take them so it will look like we've eaten them. Don't just stand there."

Camilla went into action. "What are we doing?"

"Because of my run-in with the FBI agent, some law enforcement will be here any minute, probably the local police because the FBI will be busy. Alvin sells retirement securities. We have to make it look like Alvin's been here at the kitchen table trying to make a sale since before I left this morning. Let me do the doughnuts. You run out and adjust the driver's seat of my car for you. You are the one who went for the dough-nuts, that's why the engine's hot."

"You're good at this," Alvin said. "Odd, but good. You think fast."

Vin dashed into the back room and shredded the pro-life and cam-paign papers he had taken from the truck. That done, the stage was set as Vin said, "Expect one cop to come to the front. If I'm a suspect there'll be one at the back, too, so I don't escape."

Alvin smiled benignly as if humoring a child. He started his pitch thinking he might actually pull a sale out of the chaos of the morning. "How much do you want to invest?"

"I don't want to invest anything with you!"

"I don't matter. Staying out of prison is what matters. Now, how much? Let me ask, how much do you have in a savings account earning virtually no interest?"

"A little over seventy thousand," Camilla answered as she returned from the garage.

Vin gave her a dirty look. "Okay, half of it, thirty-five thousand."

"That's not very much. Nobody would believe that. How about fifty?"

"Okay. Fifty."

"But, fifty's an awfully round number. We need something else to be believable. How about sixty-five?"

"No. Fifty-five. That's the limit. Period!"

"I don't know, that's still not very much." Alvin began rambling on about the types of investment with Vin only partly listening. A few min-utes later the front door chime sounded. He stopped in mid-sentence. Camilla answered the door.

They could easily hear from the kitchen. "Good morning. My name is Officer Higgens."

Vin leaned over and whispered to Alvin who was staring with an ex-pression of wild disbelief, "It might not hurt if you called me Mr. Wes-sen now and then. You know, groveling to get a sale."

"Gerrrrrr . . . ."

"Is there some problem?" Camilla's voice came from the front room.

"I don't know. Is Vincent Wessen at this address?"

"Yes. This is our home."

"Is he home?"

"As a matter of fact, he is. But, he's in a meeting."

"This is police business. I must insist that he see me."

"Well, come in, then."

Camilla led the police officer to the kitchen.

"Which one of you is Vincent Wessen?"

"That's me," Vin said.

"Can I see some identification?"

Vin wrinkled his forehead. "This is somewhat unusual. May I ask why? Am I breaking a law by sitting in my own kitchen?"

The rear door chime sounded. "Now what. Who could be at the back door?" Vin asked.

"That'll be my partner."

Camilla went to the door. "Might as well let him in," Vin said. "He'll come in anyway." Then to the other officer, "Come on. I don't mind showing my ID, but you can at least be civil about it."

The man looked uncomfortable. "We were only told to come out and see if we could locate Vincent Wessen. If that's you, that's it."

Vin shrugged. "Guess I can't blame you if it's your job." He pulled out his wallet and held out his driver's license.

Higgens nodded, then looked at the other officer, who responded, "One car in the garage, engine is warm."

"Been anywhere this morning?" Higgens asked.

"Doughnuts," Camilla said pointing to them and then herself.

"Hmmm," the second officer said. "Could I ask you to come to the garage with me for a minute? Bring your key ring."

She shrugged and followed.

As they left Higgens looked at Alvin. "And, you are?"

"Alvin Freidmuth. I sell retirement securities." He had his wallet out in a blink. "Here's my ID, and," he opened a three ring binder and flipped a few sheets in page protectors. "And, here's a copy of my license to sell securities. I can provide you with the original if that should be necessary."

"No. I doubt it will be."

"They're good investments, too. During that market free fall in two thousand eight, these only fell half as much as the Dow. How about you, have you planned for your retirement? No time like the present to get started."

"I'm on duty!"

"Oh. Yes, of course. No offense, I hope. This guy, ah, Mr. Wessen, that is," Alvin emphasized the "Wessen" as he smiled with his mouth showing a lot of teeth, "is no different from a lot of people. He has money in a no interest savings account when it could be earning a nice return."

Camilla and the other officer returned. He twitched his mouth, "She has keys for that car and the seat was adjusted for her size."

"Oh, that reminds me," Vin said. "Would either of you like to help me with these things? I asked for a half dozen, and guess what shows up, a dozen. I love doughnuts, but they don't like me. I get, well, constipated like I've been eating bricks. And, I can't bring myself to throw any away. Come on. Camilla, a couple of cups of coffee, please. If you don't help me out, it could be construed as police brutality, you know."

"We really shouldn't."

Camilla placed small plates on the end of the table beside the cups of coffee and drew around chairs.

The two officers sat.

Vin said, "I do appreciate this." Then, to Alvin, "How are we doing?"

"I've written it up for the Balanced Fund of Multinational Securities. That's the best performing one. All you have to do is sign these two forms." He slid them across the table. Vin signed and dated them.

"There we are. That wasn't so hard, was it? Now, to review. The initial investment will be for seventy-thousand, as we agreed."

"What! We did *not* agree on seventy thousand. You must have misunderstood, *Mr.* Freidmuth."

"Sorry. That's what I understood you to say. And, the forms are all numbered so I can't throw this one away and start over. Besides, you can afford it."

Vin glared at Alvin. "Why did I ever let you into my house? I knew it was a mistake."

Camilla said, "Vin, we haven't been putting away enough, you know that, and inflation is eating up what's in the savings account."

Vin got up, clearly upset. "Is that it? Are we done?"

"Almost. In the interest of full disclosure, I must mention that you also accepted the 'Mr. Thrifty Option.' That's where we automatically deduct four hundred and eighty dollars from you checking account each month to add to the investment."

"What? I never agreed to that. You must be nuts."

"Now, Mr. Wessen, you weren't always paying close attention, I know that, but I asked twice, and you agreed."

"Ha! That can't be right! How could you ever hope to sell anything to women with '*Mr.* Thrifty' on the form, huh?"

"Oh, for women I use the dash-S form where it has 'Ms. Thrifty.' And, of course, nine percent of each month's 'Mr. Thrifty' payment goes to me as a commission. I mentioned that, too."

"You . . . ." Vin pointed his finger at Alvin. "You . . . you worthless piece of festering dog meat!"

"Hey! Nobody's perfect!" After a short pause, "And, Mr. Wessen! By the time we're finished here, I will have invested the entire morning in you. I have to live, too!"

"I've gotta use the can."

Higgens looked from one to the other as it he were watching a tennis match. With Vin gone, he said to Alvin. "We should be going. Are you going to be all right?"

"Oh, sure. For some people, investing their money is like losing a loved one. They go through all the stages of grieving. First it's denial, followed by anger, that's where he is now. . . ."

"I would never have guessed. He's an unusual man. Never been accused of police brutality for not eating a doughnut."

"Yeah. He's different, I'll say that. After the anger, comes bargaining. Sometimes that happens before the anger. We did a lot of haggling earlier this morning. Then there will be depression, and finally acceptance. I've seen it before, and it takes awhile. That's why we have the three day cooling off period."

Higgens nodded. "Sorry to have bothered you, Ms. Wessen. Give our regards to your husband."

They made for the front door a little too fast as if wanting to be gone before Vin returned.

Alvin asked if Camilla could write the check, if Vin would allow that. She agreed. "One of us will have to go to the bank and transfer the money, so don't cash it for a couple of days, that okay?"

"Standard procedure."

A few minutes later with the doors closed, Vin reappeared. Alvin said, "Wow! That was some act. It sounded every bit like you meant it."

"I did mean it, you blood sucker."

"Say what you want, but after that they'll never forget what you signed on for. Of course, there's a three day cooling off period during which you can cancel the deal. But, you're right, the feds will be turning over rocks for years investigating that bombing. The deal must stay as I wrote it up and you signed it."

Alvin fell silent was the wheels in his head turned. "Wait a minute. If you meant it, does that include that you said at the last. That was brutal."

"I suppose the 'festering' part was a little out of place. It doesn't fit with the rest. I wasn't thinking clearly."

"But, even without that, you meant it?"

"You are what you are. I hope this is all. Can you leave now?"

"Yeah, sure."

With the front door closed, Vin sat on the sofa and let out a long breath. "That's it for now. The FBI will be around eventually, though." Almost immediately, the front door chime sounded, again.

Opening the door Vin's gaze was met by that of the man he least wanted to see at that point, Alvin's.

"Could I come in for a few minutes more. I have a favor to ask of you. If you refuse, I'll understand."

"One minute." Vin stepped back to allow him to enter.

"A one minute limit is acceptable since I have a family emergency I must tend to. It's been bothering me, not so much at first, but more recently, especially since I met you. I tried to stick an arrow in you. And, shooting you in the arm, while not my intent, was also caused by me. All around that was not very nice, and I'm sorry. I was wondering, could you find it in yourself to forgive me? I won't try again, if you're wondering about that."

Vincent was as speechless as he could ever remember being as he stood in dumb befuddlement. Alvin continued, "If you need time for another private conversation, I'll wait."

It wasn't said with the slightest hint of sarcasm or guile. He sincerely meant it.

"That won't be necessary. I'll forgive you, but you can't take it to the bank. I'll have to forgive you every night because by the next nightfall, I'll have taken it back. It'll be a case of seventy times seven."

"What does that mean?"

"It's from the Bible, and it wouldn't hurt you if you looked it up. That's the best I can do. Will you leave now?"

Alvin nodded, turned, and left.

Thursday morning, July 1

The sun sent a pattern of light and shadow on the kitchen floor as Dutch Tuley sat at the table finishing his cup of coffee. The room was his place, his center of existence. It also had become run down. The curtains hung limply on old curtain rods and the faded cotton needing to be washed and ironed. How long had it been since this room had had any attention? Nothing much since his mother died, how many years ago? Moments of reflection like this came more frequently these days something he didn't particularly like. It was a lonely life, the only one he had. The cornfield should have another run at the weeds, something he'd start this morning. Glancing at the electric clock on the top of the refrigerator, he turned on the radio to get the top of the hour news.

There was never ending chatter about the bomb and that there were no suspects in custody. No terrorist organization had taken credit for it. The surprising, almost miraculous, thing about it was there had been no deaths associated with the blast. The news commentators sounded disappointed at the fact. A number of people had been injured mostly by flying glass when windows imploded. The crater at ground zero was on every TV newscast. The Planned Parenthood building was gone and the Dairy Queen was razed. The next news story caught his attention since it was personal.

> In a related incident, Joab Feinstein, one of the President's close advisors was found dead late last night. Feinstein had been delegated by the President to be his personal representative in the bomb investigation. Apparently later in the evening he had gone to inspect the warehouse where the terrorists allegedly constructed the bomb. Those familiar with Feinstein's background know that he's an expert on terrorism in his own right. That being the case, he waved off the offers to have others from the local law enforcement agencies accompany him. He suggested they had enough to do without bothering about him. Several hours later when he had not returned, two FBI agents went to the scene. They found Feinstein dead in the warehouse. There were no signs of foul play. He was known to have a congenital heart condition, and apparently succumbed to it. The President, when informed about the death, said he would be deeply missed.

Dutch smiled as he thought about what it would take to show signs of foul play. He could imagine the FBI agents standing over the body rubbing their chins in unison.

"Hmm. Does that look like foul play to you?"

"If we had a clue as to a white supremacist who might have done it, I'd say we wouldn't have much trouble proving there was. Since we don't, we must assume he beat himself nearly to death and then had a change of heart. In a frantic effort to summon help he became entangled in fifty feet of extension cord."

"Yep. That does seem to be the way of it. True, it might not be an everyday occurrence, but strange things do happen."

"Yep."

Dutch laughed out loud. From what he had seen of the FBI, that was plausible, in fact, more than plausible. His joviality ended with an instant stab of horror. What had they said? The strange guy, the one who bought the fertilizer, the man he fought with at the warehouse, was a close advisor to the president? The name Joab Feinstein sounded familiar. That was one of the names Calloway at the Minneapolis FBI had asked him about. The man was battered, but very much alive when he had left him. Now he was dead? It seemed so. Maybe he had been injured more severely than it appeared, or someone else discovered him and used the opportunity to even a score. He could believe the guy had enemies.

Thinking back to the news story, he knew for certain there was plenty of evidence of foul play. That news release was intended to put various people, himself included, off guard. Another thing bothered him. He had to assume they'd discover that he returned the rental truck and would want to know where he found it. That meant they'd be back to see him. The question was what approach they'd take. The two attempts to arrest him had not been productive. Would they shoot to disable his tractor at the far end of the field and drag him off into the woods to interrogate him while administering their form of justice? As much has he hated to, he knew he'd have to take his rifle with him on the tractor as he cultivated. After all, he might see the cougar Danny had been after. Or maybe a skunk. He wasn't too concerned with the four-legged ones. If you left them alone, they pretty much left you alone. It was the two-legged kind that caused him some worry.

— 38 —

Vincent normally looked forward to his weekly visits with his mother even if at times she repeated stories for the hundredth time, or conversation lagged. Today was different. He was worried about her, and if he were to help her, he needed answers. If the past were any indication, she would not be happy about giving them. It still baffled him about how she refused to discuss certain aspects of her past. Most things she talked about all the time. Why were those few areas off limits?

"Hi Ma," he said as he entered trying to keep an upbeat tone to his voice. "How'd the week go?"

"Hello Vinny. My week went well. How about you? You look worried, upset. Did you lose your job?"

Vin smiled. "No. Nothing as drastic as that. There've been some odd things happening, that's all. I think I'll tell you about what's been going on. Maybe as I tell it something will occur to me that hasn't been obvious."

"Sure. That's what mothers are for," she said with a sly wink.

He couldn't help marveling at this old woman. It was as if she knew it would involve her. "Remember a couple of weeks ago when I asked about my birthday not being on Ash Wednesday as you had always said?"

"Yes." Her voice was pleasant.

"And, there was the odd thing about that girl, Margaret, who was living with you at about that time? Her name came up a few times that I can remember. Well, it's strange how things can bother a person, to the point where it interferes with their sleep. This went on until finally I decided to do more checking into the matter."

"So you asked Timmy about it, didn't you? And, he said your father and I would argue and finally I'd mention Margaret and he'd say 'We don't talk about that.' Isn't that it?"

"That was part of it. But, I took it further. I went to Sauk Centre to see what I could find out. It was a sentimental journey in a way. I went out to the old farmstead where Dad had taken me years ago."

"Oh! Is it still there? Anybody on the place?"

"No one is living there. The house is still standing but the barn is starting to fall down. The house seemed so small. One of the sheds has been kept up since it's used to store farm machinery. It gave me the feeling of quietness, even loneliness. That's only part of it, though. I also stopped at a couple of nursing homes and asked about you and dad. It surprised me that they remembered you. That was strange because you had lived there for only a year."

His mother's eyes looked a little squinty now, like a cat hearing a mouse about to make it's appearance from the safety of its hole. "It's a small town. If we had stayed ten years, they might have forgotten us. Our short stay was different, that's all."

"It was more than that. They knew something about Margaret that they weren't willing to tell me. They went as far as to say it was only hearsay, so it wasn't proper to reveal it. On a hunch, I stopped at the mortuary. There I found the death certificate of Margaret Freidmuth. Her date of death is the same day as my official birth date."

"That's an odd coincidence, I'll say that. You have to remember that Margaret was a common name in those days. You know, names come and go as to how popular they are. There were a lot of Margarets."

Vin proceeded slowly. "Yes, that may be true. There was a note on the death certificate that bothers me. It said she was an orphan, that she died of complications from the flu, and," he paused. "And, she was living on the Carl Wessen farm at the time."

Her words came somewhat mechanically, but her expression didn't change. "Poor girl. She came as a hired girl for some other family, but got off the train at the wrong town. It was snowing and she was alone when Carl ran into her at the train depot while he was picking up some freight. You know Carl. He had such a kind heart, couldn't pass a lost puppy without helping. She agreed to help out for room and board for a few days. I was due with you, and not in the best shape, so it made sense. She must have brought the flu with her, because she became ill soon after she arrived. Shorty thereafter, the big blizzard hit. We couldn't get help, and she died. We never talked about it because we felt responsible in a way. If she had stayed in town, someone might have taken her to the hospital."

Vin thought it was strange that such a logical straight forward explanation would have been kept from him, and indeed, everyone else all these years.

"Okay. There's more to it as I've learned recently. I can't go into all the details because I promised not to tell certain things. But, it's important or I wouldn't say anything at all. You know the name Norma Holleran? She's the Speaker of the House of Representatives in Washington?"

"Yes. Why is that important." Her voice had an edge to it.

"It's because her maiden name is Freidmuth, too. And, Margaret's middle name is Norma. Holleran's middle name is Margaret. Holleran's date of birth matches the date of birth of Margaret from the death certificate. You see, Holleran assumed the identity of Margaret in about nineteen sixty. I think that's the secret the old people in Sauk Centre were hiding. It was a small thing as long as she was an obscure congresswoman. But, when she became Speaker, she achieved world fame. At that point it was too late to make the truth known."

Vin's mother closed her eyes relaxing all her facial muscles as if in sleep. With her eyes still closed she said, "Why is this important?" She suddenly leaned forward and looked closely at Vin. "I haven't told you things that happened to Carl and me a long time ago and couldn't possibly affect you. Yet, you are digging away at something, aren't you? Don't deny it."

He had her attention, and it was necessary to take it further. "What happened long ago on that farm? I still don't know all the answers, but I think you do. That's why you've taken such careful precautions."

"I don't know what you mean about me and precautions."

He went to the bathroom returning with her hairbrush.

"That isn't your brush, is it?"

"Yes it is. What can you be saying?"

"No, it is not. You swiped some other lady's brush and left it on the shelf in your bathroom so if anyone came looking for a sample of your hair for a DNA test they'd think it was yours and take a few strands from it. I know of two instances when precisely that has happened. What are you so afraid of that you would go to those lengths to protect yourself? You've always been concerned about your privacy, even shunning relatives, but this goes beyond that. What is it?"

"Vinny. Have you lost your mind? Have you been working too hard? That *is* my hairbrush."

Vin took a deep breath. "I am distraught, but not from over work. During the past three weeks, someone has tried to kill me. I was wounded the last time on the arm." He took off his shirt and pulled back his T-shirt. "Another time the guy shot holes in my car on the freeway missing me by that much," he said holding up his fingers separated by an inch."

It was true that he knew Alvin had done the shooting. That didn't change the fact that he didn't know his motive. There was still the man out there who called himself Raven, and something was still wrong about the brush.

"In some way it seems to be connected with Margaret. The funny thing about my birth date got me thinking. Finally, I was one of the people who took some of the hair from this brush." he said pointing at it. "And, when the DNA of the hair from this brush was compared to this hair," he pulled at a tuft of his hair, "they didn't match. There's not a chance in a billion that the owner of this brush is my biological mother. Now, what do you say?"

It was a stinging accusation, and Vin was hurt that he had made it. His mother didn't appear as upset as he had expected.

She drew in a deep breath and let it out. "This was to be our secret to the grave, Carl's and mine. I'm sorry Carl," she said sadly. "Vincent, the brush is mine."

She never used his full first name except then it was an "Amen, amen I say to you . . ." moment. What did she mean?

"And, that logically means I am not your biological mother. Have I done so badly? I looked upon you as my own. I would have died for you as if you were really mine."

"Ma. You have been as good a mother as anyone could hope for. So, who are you?"

She looked away. The light caught her eyes looking into infinity. Slowly turning back to Vin her expression was entirely that of resignation. Softly she said, "I'm Margaret."

— 39 —

Vincent sat in stunned silence. His mother, Ruth, Margaret, didn't say anything giving him time to absorb what he had just heard. After a full two minutes he said, "You're Margaret." It was half a question, half a statement. "Then, was Ruth my mother?"

"Yes, of course."

"What happened to her?"

"She lingered for a week after you were born. There simply was no money for a doctor. Besides, she was making progress, and we thought she'd make it. She was even up and around a little. I suppose she tried too much too soon, because suddenly she was very weak again. The next day she died."

She paused. "Poor Ruth. From the first moment she saw me, she knew I'd replace her. Over the years, I've prayed for her. It wasn't my intention at first to take your mother's place. But, when I saw how bad off she was the thought entered my mind."

"So, what are you saying?" his asked incredulously.

"I'm saying Ruth, your mother, is buried in Margaret's grave in Sauk Centre."

"That can't be possible."

"It was easier than you'd think. Let me tell you about it."

Margaret related how she had come to be in Sauk Centre and ended up at Carl Wessen's farm.

"You have to appreciate the fact that there were essentially no relatives. Ruth and your father were both from southern Minnesota. Ruth was raised a Lutheran, while Carl's family was Catholic. When Carl's family learned he was dating a Lutheran girl they all but disowned him. But, just before they were married, Ruth became a Catholic. With that, *her* family did disown her. Carl's family assumed she wasn't sincere, and only did it to pull their son into the Lutheran orbit. Neither side attended the wedding. It didn't matter because, though it was in the Catholic Church, it was just the two of them and two friends. They were so young. They lied about their ages so they could marry without having parents sign for them. I suppose the priest knew that but thought they were probably better off married than having a sordid affair. It was fairly common for people to get married in their teens back then. Surprisingly, most of the marriages worked. Young people are resilient enough to make the adjustments needed.

"When they found out about the farm for sale in Sauk Centre, they decided to leave and start out anew. Shortly after they arrived on their place, she became pregnant with you. It was a hard pregnancy, with her sick most of the time. Her illness was the start of their troubles.

"The first year on a farm is hard. So many things to figure out. Each place, each set of buildings and fields are unique. A farm wife was expected to manage a large vegetable garden. They bought seeds and planted them. But, she was not up to the hoeing, harvesting, and canning. They got a few potatoes, cabbages, and whatnot. But, they were short of food. As the winter wore on, that might have been a big part of Ruth's problem, plain old malnutrition.

"Shortly after they arrived, they joined the parish in town but were only at Mass together a few times. Sometimes Carl would go alone, and other times he'd take Timmy. One or another of the women, now and then, would ask about his wife, and Carl'd tell her. She'd say, 'Oh, the poor dear. I'll have to look in on her.' But, nobody ever did. It was a small town, and cliquey as most small towns are. It takes years to break into the society, and then only if you minded your place. If you had money, you had friends. Nobody was interested in befriending a couple of dirt poor people like they were. As a result, few people really knew what Ruth looked like. I was strikingly similar to her in facial features and size. I stepped into her clothes with no alterations.

"I was sick the day you were born, too, though, not deathly sick. I had been coming down with the flu and only had a bottle of aspirin with me. Having taken too many with the little food I had that day, it caused some blood vessels in my stomach to break. I vomited blood in the early morning shortly after you were born. Carl though I was dying, and I wasn't much help for a couple of weeks. How Carl managed, I'll never know.

"Anyway, I took Ruth's place. That involved some furious discussions late into the night. But, time was short and a decision had to be made. Carl couldn't run the farm and look after two small kids. With no wife, I simply couldn't stay around as the hired help. The gossip would have been murderous. If they ignored Ruth and Carl before, you can be assured that would have changed fast when they learned about the new arrangement. Timmy took to me. It was understandable. He had hardly had a mother for the preceding nine months. When he asked, we said his mother had died and I was his father's second wife. That was good enough for a kid that young. I doubt that Timmy would even remember the change. He certainly never asked about it as he grew up.

"Carl rejected even the possibility of giving the two children to either set of relatives after the way they had treated him. I was an orphan, and all too eager to fill him in about the loneliness and rejection of growing up in an orphanage. Kids always blame themselves for failures of their parents. The nuns didn't do anything wrong. They did the very best they could. It's just that the arrangement we were contemplating held out the promise of being far better than that.

"With Ruth dead, Carl called the sheriff and said his hired girl had become sick and died. When he and his deputy arrived, I was lying in the bed in the living room with the baby, supposedly a day old. I was still pretty sick. There were questions, but it went okay. If there had been a woman along, it was likely she would have seen the baby was more than a newborn. That went, woof, right over the men's heads. The ticket agent at the train depot remembered a girl there the day I arrived in town. It all seemed a little odd, but what could they say? I'm sure someone checked with the place I last stayed in Minneapolis, as well as the hospital where I had worked. There were pay stubs and receipts in my purse. We carefully went through my effects to be sure there was nothing but what we wanted them to find. After a few inquiries, it was settled.

"Carl went to the courthouse and registered your birth the day after the sheriff was out at our place and Ruth's body was removed. That's why your official birth date is eight days after Ash Wednesday."

Vincent nodded. "Yes, that certainly does answer it. I would never have guessed the facts would be so totally bizarre, though."

"What really saved us came shortly thereafter," Margaret continued. "Out of the blue, Carl was contacted by his bachelor uncle named Fletcher who ran a farm. You know that story. He wanted to retire but stay on his place. He offered us a deal we couldn't pass up since we couldn't keep up with the payments where we were. It was far enough away so nobody knew us. Best of all, Fletch had never met Ruth. We were so short of cash that Carl went to a neighbor he hardly knew and asked if he was interested in buying a couple of milk cows. The man suspected what was going on so offered a hundred twenty-five dollars a head, exactly half the going rate. When it came to the auction sale, the bank manager noticed we were two cows short of the number on the mortgage. They kept track of things like that back then. Carl lied and said he had lost two of them during the blizzard. Don't be hard on him, he was saving his family."

She smiled. "I'll never forget the wood heater from the living room going up for auction. How Carl had struggled to drag it into the house just before the storm. I still see it setting on the grass. The auctioneer saying, 'Great heater, not even a year old.' It didn't matter. It was spring, and we got a dime on the dollar for it. Whatever it was, nobody was in the mood for paying that day. It turned out, the neighbor who bought the cows for half price over paid," She chuckled. "Wonder how he felt."

"Shortly after moving to Fletch's place, we found an understanding priest, and had our marriage straightened out with the Church. Uncle Fletch had a shop on the farm with the lathe, mill, forge, and what not that worked to our advantage. Carl took to machining and learned a lot in the off times. He never had his heart in farming, though he never complained. When Fletch died we moved to the city. It was too bad you couldn't do your last year of high school where we were. That's about it. We did fall in love and had a wonderful marriage. Carl and I never had children, though we wanted them. I didn't do so badly as a changeling mother, did I?" There was a painful pleading in her voice.

Vin could only shake his head. "No. You did fine. It's like something out of a spy movie where nothing is as it seems. And, this is my life. How did you pull it off? How did you manage never to slip?"

"It was easy for me. Being an orphan, a person learns to appear as they think others want them to appear. You sort of lose a sense of yourself. I became Ruth. I had no past, no family, to stumble over. Carl filled me in on everything he could think of about both families. The relatives, when we finally saw them, seemed a little puzzled. In one way or the other, either Carl or I would mention how sick I had been when you were born, and how I was never quite the same after that. Where I fell short I'd simply say, sorry, that part of my past is gone. It was certainly more difficult for Carl. To his credit, he maintained the subterfuge right up to the day he died. If it hadn't been for this darned DNA testing, I would've made it, too. Came awful close, didn't I?"

Vincent laughed lightly. *"The Case of the Changeling Mother.* That's a book waiting to be written. It's already been lived."

— 40 —

Six months later

The front door chime sounded and Vincent answered it knowing who it would be. He opened the door and the storm door as well. Being January in Minnesota, it was cold.

"Come in, please," Vin said.

"Thank you. I'm Fin Lions. I called earlier."

"Yes. The attorney for the late Eugene Freidmuth. I was surprised to hear from you. Having a fertile imagination hasn't helped me much in divining the reason for your call. Let me take your coat and you can explain."

They sat in the living room.

Lions began, "Let me start by saying you have heard of Mr. Eugene Freidmuth, is that correct?"

"Yes I have. A couple of months ago there were a number of news stories when he passed away. He was universally commended for his philanthropic activities."

"Very well. He had three children, one by his first wife and two from his second. The girl from the first is dead. I guess you know that, don't you? In fact, you are the one who discovered that unusual fact, something that eluded the finest PIs in town."

Vin nodded.

"You also know of his other two children. One was Norma Holleran, and the other is Alvin. Norma died this past July, as you know. It was nearly a state funeral."

"Yes, I met them both last summer."

"Very well. Now, Mr. Freidmuth had helped his son in several financial endeavors, all of which failed. It seems to prove the old adage that the children of successful people are less successful. In addition, Alvin was a bit of a spend thrift. As a result, Eugene, I was on first name basis with him having been his attorney for twenty years, did not see it as wise to leave a huge fortune to Alvin. What you don't know is your mother is some relation to his first daughter, Margaret, through, of course, her mother. We did a DNA test of a sample on your mother's hair to learn this."

Vin smiled ever so slightly realizing these were the people who had done the other DNA test on the hair from the brush.

Fen Lions continued. "You may know that DNA testing is very sensitive to contamination by other DNA. The only DNA sample we had of Margaret, the first daughter, was a lock of hair from when she was one year old. Not surprisingly, it was contaminated. Therefore, we could not place your mother exactly in the lineage of Margaret, though, there was no doubt they were related. You see, Mr. Freidmuth was looking for other relatives to whom he could leave money. As a result, a rather thorough investigation was made of you, only publicly available information, of course."

Yeah, I bet, Vin thought.

"To get to the point, we only located two relatives of Margaret's mother, your mother and you.

"What about relatives of Mr. Freidmuth's second wife?"

"There are some, but I will get to that. Eugene had the following in mind. He would leave a set amount to his son, various relatives, and several charities. The entire remainder would go to you."

Lions paused for effect expecting Vin to show some emotion, which he didn't. To Vin, it was all another aspect of dealing with this family. There was another shoe to drop, so he might as well see what else he had to say.

Lions showed a little surprise at Vin's lack of reaction, but continued. "There is good news and bad news associated with this arrangement. I'll mention the bad news first. At his death, Eugene was worth upwards to four hundred fifty million dollars. Over a period of many years, as he aged and was not able to manage so many assists, he gradually sold his interests. The realized profits were put into a high stakes international fund. The minimum transaction being one million dollars. Upon his death, I naturally had to arrange to liquidate his share of the fund. It turned out to the dismay of many to have been a Ponzi scheme with Eugene being the significant investor.

"There was virtually nothing left of his holdings in that fund. He still had other investments, of course. I was obligated to pay the set amounts as given in the will first, with you receiving what remained which should have been well over three hundred million dollars. There were terms where I would get an honest amount for administration his last testament, too. The good news, such as it is, results in a disbursement for the residual amount of his estate to you. I have a check payable to you in the amount of sixty-eight thousand dollars. Not an insignificant sum, but nothing like you were intended to have."

Vin laughed lightly. "Ever since I became involved with first Norma, and then her brother Alvin, it's been a losing proposition. I'll be grateful if it doesn't end up costing me money. What are the tax consequences on that amount?"

"Part of what I do for the money left for me is to help you with that. In short, there should be virtually none if it is managed right, and I will help you do that."

"That was very thoughtful of him to look after such details."

"He was a thorough, meticulous man." Lions opened his briefcase and presented the check to Vin.

He continued. "There is another matter. When it was all settled out, Alvin got an even million, tax free. That was the condition of the will. When he learned about you, and what had happened with the bulk of the fortune, he did something totally unexpected. He arranged to give you a quarter of his million, with the provision that taxes would be paid out of his remainder. His wife was so angry I thought she'd divorce him on the spot. But, he insisted it was his inheritance, and he'd do with it as he pleased. As an aside, he and his wife had expected to receive the bulk of the estate. In some way, Alvin learned that Eugene was planning to leave most of it to Margaret's relatives. That information was closely held, so how he found out about it we couldn't imagine. Anyway, he became angry to the point of insanity. If words could kill, I'm sure you would be dead. Back in June of last year something happened, though, and it was as if he wasn't interested anymore."

Another mystery solved—the motive for the bow and arrow shooting.

"I know the two of you met, and I cannot imagine what effect you could have had on him to cause his radical change of heart. He started going to church, gave up on the rowdy gang he had been chumming around with, and started being ever so attentive to his wife. She doesn't know what to make of it. In a way, I wish you could have received the bulk of the estate. I sense that you of all the people I've met could have used it wisely."

He handed the additional check to Vin. "That seems to complete our business for this evening, Mr. Wessen. I'll be taking my leave. Say hello to your wife for me."

Vin had rarely been stunned to the point of being speechless, but this was the second time in a half-year.

— Epilog —

And, what about the fate of Norma Holleran? That is left to the imagination of the reader. If she had been a real person, we would all eventually learn what had been her final reward. That is the reason for the General Judgement at the end of time. We'll all be there, every single person who has ever been conceived. Yes, this means all aborted babies, too. It is another place where God permits His people to see that His judgements are true. We will see how our every action, good or ill, sent ripples through society. We may be shocked to learn that even the small things we did had effects on other people and how their reactions to them influenced the way they treated others. How far does this chain of effects extend? Only God knows the answer to that. We are left with the following text which is not necessarily consoling:

> O the depth of the riches of the wisdom and of the knowledge of God. How incomprehensible are his judgements, and how unsearchable His ways. For who hath known the mind of the Lord? Or who hath been his counselor?
> *Romans 11: 33-34*

On another level, it would seem that Norma Holleran had opportunities to see that her life was not as it should be. There is also a text that says: "If today you hear His voice, harden not your hearts. . . ." *Hebrews 3:15*. The supposition of the statement implies that we can't expect to hear His voice every day. In fact, it is possible that any person may hear it only a few times in his life which means it is important to dispose our wills so we will hear Him when He speaks.